Readers Love Ashlyn Kane & Morgan James

Homecoming for Beginners
"I thought this book was just so heartwarming…I smiled, laughed, and even teared up a bit while reading—and I was there for all of it."
—Sadness or Bookphoria Reviews

Winging It
"From the terrific world building, the endearing characters and the solid plot and timelines, this book was simply so much more than I could have hoped for."
—The Novel Approach

The Rock Star's Guide to Getting Your Man
"Well paced and well balanced with emphasis firmly on the romance, but doesn't skimp on resolving the musician's professional troubles."
—QueeRomance Ink

String Theory
"Ari and Jax are two really vivid characters…I really liked the way things evolved with all the relationships in this story."
—Love Bytes Reviews

The Inside Edge
"On the surface this story is an opposites-attract sports romance about two retired professional athletes, but if you look a little closer, you will see a story about two people getting to know their place in the world."
—Paranormal Romance Guild

By ASHLYN KANE

American Love Songs
With Claudia Mayrant & CJ Burke: Babe in the Woodshop
A Good Vintage
Hang a Shining Star
Homecoming for Beginners
The Inside Edge
The Rock Star's Guide to Getting Your Man

DREAMSPUN BEYOND
Hex and Candy

DREAMSPUN DESIRES
His Leading Man
Fake Dating the Prince

With Morgan James
Hair of the Dog
Hard Feelings
Love It or List It
Return to Sender
String Theory

HOCKEY EVER AFTER
Winging It
The Winging It Holiday Special
Scoring Position
Unrivaled
An Unrivaled Off-Season
Crushed Ice
Textbook Defense

Published by DREAMSPINNER PRESS
www.dreamspinnerpress.com

By MORGAN JAMES

Purls of Wisdom

DREAMSPUN DESIRES
Love Conventions

With Ashlyn Kane
Hair of the Dog
Hard Feelings
Love It or List It
Return to Sender
String Theory

HOCKEY EVER AFTER
Winging It
The Winging It Holiday Special
Scoring Position
Unrivaled
An Unrivaled Off-Season
Crushed Ice
Textbook Defense

Published by DREAMSPINNER PRESS
www.dreamspinnerpress.com

ASHLYN KANE & MORGAN JAMES

Love It or List It

DREAMSPINNER
PRESS

Published by
DREAMSPINNER PRESS

8219 Woodville Hwy #1245
Woodville, FL 32362 USA
www.dreamspinnerpress.com

Love It or List It
© 2025 Ashlyn Kane & Morgan James

Cover Art
© 2025 L.C. Chase
http://www.lcchase.com
Cover content is for illustrative purposes only and any person depicted on the cover is a model.

Trade Paperback ISBN: 9781641088664
Digital ISBN: 9781641088657
Trade Paperback published October 2025
v. 1.0

Chapter One

AUSTIN REALLY needed a dishwasher.

So he told himself, cursing, as he scoured his kitchenette for any clean vessel he could put in the microwave. None presented itself. This was a problem. After ten hours in the garage putting on winter tires and sweet-talking a very temperamental BMW, Austin was starving—hangry even.

He should probably buy another bowl. More cutlery too, while he was at it. He didn't have time to clean the caked-on macaroni out of the ones he'd left in the sink. He might die first.

Could you put SpaghettiOs in the microwave just in the can? Metal wasn't a problem anymore, right? Or did that depend on the microwave? Austin couldn't remember and didn't want to find out the hard way.

Was it safe to eat this shit cold?

He was debating the merits of rolling the dice on that when his cell rang.

Austin was off the clock, technically. He only had one phone and didn't use it for personal reasons. But he also hadn't been a small-business owner long enough to just ignore calls. And the call ID was from a lawyer's office. Lawyers had fancy cars, and that meant fancy repairs. "Taylor's Repairs, go for Austin."

"Hello," came the polite, professional voice on the other end of the line. Not a service call, then. "This is Josephine Kelly from Keller and Associates. Am I correct in assuming that I've reached Austin Taylor?"

Oh fuck, he wasn't getting sued or something, was he? "Uh, yeah. That's me."

"Mr. Taylor, are you acquainted with a Diedre Mitchell?"

The dull ache that had lived in Austin's chest for six months gave a sharp throb. "DeeDee, yeah. Out on County Road 8?"

Austin didn't have a lot of friends. Actually, now that DeeDee was gone, Austin didn't have *any* friends. If it were left up to him, he wouldn't have had her either, but little old ladies who lived on their own in ramshackle farmhouses knew how to get their way. He was called out to fix her riding lawn mower over a year ago, and somehow he'd gone back to fix something or other once a week after that. DeeDee always insisted he stay for lunch. In the spring, they ate on her side patio, soaking up the weak sunshine; in the summer, they took refuge in the shade of her crumbling front porch. He'd never actually been inside.

Then she died, and now he never would.

"Yes, that's correct. I'm pleased we've reached the correct Austin Taylor."

Were there a lot of them? Austin wondered. "Can I ask what this is regarding?"

There was a click of a pen or a keyboard on the other end of the line. "One of our clients, Chris Mitchell, has been named executor of Ms. Mitchell's estate." Pause. "Most of it was divided up between her relatives, but there is the matter of the house."

Austin blinked, feeling hollow. "The house?"

Josephine made an affirmative-sounding hum. "Ms. Mitchell has listed you as a co-beneficiary of that particular asset." More tapping—definitely keys this time. "We've been trying to track you down so the ownership transfer can be finalized. Would you be available tomorrow to go over some paperwork?"

"Uh." DeeDee Mitchell left him a *house*? Why? She had family. Case in point, this Chris guy.

"Mr. Taylor?"

Right. Availability. Paperwork. Austin forced himself to close his mouth and consider his schedule. He only had two appointments tomorrow, both protective sprays for the upcoming road-salt season. Tomorrow was a Wednesday, so a slow day for walk-in business. "I could do sometime after two?"

Click-clack-click. "Perfect. We'll see you tomorrow at two thirty, Mr. Taylor."

In a daze, Austin took down the address of the office. Then he and Josephine Kelly hung up, and he set his phone down on the counter. He stared at it for a handful of seconds, waiting for her to call back and tell him this had all been a weird misunderstanding.

The phone remained stubbornly silent.

Austin took a deep breath and considered the yet-unopened can of SpaghettiOs.

No, he decided. If he was about to become a homeowner—or a half-homeowner, or whatever—then he was going to splurge. He snatched his keys off the peg near his front door and left the apartment. McDonald's dinner it was.

THE CLOCK read 2:11 when Joe pulled his truck into the lot at Keller and Associates. He'd misjudged the traffic from Oldcastle; he should've known the streets would be dead at this time on a weekday. But it would be brutal on the way back—nothing but school buses and parent pick-ups.

He shook off a sense of wistfulness. That was one thing he'd never miss. His kids might be mostly grown-up now, much less easy to wrangle into a hug, but on the plus side, Joe never had to wait in the kiss-and-ride line.

He clicked the lock on his truck and jogged inside.

Keller and Associates was housed in a strip mall in central Windsor, industrial beige inside and out. Joe let the receptionist know he was there for a meeting with Ms. Kelly at two thirty and took a seat in one of the beige pleather chairs. The room didn't have any other occupants, so presumably his co-owner had not arrived yet. Which made sense, because Joe was stupid early.

Why had he come inside? He could've sat in his truck and listened to music or something. Now he was in a public space. It wasn't like he could just flip through TikTok for twenty minutes; he hadn't brought headphones.

He should've known that the kids would never let him be bored… or give him a moment's peace. He hadn't even had time for his butt to warm the cold plastic before they started blowing up the family WhatsApp.

Meg Mitchell: *Okay, so who is this guy? How did they finally track him down?*

Gavin Chalmers: *Yeah, and what the hell took so long? I am DYING to go explore that place*

Alex Jones: *Dude. Too soon*

Gavin Chalmers: *Oh shit, sorry Meg.*

Meg Mitchell: *Whatever, Grandma DeeDee would've laughed. Also, same, no one from the family has been in there in 20 years*

This was news to Joe, who suddenly heard alarm bells going off in the back of his brain.

Joe Romano: *Wait, for real? She died 4 months ago!*

Meg Mitchell: *Yeah, and Dad says we're not allowed in because the house and all its contents belong to you and this Austin guy EVEN THOUGH HE'S THE EXECUTOR. He could totally go in, he's just chicken*

Gavin Chalmers: *What if there's like*

Gavin Chalmers: *Mummified rats in there*

Will Wiebe: *Ew*

Will Wiebe: *Don't speak that evil into the universe, Gavin*

Yeah, Gavin, Joe thought. *Keep that shit to yourself.* He made a mental note to buy a respirator mask and a Costco-size box of disposable gloves.

Joe Romano: *None of you gremlins are getting in there until it's been declared safe by some kind of public health authority, okay?*

Meg Mitchell: *boo*

Will Wiebe: *boo*

Gavin Chalmers: *boooooooooo*

Alex Jones: *Have you met the other owner yet? You have to tell us what he's like*

Joe didn't know why any of them cared. It wasn't like he planned to keep the house with this guy. From the sound of things, it was in rough shape. They'd probably just agree to put it up for sale and split the proceeds. Joe could use some extra money to tuck away. Meg was likely to land a scholarship or two, what with the swimming thing, but Gavin, Will, and Alex might want to go to college one day too. Joe couldn't afford to just send them, but he could help. And he could stand to put some money away for himself, since winter tended to be slow on the whole tree-trimming-and-landscape-work front.

Meg Mitchell: *Yeah, how'd he know Grandma DeeDee anyway?*

Gavin Chalmers: *Maybe he was her boyfriend!*

Alex Jones: *Gross*

Gavin Chalmers: *Yeah sorry didn't think that one through*

Alex Jones: *Is he a senior citizen?*

Meg Mitchell: *Is he a serial killer?*

Will Wiebe: *Is he hot?*

All three of them reacted to that with the finger-pointing emoji. *Et tu, Meg?* Joe thought. Evidently being uninterested in ever having a love life of her own wouldn't stop her from meddling in his. Who raised these hellions?

Oh. Right.

Joe Romano: *Oh my God*

Joe Romano: *I'm muting this chat*

He didn't. He just put his whole phone on mute.

Then he frowned, looked at the time, and opened the chat again.

Meg Mitchell: *He's just worried about you cause you haven't dated anybody since Assface*

Alex Jones: *You need to get over him. He sucks*

Gavin Chalmers: *And the best way to get over him is to get under someone else!*

Jesus Christ.

Joe Romano: *Aren't you all supposed to be in class right now?!*

He swore to God these children were going to make his hair fall out before he turned thirty, and then he'd have to kill them all.

They weren't technically his kids, even if he loved them like they were. He'd been Meg's first swim instructor, back when she was a little tadpole of a thing, seven years old and all arms and legs. Of the bunch, Meg had the best family life. Her parents worked a lot back then, but Grandma DeeDee was a steady presence; she'd supervised every lesson Joe gave. Meg also had the only house with a pool, so Alex, Gavin, and Will had gravitated to her place and often ended up waiting around for her to finish. Joe had clocked the way they watched the water, the holes worn in the toes of Alex's sneakers, the fraying hem of Gavin's shorts, and then he'd seen them all flailing in the shallow end, and—look. Meg was never going to become a Division I swim champ if she had trauma from one of her friends drowning in her pool. It wasn't like it was that hard to teach the rest of them how to stay alive.

And if Grandma DeeDee suspected Joe did it because he was an only child of divorced Mexican Catholic and Italian Catholic parents, and all his cousins had gobs of siblings and he'd always been kind of lonely, she was kind enough not to say so out loud, and simply suggested she repay his kindnesses with lunch.

But lunch and swimming lessons turned into driving them home when it started raining or got too dark to ride their bikes on unlit county roads, digging out his old clothes for the boys, and sitting with the group and DeeDee to cheer Meg on at her first swim meet. It turned into a cheering section of his own at church-league softball games, a car full of kids to take out for ice cream after, and a house that sometimes rang with laughter.

Joe was furiously glad he'd lucked into these four siblings by choice. But like hell was he going to let Gavin fail grade twelve English.

Gavin Chalmers: *Whoops gotta go bye Joe!*

Joe sighed, checked the clock again, and opened a message to Starling instead.

Joe Romano: *Remember when you said adopting four children as a teenager was a bad idea?*

Starling Bell: *Will asked you if the house guy is hot, didn't he?*

He really needed to get some friends who were less good at giving him shit.

Two thirty came around, and a door opened deeper in the building. A woman of fortyish came out, dressed in dark slacks and a purple sweater that looked like cashmere. She smiled. "Mr. Romano. Good to see you again."

Joe shook her hand and she ushered him back to her office. "Hi, Ms. Kelly."

"It looks like Mr. Taylor isn't here yet. I'll let Shawna know to send him in when he arrives. Just have a seat."

Like Joe's ass wasn't numb from sitting already. But he sat.

"So." He cleared his throat. "You found him, I guess."

Ms. Kelly dropped into her wheely desk chair and rolled a few feet with the impact. "Do you know how hard it is to find people who don't have Facebook these days?"

Joe snorted. He didn't know from experience but couldn't say he was surprised. Phonebooks were just a hazy memory of his childhood. Could you look up a private cell number?

"About four-months-long hard?" he suggested.

Ms. Kelly dipped her head in acknowledgement and smiled. "Something like that. There's no point going through all this without Mr. Taylor." She waved at the pages on her desk with an apologetic little shrug. "Can I get you anything to drink while we wait?"

Joe opened his mouth to decline, not wanting to put her out just because this Austin Taylor guy couldn't keep an appointment, but now that she mentioned it. "Water would be nice."

She nodded and turned to pour him a glass from the pitcher behind her desk.

Joe's phone buzzed in his lap and Starling's latest text popped up on the screen. *So... is he?*

Figuring such a question was better ignored than addressed, Joe turned back to the lawyer.

She passed his drink across the desk, and as Joe took his first sip, she asked after his business.

It had been a year and a half since Joe's life completely imploded, leaving him without a fiancé, home, or job. It hadn't been the most ideal circumstances to open his own tree-trimming and landscaping business, but at least he had a few contacts willing to hire him on faith and share his details with their friends. Even his mom gave him an assist and hired him to spruce up some of her properties in preparation for the market.

Fortunately, the weather had cooperated for today's meeting—it had been raining on and off all day, leaving everything soaked. Not ideal for yard maintenance or tree doctoring.

Business wasn't exactly booming, but Joe had a steady stream of work and enough of a cash inflow he wasn't worried about paying the bills.

He told Ms. Kelly as much as he awkwardly sipped his water and wondered why this Austin Taylor guy couldn't show up on time.

Her cell rang and she answered it with an apologetic smile. Whatever she was talking about was, apparently, not so confidential that Joe couldn't overhear. Or maybe she just wasn't worried about it, since her comments about having sent the email and "Did they read the document and notice subsection 2b?" were so generic as to tell Joe nothing.

His phoned buzzed once again in his lap, and he looked down in time to see a notification that Garden Depot had uploaded a new reel to Insta he might enjoy.

Before he could even think about it, he unlocked his phone and tapped. His screen was suddenly filled with Paul standing in the middle of the greenhouse. He was still beautiful, still had Ken-doll-perfect looks and blond hair that begged to be tousled. His teeth practically glinted when he smiled for the camera and made jokes about how luscious their plants were.

A giggle from behind the camera told Joe who was holding it.

So Paul was also still seeing Nikki, the mutual coworker he'd left Joe for.

Joe could have forgiven Paul for falling out of love with him. It happened. But fucking someone else in their bed and doing so bad a job sneaking around that everyone at Garden Depot knew about it before Joe found out?

Yeah, he couldn't forgive Paul that one.

Joe aggressively turned off his phone, ignoring the notifications from the group chat. Gavin might have turned off his phone so he could focus on English, but Meg, Will, and Alex shared an afternoon spare and were happy to keep pestering him with questions.

As if Joe could tell them about Taylor's relative attractiveness when the man wasn't even here. Even though their appointment was ten minutes ago now.

Joe and Ms. Kelly were back to making awkward small talk as the clock ticked closer to the hour when her PA rapped once on the door and swung it open.

"Mr. Taylor is here," she announced, and Joe and Ms. Kelly suddenly transported straight into a porn film.

Austin Taylor stumbled into the room, blurting apologies and rubbing abashed at his cheek. He wore a threadbare T-shirt under a leather jacket and over a pair of sinfully tight black jeans. To complete the cliché, he wore lace-up black biker boots. All of which would already make him hot as fuck, but the look was topped off with two droolworthy touches.

First was the hint of grease on his hands and smudged across his cheek. Apparently Austin Taylor was a mechanic of some sort by trade and in his haste had failed to properly clean up.

Second, and worse, was the hair. His jaw was covered in stubble, highlighting his jawline, and above that was a mess of long dark curls. Joe suspected, based on the apparent age and disrepair of Taylor's clothes, that he wasn't very vain or much into fashion. He probably kept his hair long out of laziness or cheapness. It was thick and glossy and fell around his face in a tousled mess of beautiful haphazard waves.

Joe wanted to touch it.

"Sorry," Taylor said again as he sat down, barely glancing at Joe.

Joe frowned. Late and rude, even while apologizing. "It's fine. It's not like our time matters or anything," he said cheerfully.

Taylor turned and eyed him. Joe smiled wider.

"Well," Taylor said, "the next time we have an appointment and an elderly client calls me while stranded on the highway with a flat tire, I'll be sure to let them know I can't help because your time is so precious."

Joe flushed, embarrassed that Taylor managed to look like the better person when he was half an hour late.

"Why don't we get started?" Ms. Kelly smoothly cut in as she slid two folders across the table, one for each of them.

Joe flipped his open and found a stack of official paperwork—a copy of DeeDee's will, a property deed.

"So, as you are aware, DeeDee Mitchell left her house to the two of you in equal share. So until you make further decisions, it's a shared asset."

Joe nodded. That wasn't unexpected. He'd had months to get used to the idea of Meg's relative leaving him half a house, even if her motives remained a mystery.

"The estate has been paying the property taxes for the past few months, so you'll be billed for that," she continued. "Last month the house was appraised and valued at two hundred and ten thousand dollars in its current condition. You can either sell the property and split the proceeds, or one of you can buy out the other."

Joe glanced at the ripped knee of Taylor's jeans and doubted the guy had a spare hundred thousand lying around. Mechanic work could pay well if you owned an established business, but someone in that position would've sent someone else to change the flat.

"Of course, before you make any decisions, you should visit the property yourself and investigate. Mrs. Mitchell left you the contents of the house as well as the structure and land, and those assets have not been evaluated." She eyed them both with a shrewd look. "As a lawyer, I feel the need to point out that as strangers, you should take on the task of cleaning it out together."

"Wait," Taylor said, "she left us the contents?" He licked his lips and finger-combed his mess of waves out of his face. It looked even more disheveled and touchable. "Like, all of them?"

Ms. Kelly nodded.

"But… that house is full." He sounded daunted by the prospect.

"Yes. All of it. In the past few years, Mrs. Mitchell had already gifted the few items of sentimental value to the relevant family members, a common act for people who want to ensure inheritance or see the enjoyment of the younger generation."

Taylor blinked. "So. She left us her house worth a couple hundred thousand dollars and everything inside?" He looked down at the closed folder in his lap, then back up at Ms. Kelly. "Was she crazy?"

Joe bristled. Where did Taylor get off? Sure, DeeDee was eccentric, but she'd adored her family. And while Joe himself was surprised by her move, he also knew that she never would have done it if it put Meg's future in any sort of peril. But Meg was well taken care of. DeeDee and her late husband were no fools, and they'd raised equally practical children. Meg's dad and his wife hadn't been hurting for funds when

DeeDee was still around, but they were even better established now that they had her nest egg. Joe suspected that not leaving them the house that Meg hadn't ever set foot in was an act of kindness. Cleaning out the house for sale would be an undertaking.

"Such gratitude," Joe muttered.

Taylor flinched and then looked at him sideways. "Sorry, but I haven't exactly lived the kind of life where someone just leaves me a house with no strings attached." Then the corners of his mouth twitched up and his dark eyes sparkled. "Or one string, I guess, in the form of an unlikely house husband."

Joe's cheeks went furiously hot and words deserted him. His hand clenched reflexively around the pen.

Austin couldn't know the sick feeling that gave him in his stomach as he thought of Paul. Joe thought it was a pretty reasonable reaction, really. Anyone who'd had a broken engagement a week before they were supposed to close on their first house together would've felt the same.

Ms. Kelly cleared her throat. "Keeping the joint asset is also a possibility, of course."

Joe wished the floor would swallow him. Jesus. He scrubbed a hand over his hair. "Uh, I think we've taken up enough of your time for the day. Maybe we should just get these signed."

Blessedly, Austin Taylor did not argue.

Filling out the rest of the paperwork didn't take long. Ms. Kelly's assistant took copies of their driver's licenses, then of the ownership transfer papers. Then Ms. Kelly slid two identical brass keys across her desk. "Here you are, gentlemen. Congratulations."

Joe stared at the key with no small amount of trepidation, suddenly aware he was being kind of a freak show. He wasn't usually this socially inept. He pasted on a smile and picked up his key, then turned to Taylor. "I kind of feel like we should be toasting to something."

Next to him, Taylor had picked up his key as well and was holding it up as though it held the answers to life's questions.

On a whim, Joe touched the keys together. "Cheers, I guess."

Taylor quirked that wide mouth again. The hint of a dimple appeared.

Joe's kids were going to give him the business forever.

Ms. Kelly looked between them and then offered, "I'm going to get a refill on my coffee. Why don't you take a moment to exchange contact information."

Subtle, Joe thought. He fought the urge to pinch the bridge of his nose like his mom did when her clients were being particularly obtuse.

The door clicked shut.

"Do you feel like you've been called to the principal's office for being naughty?" Joe asked.

Taylor smiled. Definitely a dimple. "Now what makes you think I've ever been in the principal's office?"

That smile, for one. "Call it a hunch."

"Hmm." He studied Joe for a moment, eyes mirthful. "What would you know about getting into trouble, Mr. Punctuality?"

Joe held up his hands. "Hey, I'm sorry I was a dick. I am not a great wait-around-er. But in full disclosure, at least half the time I got sent to the principal's office it was because of chronic lateness."

Austin gasped theatrically, palm pressed to his chest. "A *hypocrite*?"

"I'm afraid so."

"That's a shame." He shook his head. "Are you a hypocrite who's free this weekend?"

Joe's heart thumped too hard in his chest. Was this—Austin wasn't asking him out *now*, was he? After Joe had been a complete hot-and-cold-running disaster?

"To check out our house?" Austin finished, eyebrows raised. "I work Saturdays—hazard of the job, everybody else has it off so that's when they bring in the car to get fixed up—but I close on Sunday."

Right. Yes. The house. Duh. Joe took a moment to shake off his disorientation. "Um, let me just—" He pulled out his phone to demonstrate, opened the weather app when Austin nodded. There was a late hurricane system moving up from the Gulf, and it was still on schedule to drop buckets of rain on Southern Ontario on Sunday. Not a good work day. The jobs Joe had lined up for the week would have to wait to start until Monday. "Sunday works."

Austin smiled again. Joe told himself several things that even the kids would call harsh, because sure it had been over a year since he and Paul broke up, but that didn't mean Joe needed to react like a hot guy had never smiled at him before. This was embarrassing.

"Great," Austin said. "It's a date."

Chapter Two

AUSTIN ALMOST missed the driveway, the rain was coming down so hard. At the last safe moment he spotted the little green metal numbered sign—implemented to help emergency services find rural addresses—next to the slash of gravel, and hit the brakes. The car slowed enough to make the turn without ending up in the ditch, and Austin pulled into the long, curved driveway.

Even on a clear day, you couldn't see the house from the road. It was blocked by a tall stand of cedars. After all the Sundays Austin had spent out here having lunch with DeeDee, he should've recognized he was almost on top of the place, but sometimes it snuck up on him. Today he was blaming the rain. Everything looked different in the rain, and he hadn't been out here since the early days of summer.

The pole barn came into view first—a long flat gray building with three single-car doors, trimmed in red. To its right was another garage, this one white-sided and attached to the house via a sort of enclosed breezeway—a drafty hallway with many large windows and little insulation—that had to be an addition. Austin didn't think hundred-year-old brick two-story farmhouses usually had attached garages, but he hadn't asked DeeDee much about the house's history either.

He wished he had the garage opener. It would be nice to park out of the wet, and the slate-gray October sky promised nothing but misery for the next several hours. But he didn't, so he parked as close to the house as he could without being on the patio and settled in to wait for Joe.

The whole thing was still weird. Austin never expected to own a house. He was proud of himself for pulling together the funds to buy the garage and had spent six weeks more or less squatting in it while he outfitted the space above it with a kitchen and bathroom he acquired piece by piece from the Habitat ReStore downtown. It was ugly as fuck, sure, but it was his. In a couple years he figured he'd renovate and get some better appliances and bathroom fixtures that were white instead of their current eighties mixtape of style.

He could move that timetable up significantly if he had the proceeds from half a house to work with.

Or, said a tiny voice in the back of his head, *you could keep it.*

He squashed that thought viciously as headlights illuminated the garage and a shiny green pickup pulled in next to him.

Austin couldn't keep this house himself. He didn't have the money to buy Joe out. He could barely afford the mortgage payments on the garage. So the only way he could keep the house was if Joe wanted to keep it too. And who'd want to keep a house with a complete stranger?

Joe parked the truck. White lettering on the side read Romano Tree and Landscape Service. Austin wondered idly how much equipment he had and whether he already had an agreement with a mechanic.

Before he could reach for the door handle, Joe rolled down his window and gestured for him to do the same.

Austin wrinkled his nose at the raindrops spattering against the sill of his car.

Joe quirked up one side of his mouth in a wry half smile. "At least we won't have to wonder if the roof leaks, I guess."

Jesus. Austin hoped not.

He didn't know what to make of Joe Romano. At first he'd taken him for a jerk, what with his snarky remark about Austin's punctuality or lack thereof. Then he thought he was a homophobe, the way he'd reacted to Austin's joking *house husband* remark. And then the guy turned around and started flirting. Austin couldn't figure it out. Maybe he was trying to win Austin over only to screw him on the home thing.

Austin was leaning toward a different explanation: he was just kind of a disaster.

Speaking of disasters.

They both ran for the front porch, and after they stood a moment to shake the rain off themselves, Joe took out his key and unlocked the door into a house worthy of reality-TV intervention.

Well, shit.

"This is gonna take a while," Joe said as they stood in the front entryway, eyeing up the contents of their house.

"Did she ever throw anything away?" Austin wondered. From their current vantage point, it certainly looked like DeeDee Mitchell had never found an object she couldn't keep.

Joe sighed. "Okay. I hate to say this, but we should probably start in the kitchen. As much as I want to tackle that stack of mystery boxes"—he gestured to the living room and a pile of mailing boxes, some apparently yet to be opened—"we should probably deal with the food before we regret... not dealing with the food."

Austin swallowed and tried not to think about the mold or rodents that spoiled food could attract.

Fortunately, DeeDee's hoarding hadn't reached the stage of crowding the hallway to impassibility, so they were able to make their way to the kitchen without excavations. On their way through the dining room, Austin tore his attention away from the solid wood furniture pieces that were the stuff of interior design dreams and the box stuffed with paper and topped with a teal Pyrex bowl from the 1960s.

He locked his eyes on the kitchen doorway and followed Joe inside.

They were quiet for a handful of seconds.

Then Joe announced, "This is just depressing."

Austin had to agree. The space was minuscule. In front of them to the right as they stopped in the doorway was the fridge, sandwiched between pantry cupboards and the old chimney. To their immediate left was a pink stove from the 1980s, complete with chrome handles and analog dials. The oven sat at the end of a set of U-shaped cupboards that ringed most of the kitchen, which was so tiny the oven door would actually block access to the lower cupboards when opened. Nearly every available surface was covered with *stuff*—canned goods, boxes of pasta, a jar of pens.

"Where should we start?" he asked faintly. The prospect of trying to organize this tiny, cramped kitchen made him want a nap.

Joe, apparently, wasn't as daunted. He told Austin to avoid the fridge and waved at the countertops. "I'll be right back."

He backtracked to the front door, and Austin figured it wouldn't hurt to follow directions just this once. The countertops were crowded with jars, tins, and dishes, but at least all the horrors were out in the open. He wasn't looking forward to seeing what the cupboards had in store. Opening one might cause an avalanche.

Since the stovetop was mercifully clear, he figured it was a good place to start sorting—once he made sure all the dials were turned off.

He'd assessed a half-dozen lidless mason jars as undamaged and opened three tins to find tea, a package of unopened cookies, and several mismatched buttons by the time Joe returned with a plastic crate.

"I figured we'd need a few things." He set the crate on the floor. Inside were a couple of folded boxes, some respirator masks, work gloves, rolls of packing tape, and an unopened box of garbage bags.

"We should start with three piles—garbage, donate, and undecided-slash-keep."

Joe nodded. "Sounds good. Though I suspect the garbage pile is going to outweigh everything else." He tore open the box of garbage bags, then shook out an extra-large, extra-strength black bag. "So, what have you already found for donation?" He held the bag out like he thought Austin might start throwing.

"Uh." Austin hesitated. "Is food a donation item?"

"From this kitchen?" Joe asked, and, okay, that was a valid point. "Who knows how long some of this stuff has been here? Do you want to check expiry dates on everything?"

That wouldn't be a good use of time. Austin knew that. But the idea of throwing away food that could still be safely eaten when he knew how many families went without made his chest feel tight.

"Maybe we need a fourth pile," he said after a moment. "Food items to sort through later. Anything that's open or partially consumed can go out, otherwise we put it in a box to look at in, like…."

Joe's lips twitched. "In, like, four more months when we've finished going through the junk in the rest of the house and it's had that much more time to expire?"

Austin huffed but stood his ground. "Humor me."

Joe shook his head, but he built a box and helped Austin start packing unopened boxes of mac and cheese, Rice-A-Roni, and more cans of tuna than Austin had seen at one time outside of a Costco. Between that and getting rid of all the open food, they had a whole four square feet of counter space after only twenty minutes.

"Okay, that was a good idea," Joe admitted. He pulled a Sharpie out of his back pocket and marked the box with FOOD, then carried it out to the dining room, where it would probably get lost in the pile of other crap, but it wasn't like they could put it outside in the rain. "Let's go with 'other things that are obviously trash' next."

Stacks of old bills, decaying rubber bands, and bread tags were easy enough to agree on. But Austin protested when Joe dropped one of the tins of assorted screws and nails into the bag.

"Hey! Those are still usable."

Joe cocked an eyebrow. "You want to reach in and grab them, be my guest."

One of the things they tossed was a jar of grease from beside the sink. Austin was plenty familiar with getting greasy, but rancid cooking grease that had been sitting in DeeDee's kitchen for at least four months—and probably way longer, given the state of the house—was a whole other category of gross than run-of-the-mill WD-40. "Everyone needs a good can of hardware," he grumbled sulkily.

"Maybe, but"—Joe gestured around them—"in case you haven't noticed, we have our work cut out for us. It's not like we're not going to find another six tins of random crap. We can't save them all. We'll be here forever."

Austin wanted to argue that wasn't true—wanted to volunteer to take all those tins home with him—but where would he put them? He didn't have a ton of room at his place, and he needed to keep the shop tidy.

"Look," Joe said, "if it got dog crap on it, would you clean it off? If not, it's garbage."

In spite of himself, Austin snorted. "That's, uh… that's an interesting metric."

Joe grinned. "It's what my mom tells her clients when they're decluttering before listing a house. It works, though."

"Fair enough."

With that in mind, and the help of the extra-large box of extra-large garbage bags, they cleared off the rest of the countertops and then stopped for a water break.

Automatically, Austin moved toward the fridge—it would be great if DeeDee had some bottled water in there; that stuff didn't go bad—but Joe stepped in front of him. "Whoa, whoa. That thing does not get opened inside the house."

Austin looked at the fridge, then at the doorway to the kitchen. "Where were you planning on opening it?"

"Honestly, I was thinking about padlocking it shut and burying it in the yard—"

Outside, a car door slammed.

Austin blinked. "Were you expecting someone?"

Joe closed his eyes. "Oh Jesus," he said. "That's probably my kids."

"Your kids," Austin said slowly, eyeing Joe up. Nope, Joe still looked about his age, and barring high-school pregnancy, not old enough to have kids over the age of middle school.

"Not like biologically or legally," Joe admitted, "but emotionally?" He led the way out of the kitchen and toward the hall. Curious, Austin followed.

"I have questions."

Joe sighed. "Most people do."

Austin opened his mouth but was cut off by the arrival of four teenagers. Unless he missed his guess, they were recent high-school grads or just about to be.

They stumbled to a halt, gazes jumping everywhere as they looked around the house, clearly just as curious about the contents as Joe and Austin.

"What are you doing here?" Joe sighed, sounding for all the world like a weary single parent.

Four heads snapped in their direction. "Joe!" said the tallest and most energetic of the group. He practically vibrated.

Then all four of them caught sight of Austin, lingering behind Joe. After a beat, they burst into laughter, and before Joe or Austin could say anything, they stumbled back out of the house into the rain.

Austin blinked. "Was it something I said?"

"If anyone ever tells you they're going to adopt a bunch of preteen kids, tell them no." Joe shook his head and went back to the kitchen.

"So many questions," Austin whispered.

JOE CONTEMPLATED next steps while his devil children lost their collective shit over Austin.

His hair was pulled back into a ponytail today so that it was out of his face, and he'd tied a bandana around his head, presumably to protect it from dust and other questionable content. If Joe's hair weren't short, he'd probably have done the same.

But even without the photo-ready curls, Austin still looked extremely kissable, in spite of—or maybe because of?—the old work clothes.

"So," Austin started when he rejoined Joe in the kitchen.

Joe shook his head, but he might as well answer the questions now instead of waiting. "I taught Meg how to swim years ago, God, before she had braces. I grew fond and she came with an entourage."

"I see," Austin said, in a tone that implied that he didn't but was too polite to say so.

Joe wasn't going to drop *I was a lonely only child and so were three of them* on a guy he just met. "Meg's a good kid, and I was kind of like a big brother after a while." He pulled open a cupboard and started sorting, needing to keep his hands busy. "Which is around the time that I noticed the total lack of adult supervision happening in their lives. Meg's parents are good people but busy. The other three...." *Gavin's parents had a messy divorce and made it their seven-year-old's problem, Alex's mom didn't get sober until two years ago, and Will's family believes in conversion therapy.* Joe cleared his throat. The kids would be back any second. Now was not the time to vent his true feelings on the matter. "Let's just say there is a reason I tell them to eat their vegetables."

"Got it."

He didn't—he couldn't. But if they were going to be spending time together while they cleaned out this house and got it ready to sell, then he would eventually. The kids would be around. Alex, Gavin, and Will would be here as much as Joe let them. They didn't really have anywhere else to go.

The kids came bounding back inside, damp, Gavin and Meg in the lead—Meg because she clearly felt some ownership over the house and the adventure, and Gavin because he was always in the lead.

Will and Alex followed more slowly. Now that the initial reaction was over, they held back to better assess Austin. Will measured him up with curious brown eyes. Joe wasn't sure what Will looked for or saw, but he always read people right. After the time Will started refusing to go to the local Mac's Milk and then the cashier got arrested for child porn, Joe trusted Will's gut.

Alex sucked their bottom lip, playing with their lip ring, then tossed their head to get their hair out of their eyes. Three months ago, Alex had disappeared one Saturday afternoon to return with half their head shaved and the rest of their blond hair dyed purple. It was blue now, but they'd kept up the undercut.

"Okay, so I've prepared a list of questions," Gavin announced, because no amount of ADHD medication could curb his curiosity or dampen his energy.

"Shut up," Meg cut in, elbowing Gavin in the gut. He wheezed and whined about her pointy elbows. "Me first."

Meg held her hand out to Austin, who stripped off his right work glove and took her hand. "Meg Mitchell. DeeDee was my grandmother. Why did she leave you her house?"

"Meg," Joe groaned. Meg might not yet qualify for adulthood, but she was old enough to have some tact.

"What? I want to know! Don't you want to know? Four months looking for him. I'm dying to hear the story." Meg settled her hands on her hips. It might have looked silly on another young woman, but on Meg it highlighted the breadth of her shoulders and the muscles in her arms.

"You could at least let the man introduce himself before you start the interrogation."

"Why? He's clearly Austin Taylor, the guy who owns the other half of this house."

"How does that work, anyway? Do you divide the house up front to back, or top to bottom?" Gavin wondered.

"They're not going to saw it in half and take it home, Gav." Alex rolled their eyes. "It's not a danish."

"But, like, what if they both want to live here?" Gavin turned to Alex.

"Why would they want to live *here*?" Alex shot back, somehow managing to encompass all of the many reasons cohabitation—or, in fact, any habitation—in this house at this time was a terrible idea.

Austin's lips quirked. "There wasn't a letter," he said, addressing Meg. "So I don't know. I fixed her lawn mower once and she kept inviting me to lunch on Sundays. I came. Which, uh—" He glanced around at them, his half-smile twisting into a slight grimace. "—I probably would not have done if I'd ever seen the kitchen."

For a moment Meg evaluated him. "So you were, like, friends. Cool."

Joe was just glad they were paying attention to each other and not him, because now he was remembering all DeeDee's too-casual invitations and developing a sudden humiliating suspicion why she'd left him half a house.

She never had taken to Paul.

"Hellspawn, introductions go two ways, you know," Joe put in when he'd schooled his features. "Austin, as mentioned, this is Meg Mitchell, DeeDee's granddaughter."

Meg shook back chlorine-streaked damp hair and smiled. "Hi."

"And this is Gavin Chalmers. Don't let those baby blues fool you, he's the ringleader even if Meg's the brains of the operation."

"I resemble that remark," Gavin said and ripped off a salute.

"This one's Will"—Joe indicated his skinny twink-wannabe son in his hand-me-down jeans and flannel—"and finally Alex, the light of my life, the child of my heart, the fruit of my loom—"

"Blessed be the Fruit," the four of them intoned.

Alex added, "My pronouns are they/them."

Joe loved them all so fucking much.

Austin said, "Nice to meet you," and looked back and forth between them like he expected one of them to explode.

Good, Joe thought; obviously he'd clocked the vibe.

"So hey," Gavin said, "are we going to look around or what? Personally I'm excited to excavate—"

That was Joe's cue. He clapped Gavin on the shoulder. "Glad to hear it." He steered the kid toward the dining room, collecting the others in his wake. "Minions! Grab some work gloves from that box and let's get going. We're wasting daylight."

"It's literally dark outside," Will said.

"What's that?" Joe asked. "You volunteer to clean the bathroom?"

Behind him, he heard Austin snort.

"He means we would be happy to help," Alex translated, catching up. They smacked Will in the chest with a pair of work gloves.

"That's what I thought. Keep the gossip to a dull roar, please. I have to own property with this man for at least a few months, and he won't trust me if he realizes what a band of miscreants I've raised."

Meg booed, obviously having translated that correctly as *Don't embarrass me or I won't let you help when Austin's around.*

"If it's trash, trash it. If it's salvageable, save it. If it needs more investigating, set it aside and Austin and I will go over it later." He paused. "Maybe ask Meg if it looks like it might have sentimental value."

He weaved them around boxes and rolled-up carpets and a beat-up rocking horse that might actually be as old as the house, and deposited them in the living room. Impossibly, there was a fishtank, still with water in it, lit and bubbling, though Joe didn't see any fish. God, he hoped they died long before DeeDee, instead of slowly starving to death.

"You can start in here," he said. Nobody was going upstairs until he'd had a chance to test the floors, because even if the roof didn't leak now—and he didn't *think* it did, based on the lack of water damage on the ceilings—that didn't mean it hadn't in the past. There could be dry rot, or termites, or God knew what else.

"But we want to help in the kitchen!" Gavin protested.

"There is barely room enough for me and Austin in the kitchen." Thank God for that, even if it would make the place a pain in the ass to sell later. "This is the only room big enough for all four of you without being emptied out first. Take it or leave it."

Meg narrowed her eyes in a teasing challenge. "We could split up—"

"Nope. Buddy system. Just in case there's a mummified rat." Also because she and Alex used to be inseparable, but they had been low-key sniping at each other lately, and Joe figured witnesses would keep the bloodshed to a minimum.

Gavin perked up. "Have you found—"

"No!" Joe wondered if he had any Advil left in his truck. "Okay, well, here you are. Your work's cut out for you. Try not to get in trouble."

The four of them rolled their eyes in unison. "Yes, Dad."

Unsurprisingly, the kids were enthusiastic workers. Their curiosity to see everything meant that they happily tackled box after box, sorting, tossing, and laughing.

Once Joe got them set up with the three-piles system and several garbage bags—"Seriously, kids, if it's garbage, it's garbage."—he went back to the kitchen.

"Life tip: there's no point in having kids if you can't occasionally use them as free child labor."

Austin snorted. "Is this your pro-parenthood pitch?"

"Yes." Joe nodded, straight-faced. "If having loyal minions doesn't appeal to you, you're not cut out for parenting."

Austin barked out a laugh and shook his head. "Good to know." He pulled a box of crackers from the cupboard, frowned at the open flap, and threw it into a garbage bag. "Once I realized I couldn't accidentally impregnate any of my partners, I stopped thinking about kids."

His tone was so light, Joe suspected it hid some deeper feelings. "Uh."

Austin paused and examined the box of pasta now in his grip. "Though I guess it's theoretically possible for trans men to get pregnant." He shrugged and put the pasta—unopened—in a box.

Joe stared for a beat. *The kids can never know* was his first ungenerous—and unrealistic—thought. Once they found out Austin was gay as well as hot, they would not rest until Joe proposed marriage. This thought was followed in rapid succession by *Screw you, DeeDee* and vague surprise at how casually Austin was willing to come out.

Then again, Joe had just introduced him to his nonbinary child without blinking.

Shaking those thoughts away, he opened a cupboard a few feet from Austin and started his own excavation. Then, putting on the most casual of tones, he said, "I can't say newborns are on my radar either, what with the four kids already. But I guess an accidental baby is a theoretical possibility since I'm bi."

Two could play at this game.

"Fair enough." Austin kept sorting through his cupboard. Before either of them could say anything else, a loud gurgling noise came from the sink.

Joe froze and turned toward the source of the sound.

"Is that—" Joe started.

"Can't be good," Austin said.

The sink gurgled again, and Joe and Austin looked at each other. For a moment they were locked in a staring contest, playing chicken to see who would approach first.

"I do plants. You're the mechanic."

"Cars generally don't come with sinks," Austin pointed out, but he stepped across the room and peered down into the sink. "Well, fuck."

Joe closed his eyes. "What is it?"

"Uh, looks like the sink might back up in the rain."

Fuck indeed. Joe braced himself and took the three steps across the kitchen to peer over Austin's shoulder.

The basin was slowly filling with murky water, bubbling up from the drain. At least it wasn't as gross as Joe had feared. But it wasn't exactly an appetizing sight for the kitchen.

"Fuck," Joe repeated out loud, fighting the urge to groan. "That looks like a job for a professional."

Chapter Three

AUSTIN COLLAPSED back into his bed and rubbed a hand over his tired eyes. For the past week, he and Joe had met up at the house every chance they could to work through DeeDee's hoard.

Thanks to Joe's kids, they'd managed to empty the kitchen and living room of most of the garbage and donatable items. Yesterday they set several bags out by the curb for weekly garbage collection, but Austin wondered if they shouldn't just rent a dumpster for the next month. At the very least, the local waste collectors would thank them.

Two days ago, after they'd finished boxing up all the nonperishable unopened food, Joe piled it all into his truck and promised—hand on his heart—to bring it all to the local food bank. "I called them yesterday, and they said they'd take it and sort through it. They were excited."

Of course, there were still boxes of items to sort through in both the living room and kitchen, but at least neither room currently felt like a death trap. Which hardly felt like a victory, considering how many rooms remained untouched.

Not to mention that they hadn't been up to the second floor. Austin was all set to explore it on day two when Joe vetoed the idea. "I've called one of my mom's contacts—a house inspector—to get her out to the place. I'd like to know we won't be falling through any floorboards before we head up there."

Austin's first instinct had been to deny such a claim as ridiculous, but he couldn't do that with any sort of confidence.

So while they waited, they continued working through the contents of the main floor.

They had a usable main bathroom now, which hadn't even been terrifying on first approach since DeeDee had, thank God, kept it clean. Well, it was usable as long as it wasn't raining, at least—which it had, frequently, over the past week, and every time it did, the kitchen sink gurgled.

At least the toilet didn't back up when Joe flushed it during Friday night's downpour. Austin's shout to just put the lid down had come too late. He heard Joe swear on the other side of the door, and then it opened—Joe was using a Wet Wipe on his hands, evidently trying not to tax the plumbing further—and they met eyes for a moment before turning to the john in expectant horror.

When it became clear the toilet was not going to disgorge itself on the floor, Joe's shoulders slumped. "We really need to call a plumber." He paused and then said, "Well, once the home inspector's been through. Unless she says it's not worth it, I guess."

Austin twitched in spite of himself. "What do you mean, not worth it?"

Joe gestured around. "I mean, you read the appraisal. Most of the value in the place is in the land. Anyone who buys it is probably going to tear it down anyway."

Austin's stomach flopped. Joe would know, what with his mother's connections in the real estate world. Lots this large didn't come up often, already serviced and close enough to Essex not to be tremendously inconvenient. He could just picture someone coming along and snapping it up, then razing the place and replacing it with some horrible soulless monstrosity.

"We could fix it," Austin said.

"Maybe," Joe allowed skeptically as they trudged back to the breezeway off the kitchen to finish disposing of the forest of dead potted plants. "But how long would it take, and how much money?"

He crossed his arms. "I put in a kitchen and bathroom for a couple grand."

It wasn't *smart*, he knew. Joe absolutely had a point, the same way he'd had a point about Austin's disinclination to throw away anything that might still be remotely useful.

Joe goggled at him. "Nice ones?" he challenged after a moment.

Austin flushed, feeling defensive. "Everything works. Maybe it's a little mismatched, but that's because I wasn't trying. You can get whole used kitchens at Habitat ReStore, and you can paint most cabinets. If we rip out everything that's in here"—because even Austin had to admit that the current kitchen did not bear the effort of trying to salvage—"we'd have a blank slate. We could make a lot of different things work."

Joe's incredulous gaze turned calculating. "You really hate throwing stuff away."

The heat in Austin's cheeks doubled. He hated being so transparent to someone he'd just met—especially someone like Joe, who drove a nice newer-model truck with his business's logo in vinyl on the side, who had somehow adopted four teenagers and earned their undying mockery and free labor, who was clean-cut and conventionally handsome and unconventionally charming.

He hated the reflexive urge to explain himself, which made him spit without thinking, "You would too, if you grew up with nothing."

That effectively ended the conversation. Like bringing a gun to a knife fight, Austin thought. Well, anyway—"Come on, we're almost done with the breezeway."

Tonight, in his bed, Austin's body reminded him that he'd been asking a lot of it lately. Long days on his back under a chassis or bent over an engine, long evenings with Joe at the house, sorting through a seemingly endless pile of what even Austin had to admit was mostly crap, and then a half hour drive back to the garage before he could shower and fall into bed, at which point his brain caught a second wind and didn't want to switch off.

One of these days, Austin was going to drop a transmission on his own head because he was tired. At least then he'd be able to stop *thinking*.

Would putting in a new kitchen be so hard? Austin didn't think so. Once they pulled the existing cabinets off the wall, they'd have room to move around. They could flatten out that U-shaped set of cabinets into an elongated L that stretched into the addition, put in some better lighting. There'd even be space for a big island with seating on both sides—plenty of room for family dinners or whatever.

Not that Austin had a family to have dinners with, but *someone* would appreciate it. Someone would breathe life back into that big, beautiful, neglected house.

Assuming the home inspector didn't find anything else egregious, of course. Austin flipped his pillow over and rolled onto his side, wondering how much bad news Joe would be willing to hear and still fix the place up. The roof hadn't leaked yet. The windows were old, but only one had a crack, and Austin had experience cutting glass; he could probably fix it. The basement—God, Austin was not looking forward to the basement, but it was the next thing they had to clear a pathway to before the inspector came this week. The basement could make or break it. If the foundation was crumbling, if the joists were damaged—

And then there was the plumbing, which, what was even going on with that? On Thursday night, Austin had just pulled up to the house when the neighbor, a middle-aged woman named Linda, flagged him down for a chat; she mentioned the farmer to their rear had regraded the field a few years back and DeeDee had had trouble since.

"Something with the weeping beds," she told him. "Whatever that means."

Austin hadn't known either, but it sounded like the sort of thing Joe would know about. Very landscapey. He should ask, he thought hazily as he fell into sleep.

Days later, they had cleared out sections of the house well enough for the inspector, who arrived with a lengthy checklist and a sardonic smile.

"Let's see what we're dealing with," she quipped as Joe led her up the porch steps.

"Hiya! I'm Rita. You must be the mysterious co-owner Joe was despairing would never be found." She held out her hand, which was clean and manicured in sharp contrast to her old jeans and boots.

"I usually just go by Austin. Less of a mouthful."

Rita laughed. "Well, wouldn't want to strain anyone." She winked. "Shall we take a look at her?" She stepped through the front door. "We'll come back outside later."

Joe and Austin let her do her thing, but kept within shouting distance. Her full tour of the house took a while. Austin was practically chewing his fingers by the time she found them sorting things in the tiny main-floor office.

"So, good news or bad news first?"

"Always good," Joe said before Austin could even gain use of his tongue.

"You've got good bones. The structure is, overall, sound. The basement looks good. The roof looks okay for now, and the house shouldn't come down on you next blustery day."

Relief filled Austin. That sounded promising. Like it wasn't a write-off.

"But?" Joe prompted.

"But there's a laundry list of repairs that need doing. Wanna go see them?"

They started in the kitchen.

"I'm sure you already noticed this," she said wryly and placed a marble on the floor. It ran to the other side of the room, gaining speed.

It wasn't like Austin hadn't known about the slant, but watching the marble's race to the extension twisted his stomach.

"But that framing is sound?" Joe said skeptically.

"Hard to say without pulling up the floor, since there's no basement under the addition to get a look at it. Houses settle." Rita shrugged. "But you should be able to raise things up."

"So do you know why the sink is backing up?" Joe asked.

"The neighbor said something about weeping beds?" Austin put in.

Joe groaned and Rita nodded.

"Sounds like the change in the elevation of the farmer's field is causing more rainwater to be directed into the leaching bed of the septic tank, which means it can then back up into the house."

"How do we fix that?" Austin wanted the full to-do list.

"You'll probably have to call in someone to clean the septic system, make sure the eavestroughs are directed away from the septic bed, and maybe regrade the yard. Keeping the grass cut short should help too."

"Let's hope it's the lawn-mowing option," Joe said dryly.

She ran them through the rest of the checklist.

"There's knob-and-tube wiring in the basement, and judging by the lack of outlets and ceiling-light fixtures, I doubt anyone has serviced or changed the electrical in the last several decades. I'd put money on knob-and-tube throughout the house."

Fuck, Austin didn't need Rita or Joe to tell him that would cost to replace.

"On the plus side, the house is so old that asbestos isn't a concern. I did some scratch tests. But from what I can see, the insulation is all but nonexistent. Which is probably why it's so cold in here."

Leveling of the house, new wiring, insulation...

"So, more good news, the plumbing is copper, mazel tov. Your hot water tank, on the other hand, is leaking."

... new hot water tank.

The list was growing longer, and the stable frame that had gotten Austin's hopes up was starting to sound less impactful.

By the time Rita finished and shook their hands, Austin had a knot in his stomach and a tight band across his chest.

It was stupid. Selling the house was still an incredible financial move for him. He'd never dreamed of being able to put a hundred thousand dollars into savings before he reached his thirtieth birthday.

But he loved this house, with its original wood floors and sturdy, shady porch. They didn't build houses like this anymore. And Austin had started to dream about what it might be like to restore it to its former glory. To give it the attention it deserved.

"Hey."

Austin jumped half a foot when Joe touched his shoulder. When he looked up, Joe was frowning. "Are you okay? You're kind of… zoning."

Austin didn't have an excuse. He'd had plenty of practice, as a service industry professional, at holding his tongue. So he didn't know why his control escaped him now. Maybe he'd inhaled some mold spores. Maybe the fact that they'd been working their asses to the bone had left his defenses low.

Maybe it was the way Joe's eyes looked warm and soft in the dim lighting of the kitchen addition.

"I don't want to sell it like this," Austin said firmly. "Let's fix it."

JOE GAPED. "Let's *what*?"

Truth told, part of him had been enjoying the quest to reveal the farmhouse's actual features from under fifty years' worth of accumulated junk. It was satisfying work, if slow, and even though most of what they found had to be thrown out, the process was still interesting.

Joe had grown up with his mom in a newer raised ranch. Then he and Paul had rented an apartment. Before they could close on their first house, they'd broken up, and Joe had put the money he'd saved for a down payment toward the austere barndominium where he now lived instead, so he had a place to live and a base of operations for his business.

In this house, he felt like he was getting a view into another world— into the family that had lived here once. There were newspaper clippings and photographs and sports trophies and academic awards, all set aside for Meg to bring to her dad's; there were ancient light bulbs and a typewriter that might predate the house and a collection of dilapidated musical instruments, squashed into the office sort of room next to the bathroom.

But the house needed so much work. Sure, it wasn't going to fall down around their ears—hooray. That was a pretty low bar. Excuse Joe if he wasn't getting excited just yet.

Austin, though, had obviously made up his mind. "Let's fix it," he said. "Yeah, it'll cost money, but it'll be worth more when we sell, right?

Like, I'm pretty sure we can get out what we put in, and then some. Sweat equity. Plus there are those rebates for insulation and stuff. I bet we can do a lot of the work."

That was a terrible idea.

Not financially. Financially, it made perfect sense. Joe had read the appraisal carefully, and he had years of experience listening to his mother talk about the market. He knew that even getting rid of all the junk would improve the home's value. A cleanup, some paint, and the major repair items on the list—the septic problem and the kitchen—and the house's value would shoot up.

Besides, winter was coming, and with it, a major seasonal slowdown. That meant less money and less work for Joe. Most of his crew did different seasonal work in the winter—in retail, plowing snow, building furniture. Joe himself had driven a plow a few times, clearing out parking lots and driveways, but payment always depended on snow actually arriving. This far south, with global warming as a factor, he couldn't count on it. He'd be bored *and* broke if he didn't find something to do.

No, the problem was Austin. *Austin* was a terrible idea. Austin was smart and cute and funny, and if Joe had to watch him skillfully wield power tools, he would lose his mind. Or, God, the thought of him doing kitchen demo, swinging a sledgehammer with those broad shoulders and narrow hips—Joe would die.

Joe could not do that. His heart was a lonely himbo. It would make the dumbest possible decision and he'd end up right where he'd been when things with Paul imploded. "Where are we going to get the money for that?"

Austin gestured around. "Uh, well… now that we've cleared out some of the crap, we can sell some of the furniture. The dining set's in great condition, and it's an actual antique. I bet some of those Christmas ornaments are collector's items. The typewriter…. We haven't even been upstairs yet. Who knows what's up there?"

"More junk?" Joe suggested, because he didn't want to go down this road.

"Or more money."

Joe pinched the bridge of his nose. "Enough money to delay selling the place for months and to pay for renos?"

"If we're lucky and do it right, we might be able to make hundreds just from selling the ornaments. And if we don't have to hurry the sale, we can price them at what they're worth."

Sound logic, which, sadly, also applied to the house. If they waited until the spring to list it, the market would probably be better and they could ask more. Not to mention that any work they did to make the place livable would increase the value exponentially. Austin wasn't wrong about that.

And… if they were able to get the house in good enough condition to actually live in it, then they could sell it as their primary residence and avoid the taxes associated with selling a secondary one. Plus then Joe could rent out the living area of the barndominium to cover some of the costs building up.

"Look," Austin began, "how about we make a deal? Give me a week to see if I can sell some of this stuff. If I manage to get, say, a thousand dollars, will that be enough for proof of concept?" His eyes were big and pleading. "Please?"

"Fine," Joe said, folding like wet paper, because there was no way he could stand up to those liquid eyes and that pouty lip.

Austin lit up and beamed at Joe. "You won't regret this."

Oh, Joe already did. He was definitely regretting more time spent with an adorable, sexy man he already wanted to ruin in all the best ways. That hair was just made for being artfully tousled on someone else's pillow. Not to mention the way he looked in a pair of tight jeans.

The next several months would severely test Joe's self-restraint. He was starting to suspect he might have a masochistic streak.

Chapter Four

THE FIRST couple of weeks of their plan went pretty much exactly as Joe expected.

Austin sold the dining room furniture for an insane three grand and showed Joe an image of the money transfer. Then he sent Joe half and asked what item on their to-do list he wanted to check off first.

Of course, they couldn't tackle much of the actual renovation side yet, what with the house still being full of stuff.

So their first task was to continue decluttering. Thank God for his children, who continued to be nosy and helpful evenings and weekends.

The second order of business was to figure out what exactly needed doing, what could be done, and who was going to do it, and for how much.

So Joe called Starling.

"José! To what do I owe the pleasure?"

"How do you feel about coming round to my recently acquired run-down house and telling me how much I'm going to weep over the bill for rewiring the whole thing?"

"I'm sorry, what? You're not keeping it."

"Not forever. Just long enough to fix it up. Austin made some good points—"

"I'm on my way," Starling said and hung up.

With a shake of his head and a small amount of dread, Joe turned his podcast back on and kept sorting.

He was alone at the house that day, as it was the middle of a weekday and no one else's day job was so weather dependent. Another rainy day in November meant another day not landscaping. He was just tying up another full garbage bag when Starling's voice came booming through the house from the front door.

"José Vasquez Joseph Romano!"

"Still no Joseph in my name," Joe said, as he always did. And he hadn't been a Vasquez since his parents divorced and his mother reclaimed her maiden name. Not that he thought Starling would stop the joke now, almost twenty years after it started.

"Tell me you did *not* agree to keep owning a house with a man that your children call 'snatched'!"

"Well, you know that it's a terrible time of year to sell," Joe started.

Starling crossed her arms.

"And if we can make it livable, then it'll actually be worth more than just the land. Honestly, making it not an instant teardown will double its value."

"Joe," Starling said, her voice soft and full of concern. "They said you were vibing with this guy. Just tell me you're not—"

Joe sighed. "Look, do I want to take him to bed and mess him up until he can no longer say anything but my name? Sure. He's hot. Like, smoking. The kids weren't lying. But I'm not making an unwise decision just for the sake of a pretty face."

Starling stared him down.

"Sure, maybe the pretty face helped to talk me into it, but it really does make sense to fix up the house and sell in the spring, so long as we take the DIY approach."

Starling snorted. "Not with the electricity, you're not."

"Nope," Joe happily agreed. "Which needs a total overhaul, probably, since the inspector found knob-and-tube and there's no reason to think any of it got updated."

"Hence the aforementioned bill weeping, I guess."

"Hence the weeping," Joe agreed cheerfully.

Starling pulled out a stylus and her phone—a large tablet-like thing—and tapped at the screen. "Okay, let's get started. Walk me through the house and let's start talking about the needs."

As they went room by room, Starling added up the existing number of outlets and lights, and together they made guesstimates for additional ones. If they were going to have to pay Starling to rewire the whole goddamned house, Joe was not going to live without overhead lighting. He was tired of sorting through things in the dark.

"So, here's the thing. It's not the cost of the materials. I mean sure, you need several hundred feet of wiring and a whole new panel. But the real issue is the time, because rewiring the existing setup is enough of a bitch. But if you're willing to embrace a piecemeal work schedule and pay for materials up front, then I'll do it for cost and the promise of future earnings when you sell."

Joe hugged her.

"Also," she said, holding him tightly, "I'll be doing a vibe check on your house husband."

Joe never should've mentioned Austin called him that. Scratch that, Joe should've called another electrician. Now Starling was going to *meet* Austin, and they were either going to get along like two wet cats in a bag or bond instantly and start plotting how to divest Joe of his last remaining shred of sanity.

"On second thought," he said and tried to pull away.

"Nuh-uh." Starling squeezed one more time and then let him go. "Sorry. We hugged on it. It's a hug deal. Can't break those."

Joe wouldn't anyway—couldn't afford to—but he could see how the next few weeks were going to play out. Rather like the past two weeks, but with one more person and an exponentially higher number of third-degree burns about his love life.

At least now he could see the floor in most of the rooms on the ground level. Not *all* of the floor of course, but still. Floor. Progress.

"Fine," he acquiesced.

"Great. Now we can celebrate our business relationship with pizza."

Joe figured buying her dinner was the least he could do. But there was nowhere to sit to eat now that the dining table had been liquidated into... well, probably part of a septic repair, and anyway, nobody delivered out here. They went into Essex and hit up Woodcraft for dinner, but Joe didn't want to linger. He'd made good progress today, and if he could stick it out for another hour and a half, he could finish sorting the office and bedroom. Then he could amalgamate all the accumulated "What are we doing with this, anyway?" piles in one and pull up the kitchen subfloor to see how bad the joists had rotted.

"Just as an FYI," Starling said when they were pulling back into the driveway, their leftovers stashed safely in Joe's cooler because he was still too chickenshit to open the fridge, "you are going to need, like, so much drywall compound. Can you even use drywall compound on plaster?"

"That's a problem for future Joe and—"

The truck, and his train of thought, screeched to a halt simultaneously.

Starling said, "Dude, is someone squatting in your driveway?"

Joe blinked at the geriatric trailer parked between the two garages. A cheerful yellow light gleamed inside it, or maybe it wasn't yellow but was just picking up on the general yellow vibe of the whole patchwork metal Frankenstein thing. The trailer might have been cream once. It was tiny—so small it might've fit in the one-car garage if the garage weren't full of three lawn mowers, two rain barrels, a wheelbarrow with a flat tire, and fifteen bags of fertilizer. There were a pair of boots next to the stairs, which seemed stupid because it was fucking November; who wanted to put on freezing-cold boots?

A moment later the whole scene got even more surreal when a little whitish-yellow shape darted through his headlights, skittered under the trailer, and then disappeared around the side of the pole barn.

Starling said, "Did you get a *dog*?"

"Is that what that was?" Joe parked the truck. "Can you just—I'm going to go find out what's going on."

Starling's delighted laugh chased him out of the cab. "Wait for me."

The door slammed behind him as he strode up to the trailer and raised his hand. *Rap-rap-rap.* "Austin! Are you—"

The door opened. Sure enough, Austin stood on the other side of it, hair pulled back under a bandana, beat-up jeans hanging off his hips, yogurt cup in one hand, spoon dangling from his lips. He reached up his free hand to take it out. "Hey, be gentle on this old lady, Joe. Think it's in worse shape than the house." Those coal-dark eyes flicked from Joe to Starling. "Oh. Didn't know you had company tonight."

Joe could practically feel Starling's unfettered delight behind him as Austin waved the spoon. This was absolutely not a two-wet-cats-in-a-bag scenario. Fuck. "That's Starling. She's my friend. Also an electrician. And also not the point—did you bring a dog here?"

Austin's brow furrowed. "Why would I bring a dog here?" He gestured to encompass the property. "Like, the house is barely safe enough for your four pseudo-adult children. I'm not gonna put a dog in it."

"I saw a dog," Joe said. He sounded insane. He *felt* insane. Also, the dog was not the point either. "What's with the trailer?"

"Oh, this?" Austin patted the doorframe. It rattled. "Got tired of losing so much time driving home at night. By the time I get back to Windsor, I've got a second wind, you know? Then I sleep like shit. Or else I don't get a second wind and I'm in danger of driving into a ditch. Not great."

"We have a house," Joe pointed out.

"Yeah, and I had this thing rotting in the parking lot. Besides, every mattress in that place has mouse droppings on it."

Well, when he put it like that—"Fair point. But, like, an air mattress would've been less work."

"An air mattress doesn't have a fridge attached."

Why did Joe feel like he was getting shade for forbidding anyone to open the Schrödinger's nightmare that was DeeDee's refrigerator? "Whatever," he said. "Anyway, I guess there's a stray, so just… watch out it doesn't run off with your boots or whatever."

Austin transferred the yogurt cup to the spoon hand and held the other one up, palm facing outward. "I will protect the boots." Then he paused. "Did you ask Linda about the dog?"

Joe blinked again. "Linda?"

"Yeah." Austin gestured toward their only neighbor, a stone's throw down the road. The light on the back porch illuminated the wide stretch of recently mown lawn between the two houses. "Linda. She mentioned the septic problem to me? I guess she and DeeDee had a standing dinner date on Wednesdays."

DeeDee had had a more active social life in the past twelve months than Joe had, and she'd been dead for four of them. That was depressing.

"Right. Linda," Joe said. He wondered if she and Austin were going to continue the Wednesday dinner date.

"I'll call her." Austin stepped back into the trailer. When he returned to the door with his phone, he arrived without a yogurt and wearing a hoodie.

Joe and Starling shamelessly eavesdropped as Austin asked Linda if she had a dog.

"Uh, I don't know." Austin pulled the phone away from his mouth. "What did it look like?"

"A yellow-cream blur. We saw it sprinting away," Joe explained.

Austin relayed the information, then went pale and yelped, "What?!"

Joe and Starling leaned in. "What is it?" Joe asked, worried.

Their eyes met. "She said it might have been a coyote. A coyote?" He put the phone back to his mouth. "Linda, I don't do coyotes. I'm a city boy."

Joe and Starling looked at each other and held back their laughter.

"I don't think it was the right size," Starling said placatingly.

"Or the right color," Joe put in. As much fun as it was to watch Austin freak out, he didn't want the poor guy to have a meltdown.

Austin gave them a grateful look. "Okay, so probably not a coyote." He waited while Linda spoke once more, then hung up.

Apparently Linda didn't know the dog, but she told them to bring it to her if they did find it. "Turns out she's a vet."

Austin stepped into his boots and shut the door of the trailer behind him. "Any thoughts as to the best way to find a stray dog?"

Chapter Five

THEY DIDN'T find the dog.

Austin wanted to keep searching, but dark set in, and Joe called a halt.

"What if she's hurt?" Austin couldn't take the idea of an injured animal alone at night, especially now that it was getting colder.

But Joe refused to give in to his pleading. "It's too dark to keep looking," he said sternly, like Austin was one of his children, and dragged him into the house.

For the hour or so while they were unloading and sorting through boxes, Joe almost succeeded in getting Austin's mind off the poor dog somewhere out in wilderness, but when Austin made his way back to the trailer after Joe drove away, he couldn't help but look around for sightings of a furry tan animal hiding somewhere.

So when he got back to the trailer, he sat down at the tiny decrepit table and continued the slow task of cleaning and oiling the typewriter they'd found, until his eyes started to sting and he fell into the tiny bed.

The early drive from the house to his shop was definitely preferable to the late drive, and Austin had no regrets about the trailer that day.

A few days later, Austin made his way up to the second floor for the first attempt at a declutter.

He decided to start with one of the smaller bedrooms, as it was, surprisingly, the least horrifying—perhaps because DeeDee hadn't wanted to fill up the room that might have been a child's or perhaps had acted as a guest room. Either way, there was actual visible floor space, unlike the third bedroom to the right, which was so full Austin couldn't tell if it even held a bed.

Hours later Austin sat cross-legged on the floor, surrounded by the usual three piles—garbage, sentimental, decide later.

"Find anything good yet?" Joe asked from the doorway, and Austin jumped.

He looked up from his spot to see Joe leaning casually against the frame, arms crossed and hip cocked. Austin took a moment to appreciate the sight of the man's legs in jeans, then looked down at the object in his hands. He'd found a small bookshelf that might have belonged to a child and promptly gotten distracted by the contents.

"Found stuff for Meg and her family," he admitted.

"Oh?" Joe lifted an eyebrow, and for some reason, Austin blushed. He hadn't been doing anything wrong, but now that Joe was standing there, he felt caught out.

"Yeah. Old kids' books, school books, a couple of journals, mostly empty, I think. And a photo album."

"Oh!" Joe lurched forward and dropped down beside Austin in the only spot of empty floorspace, apparently unconcerned that it meant their thighs were all but glued together. "Lemme see."

So Austin flipped back to the beginning of the small album, and together they leafed through. The shots were mostly from the '80s and '90s, and some featured a woman Austin guessed was a younger DeeDee, but he couldn't say any of the other faces were familiar. Well, beyond a passing resemblance to Meg, suggesting a familial link.

"Definitely Meg's dad," Joe said with a laugh as he pointed to a picture of a young man in baggy clothes, looking artfully unimpressed by the cake before him with fourteen candles.

"Cute," Austin said sarcastically. Then he looked back to the bookshelf for any more finds. He didn't want to look at pictures of strangers rejecting the sort of happy childhood hallmarks he would have begged for at that age.

"Fourteen-year-olds," Joe said. "I can't say I miss that stage. The kids are definitely cooler now they're approaching drinking age."

"Harsh," Austin said as he flipped through an aged copy of *The Fellowship of the Ring*.

"Nah. Talk to me when you've got kids in the preteen, early-teen stage and then you can judge." He bumped their shoulders together to take the sting out of the words. Not that Austin was stung by the reminder that he didn't have a fourteen-year-old at the ripe old age of twenty-nine.

Joe dropped the photo album into a box with Meg's name and gestured at the book. "You ever read?"

"Yeah." Austin set the book onto a pile that he'd been setting aside. He didn't know if Meg's family would want to bother with them.

"Could never make it through the series," Joe said. "Got bored in the first book."

Austin shrugged. "It picks up." He didn't add that the copy he read had belonged to a foster parent who hadn't had a TV or the internet and whose library had mostly consisted of stuff for little children or dull, long-winded history textbooks.

Austin had read every novel in that house, cover to cover, as a way of relieving the boredom generated by a 5:00 p.m. curfew and no TV.

He pulled out a few more books and set them aside. Joe broke the silence as he flipped through a copy of *Call of the Wild*. "Still no sign of the dog?"

"No." Austin's mouth twisted. He was beginning to think they wouldn't find it. He hoped that was because it was safe and not because it had gotten hurt. "What if we left some food out?"

Joe turned and gave him a look. "Yeah, no. Not unless you want something else to come visit, like racoons or worse—like the coyote that Linda suggested our mystery dog was."

Austin conceded the point but couldn't help but pout. "Fine." He pulled over a new box, flipped it open, and stared. Then he slammed it shut, face burning. "Why would DeeDee have a box of *Playboys*?"

"What?" Joe lunged for the box and leaned into Austin's space, practically sprawling across his lap. He tore the flaps back and breathed with delight. "Oh my God." He reached into the box.

Austin covered his eyes.

"Why are you hiding?" Joe demanded. "This is amazing."

"Did you forget the part where I'm very gay? Besides, I don't want to see someone else's *magazine* collection."

"Okay, one, you are making assumptions here, buddy. Because, two, these are from, like, the '70s, and in pretty decent condition, and—" Joe looked back in the box and shifted some magazines around. "There's also some Archie comics and gardening magazines in here, so I bet this is another one of her thrifting or junk collections. You know, the old *Playboys* can have value, like anything else vintage."

Austin's shoulders untensed, though he didn't want to take a closer look at the magazine Joe was actually flipping through.

Joe sat back and then shot Austin a look. "Ooor, maybe they were DeeDee's and she kept them for the articles."

Against all Austin's better judgment, he opened his mouth. "What kind of articles does *Playboy* have?"

Joe shrugged. "I don't know—let's find out." He plopped a magazine in Austin's lap and flipped back to the beginning of his own, like he was looking for a table of contents.

Austin still felt like he should be wearing gloves, but so far none of the magazines had crackled with anything suspicious, so he opened the cover.

And—all right. The pictures of naked or nearly naked women didn't do anything for him, but they weren't *gross*, other than in the exploitative way pictures like this were inherently gross. Bisexual or not, Joe didn't seem to be lingering on them either. Maybe he thought so too. Or maybe he was having the Dad Reaction, imagining Meg being photographed like that.

Austin grimaced and put *that* thought out of his mind, to focus firmly on the words in front of him.

Then, blinking, he flipped back to the front cover to check the magazine's date.

"Huh."

"Mmm?" Joe asked beside him and leaned to look over Austin's shoulder.

Austin paged back to the article and read the line that had caught his attention. "About AIDS being a 'gay' disease: It's not. There's no such thing. Germs can swing both ways, and they don't care whom their hosts sleep with." He paused and let that sink into him—the reality of a magazine printing those words in October of 1983. "Is it weird that I'm now kind of hoping these actually were DeeDee's and that she *did* read them for the articles?"

Joe already had his phone out. "I mean, I'm asking Meg right now, so...."

"In the group chat?" Austin asked, imagining the chaos that would ensue.

Joe glanced up, warm eyes dancing in the light of the single lamp plugged in on the floor two feet away. "They give me so much shit, you don't even know. It's karma."

Needless to say, they didn't get much sorting accomplished that night. Instead, they spent an hour reading each other bits and pieces of the unusual treasure they'd found. Many of the magazines had short stories by authors Austin had read before—Vonnegut, Oates, le Carré. At the bottom of the box, they found a truly ancient issue that had a story set in a dystopian future where everyone was gay and people marched against heterosexuality.

"I'm not going to lie. My mind is totally blown right now."

"Same," Joe agreed. "Mind blown, ass numb."

Now that he mentioned it, Austin was feeling the lack of circulation himself. He glanced at his phone. "Jesus, it's eight o'clock."

"That explains why I'm so fucking hungry." Joe used Austin's shoulder to leverage himself to his feet, then offered his hand. "Come on, you want to go find dinner?"

For a second, Austin stared at it, uncomprehending.

Joe waggled his fingers.

Austin let Joe pull him to his feet. It left them standing close enough for Austin to feel the heat of Joe's body from his shoulders to his knees.

But it wasn't just body heat, was it? It was something else, in the light of Joe's eyes and the fondness in his smile. Something in the way the touch of his palm on Austin's seemed to linger even after they let go.

Or maybe he was just delirious from hunger. That had to be it.

Austin cleared his throat. "Uh, I mean, I was just going to make mac and cheese with hot dogs in the trailer. But you're welcome to join me."

"Well, if you're rolling out the red carpet like that...."

"It's not too plebian for you?" Jesus, Austin's knees had forgotten his feet even existed. He was all pins and needles. On the way down the stairs, he held tight to the railing.

Behind him, Joe huffed a laugh. "Nah, it'll be just like the dinners I made the kids before I learned to cook things that didn't come out of a box. Nostalgic, practically."

Austin shook his head. He'd seen the evidence firsthand, and it still seemed impossible that a teenage boy could collect seven-year-olds like orphaned ducklings—that he would want to. How different would his life be now, if he'd had a Joe when he was that age?

"I'm not much of a cook myself. Never seemed much point."

They trotted out the side door, down the steps, and across the driveway to the trailer. Austin gestured Joe toward the tiny table while he filled a pot with water and took out the milk and butter. There wasn't really room for Joe to help.

"Not much family?"

Joe asked the question mildly, in a way that would've let Austin brush it off, but he didn't. Maybe *because* he knew Joe wouldn't judge him and maybe because Joe didn't feel sorry for the kids. He just cared for them because someone had to, and he could. "Foster kid," he said.

Joe didn't need to know all the details. "No one really took the time to teach me when I was young, and once I was on my own, it seemed pointless to cook for one."

"I hear that. I don't even do it most of the time, and I *like* cooking."

Austin had a vision of the farmhouse kitchen, torn up and redone in secondhand cabinets, Joe standing in front of an oven that didn't match the fridge and the kids crowded around an island or snatching pieces of roasted turkey off a cutting board while his back was turned. He dismissed the thought with a shake of his head. Just because they were fixing up the house didn't mean they were keeping it. But maybe they'd have time for a celebratory meal before they sold it.

"Well," Austin said without thinking, "if you're willing to cook, I'm willing to eat. Or, you know, do cleanup or grocery shop or whatever."

"Careful or I'll take you up on that." He paused. "Though before I cook anything in that kitchen, we have to deal with the fridge."

Austin snorted and dumped the macaroni into the pot, the hot dogs into his little frying pan. "If you'd let me handle it two weeks ago—"

"We didn't even know if we could open the windows yet then. They could've been painted shut."

"Well, it's getting kind of cold to open them now."

"It's not like the pipes are going to freeze. And no one's sleeping in there at the moment. It'll be fine."

For God's sake. Austin shuffled the hot dogs over, pulled out the colander to drain the pasta. "Why are you okay with it now when you were dead set against it before? And don't give me the window line."

When he didn't get an answer right away, he looked over. Joe was sitting at the tiny chipped Formica table, looking at his hands. "Would you believe me if I said I had fridge-related trauma?"

Fridge-related...? Austin poked at the hot dogs. "Not without follow-up questions."

The pasta had finished cooking, so he drained it in the tiny sink and scraped the last of the margarine out of the container into the pot. He crossed the two steps it took to open the door and drop the empty container in the blue box next to the step.

When he turned around, Joe was looking up at him, smiling. "Give me a second to come up with a good lie, then."

Austin gave him a moment while he finished dinner and plated it up in a couple of plastic bowls he'd salvaged from DeeDee's. They had scenes from Peter Rabbit on the insides. But before either of them could take more than a few bites or Joe could spin his wild tale of refrigerator terror, there was a shuffle of noise from outside the trailer, the rattle of plastic and tin.

They met eyes over the table. Underneath it, their legs tangled for a fraction of a second as they both sprung to their feet.

"Is it—"

"The dog—"

Austin half tripped as he went for the door and grabbed the plug-in flashlight from the bulkhead as he went. The trailer door flapped behind them.

The recycling bin had been tipped over—no shock there; he should've realized keeping it outside was a bad idea—and the margarine container, which he'd dropped in without its lid, had wandered off. They stood on the driveway for a moment, listening, and then after a moment, Joe pointed around the back of the house. "That way, I think."

Part of Austin recognized that chasing a dog that was running away would likely not result in the dog trusting them, but what else was he supposed to do? It was a dark country road, and the thing could get hit by a car. If it was out here scavenging in his trash, it was obviously hungry. And Linda had said there were coyotes around.

"So, foster kid." Joe paused like he was making a point. "You always wanted a dog?"

"Fuck off," Austin said automatically, even as the guilt set in, because—well, yeah. "Every kid wants a dog."

Joe snorted as Austin played the beam of the flashlight around the side yard. No little-to-medium-size dog revealed itself, though he did catch an opossum trundling along next to the breezeway. It stopped its lopsided waddle to hiss at him.

"I mean, true. Mom would never let me have one, said it'd get dog hair all over the house."

"Not a fan of messes?" Austin asked, casting the beam about.

Joe hummed. "She kept her house showroom ready."

Interesting. "She's a Realtor, right? So it's not like she was selling *your* home...."

"Live like you wanna be, and all that." Joe shrugged. "Mom understands the value of a good impression and of appearances. If she's going to tell clients to have their houses in order, then she should too. Not to mention, how can you trust someone to know the value of your home if they don't know the value of their own?" He gave a rueful smile.

"Sounds like she has… high standards," Austin offered tentatively.

Joe shrugged and moved forward, visibly searching once more for the dog, making Austin suddenly aware of the fact that he'd stopped in his curiosity about Joe.

"High standards is one way of putting it. Another would be that the house, the husband, the kid were all… checkpoints. She had a kid because that's what successful women did, but she didn't know what to *do* with us… me. Especially after I got too old to be an adorable showpiece and her marriage ended anyway so there were fewer family-style holiday parties."

"I'm sorry," Austin said feelingly.

Joe shrugged again. "Poor-little-rich-boy problems." He shot a grin over his shoulder. "Though I guess my whole teen-adoption thing makes more sense now. I have Mommy *and* Daddy issues."

"Doesn't everybody?" Austin said, letting Joe change the conversational flow. "I mean, I'm given to understand even good parents leave their kids with issues."

"You're probably right," Joe huffed as they rounded the house, still no sign of the dog. "Should we keep searching?"

As much as Austin wanted to say yes, common sense prevailed. "Maybe we'll catch sight of him on the way back to the trailer?"

"Maybe."

They kept checking the greenery and under and behind objects, but they had no luck as they approached the trailer again.

Austin tripped up the steps and stopped in his tracks. Their dinner— or rather, the empty dishes of what remained of it—lay on the floor.

"Uh…."

"Austin?" Joe followed up the steps, but since Austin was frozen, Joe had nowhere to go but into him. His chest pushed up against Austin's back, broad and warm, and he hooked his chin over Austin's shoulder. "What's—oh."

They stood in silence, staring at the floor.

"Hey, Austin? I think we found evidence of the dog."

"Yeah," Austin said glumly. He sighed and stepped forward to clean up. The trailer was too small for the dog to be hiding in it. He must have snuck in after they left and made a rapid escape. "I think we're going to need a backup plan for dinner."

Joe cleared his throat. "I'll pick something up while you take care of this. What's your order?"

SUNDAY MORNING found Joe at the farmhouse bright and early, wincing against the mean morning sunshine that glinted off the lurid green dumpster parked next to the trailer.

"Think it's big enough?" Austin asked, voice morning rough. His breath steamed in the chilly air.

"Based on how much you hate throwing things away?"

"Hey. Rude. See if I offer you a coffee."

Coffee. Joe knew he'd forgotten something in his haste to get out of the house this morning. He turned beseeching eyes on Austin.

"God, put those away." Austin shoved his arm. "Come on. I'll caffeinate you, and then we should get started. The kids coming to help?"

Joe waggled his hand and followed him into the trailer. "Gavin and Alex are coming later—you know what teenagers are like in the morning. Will's got church with the family, and Meg has practice. Wouldn't ask her to help anyway. I'm not risking her swimming career."

"That's fair." Austin poured a mug from a tiny coffee maker on the trailer counter and passed it over. In chipping enamel paint, the side read, *1979 Harrow Fair.* "Sugar?"

"Please. And milk, if you have it."

Austin *tsk*ed. "Such a princess." But he handed over actual creamer, not just milk, so obviously he loved Joe and wanted him to be happy. Or at least caffeinated.

Joe poured in enough liquid fat to cool the coffee to chugging temperature, then downed it and handed the mug back. Austin watched with raised brows but didn't comment as he set the mug in the sink. "Okay," Joe said. "Let's go. Operation Dumpster Fire."

"If you pour gasoline in that thing, we're getting a divorce."

They emptied the garage first. Austin had already repaired and sold two of the lawn mowers, and the cash was now sitting in an old coffee can in the kitchen because they weren't opening a joint checking account just for the next six months, and trying to split all the bills fifty-fifty was insane. Now they rolled out the rain barrels. One had a long crack in the side. Austin opened it up and they filled it with other garage detritus—old newspapers and trash, wood scraps too small to be useful, holey boots and broken gardening tools. Then they tilted it onto its side and slid it into the dumpster.

That left a few useful implements—a snow shovel, pruning shears, a rake, and a snowblower that impressed even Austin by starting on the first try. Joe tidied up some plywood and two-by-fours that might yet find a home during this impromptu reno project. He leaned them against the outside wall so Austin could use his miniature blower to clear out the dust, which he did with his bandana pulled over his face.

Joe stayed out of the way. He didn't want to inhale whatever had been growing in that garage for the past forty years either.

Finally Austin surveyed the space and declared, "Okay. Looks good, let's do it."

The next thing to go was the demon fridge. Austin gave Joe bombastic side-eye when he secured ratchet straps *and* a padlock around the doors before they managed to wrangle the thing onto a dolly and out to its final destination.

Joe sighed with relief when the job was done.

Austin only shook his head.

For the next hour, they wrestled the mouse-eaten "soft goods" furniture out of the main floor of the house and into the dumpster. The decaying couch was the first thing to go, though Austin thought the armchair looked like it was in decent-enough shape, so that got moved to the garage instead.

With several pieces of furniture out of the way, they were able to pile the boxes more efficiently and finally excavate parts of the house that were previously unreachable.

In the living room, behind towers of boxes, newspapers, and magazines, they found a piano—an antique upright with carved details on the front legs and panels. The old mahogany-stained wood was battered, but it looked in good condition from the outside. Unable to resist the temptation, Joe lifted the key cover. Over the keyboard, in gold lettering, was the name Sherlock-Manning. Joe loved it.

Still curious, he pulled out the old bench, tested it gingerly to make sure it would stand up under his weight, and then sat down. Cautiously, he plunked a few keys to test them out. He tapped out a quick melody and didn't want to cringe. He wouldn't say it was in tune, exactly, but it wasn't as catastrophically off-key as he'd expected.

"Do you play?" Austin asked, stepping in close.

"Took lessons as a kid. Mom insisted." He tried a few quick scales to warm up his fingers.

"You any good?" Austin teased. "I mean, you haven't been a kid in a while."

Instead of answering, Joe smirked and then, with a quick prayer to the music gods that his fingers would remember what to do, he began. The first few notes were a bit rusty, but he quickly fell into the swing of the old Queen song. Muscle memory took hold, and when he reached the verse, he began to sing "Love of My Life."

No one would claim that Joe was brilliant—he wasn't about to put Michael Bublé or Harry Styles out of a job. But he could carry a tune.

Caught up in the song, one of his favourites, he kept playing all the way through to the end.

When the last notes faded, he opened his eyes and found Austin still standing to the right and staring somewhat wide-eyed. Looked like Joe had finally managed to surprise him.

"What do you think? Should I take my show on the road?" Joe batted his lashes.

Austin coughed and rolled his eyes. "You'll need a better instrument if you plan on going professional."

"Hey, she's a fine instrument." Joe swiped a hand across the open lid.

"I mean. It's shockingly okay-sounding," Austin agreed. "What's the make?" He fished out his phone.

"Sherlock-Manning."

"What, seriously? Okay. Hmm, looks like a Canadian company. They opened in 1902 and existed until the eighties."

"So what you're saying is that this thing is anywhere from forty to a hundred and twenty years old."

"I guess so." Austin looked at the piano again, as if he could guesstimate the age by the look alone. Joe had respect for Austin's varied knowledge of antique and vintage items, but he doubted it stretched that far.

"I'll buy you out of it," Joe said quickly.

Austin looked up and blinked. "What?"

"Just...." Joe couldn't explain it, the sudden panic he felt at the idea of Austin trying to determine the instrument's value, offloading it on some Facebook Marketplace ad. "I want to keep this one."

It wasn't that weird, right? Austin had kept those bowls and a few of the dishes—nothing worth as much as a piano or anything, but—

"You don't have to buy me out." He put his phone back in his pocket and the thing in Joe's chest that had tightened at the idea of the piano leaving him loosened again. "But you do have to get off your ass and help me clean out the rest of the house."

Half an hour later, he was trying to move the filing cabinet in the office, but when he called out to Austin for help, no one answered. Annoyed, he squeezed his way around the various furniture toward the dining room. "Austin?"

"Joe? Thank fuck," came the muffled voice—from behind him. Joe turned around. The noise had come from the closed bathroom door. "I'm stuck and don't have my phone."

"How exactly did you get stuck?"

A deep sigh. "The fucking door handle came off."

Joe blinked. It was still attached on the outside. But when he reached out to open the door, his side came off in his hand. "Ah." He knelt down to peek through the hole where the doorknob was supposed to go. He could see the light on the other side, as well as some kind of mechanism that obviously worked the lock and latch. "Okay, so... any idea how to open the door?"

"You could pop the hinges off, but that's probably overkill."

God, Joe hoped so. This door looked pretty heavy. It would be awkward as fuck to try to get it back on. "Yeah, let's call that Plan C." He registered movement on the other side, then made out the dark brown of Austin's iris peering back through the hole. "Did you lock it?"

"Unfortunately."

Shit. "Did you *unlock* it before the handle came off?"

"I fucking hope so. I really don't want to spend the rest of my life in the john."

"I don't want that either. At some point I'm going to have to pee."

"I guess I could go out the window."

Despite much coaxing, that window had never opened more than four inches. "Plan Z," Joe said. "I don't want to buy a new window for Christmas." He squinted at the various metal bits that made up the handle. "I'll go get a screwdriver."

The screwdriver, despite its many interchangeable tips, did not appear to be the correct tool. Whatever Joe managed to unscrew didn't seem capable of unlatching the door.

"Maybe I can get it from this side," Austin said impatiently. "Can you push it under the door?"

Joe couldn't. It didn't fit.

Something thunked against the other side of the door. Probably Austin's head. "So… back to those hinges."

Joe tapped the screwdriver against the lock guts. There was a spring *there*, and that bit obviously attached to the doorknob, so…. "This would've been easier if I were the one stuck in the bathroom, huh?"

Austin snorted. "Little bit." The door shifted and the light changed; he must be looking through the hole again. "Hey… do you think you can fit a butter knife through there?"

The butter knife didn't fit through the hole, but it did fit under the door, and a few seconds later Austin jammed the blade into the slot left by the handle and twisted.

The door opened.

"Freedom!" Austin said, mock jubilant, his hands raised in victory.

Joe yanked him out of the bathroom by the hand. "Move. I have to pee."

By the time Gavin and Alex showed up, the dumpster was just under half full and Joe had worked up enough of a sweat to ditch his hoodie in Austin's trailer. His work T-shirt stuck to his back. Austin had tied his flannel overshirt around his waist and the bandana back in his hair again. Joe was half tempted to offer him one of the dozens of hair ties he'd accumulated in his truck, some left there by Meg and Alex and Starling and some he'd bought to have on hand when they needed one.

He didn't get the words out before the side door banged open. Damn kids were going to dent the plaster. Not that you'd be able to tell.

"Manners!" Joe hollered anyway.

"Child labor!" Gavin yelled back.

Austin snorted.

"You're almost eighteen," Joe pointed out. "Move, please." Gavin was in the way of Joe and Austin getting the fuck-off heavy dresser from the front bedroom into the garage.

Alex held the door from the outside, because at some point Joe's lessons on courtesy had stuck with them in a way they hadn't with the other kids.

"Thank you, Alex. You're my favorite."

"Hey," Gavin protested.

"Hay is for horses," Joe and Alex chorused.

Austin tripped over the threshold. "Jesus Christ, you *actual dad*."

Alex and Gavin stepped forward before the dresser could come to any harm, but Austin didn't need help, even if his facial expression said he thought Joe did.

Joe only grinned at him. "If you think that's bad, you should see the Father's Day presents I get." He steadied himself to take his first step down the porch stairs. "Now—lift with your legs."

Chapter Six

EMPTYING AND cleaning the remainder of the first floor—including the horrible kitchen cabinets and appliances—took until early afternoon. Joe sent the kids into town for pizza while he and Austin panted in the camp chairs they'd set up in the dining room.

"Septic guy confirmed for tomorrow?" Austin asked, wondering if he could get away with sneaking out to the trailer for a catnap before lunch. He'd cleared tomorrow's appointments from the garage schedule. Frankly he was looking forward to spending the day in the trailer, possibly with the space heater cranked since the temperature was finally supposed to drop, and reading, hilariously, a couple decades' worth of *Playboy* short fiction.

"Yeah." They both looked at the kitchen sink—housed in the only remaining cabinet, left in case the septic guy needed to inspect it to diagnose their issue.

"Fingers crossed."

"Ripping up the floor next weekend?"

Austin waggled his hand back and forth. "Maybe. Could start sooner." Especially since he had Monday off. "At least get a feeling for what we're working with. I'm not an expert carpenter, though."

"Eh," Joe said, half smiling, "that's okay. I'm pretty good with wood."

"So your shirt says," Austin said wryly. This one said I Like Big Birch. It had the logo for Joe's company on the back.

He preened. "Gavin designed it. Birthday present from the kids. Have to give him credit for finally picking a slogan I can wear in public."

Oh God. Austin had to ask. "What do the other ones say?"

"The one the kids like best is I Heart Hardwood."

Austin choked. "Of course it was."

Joe grinned.

"Your children are menaces."

"Only most of the time. The rest of the time, they have redeeming qualities."

At that moment, Gavin and Alex returned with the pizza and once again made a loud entrance.

"I found you a girlfriend." Gavin grinned at them over the boxes. He had the appeal of a cherubic kindergartener—innocent enthusiasm that made you want to give in to his schemes and avoid disappointing him. How he managed to pull that off while meddling in Joe's love life, Austin wasn't sure.

"A girlfriend," Joe repeated.

Next to Gavin, carrying a bag with their ordered drinks, Alex nodded. "Yeah, we ran into Ms. Kent, our math teacher, at the pizza shop."

"And she's totally single," Gavin added, "because she never talks about dating anyone, but she talks about her brother and niblings all the time."

Austin bit his lip to keep from laughing as Joe literally facepalmed.

"Your teacher," he muttered. "I do not want to date your teacher."

"Why not?" Gavin asked.

"Yeah, why not? Ms. Kent is really pretty, and you know she's into family and kids, what with the talking about her own all the time." Alex crossed their arms, clearly annoyed at having their reasonable suggestion brushed aside.

"Ms. Kent isn't *pretty*. She's totally snatched—I mean, for an old math teacher."

Joe pinched his nose. "I know I'm going to regret this, but how old is she?"

"Um. I mean, I think she mentioned something about being a young millennial once...."

"I don't know if I should be insulted that you called me old or relieved that you've shown some sense in your matchmaking efforts."

"Definitely the first one," Austin said. "You're not the only one they called old."

"We didn't call you *ancient* or anything," Gavin said. "And why don't you want to date our teacher?"

"Gavin, more to the point, why *would* I want to?"

"Um, did you miss the part about hot?"

"So you want to look at the person giving you math tests knowing I kissed them?"

Gavin opened his mouth, shut it, and wilted. "Fine." He put the pizza boxes down, and Alex passed around their drinks.

They each grabbed a slice, and for a moment, everyone was too hungry to talk. But of course, it couldn't last.

"I just don't get it," Gavin said. "You're terminally single. If I looked like you, I'd be drowning in pussy."

"Ick," Alex yelped.

"Or ass, I guess," Gavin amended, with a nod toward Joe.

"So, you're stealing his looks *and* his sexuality?" Alex snarked.

"Young one," Joe said seriously, "with great power comes great responsibility."

Austin nearly snorted cream soda out his nose.

"Excuses," Gavin said. He waved his pizza in the air while he spoke. "You just don't have any game."

"It's true," Alex agreed. "No game."

"I've never even seen you flirt."

Joe stared. "Did you want to?"

Alex made a face, and Gavin shrugged.

"Aren't you supposed to model healthy adult relationships for us and shit?"

Joe looked at Austin. "I regret my life choices."

"But they're so entertaining." Austin wiped a smear of pizza grease off his chin. "Being a single dad must be so hard."

"If it is," Gavin said sagely, "he's taking care of it by himself."

"*Ugh.*" Alex threw down their pizza. "Gross. Really, Gavin? While we're *eating*?"

Where had his paper towel gone? It took Austin a moment to locate it, stuck with cheese to the bottom of his paper plate. "Kid," he said, meeting Gavin's eyes across the room. "You say he's got no game."

"He categorically has no game," Gavin proclaimed. "He's been single for *so long*. It's sad."

Austin glanced at Joe, who had taken the teasing with good grace, mostly, but now looked kind of miserable. Austin could only guess he was thinking of his last relationship and its untimely demise, and Gavin's well-meaning interference wasn't helping.

"He owns his own business," Austin said. "He plays piano. Good body. *Great* ass. His face is okay."

Alex cackled. Joe said, with furrowed brow, "Thanks?"

Gavin only raised his eyebrows and gestured for Austin to continue.

"From where I'm sitting, he's got plenty of game." He paused for dramatic effect and threw his napkin at Gavin's head. "He just ain't playing."

It would've been a good mic-drop moment, but Joe ruined it by clapping once and then pointing, like a dad. "*Yes*," he said. "Exactly."

Austin sighed and shook his head. "Never mind."

They packed the rest of the pizza into the trailer fridge and split up to go back to work. Joe and Gavin stayed downstairs to start moving boxes out to the garage or the pole barn or the dumpster, and Austin and Alex went upstairs.

"Keep an eye out for any little typewriter bits," Austin said as he unfastened the headboard for the twin bed. "I'm missing a couple keys."

Alex peered at him from where they were holding the wood steady so it didn't crush Austin's noggin when the bolts came out. "I thought it didn't work."

He snorted, then grimaced and put a little more elbow grease on the wrench. "Yeah, but I can fix that if I find the letters." The nut finally eased, and he picked up the drill with the socket attachment from the floor beside him to finish the job.

"Cool."

He looked up. "Yeah, it is. I like saving things from being junk."

They grinned. "This house is really testing you, eh?"

He laughed and started work on the second bolt. "You're not wrong."

The hardware went in a small paper bag he taped to the headboard with painter's tape, and they carried the bedframe down the stairs in pieces.

Up and down and up and down and up and down they went, until the sun was kissing the horizon and Alex and Gavin waved goodbye to go home to their families for dinner.

"Almost done?" Joe asked.

"Couple mattresses left," Austin said. He hadn't wanted to ask Alex to help with those; they seemed pretty strong, but the stairs were narrow and steep and one of the mattresses had a rusted spring poking out. "And a surprise."

Joe looked exhausted, but he nodded grimly. "Mattresses first."

They trudged back up the stairs.

The first mattress was full-size. It barely squeezed down, the top just brushing the ceiling at the narrowest part of the staircase.

Maybe that lulled them into a false sense of security, because the second one didn't go nearly as smoothly.

"You're gonna have to push," Austin called from the bottom. They'd pulled down on the queen-size mattress to compress it enough to get it this far, but they couldn't reach it now, and it was stuck. "I knew we should've used the ratchet straps."

"You and your goddamn ratchet straps," Joe grumbled. Austin could hear the forced huffs of his breath as he put his shoulder into trying to unjam the mattress. "Okay, pull on three. Ready? One." Austin adjusted his grip. "Two." He braced his shoulder against the wall. "Three!"

Joe pushed. Austin pulled.

The mattress gave not at all, and then all at once. Or so Austin thought—until he heard the crack and his foot went out from under him. "Oh *shit*—"

"Austin?"

He flailed out one-handed and latched on to the railing, which steadied him for a moment before it pulled free of the plaster with a lurch.

His foot sank lower.

"Austin! Are you—"

Austin looked down. His left leg was bent at the knee in a squat, his left arm stretched out grasping the useless railing.

His right leg was dangling below him, having fallen victim to a sudden hole in the staircase.

"I'm stuck," Austin said succinctly.

"Jesus Christ," Joe said. "*Again?*" Perhaps he hoped Austin was joking, or maybe he had already seen the problem. Joe couldn't do shit to help. He was stuck upstairs so long as the mattress was blocking the way down.

Austin dropped his forehead to the mattress—then jerked back when he thought about putting his face on that gross thing. "Yes. Stuck."

"What happened?" Joe sounded like he didn't actually want to know.

"Well, I can't see my right foot. It went right through."

"Right through the step?"

If Austin weren't currently wondering if he was going to be stuck here for the rest of his life, Joe's tone would have been hilarious. He almost wished he hadn't left his phone downstairs so that he could record it. "Yes. The step. I'm up to my knee."

"Oh. Fuck."

"Yup."

"Can you get unstuck?"

"Without you?"

"Yeah."

"Honestly? Not sure, but I guess I don't have much choice, do I?"

"Nope."

"Yeah." Austin took stock. The handrail shook under his grip. He doubted it would hold his weight if he tried to use it to pull himself up, so that was no good. He considered other options. His left foot, thank God, was on another step and solid. But was there anything to brace against with his right arm?

"Hey, Joe?"

"Yeah?"

"You have your phone, right?"

A pause. "Yeah," he said slowly.

"Oh good. I left mine downstairs. At least one of us can call for help."

"Do I need to?" He sounded nervous now. Austin wondered if his lack of panic was more that he'd gone far enough to go out the other side.

"Nah. But figured I should check before I give this a go. You know, just in case."

"Oh. Okay."

Austin braced his shoulder and his right arm against the wall, settled his left foot, and adjusted his grip on the old railing. *Don't pull*, he reminded himself. "Okay. Here goes."

He pushed. For a second, he thought nothing would happen. Then his knee shifted and he was all but popping up. He gripped the railing and mattress and panted, adrenaline spiking once more.

"Austin?"

"Yes. Out. I'm good."

"Oh thank God." He paused. "You're not bleeding or injured or anything, right?"

"No, but the hole in the steps is gonna make this a bit harder. Also, I'm condemning these stairs."

Joe sighed. "Yeah. I guess we better move replacing them up our list of repairs. Think we can buy that at Habitat?"

Austin snorted. "Don't know, but now is not the time to figure it out. Can we focus on getting off these death traps for now?"

It took another five minutes of pushing, pulling, and grunting, but at last they got themselves and the mattress downstairs.

"I'm assuming that wasn't the surprise you had for me."

Austin snorted. "Definitely not."

They didn't go back upstairs. Instead, they went to Austin's trailer to crack open a couple of beers, because if there was ever a day that called for alcohol, this was it. The goddamn house had tried to eat him twice in one day. Austin deserved so much beer.

Once they were settled into whatever seating they could find and Joe had taken a couple of long gulps, Austin let his curiosity take hold. "So, we gonna talk about the pachyderm your children dragged into the room and left behind?"

Joe snorted. "You mean my benchwarming?"

"Your benchwarming," Austin agreed. "I mean, you don't have to tell me squat, but I gotta admit I'm curious."

"A while back I had a boyfriend. We worked together at a local nursery—uh, for plants, not children—"

"I figured."

"—and we were at the permanent cohabitation stage. Found a house and everything." Joe drank more beer.

"I'm guessing this doesn't have a happy ending."

"Nope. The day before we were set to sign the paperwork, I caught him with his pants down, metaphorically."

"Shit. As in—"

"Yup. I got home after a week in Mexico for my cousin Fernanda's wedding. Paul couldn't get the time off to go along with me, or so he said." Joe sipped his beer. "So I get home after eight days away, opened the fridge to pour myself a glass of water, and suddenly I'm looking at a whole array of temperature-play sex toys. Which, like, okay, he could've just been missing me, but three of them were designed for parts he didn't have, and the used condoms in the kitchen trash kind of gave it away. And to add insult to injury, he left the previous week's stir-fry rotting on the shelf." He snorted. "Asshole didn't even bother remembering when I was getting back. He got home a few hours later. By that point, I'd gone through denial and anger and had landed on resignation."

"You figured it out."

"Yeah. Suddenly the other signs were obvious and I couldn't ignore it anymore. He didn't bother denying it when I confronted him. Out with the old and in with the new."

"Jesus. I'm sorry."

"Me too. I mean, not that I found out he was a cheating scumbag before I signed the offer, but… it sucks to find out your taste is that lousy." He gave a rueful smile that held little humor. "Told you I had fridge trauma."

Austin grimaced.

"It gets worse," Joe went on. "We all worked together."

"Wait—he cheated with your mutual coworker?" Austin said, aghast. Jesus, how low could this asshat ex get?

"Yup. So there went my relationship, my house, and my job, all in one go."

"Wow." Austin kind of wanted to hug Joe about it, which was super weird. Austin didn't hug people. "I can see why you thought a season or two benchwarming sounded like a better option."

"Yeah. It was a pretty bad burn." Joe contemplated his beer bottle. "The kids don't know. I mean, they obviously know Paul and I broke up, but I didn't tell them why."

"Why not?"

"Honestly? At first I was ashamed. And then I wanted to keep them out of jail. Gavin and Meg are hotheads. I mean, Will is devious enough not to get caught, but he's also only just out of his closet and pretty vulnerable about it, so I couldn't be sure that between the four of them they wouldn't do something dumb like slash his tires."

Austin snorted. "That's not fair. Your kids are definitely more creative than that."

"Yeah," Joe said fondly. "But I'm not."

"So avoiding the cost of bail is why you've kept quiet?"

Joe tipped his head back, drained the last of his beer, and then plunked the bottle down on the table. He leaned over, opened the fridge, and pulled out another. He tipped it in Austin's direction, and after his nod, handed it over and grabbed a second.

Joe opened it and took a drink. "For a time. But now I just can't bear the thought of proving to them how much some people suck."

That was… endearing and adorable.

"I mean, don't they already know that lesson?" They must, considering three of them apparently had parents so unworthy of them that they turned to a guy who was little more than a kid himself to love them unconditionally.

"Yeah." Joe frowned glumly at his bottle. "You know what the worst part was?"

"Worse than a cheating boyfriend who sleeps with your coworker and chases you out of your job?" How could it possibly be worse?

"He cheated with a woman, living down to all the negative stereotypes about bisexuals."

Of course Joe was more bothered by the idea of what others might think about bi men in general than about the personal hurt. Would it kill him to be a little bit selfish once in a while?

Joe answered his unspoken question by prodding his leg—the unbruised one—with his toe. "Come on. I showed you mine."

"What, you want to know why I'm perpetually single? You can't guess?"

"Oh, a challenge?" Joe smiled a little and tilted his head as he assessed Austin head to toe. "Hmm... you have a very needy cat who's jealous of all your attention?"

Austin spread his hands, gesturing around the trailer. "Obviously not."

A little light came into Joe's eyes. "You hate leaving the house after five o'clock."

Austin laughed. "Rude. And true, but no."

Joe tapped a finger against his lips. "Porn addiction?"

"Oh, he's got jokes. Here I am ready to bare my soul—"

Joe raised his hands in surrender. "Hey, hey, you're the one who wanted me to guess."

"Dick." Austin flicked his bottle cap at him. "I mean, the truth is not, like, less shitty than your season-ending injury. It's mostly the trauma. The non-refrigerator variety."

He wasn't usually that forthcoming about it, but, well, he co-owned a house with the guy. Plus, tit for tat or whatever. Joe knew enough about Austin's childhood to guess anyway.

"General or specific non-refrigerator trauma? Or can I ask?"

Austin drummed his fingers on the table. "Most of it's pretty old. I mean, I don't remember my mom dying. She, uh, she got postpartum pretty bad, so it was me and my dad until I was six or seven." When the drinking caught up with him. Austin didn't say that part out loud. "Then he died and I stayed with my great-aunt for a few years, but she got sick and couldn't look after me, so…." Group homes, foster homes. He shrugged. Joe knew that part too, or as much of it as Austin cared to tell anyone about. "I learned to be independent maybe too well, but I never got really good at relying on anybody else."

Not that he'd tried particularly hard.

In his weaker moments, Austin would've admitted that he wished things were different. It wasn't like he wanted to be alone forever. But everybody died eventually—his mother, his dad, his great-aunt, even DeeDee. And as Joe had just demonstrated, people could leave you in lots of other painful ways too.

Austin might not have everything he ever wanted, but he had a good life now. He had a business that earned him a decent living and kept a roof over his head—and now he had an extra roof, even. He liked his work, which even five minutes of idle conversation with someone could tell him was a blessing most people didn't get. And when he got an itch, it wasn't hard to go out to a bar and find someone to scratch it. Hell, as Joe had pointed out, the worst part was having to leave his house after 5:00 p.m.

"Not much of a team player?" Joe said after a moment.

Austin snorted. "Well, it's not my strong suit." He'd spent more time with Joe in the past few weeks than he had with any other person since he was twelve years old. "Call it a work in progress."

"Guess you got thrown in the deep end with this house thing and my seventeen kids." Joe grinned. "Good thing I'm such a good swim teacher."

Austin was debating whether to throw something else at him, but the only thing at hand was the beer bottle, and that seemed extreme and also wasteful. He made a face instead, even if he appreciated the levity. He was about to ask if Joe wanted another drink when a soul-piercing yowl split the night.

Without a word, they shot to their feet. Austin had two flashlights plugged in on the bulkhead now, and they each grabbed one as they stumbled out of the trailer.

This late in the year, the sun set around five, so it was fully dark except in the little halo around the trailer.

"Where do you think—"

Another sound, this time a snarl, yelping, the scrabble of claws in gravel and dirt.

"Behind the garage," Austin said, but they were already moving. His heart beat in his throat. That was the dog, he was sure of it. But what was *happening* to it?

The flashlight beams crisscrossed the yard as they jogged. Joe slowed by the side of the garage long enough to pick up a length of two-by-four, which was a frankly insane thing to do, but probably so was running toward noises that made the hair stand up on the back of his neck like this.

It didn't take long to find the source of the commotion.

In the muddy light of their torches was a tangle of snarling limbs and blood and fur.

It had to be the dog, Austin thought. The dog and one of the coyotes Linda had warned him about.

The dog had gotten the worst of it. She was on her back now, yelping in terror as the coyote latched on to her hind leg. Any second it would let go and lunge for the poor thing's throat, and all Austin could do was stand there and gape, frozen in horror.

But not Joe. His flashlight hit the dirt as he stepped forward. Half a second later there was a solid *crack* as he swung the two-by-four hard into the coyote's flank. "Get out of here!" he shouted. "Go on—get—"

For a moment the commotion stopped and the coyote froze, head down as it considered this unexpected threat.

Then it squealed, bared its bloody teeth, and fled into the field behind the pole barn.

"*Shit.*" Joe dropped the wood and fell to his knees beside the dog. Austin was still staring at him, thinking *What the hell?* Who did that? Who went and fought a wild animal with a piece of scrap lumber? This wasn't even his dog.

The dog didn't get up. It was whining now, panting. The whites of its eyes showed when it looked at them, obviously terrified.

Austin dropped to his knees too as Joe ran a gentle hand along the dog's side, making hushing sounds. "Hey, girl," he murmured. "Hey, hey, it's okay. We've got you." He ripped his sweatshirt over his head, covered her with it, and wrapped one of the sleeves around the injured back leg.

The dog cried like it was being murdered. Austin's heart squeezed. "Help me get her up? We've got to get her to a vet."

"Better idea," Austin said. He worked his hands under the dog's head and neck, surprised when she didn't try to bite him. Instead, she licked at his arm. "We bring the vet to her."

Joe blinked at him.

"Linda," Austin said. "Come on, her car's in the driveway. She's gotta be home."

Chapter Seven

THE NIGHT was a bit of a blur after that.

Linda must've heard the noise too, because Austin had barely touched his knuckles to the back door before she threw it open. She had her hair pulled back in a no-nonsense ponytail, and she took one look at the dog in Joe's arms and said, "Put her in my back seat and we'll take her to the clinic."

Joe and Austin didn't argue. Joe got in the car with Linda and the dog, and Austin followed them into town, then into a tidy little building that certainly was not normally open after eight o'clock on a Sunday. They'd been there only a handful of minutes before the door swung open and a harried-looking young woman came in wearing scrubs and Crocs. She spared them a quick look and then disappeared into the depths of the building.

Austin had no idea how long they sat there. He'd left his phone in the trailer. He was barely aware of the press of Joe's shoulder against his.

Finally the door to the clinic opened and Linda stepped out. Austin stood automatically and was peripherally aware of Joe doing the same.

"Well," she said. "That was more excitement than I expected for a Sunday night."

That sounded—good? That didn't sound like *I'm sorry*. Austin swallowed. "Is she—"

"Stable, for now," Linda said. "But we need to talk seriously before I go much further."

That sounded… less good.

Something touched Austin's hand. He looked down. It was Joe's. Their fingers laced together. Joe squeezed.

Austin looked back up again. He didn't think Joe knew he'd done it. Maybe he just needed someone to hold on to.

He nodded for both of them. "Sure, yeah," he said.

"Most of her wounds are superficial," Linda said. "But I'm not going to lie, her leg's a mess. It's possible I could save it, but it'll be multiple surgeries, and even then, she could lose the leg. My recommendation is to amputate."

Fuck. Jesus.

Joe said, "Can she—I mean, with just three legs…?"

"Lots of dogs live healthy, fulfilling lives on three legs. There's no guarantee, but she can still have a good life." She paused. "But it's a long recovery. She's going to need help, antibiotics, attention, dressing changes. We don't know how long she's been on her own, if she ever did have people—there's no microchip. She might not be housebroken. That's going to make it harder to find her a home. And she *needs* a home if she's going to have this surgery. It would be cruel to amputate and leave her to recover in a shelter."

Suddenly Austin understood what she hadn't said.

This dog needed a home, needed a family, right now—or the kindest thing would be to end her suffering.

He didn't even have time to think about it before he said, "I'll do it."

Linda locked eyes with him and asked seriously, "Are you sure?" She held up a hand. "This is a commitment. She's going to need extra time and extra money."

"She makes a good point," Joe put in. "Not sure the house has enough old dishes to cover the cost of renos *and* vet bills."

"I'll figure it out," Austin said stubbornly. He couldn't stand the thought of doing anything else. Especially not if it meant that poor creature would have to be put down.

Joe shook his head and turned to Linda. "I guess we're getting a dog."

Austin jerked and stared at Joe. *We?*

Linda smiled then, small but genuine. "Good. Let's talk fees and care."

"Shouldn't you—" Austin gestured and glanced at the door she'd just come through.

"Five minutes to make sure you're giving informed consent won't make a difference."

Joe snorted. "Let's hear it, Doc."

Linda walked them through the fees involved in the upcoming surgery, but Austin barely paid attention. What difference would the cost make? Austin wasn't changing his mind. Though figuring out how to pay for everything without having to take out loans or relinquish the house would be a task.

Unless…. He was barely sleeping at the garage these days. He pretty much lived full-time in the trailer. If he rented out the apartment, that would help. Besides, he was pretty sure he wouldn't even have to advertise or go looking for a tenant. The baker who rented out the shop next to Austin's garage had been grumbling about his long morning commute and his horrible landlord.

"Okay, that covers the basics. I'm going to get back to her," Linda said. Austin hoped Joe had been paying attention. "Afterwards, one of my people can get all the paperwork sorted and we can go over aftercare in more detail." She slapped her thighs and stood. "Oh, by the way, any thoughts on a name? We'll need one eventually for paperwork."

Austin answered without thinking. "Josephine."

Linda grinned. Joe gave him a look.

"Why, exactly, are we calling our new dog Josephine?"

Austin shrugged. *Because it feels right?* "It's about time one of your kids was named after you."

"We can talk about late-life adoption and naming rules another time."

"Okay. I'm going to go do the surgery. You two should head home."

"What?" She wanted Austin to *leave*?

"There's nothing else you can do for her tonight," Linda said kindly, "but you're gonna want to be well rested tomorrow when you come to pick her up."

"Come on," Joe cajoled. He knocked their shoulders together. "We both need sleep. Josephine"—he pulled a face—"is in good hands."

Austin chewed his lip, but he could see their point. With a sigh, he nodded and let Joe pull him toward the door.

Then, surprising himself, Austin gave in to the impulse to lean forward and pull Linda into a hug. "Thanks."

"Don't thank me for doing my job."

"Can't stop me," Austin said with a grin and waved goodbye.

THE NEXT morning, Joe woke up at 5:26 a.m.

He groaned, rubbed his face, and cursed beating his alarm by half an hour.

He was used to early starts, what with working in landscaping—one didn't waste the coolest hours of the day—but Joe wasn't exactly an early bird. He liked sleeping in on days off, and usually the only perk of cool weather and shorter days was getting to do just that. But with a house in need of renovations, Joe had glumly kept his alarm set even on days off.

He thought about rolling back over. After all, what would it hurt if he slept past the alarm?

He pressed his face into the pillow when the memories suddenly came back to him. Josephine. (God, that name.) They had to pick her up this morning, and Austin wouldn't want to be late.

Joe wouldn't be surprised if Austin was already awake and pacing the trailer.

With a groan, he rolled out of bed and headed for the shower.

By the time he got to the house, he was fortified with coffee and donuts and ready to take on the day.

As he got out of the car, he glanced at the trailer but figured he should leave Austin to it if he was actually sleeping and headed for the house.

Of course, Joe had only just stepped into the front hall when he realized his hopes were in vain. From the sound of it, Austin was moving things around in the living room.

"You're my favorite," Austin said when Joe dangled the coffee cup in front of his face.

"And all it cost was a cup of a coffee? Guess I shouldn't have splashed out for the donuts, then. Maybe I'll keep them for myself."

Austin made grabby hands. "Don't you dare."

Joe handed over the box and settled next to him in one of the camping chairs. "Whatcha up to this morning?"

Naturally, Austin was mid-bite. He pulled a face while he chewed. His affronted look over Joe's bad timing was nothing short of adorable. "Figured I might as well do some sorting, assessing, and cataloging for selling. What with all the vet bills coming."

"Probably a good idea. Want a hand?"

Neither of them mentioned that they were just filling time while they waited for Linda or one of her people to call and tell them it was time to get their new dog. They also didn't talk about the logistics of a shared pet.

A few boxes and two cups of coffee and three donuts in, Austin broke the silence on the topic.

"We'll have to stop at the pet store on our way to get Josephine."

True. They definitely didn't have anything they needed. Still, that hardly seemed the most pressing point to Joe.

"You're serious about that name?"

"Deadly," Austin said, smirking.

Joe shook his head. "Fine. If you insist, then we can call her Josefina." He pronounced it the correct Spanish way. Austin lifted a brow but didn't argue. "But I'm not calling her that—I'm not yelling for Josefina in a park."

"We can't call her Joe," Austin said. "That would be confusing."

"Of course not. We'll call her Pepa."

"Pepa," Austin said slowly. "Why would we call her Pepa?"

"It's the Spanish nickname for Josefina."

"What?" He paused mid-sort of a box and stared at Joe like he thought Joe was putting him on. "How the heck do you get Pepa out of Josefina?" His accent was terrible, but Joe was mature and didn't mock him for it.

"How do you get Dick out of Richard? A mystery."

"I don't know, maybe Richard likes having dick in him," Austin shot back.

Joe laughed. "Touché." He shook his head. "So…. Pepa?"

Austin nodded. "Pepa."

"So should we go upstairs and find some vet bills?"

They wandered over to the base of the stairs, where Joe turned on the flashlight on his phone and knelt to look at the offending step. The whole tread had come off the stringers and been pushed through the plaster underneath and into the basement—likely from the force of Austin pulling. Joe whistled under his breath. "This could've been worse."

"Tell that to the bruise I have this morning, man," Austin said ruefully. "Although at least it's not tetanus."

"Dodged a bullet on that one," Joe agreed. Some of the nails poking out looked nasty. He stuck his finger into the wood where the tread had been attached, and it crumbled. "Huh."

"What?"

"Can you find the piece that broke off?"

Austin trudged off to the basement and returned a moment later. He handed over the board.

One touch confirmed it. "Okay," Joe said. "Fun. Dry rot." He debated for a moment. "Is my crowbar still in the kitchen?"

Austin brought that too, and Joe pulled up a couple more treads and checked the stringers, but the dry rot hadn't spread too far—just around that one step, it looked like. He put the crowbar down and sat back.

"Well, the good news is the rest of the stairs are sound and the repair is more of a pain in the ass than anything." They'd have to replace the stringers on both sides, just to be safe, but the treads and risers could be reused. "Bad news is we're gonna be skipping a step until then."

"At least nobody's sleeping upstairs right now. Kind of a nasty shock if you go downstairs to pee in the middle of the night."

"Not recommended," Joe agreed. Then he remembered their conversation from yesterday. "Hey—you said you found something cool?"

Austin pulled him to his feet. "Oh—yeah. Uh… after you, though."

"What, you don't trust me?"

"My abs still hurt from pulling myself out last night. Give me a break. At least I'll be able to help you if we go up one at a time."

Joe couldn't argue with that, and he did actually trust his assessment of the stairs' condition, so he trudged up, skipping over the ones he'd removed. He'd nail those back down later.

Austin followed and then led the way to the smallest bedroom, where two items remained—an ancient radio covered in dust, with a walnut veneer that had once been glossy but was now cracked and warped; and a blue Rubbermaid container on a shelf.

Austin took the container down and opened it with a flourish. "Voila."

Joe hadn't been that excited about the radio—it looked like it needed a ton of work—but the box was a different story. Grimy on the outside, sure, but inside it was neat and orderly and absolutely packed with old vinyl records.

Joe didn't know a lot about record collecting, other than that it had come back into vogue. If that little radio had a working record player and they could get it looking good again, it might be worth something, but this bin could be worth five bucks for the plastic or five grand for the vinyls, depending what was in there.

"Am I supposed to be impressed?" he asked after a minute.

Austin reached into the bin and pulled out a handful of LPs. Most of them were bands Joe didn't recognize, with the cardboard sleeves a little battered. He did recognize a few names, though—Jimi Hendrix. The Stones. And—

"Jesus Christ, what the hell is that?"

"That," said Austin, "is the Beatles' *Yesterday and Today*."

Joe stared at it, appalled. "Why are there decapitated dolls? And… meat?"

"This is like the Pepa question all over again." Austin shook his head. "But it doesn't matter." He turned the album over. The weak light of the bare, pathetic bulb overhead glinted on the plastic wrap. "It's in perfect condition. And this cover is rare. Apparently the 1960s were not ready for political commentary in the form of dead fake babies, so they pulled it and released it with a different image."

Joe thought that was probably fair.

"But like I said," Austin said, "it doesn't matter, because it's not an album."

Joe blinked. "It's not?"

"Nope. It's a three-legged dog and some stair stringers."

Huh. "Maybe we should've called her Yoko."

"You said yes to Pepa. No takebacks."

They carefully carted the record crate downstairs to sort through, and then it was late enough to hit Pet Valu for the essentials before they picked up Pepa.

The definition of *essentials* was pretty broad when you'd never owned a dog before.

"What's, like, a good number of toys?" Austin asked ten minutes in. He was holding a sleeve of tennis balls, a larger knobbly ball, a porcupine stuffy, a rubber chicken, and a frisbee. It was possible the idea of *essentials* became even more impossible to define when you hadn't had anything as a child. Then: "Do you think we need a cart?"

Joe got a cart.

They picked out a nice soft bed… and then a second firmer one in case she liked that better. A raised set of food and water dishes, because Austin had read online that it was helpful for dogs that had amputations. Joe thought that probably was more for dogs with front-limb loss, but whatever, the dishes looked nice. Three different bags of treats and a handful of what the sales girl called "bully sticks," which Joe knew just enough about to avoid asking questions.

Joe selected a leash and harness while Austin chose a collar, and then they had a three-minute argument about whose phone number would go on her tag, which they eventually solved by flipping a coin.

Joe tried not to pout that Austin won.

It was probably a good thing Linda called when she did, or there might not have been room left for the dog.

The tech from the night before wasn't present at the desk—Joe hoped she'd gone home to get some rest—but Linda was, with dark circles under her eyes but a bright smile. "Hey, boys. Your little princess is just starting to wake up. Did you finalize the name?"

"It's Pepa," Joe said. "I didn't really want the dog named after me, but Austin insisted."

Austin's cheeks were still red from the early morning chill when he said, "If you save a stray dog by attacking a wild animal with a two-by-four, the dog gets named after you. Those are just the rules."

Linda raised her eyebrows as she slid a form across the desk. Joe picked up a pen and started filling it out. At least this one had room for both of their names and contact info. "You two left out a few details last night."

"We were kind of preoccupied." Austin tapped his credit card on the desk. "Can we see her now?"

Linda presented Joe with a mountain of discharge instructions and a small pharmacy worth of pills, which he shoved into his jacket pockets while Austin followed Linda back to retrieve their new friend.

"She's going to be groggy for a few days," Linda told them. "She might not want to eat much, and she'll be extra clumsy from the anesthesia even without the missing leg. Keep her somewhere she can't stumble around and hurt herself. And she'll need to be kept warm. The anesthesia interferes with their ability to regulate body temperature."

"Blankets and space heater, check," Joe said, thinking about the best place to set up a recovering three-legged dog.

Linda opened the door to the recovery room, which held a series of cages. Pepa lay in an open-top pen that looked more like a playpen for a toddler than a crate for a dog. Her half-lidded gaze stared blankly until Austin said quietly, "Poor baby." Her eyes rolled and landed on them, and then, to Joe's surprise, she let out a pathetic whine, wiggled, and thumped her tail.

"Does she—" Austin swallowed the rest of his words in favor of getting closer.

"Looks like she remembers her rescuers," Linda said softly.

Austin leaned over the side of the pen, reached down to touch her head, and stroked gently, murmuring to her. Joe was only a half step behind him.

"You can open the gate, you know," Linda said, a clear smile in her voice.

Joe's back would definitely appreciate that.

Delighted that her heroes were getting closer, Pepa tried to wiggle onto her feet—and failed as her front paws slipped and her bandaged back end sort of flopped. Austin dropped to his knees and settled her head in his lap.

Now that he was no longer running on adrenaline and terrified for the life of another living creature, Joe finally got a good look at Pepa. There was something golden retriever–like in the color of her coat and the shape of her face, but she was smaller, slimmer than the average retriever. Her coat was shorter too, and she had a pure white stripe on the top of her head.

Joe crouched next to Austin, and Pepa brought her adoring gaze to him. Her tail thumped again.

"Hello, Pepa," Joe crooned. "What a brave girl you've been." He stroked her ears, and she whuffled and sighed into Austin's lap, clearly delighted.

The door swung open, and Joe turned to see Linda walking back in—he hadn't even noticed her leaving.

"All right, boys. You're all set to take her home. You can wrap her up in the blanket that she's on and take that with you."

"We can't take your blanket," Austin said.

"Yes, you can. It'll help make her feel better to have something that smells like her in her new home." Linda smiled. "Think of it as a new-baby present from your neighbor."

Joe snorted and started to roll Pepa up in her blanket burrito. There was no way this doped-up tripod was walking anywhere right now. He scooped her up and carried her out to the car, winning the fight by not even asking, while Austin huffed about him being a dog hog.

But Austin won the car seat battle by virtue of opening the back driver's side door for Joe to set her in, then scurrying around to the passenger side and wiggling onto the bench next to her. Pepa sighed as she settled her head on Austin's thigh and fell into a drugged doze.

Joe snorted and got into the driver's seat.

Back at the house, Joe put his plan into action. He carried Pepa to the breezeway, while Austin followed behind.

"I figured she'd be more comfortable here. Single story, empty of too many obstacles. And we should be able to easily keep it warm and cozy with a space heater."

"Good idea," Austin said approvingly and settled both of the beds on the floor. Joe eyed them up and then set Pepa down on the firmer bed, figuring that she could use all the help she could get when it came to moving around. He didn't want her to have to fight against mounds of unpredictable fluff while trying to get her limbs under her.

They pulled in all of their new purchases and set up a cozy little den with some of the old wool blankets they'd found in the house.

In one corner, Pepa lay in her new nest, and spilling out around her were more soft things—blankets, stuffed toys, her other bed. In the neighboring corner were her food and water. Austin took the bowls inside to wash and dry them while Joe set up the stand, then turned to the other side of the room. He'd set down the puppy pads, a just-in-case move, when Austin returned with water and food.

Per Linda's instructions, the bowl was pretty empty, but if Pepa was able to keep those bites down, they'd give her as much as she wanted later.

Not that Pepa was showing much interest in food. She was alternating between staring into space and wiggling and grunting in her nest.

Joe took a video of one of her doped-up wiggles—her face was burrowed in the soft fabric, and she was letting out happy little "grrr-ump" noises while her tail wagged her lumpy lopsided butt.

Then, on impulse, he sent the video to the family group chat.

Figuring he should probably do something productive before his kids took over his life, he switched over to his contacts and called Greg. Joe was supposed to meet his crew on a job later to help out, but he knew he could trust Greg to make sure everything was done right and on time. They didn't need him today, and he told Greg there was a family emergency keeping him away.

"Hope the kids are all right, man," Greg said kindly and promised Joe didn't have a thing to worry about.

"Thanks," Joe said wryly, and hung up.

The kids, human and dog alike, were going to be just fine, judging from the way Pepa melted into her nest under Austin's belly rub and the way the family chat was blowing up.

OMG DOGGY!
its so cute!
Whose dog is it?
Joe???
DAD?!
DID YOU
GET
A DOG?!?!
JOE!
I'm coming over right now
WE are coming over
JOE!
Just so you know, I have already named it, and I'm severely emotionally attached and will be scarred for life if we don't get to keep it.

Joe snorted.

Noted, Will. Though, fyi, she's already been named.

He snapped another picture, this one of Austin kissing the top of her head as she snuggled into him.

Meet Pepa. Stealer of mac and cheese and fighter of coyotes.
WHAT?!
COYOTES?!
GAVIN, YOU'RE TAKING US TO DAD'S AFTER SCHOOL SO WE CAN INTERROGATE HIM IN PERSON!

Laughing, Joe pocketed his phone once more. He figured they had about an hour before the kids invaded the house.

"Hey, Austin, what do you think we can get done in an hour?"

"A lot of belly rubs?" he said ruefully. Under his hand, Pepa let out an enormous sigh and closed her eyes. "I kind of don't want to leave her. How do people with dogs get anything done when they're sick?"

"They probably don't," Joe decided. He didn't want to leave the room either, but they would have to eventually, and Pepa needed to sleep to recover. Soon enough the painkillers would start wearing off—she'd need them more then. They should let her sleep while she could. "But they also probably don't have a hundred things to do before they can move into their house."

Austin raised his eyebrows. "You moving in?"

Joe gestured around them. "I mean, we've got a lot of work to do. And now we have a dog to look after. You think I'm going to miss out on my baby's childhood?" He shook his head. "Besides, if I make it my primary residence I don't get dinged as much on taxes when we sell it."

You should move in properly too, he thought. The idea of Austin staying in the trailer when there were coyotes in the yard—when it was halfway through November and the smell of snow had started to hang in the air—sat wrong with him. But Austin wasn't Joe's kid; Joe couldn't tell him what to do.

"Point." Austin heaved out a breath and then dragged himself to his feet. "Okay. Let's go rip up the kitchen floor."

Chapter Eight

MONDAY QUICKLY became very expensive.

Between Pepa and the septic servicing, the Beatles album was a write-off. That was okay; they'd make it back when they sold the house.

At least Austin had a contact he could unload the record on pretty quickly. They wouldn't get top dollar, but they wouldn't have to wait months for the right buyer either.

While the septic guys went in and out to test the drainage or whatever the fuck, Austin and Joe pulled up the floorboards and then the subfloor in the kitchen addition.

"That's not dry rot," Austin said, wiping the back of his wrist over his forehead.

"No, that's just the regular kind," Joe agreed. He kicked his work boot into a joist. From Austin's understanding of construction—and what he could see of the boards that were in better condition—it should've been a two-by-ten. Three or four inches had rotted away. No wonder the kitchen floor was more like a skate park.

Austin nodded. "So can you fix it?"

Joe gave him a look. "You're the mechanic, aren't you? The one who said, 'Oh, we should fix it up'?"

Austin sincerely hoped Joe was fucking with him. "I fix metal things," he protested. "You want me to weld something, grease it, use a wrench, change a tire, replace an exhaust system, I'm your guy. This?" He gestured to the floor. "This organic-material bullshit? That's your job."

For a minute he was sure Joe was going to tell him he didn't know what the fuck he was doing either.

Then he grinned. "Yeah, man, I'm good with this shit. Let me just get my I Heart Hardwood shirt."

Austin laughed in relief. "Fuck off, you had me going."

"I'll make a shopping list if you wrangle the kids."

"You don't want to be the one to introduce them?"

"I don't want to send you to the hardware store," Joe corrected.

Okay, that was fair. Austin didn't mind the hardware store, but he didn't fuck with the lumber section. "Guess I'm on babysitting duty."

On cue, the door banged open and the kids—minus Meg—piled in.

"Dude, your yard is *gross*," Gavin commented. Then he peeked into the kitchen and said, "Oh shit, your floor is bad too."

"Are you giving me crap when you're literally cutting class to meet my dog right now?" Joe asked.

"It's *our* dog," Austin corrected.

Gavin looked at Alex, then at Joe, and then said, "What, co-owning a house wasn't enough for you guys?"

"Maybe he has game after all," Alex suggested.

Austin rolled his eyes and dusted off his hands. "Come on. Your father's got to go deal with his wood situation. I'll take you to meet Pepa."

The kids dutifully followed him through the kitchen to the breezeway door, which they'd closed to keep Pepa contained and warm. She didn't look like she'd moved much, not that Austin blamed her, and the dressing on her back leg was still clean, which was a relief.

But her eyes were open, and now that he was standing in front of the door, he could hear her soft whines.

"Maybe one at a time," he decided. "She's not feeling great, and we don't know what her history is like. She might not like people."

She liked Joe, but everyone liked Joe. And she seemed to like Austin too, which was a gift Austin wouldn't take for granted.

"Me first," Gavin said, shoving forward.

"Will first," Austin corrected. "He's the quietest. Let's ease her into you."

Will flushed with pleasure. By some miracle, Gavin didn't argue.

Despite the general lack of insulation—something on the mile-long list of things to address—the breezeway was plenty cozy with the space heater from the trailer set up in a corner and blocked off by a couple of chairs they'd dragged in from the garage so Pepa couldn't accidentally burn herself.

She raised her head when she saw Austin, and her tail thumped on her bed, but she whined too. Poor thing. Austin had memorized Linda's instructions by now—no more pain pills until evening.

"Hi, sweet girl," he said, kneeling next to her and gesturing Will to come closer. "This is Will. I guess he's your half brother." He held out his hand for Pepa to sniff; she licked it.

Will copied Austin's greeting, and Pepa consented to gentle ear pets. "Did she really fight a coyote?"

"She started it," Austin agreed. "Or, well, maybe the coyote did. Joe ended it with a two-by-four."

"Seriously?" His blue eyes went wide. Then he lowered his voice and glanced back toward the door, which Austin had closed behind them to keep the heat in, and said conspiratorially, "Sounds hot."

Jesus, these kids were going to kill him. "I'll tell him you said that," Austin threatened, barely holding in a laugh.

The blood ran out of Will's face. "Oh God, please don't. Someone will ask if I have daddy issues."

Austin kind of assumed daddy issues were a prerequisite of being one of Joe's kids. Then again, if Will *didn't* have any, it was probably down to Joe.

Will stroked Pepa's head again. "She's sweet. I always wanted a dog."

"Me too."

Not just a dog, of course. Parents who loved him, siblings, a partner. But just because you wanted something didn't mean you'd get it. He'd learned that hard lesson. And you could lose anything you did get. Austin was better off alone.

But Pepa was better off with him. He could take care of her. He couldn't let her suffer. He didn't want her to be alone.

Besides, dogs were loyal. Pepa would never leave him.

She licked his hand once again as he stroked her neck. "All right. Let's give Alex a turn."

WITH THE addition of Pepa to their family, having a habitable house where they could safely and comfortably sleep and eat was more urgent than ever, and Joe and Austin stepped up their efforts to cross things off the to-do list. First up was patching the stairs, which Joe did the day they brought Pepa home.

The day after her arrival, Austin watched Pepa take her first steps, and her unhappy first fall. Miscalculating her weight, she overbalanced and landed on her bandaged hip, letting out a pained yelp. Austin was at her side, petting and soothing, before he thought about it. As she panted in his arms, he buried his face in her fur and hid his own tears.

Thank God she quickly picked up how to manage a three-legged walk. Austin didn't think he could take seeing her in such distress again.

On Tuesday, the exterminator came to deal with the mice.

Since neither Joe nor Austin could get their work done in the house, they spent the time at their day jobs. Nervous about leaving her alone, Austin brought Pepa to the garage and kept her snugly cooped up in his office. Between changing the oil on a Ford and replacing the carburetor in an old Chevy, Austin popped next door to his neighbor and asked if he was still thinking about renting a place closer to his work.

At home that evening, they got to work implementing the rest of the exterminator's advice. Joe took the lawnmower and weedwhacker to plant life near the house, and Austin picked up airtight containers for food and garbage.

After dinner they settled in the breezeway with Pepa, who was growing antsy now that she had recovered from anesthesia and the harsher drugs, and argued the merits of accepting the last piece of advice from the exterminator.

"I'm not saying a cat is a bad idea." Joe jabbed the air with his sandwich. "I'm just saying that now is probably not the best time for more animal adoption."

"Okay, but isn't an animal that will help us maintain the house one that's worth putting the money into?"

"Sure, but a pet isn't a temporary thing. What are we going to do with it when we sell the house?"

Austin threaded his fingers in Pepa's ruff and pursed his lips. He didn't appreciate the reminder that Pepa's future was undecided. "Oh, so it's fine for the dog—"

Pepa whined and settled her chin on his thigh. Austin stroked her silky ears. She'd been so unhappy as the painkillers wore off. Maybe Linda could increase her dosage?

Then again, getting the dog addicted to drugs didn't seem great either.

With a roll of his eyes, Joe stood up. "All right. I'm going back to the subfloor." There was something pointed about the way he looked at Austin when he said it, like Austin was slacking off by giving Pepa much-needed comfort, but Austin wasn't taking that bait.

Pepa whined again, and this time she stood up and hopped to the side door. Austin didn't need to be a dog whisperer to understand what she wanted.

He clipped her new leash onto her collar and took her out for a pee. She wouldn't need it forever—the property was big—but neither Austin nor Joe trusted her yet not to accidentally hurt herself if she had free rein.

Pepa whined and pulled on the leash; clearly she knew where she wanted to do her business. Seeing no point in arguing, Austin strolled behind her as she led the way to—

The spot where the coyote attacked her.

"Why do you want to go there, baby?" Austin muttered, but he reluctantly let her drag him on.

Pepa snuffled in the grass and—

Was that a meow?

Austin shuffled forward and looked over Pepa's head.

Well. Looked like Austin was winning that argument after all.

"AUSTIN!" JOE had reached the point in the subfloor installation where he needed another set of hands. Maneuvering a twelve-foot-long two-by-ten into a joist hanger was a two-person operation. "Quit petting the dog and come help me with this!"

When Austin didn't show up right away, Joe thought back. Had he heard the breezeway door opening? He dusted off his hands and walked down the three steps to what he'd come to think of as Pepa's hospital room. Sure enough, it was empty, but Austin and Pepa were on their way back to the house, illuminated in the yellowy glow of the motion-activated floodlight.

Austin had taken off his sweatshirt and was cradling it against his chest, half his attention on the bundle, half on Pepa.

It was only polite to get the door. "Hey, can I get some—oh my God, what are those?"

"Don't look at me," Austin said. "This was all Pepa. Naming her after you was obviously the only thing to do."

Wrapped in Austin's sweater were three tiny mewling kittens, two orange tabbies and one bedraggled-looking black.

Joe should open his mouth and say *We're not keeping those.* At the very least, *Put two of those back.*

But Pepa hopped over to her bed and sat, tail wagging more than it had at any point since they met her, gaze fixed adoringly on Austin and his precious cargo.

"What?" Joe said weakly.

"Think I know why she picked a fight with a coyote," Austin said as he knelt to set the kittens down next to Pepa on her bed. "Protecting her adopted children, obviously."

Two of the skinny, pathetic, damp-looking cats toddled unsteadily out of the sweater and yowled at Pepa, who licked each of them in turn. Joe wasn't an expert, but they looked scrawny—he doubted their mother was in the picture.

The third cat—the black one—declined to exit the sweater the same way as its siblings and instead turned around and climbed up Austin's pant leg.

"This isn't fair," Joe said as Austin collected the kitten in one big hand and pulled it close to his chest. "You and Pepa ganged up on me."

Austin fluttered his lashes over dark eyes and held the kitten next to his face. "C'mon, Joe. How would you feel if someone took your kids from you?"

"Mew," said the black kitten.

Jesus. Fuck, how was Joe supposed to make good financial decisions faced with that cuteness? "Fine. Fine." He huffed. "But I'm naming these ones."

"Deal," Austin said immediately.

"And you get to call Linda and explain we need to know how to look after three tiny cats."

"Okay," he agreed placidly.

"And none of them better need a leg amputated unless there's another rare Beatles album in that Rubbermaid bin."

"Mew," said one of the orange kittens, which had rolled off the edge of the bed and was now attacking Joe's work boot.

"God fucking damn it, that's adorable," he sighed, bending to pick it up. "Okay, seriously, call Linda so we can make sure they're not going to die, because I need your help hanging floor joists if we're going kitchen shopping on Thursday."

Linda came over right away. Joe had the distinct impression she was laughing her ass off on the inside, but she let him maintain the illusion that this had been a joint decision.

"They're not quite old enough to be on their own, but they'll probably be okay eating softened kitten food. I've got a bag at home from some fosters a few months back you can have and a spare litter box that'll do until you can get your own. We'll do shots when they're a bit older." She stroked the creamsicle one under his chin. "Have you named them yet?"

Joe had spent the forty-five seconds between Austin's phone call and Linda's arrival coming up with the most vindictive names possible. "Ozzy," he said, pointing to the black one. "Dallas." Creamsicle. "And that one's Walker Texas Ranger."

Austin gave him a flat look. "Really? Not Houston?"

"The orange ones are trouble," Joe said. "The whole internet knows that."

He didn't have brain space to defend his naming choice. He was too busy trying to figure out how to tell Starling, who *had* laughed in his face when he mentioned they'd gotten a dog and Austin had named it Pepa, that the number of legs in the house had just gone up exponentially. "Moving in together and adopting a three-legged rescue dog? You're never beating the U-Haul lesbian allegations, babe. That's straight out of the playbook."

Naturally it was another twenty minutes before Austin was any use in the kitchen. Joe spent them on the phone with Starling so she could get the mockery out of her system before he had to see her in person.

"Are you *sure* you didn't run off to Vegas and get married without inviting me?"

"I wouldn't go to Vegas," Joe protested. "I'd go to Niagara Falls, it's way closer."

"But seriously. There's nothing going on? I know I'm not the target audience, but I know when a guy is hot, Joe. Austin is hot."

You should see him holding a tiny kitten. But the cuteness factor changed nothing. "There's nothing going on. We're basically business partners. You know I don't like to make the same mistakes twice. Don't shit where you eat." If he hadn't been dating a coworker, he wouldn't have had to quit his job and start his own business. Sure, it had worked out okay in the end, but it had taken work and time and the money he inherited from his grandfather's death—money he'd intended to put toward a house.

He'd still gotten a house eventually... half a house.

Whatever, that didn't make it okay.

"I know," she said softly. "It's why I worry."

"Well, please don't."

"Okay. But how are you going to divide an undividable dog when you sell?"

Joe had been avoiding that same question for the past few days.

Starling let his silence speak for itself. "Just remember, I'm here if you need me."

"Yeah. Thanks, Star."

When Austin finally joined Joe in the kitchen, sans kitten, his curls were a jumbled mess. He pushed them out of his face as Joe explained what he needed. As they got positioned to shift the hanger in place, Austin's hair fell into his eyes once again. He grumbled quietly and flipped his head to clear his vision, and Joe broke.

Once their hands were free, Joe reached into his pocket for the hair tie he'd started carrying around and passed it over. "Seriously, man, just do us both a favor."

Austin blinked, then huffed. "Why do you have a hair elastic?" But he took it anyway. With a practiced flip, he slipped it around his wrist, then started finger-combing his curls into order.

"I don't know if you noticed, but my best friend and one of my kids have long hair. Alex used to as well but cut it shorter."

"So you can carry around ties for them?"

"It can't surprise you that they're all forgetful," Joe evaded instead of admitting that he didn't usually keep them in his pocket.

Austin snorted.

Apparently curly-hair ponytails were more involved than straight, Joe thought, as Austin finally seemed satisfied with the placement of his hair and wrapped the tie around it three times.

"So, what's next?" Austin swiped a too-short curl off his forehead.

"Hm?" Joe had miscalculated. He could not handle Austin with a ponytail.

"What's the next step with the floor?"

"Right." Joe shook his head to clear it. "We need to finish installing hangers, put in the joists, make sure they're level, and then install the subfloor."

Austin nodded. Had his neck always been that long?

Two joist hangers later and Joe was certain that he'd made a horrible choice. Every time Austin leaned over to check level, he turned his back to Joe and leaned forward. With his hair tied out of the way, Joe could see his broad shoulders and, upsettingly, his nape.

Why was his nape sexy?

Also, Joe was starting to get specific fantasies about that hair. He'd thought Austin kept it long out of practical reasons, but what if he had a more salacious motive? Joe could picture those beautiful curls tangled around his fingers—

"Joe?" Austin glanced over his shoulder.

"Right." Joe stepped forward and—good Lord—drilled Austin's joist into the wood.

By the time they'd finished the joists, Joe was sweating and wondering why DIY was so sexual. Also, he wondered if Austin liked taking it from behind while his top pulled his hair and chewed his neck. Purely as a thought experiment, of course.

They took a break for water and a snack and then pushed forward, hanging some strapping, shoving some insulation bats between the joists, then screwing down the subfloor. Holy crap, this place might actually have a kitchen again someday soon.

Joe had a brief fantasy about it—not a perfect kitchen but a functional one that saw a lot of use, mismatched mugs in the cupboard, everyone with their own favorite. A table or island big enough for eight or ten, more if they got a little friendly, perfect for birthdays and holidays and graduation parties.

"Hey," he said before he meant to, "you said you'd installed cabinets before, right?"

"Mmm," Austin agreed. He was leaning against the wall of the house, head tilted back. His ponytail, squashed against the wall, stuck up around his head like a curly dark halo. He looked exhausted. Joe knew how he felt.

"How fast you think we can finish it?" Joe asked. "I mean, uh. Think we can host Christmas?"

Austin's eyes opened, fathomless as ever. "I think," he said after a moment, "we shouldn't put up cabinets until Starling's done the wiring in here. But if we're doing a simple layout and the ReStore has something suitable in stock, yeah, we can probably get the cupboards installed in a day."

Sweet.

"But let's go back to the thing where *we're* hosting Christmas."

Joe rubbed the back of his neck. "Well, I mean, it's your house too. I'm not going to, like, kick you out of it—"

"What kind of Christmas are we talking about?"

What did he mean, what kind of Christmas? The kind with people and dinner and presents, obviously.

Except—maybe not obviously. Not if Austin didn't have any family. Not if he'd grown up in foster care. Not if DeeDee had been his closest friend in the area.

For once, Joe was glad he'd been momentarily tongue-tied. "Just, you know, dinner. The kids, maybe their parents if they don't have other plans. Will's won't come, and Gavin's are divorced, but they get along. Alex's new stepdad is cool, and their mom's sober now. They'd probably come. Starling, maybe Linda...."

Austin stared at him. Joe felt like he was being scrutinized. Finally he said, "You know I don't cook, right? Who's going to make dinner for, what is that, twelve people?"

"Well, Meg probably won't come until after dinner if we're doing it on the twenty-fifth, but I probably have to invite my mom—"

"Jesus," Austin muttered. "Like I said. Who's cooking for all these people?"

"I will. You can be my sous chef." Will and Gavin would probably volunteer to help, and Alex and Starling would each want to bring a dish. "We don't have to do, like, presents and stuff. I just... I don't know, I thought it would be nice."

"It is nice," Austin agreed, though something in his tone made Joe think it wasn't that simple. He seemed to be weighing something in his mind. "Fuck it. Let's give it a shot. But we're going to need more furniture. Like, there's nowhere for anyone to sit, for one thing, unless you count the toilet."

"I think my mom's got someone lined up to rent my place," Joe said, "so I can bring my stuff when I move in. It's not a lot, but I've got a dining table and chairs and a couch and whatever. It won't be naked. And I have a Christmas tree." He barely spent any time at home anymore anyway, with how much work they had to do here. Besides, now he had Pepa and the kittens to think about.

Austin shook his head. "Okay, well. Looks like we have our work cut out for us."

Chapter Nine

THANKS TO Joe's new self-imposed deadline, the pressure was on for a livable space, at least on the ground floor.

Starling arrived the following day to put in another couple of hours and a few hundred feet of electrical cable. Given her piecemeal schedule and their need for electricity in the meantime, she suggested running the new wiring but leaving it unconnected until they could hook everything up.

But when she let herself into the house, she first beelined for the breezeway and cooed over their new additions.

"They are so cute," she sighed as she eyed the kittens' furry tangle next to Pepa.

The kittens and Pepa both loved when they could settle into the hollow of her belly. They even kneaded Pepa and purred at times, as though longing to nurse.

Austin should probably ask Linda about that, for the kittens' and Pepa's sakes. She always looked so content that Austin wondered if Pepa hadn't had puppies in the past. They definitely didn't want any more of those, though putting her through another surgery right now would be brutal.

Once Starling was busy in the kitchen, Austin dragged Joe to the ReStore.

Austin loved the Habitat for Humanity store. He had a habit of perusing it for objects in need of some TLC. Fixing them up for resale wasn't a bad hobby; it kept him busy and tended to fund itself and make him a few spare dollars.

Fortunately, luck was on their side, and they found a suitable straight section of cabinets on their first visit, as well as enough wood-look laminate tile to freshen the room (and cover their brand-new subfloor).

The tiles themselves took most of an evening to install, but as Austin had predicted, the cabinets went in quickly once Starling had finished in the kitchen. Without the awkward section of counter that divided the kitchen from the eating space, it was almost roomy.

Days passed in a blur of painting, moving furniture, cuddling and feeding Pepa and her kittens, dodging mockery from Starling and the kids, putting them all to work, and casual physical affection from Joe.

Austin couldn't say when it started. Joe definitely didn't touch him at first. But sometime between their first rocky meeting and the decision to host Christmas, Joe got handsy.

Not in a creepy or pushy way. In fact, Austin wasn't sure Joe knew he was doing it. After he saw Joe with Starling and the kids, it became obvious that Joe was just a physical guy. He patted backs and heads, gave high fives, bumped shoulders, played footsie, moved people out of the way with a hand on the back, shoulder, or hips.

Austin could take the more casual touches. Knocking shoulders or boots together when they were chatting to make a point or get Austin's attention didn't bother him. But he didn't know what to do with the more intimate touches.

The day they painted the dining room and kitchen, Joe grabbed Austin by the hips to move him a step to the right and out of his way. Austin was so shocked by the casual proprietary nature of the act, he couldn't even protest. Then, later, after an hour of painting, Joe laughingly told Austin he got paint on himself, cupped his face, and tenderly swiped the drips from his cheekbone. Or tried to, rather, since it had already started to dry. It took a good few seconds for Austin's brain to reboot.

What were you supposed to do with a guy who looked like Joe and didn't stop touching you but who you also couldn't have a one-night stand with?

Which he definitely could not. For one, they were essentially business partners. Also, they were becoming friends, and Austin didn't want to ruin that. Not to mention that Joe didn't seem like the one-night-stand sort. He was too sweet.

A few days after his grudging adoption of the kittens, Austin arrived at the house to find Joe working in the kitchen with Walker Texas Ranger curled up on his shoulder. The cat looked for all the world like he'd appointed himself Joe's supervisor, and he was hanging on his every word as Joe softly narrated his actions.

"We have to adjust these screws or the door to the cabinet will always hang crooked."

"Me-ew."

"Exactly. We wouldn't want to embarrass ourselves with wonky cabinetry."

Austin tiptoed back out of the room. The moment felt too precious to be ruined by Joe's potential embarrassment. Besides, there was plenty of work to do elsewhere. He went back to winterizing the windows in an effort to keep their power bills out of the stratosphere now that the cold weather had hit. The past few mornings he'd had to scrape frost off his windshield before driving into work, so he was glad to start emptying the garage now that the painting was done. It would be nice to park indoors. They'd sold some of the furniture, but they'd kept a simple bed frame and a dresser for one of the upstairs bedrooms. Joe managed to convey, without saying the words out loud, that he was keeping them in the eventuality that Will's parents realized he was gay and kicked him out.

Austin couldn't think about that any more than he could think about Joe's new shoulder ornament.

"What do you think?" he asked Pepa as he finished wrapping the window in the breezeway. "Nice and cozy?"

Pepa nudged his hand for pets, which Austin happily provided. She was getting around well enough that she wasn't confined to her sickroom anymore, and Austin was starting to think about how to build her a prosthetic. He had all the skills needed, and the knowledge he didn't have, a half an hour on YouTube could provide.

"Just in time for the storm, huh?"

Outside, the wind had picked up and was howling through the trees. Though the sky had been overcast all day and the air smelled like snow, nothing had fallen yet. Austin figured it would happen overnight; he didn't look forward to the drive in to work tomorrow if it did. Back county roads like this one often had drifts.

At least Joe would be here to help pull his car out of the ditch if that happened. He'd brought over his couch, TV, dining set, and mattress crammed into the back of his pickup, and they unloaded it all this afternoon.

"You don't want to sleep in the house?" he asked Austin. "Like, no judgment, just… it's cold, man, and I've sat on the mattress in there. It sucks."

The trailer mattress did suck, and it felt extra-hard when it was cold, but Austin wasn't fussy. "I will eventually. I just haven't had a chance to pick up my bed." He didn't have a truck, though the ability to haul things was a consideration he'd be making the next time he traded his beat-up car in for another, slightly newer, slightly less beat-up model. Now that he'd leased out his place, his disassembled bed was sitting against the wall in his office at work. His dresser was taking up space in the garage bay.

"We can go tonight, if you want," Joe offered. "Still two unclaimed bedrooms upstairs."

Austin shook his head. "This weekend's soon enough. I want to finish up a few projects first."

He regretted it now, though, as Pepa followed him into the front main floor bedroom—the one Joe had claimed as his own. The house had a double fireplace, with one side in Joe's bedroom and the other in the living room. There was no overhead light, so the space was currently lit by the trouble lamp they'd been carting from room to room as they painted, set on top of a folding ladder. But even with its limited furnishings—just the bed and the dresser—the tall wood baseboards and deep windowsills made the room feel charming.

Part of that was the color Joe had chosen—a deep foresty green that, combined with the scarred wood floors and original trim, gave the room a cozy, earthy feel. Part of it was the furniture too. The pieces might not be antiques, but they were real wood, stained a rich dark brown, and well-made. Austin didn't have to Google to know they were expensive.

For the first time in weeks, he wished that he'd moved up the arrival of his own bedroom furniture. The mattress was eighteen inches thick and covered in soft gray-green sheets, a comforter with a foliage pattern, a kitten-soft knitted throw in earth tones, and more pillows than Austin had ever seen outside the bedding aisle at Home Sense.

Ozzy and Dallas had made themselves at home on the throw blanket, likely via the step stool someone had parked at the side of the bed. There was no way they could've jumped that high yet. Joe might still be pretending he'd adopted the kittens at gunpoint, but Austin hadn't put the stool there.

With a fire lit in the double fireplace—"I didn't spend all that time cleaning it out to not test it," Joe protested, wide-eyed; Austin was pretty sure he was just one of those guys who liked lighting things on fire, and decided to be glad they had the appropriate venue for it—the bedroom was….

Austin wasn't going to think about what it was. He wasn't going to think about how all it needed was a nice hand-knotted rag rug in front of the fireplace with a bed for Pepa and a small desk and chair in the corner. A nightstand instead of the ladder.

There was even an en suite bath, although its current state was unusable.

Austin would've been annoyed about Joe claiming the best bedroom for himself, but it wasn't like they were *staying*.

He regretted his choices even more as night fell and he left the warm cozy house for his dilapidated trailer, which did little to protect him from the late fall weather.

The trailer had never felt more rickety than it did right in that moment as the wind howled and buffeted the sides. The space heater couldn't fight back against the cracks and holes he was now discovering.

Of course, he thought bitterly when lightning flashed, it couldn't be a snowstorm. No, it had to be rain, thunder, lightning.

Another flash and boom and Austin winced. He huddled down in his nest of blankets and wished they were enough to keep warm.

He was thoroughly regretting all his life choices and was convinced his trailer was going to fall apart around him when a bang rattled the door.

For a second, Austin thought this was it—the trailer was going to give way with a shudder. Then common sense prevailed and he realized someone was at the door.

"Austin! Open up!"

Austin stumbled to the door and let a grumpy Joe inside.

"Why is the door locked?"

And okay, sure, mostly Austin didn't tend to lock it, but—

"So no ax murderers find me in my sleep?" Austin snarked, which was bullshit, but his toes were cold, so he thought he could be forgiven.

Joe gave him a look that was 100 percent Dad, and Austin relented. "It's windy. I didn't want it to blow open," he finished saying as a gust of wind did just that.

Joe pulled it shut and huffed. "Pack your bags, you're moving in."

"What?"

"Austin, you cannot stay out here. It's freezing and storming and the house is actually, finally, semilivable. So put on your coat and boots and let's go."

"Uh." Austin didn't move—couldn't move—because his brain was stuck on one crucial fact. The house only had one bed. Joe's bed. Joe's very comfy, luxurious, cozy-looking bed.

"Austin." Another Dad look. "I can't let you stay here. I also don't want to stay here. Please put us both out of our misery and come sleep in the house. You can share my bed," he added, like that was an enticement, not a caution. "I promise not to bite."

Why did that also feel like a con?

"Pepa misses you," Joe added hopefully.

"That is dirty fighting," Austin said, pointing a finger Joe's way. But he relented. He gathered his boots and coat.

Then they braved the elements. The trek from the trailer to the house had never felt longer.

Inside, Pepa greeted them at the door, especially excited to see Austin, proving Joe's cheap shot might have had some truth to it. Damn.

As much as Austin was not looking forward to climbing into bed with Joe—seriously, what a bad idea—he couldn't deny that it was warm and cozy and inviting. And when a particularly loud clap of thunder and its accompanying blue flash split the night, then plunged the house into darkness, that sealed the deal.

"See?" Joe said.

"No," Austin pointed out dryly. "I can't see shit, man. The lights just went out." This wasn't quite true. The warm glow of the embers in the fireplace provided plenty to see by.

"No power, no space heater. No freezing to death." Joe waved him toward the clearly unused side of the bed. "Just get in."

Austin had never shared a bed for sleeping before. In his mind, that was something reserved for couples and, occasionally, parents with kids.

He would've been nervous about it, but actually the parents with kids thing made it easier. Joe would've let any of the kids crash in his bed with him, probably. Well, maybe not Meg or Alex, but only because of how that would look to outsiders. He'd probably shared with Starling too.

It only meant he didn't want Austin to freeze to death.

"Is this a bad time to tell you I sleep in the nude?" he joked as he pulled off his sweatshirt.

He had a T-shirt underneath, but still, if Joe was going to give him shit, Austin was going to hand it right back.

Joe apparently shared the philosophy, because he said, "No, that's cool, me too," as though he'd expected this, and then dropped his sweatpants.

In the dim light of the fire, Austin could just make out that his boxer briefs had flamingos on them. The flamingos wore little Santa hats.

Austin gave up. It'd be easier to deal with that when he didn't have to look at it. Besides, his feet were icicles. He crawled into the bed and pulled the covers over himself while Joe flung his sweatshirt over the ladder.

"Where's—okay, good, they didn't get up."

Austin squinted and just made out the forms of three tiny kittens curled up at the foot of the bed. "I dunno, not sure there's gonna be room for you. Is Pepa getting up here too?"

"I don't want her up here yet in case she hurts herself getting down when I'm asleep. I put her bed by the fireplace. C'mon, Pepa, there's a good girl. Go back to sleep, sweetheart."

Austin couldn't see from his vantage point, but he could hear her turning in her habitual circles, getting comfortable. Then the mattress dipped just perceptibly as Joe got in.

The bed was everything he'd hoped for—warm, soft, cozy. The pillows, Austin was pretty sure, had actual feathers in them. It was hands down the most comfortable bed he'd ever been in.

But how the fuck was he supposed to sleep with Joe six inches away?

The mattress shifted underneath them as Joe rolled onto his side to face Austin. "You can relax. I told you I don't bite."

"You did say that," Austin agreed. "I just don't believe you."

Joe cackled. "Wow, okay, I see how it is. You invite someone into your bed out of the goodness of your heart—"

"Is that what this is? I thought you were just a control freak."

"—and they impugn your honor and malign your character—"

Austin pressed his toes to Joe's bare leg.

"—*Jesus Christ*, and then they try to give you a heart attack with their ice-cube feet, what the fuck, Austin? You wanna put some socks on, maybe?"

Ew. "I can't sleep with socks on. That's gross."

"Well, you can't sleep with your feet on my leg either."

"What kind of host are you?"

"I'm not your host. This is your house too, dumbass." Under the covers, Joe poked Austin's stomach. "Now go to sleep. You're disturbing the kittens, and they need their beauty rest."

Chapter Ten

JOE WOKE to predawn light and to the stomach-wrenching, blood-warming sight of Austin in his bed.

Austin lay curled on his side, tucked into the fetal position, the blankets snug around his shoulders. He lay facing Joe, his hair spilling enticingly across the pillow.

Joe wanted to crawl into that cocoon, kiss Austin awake, and then really mess up those curls. Or maybe crawl under the blankets and see if he couldn't use his mouth to get Austin to unbend from that protective pose.

Joe knew a sleep pose could just be a sleep pose, but somehow it felt meaningful that Austin was curled up in his sleep, as if protecting his vulnerable parts or trying to take up less space.

Of course, Joe couldn't do any of those sexy things, and not just because Ozzy had migrated to settle into the space between Austin's neck, chest, and arms. At least they'd both definitely been warm last night.

His blood pumping with thoughts of the company in his bed, Joe gave up on getting any more sleep, eased his way out from under his comforter, and tiptoed out of the room.

He couldn't claim surprise when Pepa didn't follow—their girl liked her sleep and had a clear favorite—or when Walker perked up with a soft mew and padded eagerly after Joe.

Once in the kitchen, Walker sank his claws into Joe's sweats in an attempt to climb—a trick that only really worked with jeans—and Joe sighed and bent to rescue his calves and his kitten.

"You are pure trouble," he said softly. "Don't think I haven't noticed what a nosy busybody you are. Your name is totally apt. Wandering around sticking your nose in everyone else's business. God, you'll probably be the boss once you're all grown." Already there were signs that all mischief could be sourced back to Walker, no matter which cat was actually caught mid-mess.

Unperturbed by Joe's aspersions on his character, Walker snuggled in and purred in Joe's ear. Soon he'd be too big for this, and Joe would miss having the soft warm weight pressed in close.

With his preferred energy outlet off the table—or bed—Joe channeled his restlessness into something more productive and started prepping the dining room to paint. This wasn't the first time he'd had an inconvenient crush, or a dry spell for that matter, since he'd never been fond of one-nighters. He could ignore the pressure from his libido. It wasn't as if Austin would keep sleeping in his bed. Joe would be able to work out some of his frustrations solo later, and they could go back to their easy platonic cohabitation.

Well, maybe not fully easy. But they'd done an acceptable job of ignoring the sexual tension so far. They could keep it up, Joe was sure.

But he was also pretty sure he wasn't alone—that Austin felt it too. He'd caught Austin looking once or twice.

But looking wasn't touching, and touching was definitely a bad thing right now. It would make everything even more messy. Joe had learned his lesson about getting involved with someone when you had business entanglements. Therefore no mess. Right?

Joe put a second coat of paint on the dining room walls. At least that kind of mess, he could clean up.

Then, figuring it was late enough that he no longer had to worry about disturbing Austin's beauty sleep, he headed to the kitchen for coffee and pancakes, a perfectly normal, *not* morning-after, breakfast choice.

Whether it was the hour, the smell of coffee, or the sound of Joe in the kitchen, Pepa hopped into the room as the skillet was warming, Dallas riding on her back and Ozzy following a pace behind, uttering anxious mews like his mom might leave him behind or forget to feed him.

"Good morning," Joe murmured.

Pepa answered with a happy rumble and a press of her face into his leg.

"Are you hungry, sweet girl?"

He stepped away from the stove to dish up breakfast for his three- and four-legged babies. Walker and Dallas abandoned their perches immediately and without grace as soon as Joe opened the can.

Joe had a plateful of pancakes warming in the oven by the time Austin shuffled into the kitchen, looking for all the world like Joe had made good on every fantasy he'd had this morning.

Which Joe definitely could not think about right now, as he stood in loose boxers and sweats.

"Morning, sleepyhead," Joe's mouth said, apparently better at faking coherency than the rest of him.

"Morning," Austin mumbled. He blinked at Joe and the skillet. "Did you make pancakes?"

"Yes, because cold nights deserve pancake mornings." He took a plate from a cupboard and used the kitchen tongs he'd brought from his place to deposit some breakfast upon it. "And because I have big plans for the day."

Joe remembered too late that they didn't have any maple syrup, still dealing with a kitchen that had only recently become functional and thus an incomplete pantry, but this didn't perturb Austin, who opened the fridge and withdrew a jar of homemade raspberry jam Linda had bequeathed him when he fixed the heater in her car the week before.

Austin rattled in the drawer behind Joe for a fork and knife. "Plans?"

Joe could feel the sleep warmth radiating off of him, caught the faint whiff of sweat, and immediately stuck his face back over the frying pan. He was flying by the seat of his pants here, but he knew the old saying about idle hands. He might not believe in the devil, but his hands or his eyes would definitely wander all over Austin if he left them idle. He just needed to keep busy until he could get some time to himself and give his hands a more appropriate and helpful job to do.

"I figured we've been working pretty hard on the house, and it looks great. Kitchen's done, right? We've got some cleaning up to do, and we need to grab some more furniture, but we're totally on track for hosting Christmas." He paused as he worked himself up to the point, suddenly realizing how perfect it was. "So we should do a test run of the kitchen, make sure everything's up to par. Call it a celebration dinner."

Austin hopped up on the counter beside him. Joe wanted to scold him—*Were you raised in a barn?*—but he bit his tongue on it in time. The words sounded like his mother. Besides, that remark would've hit way too close to the truth.

It wasn't like Joe even minded Austin sitting on the counter, except now he was looking at Austin's bare feet tapping against the cupboards and feeling like a repressed Victorian.

Austin shoveled in a forkful of pancake and then spoke with his mouth full, which broke the spell before Joe could burn the latest batch. "We worked our asses off getting the house ready, so you want to work our asses off on a fancy dinner?"

"Shut up. I like cooking." This would totally work. Joe downed half his cup of coffee. Caffeine was integral to this plan. "It's like… relaxing. Not all the time, just sometimes."

"Well, your pancakes pass the test, at least. I'm in."

Joe tipped the last few onto a plate for himself, added a slathering of jam, and debated. He could go sit in the dining room like a civilized person.

He hopped up onto the counter next to Austin instead, then reached down and pulled open the cutlery drawer for his own fork. "Okay, let's talk menu. You like Italian?"

Austin dragged a pancake through a smear of jam. "You mean like pasta?"

"I was thinking more like—veal parm? Or do you like seafood? I make a pretty good seafood linguine, but it can be tricky getting good-quality fresh ingredients. I'd definitely have to drive into Windsor for groceries. I can probably get the veal at Schinkel's in town, though. Or I could do chicken marsala and a mushroom risotto—"

"I don't know what half of this stuff is."

Ah. Well, not everyone grew up in an Italian family that loved to cook. Joe awkwardly rubbed the back of his neck. "Are there foods you don't like?"

Austin hopped off the counter and put his plate in the sink, plugged the drain, ran the hot water. "I'm not big on seafood. I think I could be, just never… had much."

Translation—shrimp and mussels were expensive, not the kind of thing you'd make for yourself as a treat unless you already knew you liked it.

That was fine with Joe; he didn't really want to drive all the way to Erie Street anyway. "Mushrooms are okay, though? Rice, butter, cream…?" A horrible thought occurred to him. "You're not lactose intolerant, are you?"

Austin looked up from adding soap to the sink. "You've seen me eat pizza."

Joe sagged in relief. "Okay. Good. I'll make a shopping list, then. How do you feel about tiramisu?"

Austin blinked at him. "What's tiramisu?"

It took everything in Joe not to gasp in horror.

Austin grinned. "I had you going, didn't I?"

"Fuck off," Joe laughed. "Tiramisu or biscotti? Or maybe cannoli?"

"Jesus, how many courses are you planning?"

Shopping took an hour and a half because Joe had to go to three grocery stores before he found fresh basil that met his standards. When he got home, Austin had finished washing and putting away the breakfast dishes, and Joe could hear a load of laundry thumping around in the washing machine, but Austin and Pepa were nowhere to be found. Out for her morning physiotherapy slash walk, then.

Joe could've taken the opportunity to jerk off in the shower, but if he wanted to cash the checks his mouth had written earlier, he needed to get a move on in the kitchen. He could shower while the biscotti baked.

The day passed in a parody of domestic bliss. Joe cooked, baked, and cleaned the kitchen (he hated leaving the mess until the end), while Austin passed in and out, moving through the house to work on various small jobs.

"I've been thinking," Austin said during one of his visits to the kitchen for water and a snack, "that we should put a more permanent heat source in the breezeway."

Joe considered that. It was an enclosed structure with some insulation. If they added more and a heat source, there was no reason why it couldn't be comfortable all four seasons. "Like?"

"I'm not sure. Maybe an old-fashioned wood stove? It could be functional and atmospheric."

Joe deferred to Austin's judgement, and the man wandered off in the direction of the breezeway with his water, muttering to himself. Joe figured a fully insulated and heated breezeway was in his future. At least at Christmas they'd have a handy place to sequester the pets so they didn't get their furry little paws all over Joe's feast.

By the time dinner rolled around, Joe could admit he might have gone a little bit overboard, but Austin said he didn't know what risotto was and Joe's Italian heart couldn't handle it.

Of course, it took all of three minutes for Joe to realize his mistake.

Austin eyed up the various dishes with curiosity while Joe set them out, and happily accepted his plate. Then he took his first bite and moaned like a porn star trying to entice viewers past the paywall.

Okay, that was probably an exaggeration brought on by Joe's libido, which was cursing his poor time management. What had he been thinking? He should've skipped the biscotti.

Joe took several gulps of red wine and tried to remind his dick that Austin was not talking to him. Austin was currently making heart eyes at his plate like it had offered to put a ring on it. He was not going to suck Joe's dick, no matter what Joe's dick thought, because Austin was too busy sucking back veal marsala like it was his job.

Joe drank more wine. He'd picked up two bottles of his favorite Chianti; Austin gave it a curious glance and then shrugged and let Joe pour. He must've liked it well enough, because they managed to kill one bottle between them over dinner.

"I gotta ask, where did you learn to cook like this? And please don't say TikTok."

Conversation. Good—Joe could do that. "My nonna. Stereotypical Italian grandmother stuff. This is nothing; you should try her peposo. Uh, it's a beef stew. It's not fancy, it just tastes like it." He paused. "And don't you learn all kinds of shit from TikTok? You told me that was how you fixed the typewriter."

"That was YouTube," Austin corrected. He swiped a piece of fresh bread—Joe cheated and got that at a bakery because he only had so much time and kitchen space—through the marsala and popped it in his mouth. "Which is fine, because the typewriter does not have a soul. This"—he indicated the risotto and the plate of caprese salad they'd demolished—"has a soul."

Joe might have preened a little, but he wasn't going to own up to it. "Think that might be the Chianti talking."

Austin polished off his glass. "Well. You might be right."

The wine had stained his lips dark red. Joe needed something to talk about stat or he wasn't going to be able to look away. "So, you know what *I* did all day. What did you get up to?"

Austin pulled his lips between his teeth, almost like he was nervous. The apples of his cheeks were pink. "Okay, uh… it's probably better if I just show you?"

They'd more or less polished off dinner anyway. A little movement would be good. "Sure."

They took their wineglasses along—refilled from the freshly opened bottle—as Joe followed Austin into the breezeway. Somehow, while

Joe was busy with dinner and dessert, Austin had found and installed a wood-burning stove, complete with a round pipe that exhausted through the smaller window.

"Dude," Joe said. "So when you said you thought the breezeway needed a heat source, you meant, like, today?"

Austin rubbed the back of his neck. He had his hair up again, the better, he said, to not get any risotto in it. Joe reminded his eyes they should be looking at Austin's face, but that didn't help much. "Well, I mean… that was after I found this stuff in the pole barn. They must've had something like this before, or maybe they used to heat the barn."

"Either way, a pretty handy find." Pepa would be thrilled to discover her favorite room just got cozier.

They moved to the living room and settled on the couch, the bottle of wine on the coffee table between them.

"So. I'm guessing your ex is the biggest idiot on the planet to give you up. No way his new squeeze is hotter or better at cooking."

Well, that was forward. Also, a bit out of left field. "I mean, he never appreciated my cooking," Joe admitted with a grimace, "which should have been a signal to me that we were incompatible."

Austin eyed Joe over his wineglass. "Biggest. Idiot."

"Thanks." Joe sipped his wine.

Austin twirled his wineglass and eyed Joe up. "Though maybe next time, don't keep dating someone that dumb."

"Ha ha," Joe said dryly.

"I'm serious." Austin laughed. "Though I gotta say, I'm also curious, 'cause what were your dates even like? I mean," he continued with a handwave to take in Joe's everything, "you're clearly a romantic of the red roses and candle-lit dinner variety."

"Oh, am I?" Austin wasn't wrong—Joe did like an intimate dinner—but he didn't want to admit it, especially after the meal they'd just had.

"Uh, yeah?" Austin sounded confused by even the hint of a contradiction.

Joe snorted. Curious about this game Austin had started, he said, "And you aren't?"

Austin shrugged.

Joe considered him. "You probably make your date pick every restaurant because you can't decide."

Austin was mid sip and nearly choked.

Joe grinned. "Was that a yes or a no?"

Austin wiped his chin and glared. "It was a neither. Also, you definitely always pick and refuse to let anyone else have final say."

Joe shrugged. "Only because most people have terrible taste." Plus, there were a lot of Italians in the area, and everybody talked. Joe knew every decent restaurant in a fifty-kilometer radius and whether the owners were assholes. He eyed Austin again. "Don't tell me you like a coffee date."

Austin pulled a face. Joe hadn't thought so. That had been a long shot, but he struggled to imagine Austin on convoluted dates. He struck Joe as someone who liked simple. He probably enjoyed strolls through antique shops and farmers' markets—places he could find projects, or inspiration for the same.

"You probably love a coffee date if it's in a fancy hipster café with pour-over and handcrafted baked goods," Austin guessed. Damn it, why was he better at this?

"Let me guess—the ReStore is your ideal date."

Austin pulled another face.

Joe gave up. "Okay, enlighten me, then."

"I don't really date." He shrugged.

Joe gasped. "*Cheater*." Here he'd thought they'd been playing a game and it turned out Austin had just thrown out the rulebook.

"I thought that was already established."

"Not hardly." He sipped his wine and pondered. If Austin didn't date, then Joe only had one avenue to even the score. "Hmm. I bet you call all your one-night stands 'baby' because you can't remember their names."

As soon as he said it, he knew it had been a mistake. He'd spent the whole day trying *not* to think about this. Now he was not only thinking about it, he was voicing those thoughts out loud and inviting Austin to speculate right back.

Austin flushed, his mouth dropping open in offense. A direct hit. Austin Taylor was kind of a slut, and now Joe could never unknow that. "Oh, so we're moving to that side of things?" He stuck out his chin. "Two can play at that game too." He pointed a finger in Joe's face. "Pillow princess."

The accusation momentarily jolted Joe out of his more X-rated musings, and he cackled. "Swing and a miss." *Huge* miss, even. He let that give him confidence as he shot back, "You probably have your hookups saved in your phone as 'hot blond (name of gay bar) bathroom handy.'"

That got a laugh, at least. "First of all, that would never work. There's only one gay bar in town."

Oh, yeah. Good point.

"Also," Austin added, "I just don't get their numbers."

Joe inhaled sharply. Fuck, was that... kind of hot? Or had it just been too long since he touched another person with sexual intent? He cleared his throat. "Wow. Love 'em and leave 'em, huh?"

"More like fuck 'em and leave 'em," he countered.

Nope, nope, nope. Joe wasn't thinking about that—not analyzing the slight drop in his stomach at the thought of how lonely that sounded. "Touché. Let me guess. You're into back rooms or their place, never your own."

"Obviously." Austin tilted his head. "And *you* are a control freak."

"How is that supposed to work? I thought I was a pillow princess?" Joe didn't want to admit that the second accusation was closer to the mark. Maybe because "control freak" made him sound unreasonable, or maybe just because he didn't want to lose this weird game.

"You're a complicated guy," Austin said with a shrug. A stray curl fell out of his ponytail and across his forehead. His lips were stained red from the wine, and Joe should really have remembered before now that red wine always hit him like this.

"And I guess you like it simple? Hand jobs in bathrooms? Back-seat blowjobs? Fucking in alleyways?"

Color rose further in Austin's cheeks, and he defiantly met Joe's gaze. "I'm not telling you which of those is right."

"Cheater," Joe said for the third time. How could he win if Austin wasn't honest?

"Usually a guy at least buys me a drink before I reveal this sort of information."

Joe pointedly looked at the wine bottle, then back at Austin.

Austin's flush deepened. It looked unfairly good on him. "You know that's not what I meant."

"Uh-huh. So what, you saying I gotta buy you something fancier—or maybe it's trashier?—for you to be honest? Rude."

"You wouldn't tell me either," Austin pointed out, cheeks still rosy. "You neither confirmed nor denied anything."

"Yeah, well. I didn't want to get too far into it in case I couldn't get back out again."

Fuck, he hadn't meant to say that out loud.

Austin blinked at him, tilting his head. A teasing smile lifted the edges of his lips. "You have trouble pulling out?"

God damn it. Joe groaned, slouching on the couch. "Give me a break."

"I mean, that would explain how you ended up with four kids—"

Joe flipped him off. "Don't make fun of me. It feels like it's been that long since I got laid."

Austin hooted. "God, and I thought fixing up the house was putting a crimp in my sex life. How long's it been for you? I'm guessing eighteen years is a stretch."

"I don't wanna do the math. It's depressing. Spring sometime, I think." *Last* spring, but Austin didn't need to know that.

Austin made a noise of disbelief. "You *think*?" He looked aghast.

Joe groaned again. "We gotta talk about something else," he complained. "Fucking red wine. Disaster."

A glance into the wineglass, then back at Joe. An eyebrow went up. "I'm not making the connection."

Fuck, Joe was going to have to say it out loud? He sighed. "I forgot red wine makes me horny."

"Are you sure it's not just the dry spell?"

Joe rubbed his fingers against his thigh in an attempt to distract himself, uncomfortably aware of the fact that the subject had had a predictable effect that was probably visible in his jeans.

"Although…."

Something in Austin's tone made Joe look over. He swallowed, his throat suddenly dry. "What?"

"I was just thinking the wine would explain my problem too."

Joe's heart thudded in his ears. Was Austin suggesting…? "Oh?"

"Maybe we could help each other out with that."

Somewhere in the back of Joe's brain, a little voice started to say, *Hey, remember why this is a bad idea?* Joe's neglected libido shoved a gag in it and took over Joe's stupid wine-drunk mouth to say, "Flip a coin to see who tops? Loser gets next time."

It wasn't the best idea he'd ever had for more reasons than Joe was going to give passing consideration. The only one that mattered right now was *What if Austin loses this coin toss and backs out of the whole thing because he's not into being fucked.*

But Austin didn't back down, he just laughed. "Seriously?"

Joe narrowed his eyes. "We could wrestle for it if you prefer." He dug in his pocket and came up with a nickel. "Call it."

Somehow he still expected Austin to flinch. To back out. To roll his eyes and pass the whole thing off as the same kind of joke as his pillow-princess accusation.

But the coin had barely left Joe's thumb when Austin called, "Tails."

It was kind of funny, Joe thought, when the thing landed. "Huh," he said.

Across the room, Austin's eyes had gone dark. "Hmm?"

Joe flicked the coin toward him. "Bet you've never been so glad to see a beaver."

Austin's gaze went predatory. That was cute, Joe thought. Maybe that control-freak allegation had been as much a shot in the dark as the pillow-princess one.

But no way was Joe leaving this up to chance. He pushed himself to his feet and crossed the living room until he was standing in front of Austin's chair, their feet almost touching. "Unfortunately for you, I don't have an alley handy—"

He reached down and hauled Austin to his feet. The minuscule space between them crackled with electricity.

"—and I don't think the bathroom counter is really up for the job unless you wanna redo that before Christmas too—"

"Should I make another guess?" Austin asked. "You're all talk and no action?"

Joe barked a laugh. "You're so bad at this. Some of us can talk and fuck at the same time."

"Prove it," Austin said, eyes flashing. And then he added, because he was hilarious and kind of a shithead, "*Baby.*"

Oh, this was going to be fun.

Joe kissed him.

They stumbled toward Joe's bedroom, half tripping over stray furniture, occasionally bumping into walls. They really needed to get some overhead lighting. But by the time they got to the bed, the only casualties were Austin's hoodie and Joe's T-shirt, along with the cats' respect at their clumsiness. Austin shut the door behind them, and Joe dragged him onto the bed and tumbled them onto it.

How long had it been since he'd felt this kind of rush? The anticipation burned through him as they pulled at each other's clothing. Austin tasted like Chianti and kissed like he hadn't eaten in a year. His skin was hot and smooth under Joe's hands, his fingers demanding and firm on Joe's body. When Joe rolled them on the mattress so he could reach for the bedside table, he braced himself on his right hand and accidentally caught Austin's hair under it. Austin hissed and arched his back, rubbing his dick against Joe's ass.

Yeah, it had definitely been too long since Joe took someone to bed. He dropped the lube and condoms onto the mattress.

There was a fruitless scramble to get out of the rest of their clothes. The wine buzz didn't help. Eventually Joe laughed into Austin's mouth and pulled back. "Fuck it, take off your own pants."

For a second he thought Austin would argue on principle, but after a beat he just said, "You know what? Good plan," and pushed Joe off him.

Rude.

But then they were naked and Joe could drink his fill of Austin's lean, compact body—the muscle definition in his arms and chest, the dark trail of curly hair between his pecs leading down, the frankly gorgeous cock lying plump and hard against his stomach.

Okay, yeah. Joe could definitely work with this.

"Nice," he said appreciatively as he reached out to give Austin's dick a slow stroke.

Austin made a close-mouthed sound and thrust into it. Then he fumbled in the covers for the bottle. "Wait 'til you feel it from the inside."

Joe wanted to laugh—would've laughed—but somehow Austin already had the lube open and his fingers wet, and he smeared them over Joe's hole without preamble. The laugh died before it could escape his lungs. "Jesus—do those lines *work* on people?"

"Who needs lines?" Austin said breathlessly and pushed his fingers inside.

Brat.

Joe leaned into the touch, savoring the feeling.

Austin crooked his fingers, and Joe cursed. Why had he let it go so long? Sure, he maybe would prefer to top most days, but tonight he had no complaints. He tipped his hips for a better angle and demanded, "There. Like that."

Austin huffed. "Bossy. Should have known." But he followed Joe's directions.

"Don't you want to know that you're making me feel good?" He moaned as Austin got the angle just right. Austin's eyes went darker, and he redoubled his efforts. No matter what else he said, he clearly liked the feedback and encouragement—and some direction.

"Of course I do… baby." Austin smirked and pressed.

Joe was too busy moaning to protest the dumb pet name. "Get dressed so we can do the fun part." Then Joe proceeded to ignore his own words, snatched up the condom from the bed, and tore it open. With fumbling hands—stupid wine, stupid fingers—Joe slid it down Austin's perfect length.

Austin grunted under Joe's touch, and he paused for a few more strokes. God, it was such a pretty cock. Joe couldn't wait.

Speaking of….

Joe pulled himself off Austin's fingers and straddled his waist, keeping hold of Austin's dick so he could hold it steady as he sank onto it.

Austin clung to Joe's hips and gasped openmouthed. When his ass met Austin's hips, Joe paused a moment, adjusting to the feel. He squeezed down and then released. Austin grunted and stared up at Joe.

Joe could work with this.

He pulled up, and when only the head of Austin's dick remained, Joe clenched and slid all the way back down.

"Fuck!" Austin bucked and tightened his grip. Joe was going to bruise. "You're—you're so good at this." Austin licked his lips. "*Baby*."

Joe narrowed his eyes, and Austin smirked. Right. Time to get Austin to scream his name. Just because it had been a while didn't mean Joe had forgotten how to do this.

Adjusting his stance, Joe went to town, riding Austin like he was the prize bull at the rodeo. Beneath him, Austin panted and groaned, staring up at Joe wide-eyed and heated, clearly enjoying the view.

But that was a little *too* good. If Joe was going to get only one ride on this cock, he was getting his money's worth. Austin could lay back and look pretty and let Joe have his fun.

Joe slowed to a grind, hardly lifting his hips, clenching and watching Austin fall apart beneath him. The stimulation definitely wasn't enough for him. He squirmed and tried to buck, but Joe's thighs were stronger.

Joe twisted his hips, breathless. That delicious length was pressing just right against his prostate. He leaned forward, ran his nails over Austin's pecs, and caught his nipples.

"Fuck," Austin gasped as he raked his fingers down Joe's thighs, trying to spur him on. "Move. Baby."

"That's not my name." He pinched and clenched, and Austin lost it.

"Fuck. Joe. Please!" He scrambled to find purchase on Joe's hips, trying to push and pull him into movement.

"Say it again," Joe teased.

"Please," Austin begged, "Joe."

Such good behaviour deserved a reward. "Good boy," Joe teased and pecked a quick kiss to Austin's slack mouth. Then he straightened up, leaned back, and fucked himself until Austin was groaning and coming beneath him.

He looked obscene doing it, head thrown back, skin flushed and sweaty. It was that as much as the sweet pressure of him in Joe's ass and his hand, loose on his cock because the lube was drying out, that pushed him over the edge.

Finally his thighs wouldn't lift him anymore, so he rested his weight on Austin's hips and legs, his chest heaving, as he came back to himself. Austin's eyes were still closed. When he opened them a second later, they were dazed, unfocused. He looked like someone had slapped him silly.

Joe was going to feel really smug about that. Just as soon as he got enough blood circulating in his brain to feel more than *hnnng*. He'd come all over Austin's chest. He was going to be smug about that too.

Who's the pillow princess now?

But he only got a few seconds to bask, because Austin took a deep breath, regained his faculties, and complained, "You're heavy."

"Yeah, well, you're filthy," Joe shot back, but he wrangled himself up and off to the side almost without falling over. The red wine reminded him it existed at the last moment, and he lost his balance and went face-first into the pillows. "Go bring me a washcloth."

Austin wrinkled his nose. "Why do I have to get it? I'm the one who's going to drip everywhere."

"Top handles cleanup. Them's the rules."

"I feel like these rules should've been negotiated along with the coin toss," Austin grumbled, but he got up. A few seconds later, Joe heard the water in the bathroom come on.

When he returned, he threw a washcloth at Joe's head, and Joe caught it without looking—pure luck.

Austin didn't get back into bed, so when Joe finished with the cloth, he looked up.

Austin had put his boxers back on, and he was standing awkwardly in the doorway. His hair was a whole disaster. Joe could've spent the whole night running his hands through it, the way it looked. He was pissed he hadn't, and equally pissed he was going to pass out now before he had a chance to.

Joe blinked at him. "What are you doing? Get back in bed before you freeze to death, Jesus. Or, shit, do you think we have to let Pepa out first?"

"I'll get her," Austin said. "Yeah… be right back."

The wine and the orgasm combined with the busy day and conspired to drag Joe's eyelids down. Somewhere in the house, a door opened and closed.

The pillow swallowed Joe up.

Some time later, the mattress dipped once, deeply. Then three more dips, just in the covers this time, as the cats rejoined them. One of them walked unsteadily up the mattress until it was curled up by Joe's head. Walker, he assumed.

"Night," Austin said.

Joe didn't answer, already mostly asleep.

Chapter Eleven

AUSTIN WAS a foster kid. He had a misspent enough youth. Hell, he still liked to go out and tie one on now and then; the only way to tolerate the club scene was with copious amounts of alcohol. The point was, Austin knew hangovers.

So it was *really annoying* to wake up after a night of only moderate drinking feeling like deep-fried ass.

"Kill me," he said into the pillow, long before he had the courage to open his eyes.

Beside him, Joe said in the same tone, "Your dick is too pretty to die."

Austin was wide-awake, the influx of adrenaline momentarily sidelining the sick throbbing in his head.

It didn't last, though. Like, it was great that they weren't going to have to pretend last night never happened, but that didn't stop Austin from wanting to crawl into the bathtub and disintegrate. "I didn't drink enough to deserve this," he whined. "What the fuck."

Joe grunted and shoved the covers down. Thank *God*; Austin was roasting to death. "Red wine," he said.

"You knew this was going to happen and you *still drank it*?"

Joe slapped a hand over Austin's mouth, which, fair. "Shhhhh."

Austin would've licked it, but his mouth already felt drier than a geriatric nun in the Sahara. He rolled over instead and regretted it when his stomach stayed put. It took him a moment to recover without vomiting. "Do we have Advil?"

For a moment Joe lay there without speaking, and Austin was afraid the answer was no.

Then he said, "In my truck, I think." Which—right. Austin had some in the trailer too.

That was a good start. Things were looking up. Then Austin's hungover brain had a moment of divine inspiration. "How much do you think we have to pay your fruits to bring us McDonald's breakfast and Gatorade?"

Joe made a garbled noise and started flailing for his phone. "Fuck, you're a genius."

They managed to get themselves dressed and into the kitchen just in time for the fruits' arrival.

Gavin, because he was a chaotic neutral troll, laughed when he saw them slumped at the table.

"What did you do to yourselves?" Will asked.

"Red wine," Joe grunted and made grabby hands at the food. "Let this be a lesson to you, children—never drink."

Alex rolled their eyes. "You're so old."

Austin contemplated this accusation as he sipped his Gatorade. "Nah, I've never felt like this before. The lesson here, kids, is don't drink red wine. When it comes to booze, be trashy, not classy."

"Austin, don't corrupt my children."

Austin glanced at said children. "You've got to be almost done high school, right?"

Alex dimpled. "A couple more months."

"Yeah. That barn door is open," Austin said without pity and patted Joe's head condescendingly.

"People who mock my children don't get to use them as DoorDash or free labor."

"Talk about cutting off your nose to spite your face," Will said.

"Nice." Austin held out a tired hand to fist-bump. "Keep this up and you'll be my favorite." He winked and the kid went adorably pink.

Once Austin and Joe were approaching human, they put the kids to work walking Pepa, feeding the kittens, and handling the box of Christmas decorations they hadn't gotten rid of. Then Joe said, "So, should we go get your bed?"

Austin wasn't an expert on navigating potential repeat-night stands, but he was pretty sure the subtext here said that last night might have been good, but there wouldn't be a repeat.

Thank God for Joe's work truck. They loaded Austin's bedroom furniture into the back and had just started to secure the mattress when Austin had a thought.

"Hey, Joe?"

Joe glanced his way and grunted. Austin was pretty sure Joe was looking at him, but it was hard to tell behind the sunglasses.

"How are we gonna get the mattress up the stairs?"

Joe looked at the mattress. He looked at Austin.

Wordlessly, they took the mattress out of the truck bed and put it back against the wall of Austin's office.

"Plan B," Austin said. "As in Bedroom Depot."

They made it to the store just as it opened—noon on Sundays—and Austin dipped inside long enough to sit on three different foam mattresses that came in boxes. He picked the medium-soft one. He and Joe loaded it into the truck five minutes later.

"I should pay half of it," Joe said once they'd gotten back on the road home. They were taking Walker Road, which was a big industrial and shopping street in the city and somehow transitioned to farmland and would deposit them more or less at their doorstep. It felt wrong.

So did Joe's offer. "Hell no. That's my mattress," Austin said. "First brand-new one I've ever had. Merry Christmas to me. Besides, it was still on sale from Black Friday." It might've been a stretch at any other time, but his credit card company gave him an extra month to pay at Christmas.

"Yeah, but if I hadn't taken the bedroom on the main floor, you wouldn't have had to buy one."

Austin was too hungover for this. "Joe. You literally just saw my mattress. It basically had springs poking out of it. There's a reason I didn't mind sleeping in the trailer."

Joe huffed. "Fine."

Back at the farmhouse, Joe conned his male offspring into helping unload the truck while Alex strung lights on Joe's Christmas tree.

"This doesn't feel too gender essentialist?" Austin asked them as Joe and Gavin wheezed past with Austin's dresser.

"I'm cool sitting out the hard labor," Alex said seriously. "Besides. One time Gavin got bored putting up Joe's tree and just left the lights all bundled up together in the middle."

"Right, yeah. I think you've got the right job, then."

They heated up leftovers for lunch, and soon they were crowded around the dining table. Joe looked so content to have his children at hand, though Austin did have to wonder....

"No Meg today?"

"She's gearing up for a big competition," Gavin said between bites.

Alex pulled a face. "Don't talk with your mouth full."

Gavin stuck out his tongue.

"Children," Joe said mildly, in the tone of a man who wasn't about to be put off his leftover risotto.

Alex elbowed Gavin. "He's talking to you."

Gavin swayed under the touch. "Nah. I'm the favourite."

Naturally, that started a heated debate, Alex loudly explaining why Gavin was wrong and Will backing them up with well-timed jabs.

Joe caught Austin's gaze and rolled his eyes, so Austin took his cue from the experienced parent in the room and ignored the bickering in favor of his lunch.

Afterward, Joe abandoned them for paid work. "There's lots of post-storm cleanup still to do," he said with a shrug on his way out.

By this point, Alex and Will had caught sight of the boxes and boxes of seasonal décor and couldn't be stopped. They approached the boxes with the enthusiasm of children who had been denied the experience in the past. Part of Austin definitely got it. The greater part thought it was probably best to stay out of the way. Maybe they could convince Gavin to help too.

Austin set up his bedroom and was gathering the last of his stuff from the front hallway, where the boys had left it after they pulled it out of Joe's truck, when Starling entered trailing her gear.

"No furry children today?" she asked with an arched eyebrow, noticing the empty space around him.

A fair question, considering Pepa and the kittens had taken to following him and Joe around the house. "They found better entertainment," Austin explained as laughter rang out from the living room.

"Teenagers?"

"Teens with Christmas decorations."

"Oh. Shiny, hangy things," Starling said, nodding.

"And teens who think you're the cutest thing they've ever seen," he agreed.

She followed him upstairs. "I think I'll be able to finish things up today. Should be ready for inspection once I'm done."

"No shit?"

She laughed.

"That was faster than I was expecting."

"Well, call me crazy, but I wasn't thrilled about the idea of my best friend living in a house with knob-and-tube."

Austin pulled a face and once again pushed away the ominous thoughts about the outdated system and why it was retrofitted.

He left Starling to her work in the other bedrooms, finished unpacking in his own, and figured it was time for Pepa's walk.

They'd slowly been increasing the distance they travelled each time, and Austin was so proud of how well she was adjusting.

The kittens were sleepily watching the children decorate—evidently they'd already tired themselves out chasing bits of garland—so Austin felt no guilt about leaving them behind and pulling Pepa out into the cold. Well, maybe he felt some guilt about that, but Pepa was happy for the fresh air.

She tugged him along, following her nose and inspecting grass and trees. Before Austin knew it, she'd dragged him to the border of Linda's property. She sniffed aggressively at a tree near her driveway and then—as was her wont these days—peed on the tree without squatting. Austin couldn't fault her for using her disability to her advantage.

"Well, hello there."

Austin and Pepa turned at the sound of Linda's voice, though Pepa was the only one to wag her tail. She hopped over, lifting her head for pets and waggling her butt with delight.

"How are you doing?" Linda asked softly and stroked her ears. Pepa answered with happy woofs and snorts. "She looks good," she added to Austin. "Healing up well?"

"Yeah," he sighed with relief and pride. "She's a trooper."

"So I see," Linda agreed, still paying Pepa her due attention.

Austin wasn't quite sure how their small talk turned into an offer to join Linda inside, but a short time later found him in her kitchen, nursing a cup of hot coffee while Pepa lounged in front of her old wood-burning fireplace.

"You don't mind if I cook while we talk?" Linda asked. She had something in the oven in a cast-iron pot, and she pulled it out and set it on the stove. "I have to get the potatoes in the pot or they'll be rock-hard when it's time to eat."

One of these days Austin was going to have to learn to cook, he thought. When he and Joe sold this place and went their separate ways, his usual SpaghettiOs were not going to cut it, and he didn't have the budget for constant takeout. "No, of course not." He paused. "Um, do you need help? I don't really cook, but I can chop things."

She shook her head, smiling. "No, I already did all the prep work. I just have to add the potatoes. They take forever in this old oven, though." She removed the lid with an oven mitt, and the aroma of slow-cooked beef filled the kitchen.

Austin should not have any room in his stomach after breakfast and lunch, but his stomach suggested it could make room. "Oh—do you want me to take a look at it?"

Linda blinked at him. "You fix ovens?"

He smiled. "I fix just about anything."

"Well, I didn't invite you over for that, but I'd appreciate it. Maybe after dinner, though. Seems like a bad idea to do it while it's hot. And you have to let me feed you."

"Deal," Austin said immediately.

Linda gave him a smug look; she'd obviously clocked him drooling. Oh well. "I won't be taking you away from Joe?"

That was kind of a weird question, but—well, they did live together; it made sense she'd think they had meals together too. "No, he's out working after the storm. Trees down everywhere, I guess."

"I believe it," she said. "You boys are finally all moved in, then?"

Austin brightened and reached out with his foot to rub Pepa's belly. "Yeah," he agreed. "It's kind of wild. Don't know what I'm going to do with myself now that the majority of the work is done." He paused and thought about his bank balance. "Okay, no, that's a lie. I definitely have to do actual work that I get paid for."

"Renovations can be expensive." She stirred the potatoes into the pot and returned it to the oven. Austin looked over her shoulder; he was pretty sure she needed to replace the seal. That shouldn't take long.

"Renovations and dog surgery," Austin agreed. Then he realized that made him sound like an asshole. "Not that—uh—I mean, it was worth it and everything! Just... you know. Unexpected."

Pepa licked his sock as if in thanks.

"No, no, I get it," she assured him as she resumed her seat opposite him. "Honestly. It's one of the hardest things about being a vet, trying to balance the need to keep the lights on and pay everyone fairly and knowing that paying for veterinary care is a real hardship for people."

Austin took her at her word. But that reminded him—"Actually, I wanted to ask, uh. You said dogs can do well on three legs, and I mean, she's come a long way already. But they make canine prosthetics, right? Like... that's a thing?"

She nodded, sipped her coffee, set it back on the table. "They do," she agreed. "There's a lot of custom fitting involved, which is why most people don't do it. It gets expensive—in the thousands."

Not surprising. "But it can be done," he prompted.

"Well, sure. With the right—oh." She smiled. "You're going to build her one."

Austin flushed. "Uh, I mean, only if I can get your professional advice on how to do things without hurting her. I don't want to, like, make it too long and give her back problems or whatever."

Linda tapped her fingers on the kitchen table for a moment and pursed her lips in thought. Then she looked down at Pepa, stretching out next to the fire. "You know, I think I have a sewing tape around here somewhere."

Chapter Twelve

JOE RETURNED home smelling of sawdust and sweat, somehow chilled and overheated at the same time. The wind and ice storm of the day before had hit Amherstburg and LaSalle particularly hard. Joe's employees had handled the cleanup the previous day, when Joe was so discombobulated with thoughts of Austin that handling power tools would've posed a danger to his health. Today, though, Justin had called out sick, and clearing away the rest of the fallen trees couldn't wait when it might mean losing business.

Besides, he needed the money.

At least today he was able to concentrate without the constant thrum of arousal under his skin. Even if he mostly assigned himself to the rote physical labor of dragging branches and logs from the backyard to the front, where Eric would toss them into the chipper.

He walked in the front door to find the kids and Austin gone. Starling was in the basement, labeling the brand-new electrical panel.

"Hey."

"Hey, he says," Starling mock groused, turning just long enough to give him a wry look. "Leaves me alone in his house all day doing manual labor, didn't even save me any risotto—"

"I did hide the biscotti, though."

Starling narrowed her eyes and gave him a long look.

"Right. The power's back on, but I need to finish labeling this panel. You're going upstairs to make me coffee to go with that biscotti, and then you're going to confess to me whatever it is that's making your face do that thing."

"What thing?" Joe grumbled but did as Starling directed. He wasn't about to risk the wrath of his best friend, or the electrician that basically wired his house for free.

"And shower!" she yelled after him as he headed out the door.

Once they were settled in the kitchen with their coffee and biscotti between them, Starling dipped her treat in her coffee and said, "So, what's going on?"

Joe considered lying, but truthfully, he was glad she was here. He needed to tell someone, and based on Will's blushes that morning, the kids were the last people he should confide in.

"I slept with him."

Starling paused with her mug halfway to her mouth. "By him, I'm going to assume Austin. And by slept, I'm guessing you don't mean platonically."

"That was two nights ago."

Starling stared.

"I couldn't let him sleep in the trailer during the storm," Joe protested.

"Right. So you decided to compound the first questionable choice with another?"

"There was red wine involved," Joe muttered petulantly.

Starling glanced once more at her coffee, which she'd yet to take a sip from. "You got any whiskey?"

"Will Baileys do?" Joe offered. He had a weakness at Christmas time.

"I guess it'll have to."

Once their coffee was fortified with some healthy glugs of Irish cream, Starling resumed the interrogation. Not that she had to do much interrogating. Joe had already folded like origami in the rain.

"You flipped to see who would top."

"It seemed like a good idea at the time?"

"Why didn't you just offer? Obviously he didn't mind you throwing yourself at his dick ass-first."

"It seemed more fun?"

"Joseph. You are such a disaster bisexual."

Joe sighed. "I know. But what am I going to do?"

"Didn't you already do something? I thought that was the problem."

"Starling. I slept with him. It was good. I wanna do it again."

She caught and held his gaze. Despite her earlier teasing, her face was serious now. "So, either don't sleep with him again, or talk to him like an adult, have a relationship, and sleep with him again."

Joe groaned and dropped his forehead to the table. "That would be a terrible idea, right?" He turned his head so he could catch her eye. Joe did not want to enter into a relationship with a parodic house husband.

That was a foolish idea that would end in heartbreak, and he definitely couldn't do casual with Austin. He widened his eyes at her. "Like, objectively."

"Yes, Joe, all your ideas are inherently terrible, so… definitely don't do that."

Joe pouted. "You weren't supposed to agree so quickly."

"Hey, I'm your bestie. I'm not supposed to lie to you either." She reached out and combed her fingers through his hair. "The truth hurts."

The truth was that Joe was a hopeless romantic who preferred love and candlelit dinners to one-night stands, who loved having a partner and who had maybe, kinda, sorta settled once or twice instead of calling time of death on a relationship. And Joe didn't want a relationship with Austin because of all the entanglements. Super messy.

Not that he had to worry about that, since Austin didn't do relationships or dating. Come to think of it, that made him kind of the ideal candidate for a friendly one-nighter.

And a terrible candidate for a longer-term arrangement.

"Keep it in your pants, Casanova," Starling intoned seriously, the words at odds with the amused twist of her lips.

Sighing, Joe held up his first two fingers. "Scout's honor."

He actually had been a scout too. He could never tell Austin that; he'd never hear the end of it.

"Good. Now that that's over with, can I get a fist bump?"

Joe blinked. Starling had her hand held out toward him, fingers closed around the palm. "I'm getting kinda mixed signals here, babe."

"Please. Austin was absolutely the wrong guy to play prod the peach with, but how long has it been since you had an orgasm with another sentient being? Note that I am explicitly excluding Paul."

"Why is everyone so hung up on the numbers?" Joe whined. His mind shied away from doing any kind of calculation. It was winter. Things were depressing enough. "Everybody's so mean to me."

"What, who else asked you? The kids?"

"Worse. Austin."

Starling's lips twitched the way they did when she was fighting a smile. "Did you lose it early or something?"

Joe gasped theatrically. "First of all, how dare you. Second of all, technically I was bottoming, so that wouldn't have mattered—"

Starling cackled.

"—*not that it was a problem*. And finally, this was the conversation we had *before* the pants came off."

"Oh, so you were just setting realistic expectations."

He tossed the remainder of his biscotti at her. "Fuck off."

She picked it off the floor and popped it in her mouth. "Nah. That's your job." She slugged back some more Irish coffee and grinned impishly. "You telling the kids?"

"Oh my God, no, why would I do that?" What a shitstorm that would cause. Gavin and Alex would roast his ass from here to next Tuesday and—"Will would cry. He totally has a crush."

"Joe. *Joe*." Starling put her mug down and leaned forward, reaching for his hand. "You cannot make Austin his stepmom. At least not without installing cameras and some kind of livestream. Seriously, there's good money in that—"

"Starling—"

"Please, I'm begging you. If he finds out, you have to get it on video—"

"That's *mean*," Joe said, but he was giggling too. He blamed the coffee. "I don't think Austin's noticed, which makes it funnier. I feel bad for Will, though."

Starling nodded sagely. "Where are the age-appropriate queers when you need 'em."

"Right?" He shook his head. He got it, though. It wasn't like Will could date anyway, with his fundamentalist parents. It was safer to crush on someone he couldn't have.

Now *that* was depressing. He pulled his mind back to more cheerful matters. "Anyway, now that we've got the place more or less ready to go—we're thinking Christmas Eve dinner. You, us, the kids, probably my mom. I'll invite Linda. Bring a friend if you want."

Starling had this unique ability—she could give you the side eye right to your face. "So this thing where you need to draw a line between your personal life, your sex life, and your partner in temporary homeownership—how's that going for you?"

Joe flipped her off again. "Shut up. You want another biscotti?"

Chapter Thirteen

TUESDAY, THE shop was dead, which was not a great sign. Austin spent most of the day taking inventory—oil filters, windshield fluid—and tidying up, just to have something to kill time and an excuse to keep the sign lit up. He got one college kid who came in to get a quote on her 2004 Malibu, which needed the exhaust replaced—not a worthwhile repair on a car that was old enough to vote, but Austin knew a scrap yard where he might be able to get a used one for cheap, so he took her number and said he'd call her back.

As if to make up for it, Wednesday was brutal. Austin fixed a heated seat, a fan belt, a tire puncture, and a chipped windshield before he got a break long enough to hit up the bakery next door for lunch. He spent the afternoon under the Malibu, replacing the entire exhaust system.

God, he needed a shower.

That evening, he found Joe in the kitchen with an unfamiliar woman, who stood cradling a glass of bubbly water while she watched Joe cook.

She was dressed casually in jeans but wore them with the primness and authority of a well-tailored pantsuit. Austin immediately felt grubby in her presence and felt the urge to apologise for not having showered.

He wondered if he could sneak away unseen. He doubted very much that this stranger admired mechanics for their skilled labor.

Of course, she lived up to the expectations set by her first impression and immediately caught Austin in her calculating gaze.

"Hello. You must be the mechanical half of the DIY dream team." She arched an eyebrow and looked at him with Joe's eyes.

Yeah, definitely Joe's mom.

"Uh, hi. Austin." Smooth.

"Austin," Joe echoed, "you're home. Obviously. Meet my mom, Maria Romano. Mom, meet Austin Taylor, co-owner, mechanic, finder of valuable vinyls."

"A Renaissance man," Maria said, and Austin couldn't tell if she was impressed or mocking him. Or maybe she was just neutral.

Before Austin could figure out what to say in response, Joe jumped to his rescue.

"Dinner will be another twenty or so. Plenty of time for a shower."

Austin gave a thumbs-up—what was it about this lady that turned him into a dumbass—and backed out of the kitchen.

As much as Austin didn't want to return to Maria's company to be judged, he couldn't deny his stomach or his nose. He needed to investigate the source of those delicious smells. He was getting spoiled living with Joe, he thought ruefully, and definitely did not think about no longer living with someone who moonlighted as a gourmet chef.

He was too busy not thinking in general, apparently, because after a five-minute shower that blasted the grime off and abated the muscle stiffness from a day spent in the cold garage, he realized he had his towel but no actual clean clothes, because—well, who cared if he walked upstairs in a towel if Joe was the only other person home? It wasn't anything Joe hadn't seen before.

Joe's mom, on the other hand....

Fuck.

He could put his work coveralls back on, but they were filthy to the point he'd need another shower. And there was no way he could get upstairs to his room without Joe's mom noticing. But Joe's bedroom—that was only a few steps away.

Nothing for it. Austin scrunched up his curls in the terry cloth to dry them as best he could in a minute, then scrubbed the towel over the rest of his body and wrapped it around his waist.

He opened the door a crack and peered out. He could see Maria's back in the kitchen doorway.

Good enough. He made a break for it.

He was just feeling the relief of the door closing behind him when Walker tried to murder him by tripping. With a curse, Austin caught himself on the edge of the dresser.

"I rescued you from the great outdoors and this is how you repay me?" he grumbled.

"Mrow," Walker said proudly. His orange tail stuck straight up as he rubbed against Austin's bare legs.

At least Austin knew where Joe kept his underwear. Fuck, was that weird to steal?

It was probably weirder to steal his jeans without underwear.

He put the questions out of his mind as he dragged on a T-shirt and then a hoodie. Joe had six hundred of them and the house was freezing.

Then he scooped up the cat and went back to the kitchen to face the music.

"—a kitchen island," Maria was saying when Austin came in. "Throw a coat of white paint on the cabinets, upgrade the counters...."

Austin twitched.

At the stove, Joe hunched his shoulders. "It's not really in the budget, Mom."

"Sweetheart. You know I'd loan you the money. You can pay me back when you sell. Or just let me list it for you. You've done a lot of work—it's going to pay off. I'll give you a deal on commission."

Austin didn't know a lot about healthy parent-child relationships. The closest he'd ever been to one was on TV. But he understood body language, and he didn't think Joe's mom was making him chafe on purpose.

Which meant she didn't see that her remarks were upsetting Joe, but Austin did.

Austin could think about *that* later too. Or, more likely, avoid thinking about it. He took a sharp breath, then cleared his throat. "Sorry about that," he said, forcing a smile. "Long day at the office. Can I help?"

Joe threw him a shocked and bewildered look over his mom's head, because Austin had been clear about his uselessness in the kitchen, but then they met eyes and he must've understood Austin was just there to change the subject. "Looks like you have your hands full," he pointed out.

"Well, my favorite wasn't available. Where's Pepa?"

Joe's mother blinked. "Who's Pepa?"

Wait, Joe hadn't told her about the *dog*? Austin opened his mouth, caught Joe's eye again. Was he supposed to lie?

"Austin's dog," Joe said.

Maria arched a curious, nonjudgemental eyebrow, so Austin supplied, "She was a stray in the neighborhood. She stole my dinner one night, so I took her home."

"Did you, now," Maria said, clearly amused.

"She's in the breezeway," Joe explained with a look that told Austin his need for Pepa cuddles was transparent.

Austin took the offered olive branch and excused himself from the awkward small talk in the kitchen. Besides, his girl probably needed a bathroom break before dinner.

Austin set Walker down on the floor and watched with fond amusement as he immediately trotted across the kitchen and climbed Joe's jeans. Joe didn't flinch, just reached down and scooped the kitten from his hip to his shoulder.

Shaking his head, Austin turned toward the door and caught sight of Maria watching this with a smile.

Then, to his surprise, as he headed toward the door, Maria said, "I'll tag along. I'd like to meet this Pepa." The slight stress on the name told Austin she knew everything about its meaning.

"Uh, sure. The breezeway is heated, so you don't need a coat or shoes. Unless you wanted to come for the walk."

She followed him to the breezeway without collecting boots or coat, so Austin figured she just wanted to get a look at Pepa. She clearly wasn't a dog person, though she did bend down to pat her head once Pepa abandoned Austin to greet her guest. Austin put on the outdoor gear that he left in the breezeway, and Pepa danced happily at his feet.

Ozzy eyed them from his cozy spot on the dog bed and then closed his eyes and went back to sleep.

Maria left him as he clipped on Pepa's leash, and he figured that was it, but two minutes after they got outside, Maria came around the side of the house, dressed in casual boots and a coat that looked just as picture-ready as her jeans and sweater.

Okay. Apparently they weren't done hanging out. Austin could totally do this. Make small talk with a woman who had such exacting standards that Joe still acted as if any sort of dirt or chaos was some sort of rule-breaking thrill.

"So, you can tell me the truth. Did Joe want to help her because she needed a home or because she had special needs?" Maria shot Austin a quick small smile, as if they were sharing a secret.

"Er, well, I mean, I was definitely the one handing over the credit card at the vet, but he didn't dissuade me," Austin said, trying to stick to the truth without revealing Joe's sort-of lie. Technically Pepa was Austin's dog, but she was also Joe's. "And he's never said why, but probably for both reasons. Though considering he saved her life from the coyote that took her leg, I can't say I blame him for being attached."

"Well, that's a story I need to hear," Maria said, so Austin recounted the Pepa saga, start to finish, including the finding of the kittens.

"Honestly, I should have been more surprised if he hadn't found strays after moving out here." She shot Austin a sly look. "He ever tell you about the time he tried to adopt a kitten?"

They were on their way back to the house now. Pepa had finished her business and was starting to shiver. "Can't say he did."

Maria happily launched into the story, voice laced with warmth as she recounted it, which didn't quite match the picture of her Joe had painted. Though he'd said she was trying to do better these days, hadn't he?

By the time they stepped back into the breezeway, Austin was wheezing with laughter, picturing a tiny nine-year-old Joe thinking he was being in any way subtle about his hidden prize. As if his meticulous mother wouldn't have noticed the missing guest towels from the bathroom or the pilfered cans of tuna or, most tellingly, the sounds of a lonely baby looking for its surrogate parent coming from his bedroom closet.

"You could hear it howling all throughout the house. Poor kid was so alarmed at having been caught. He tried to tell me it was ghosts, and maybe I should put in a call to the Ghostbusters." She shook her head. "I almost caved and let him keep it," she said thoughtfully, then gave a self-deprecating huff. "Can't change the past now, though. And he really was probably too young for full responsibility of a pet."

Austin hummed, not sure how else to acknowledge that statement without sounding like a douchebag. Obviously there was more to the relationship between Joe and his mother than Austin had gleaned from their months of acquaintance.

When he didn't offer a verbal acknowledgment, Maria prompted, "So is it just the dog and the three cats, or does he have a terrarium somewhere too?"

"The kids wouldn't fit," Austin told her as he held open the back door. She laughed and preceded him into the breezeway. "And I make Joe take the spiders outside and release them."

Now she paused, shaking her head as she removed her coat. Rather than hang it on the hook where Austin kept his—perfectly serviceable for a puffer jacket—she folded it over her arm to take back to the front hall closet. "You make Joe deal with the spiders?"

"Ah, well." Austin was too gay—and had too macho of a job—to feel emasculated by his fear. "I think they're creepy, so...."

Maria tilted her head at him. He thought she'd taken his measure inside, but he could see her reevaluating him now. He didn't know why until she said, "Joe's been afraid of spiders since he was a kid. We had a neighbor with a tarantula. Awful brat. He made Joe put his hand in the tank once."

Jesus, what the fuck.

Joe was afraid of spiders?

Austin turned over this piece of information, fitting it into his understanding of Joe as a person.

Joe collected strays. That was obvious. He had too much heart by half; he'd adopted four feral children as a teenager; he had a whole contingency plan in place for when Will got outed to his family and had to move out. He'd given Austin grief about Pepa and the kittens, but it was all surface level and none of it directed at the animals; he was sweet as anything with them.

Austin had thought Joe had exempted him from the collection. After all, Austin was an adult. He didn't need looking after.

Except Joe kept feeding him, didn't he? And taking out the spiders, even though he was afraid. He'd come to collect Austin from the cold the night of the storm, made sure Austin was warm in his bed.

And then there was the sex, the way Joe'd micromanaged everything until Austin had been overwhelmed with pleasure.

Perhaps Austin had been adopted after all, except not in the same way Joe had taken in the kids, the dog, the cats. And not *openly*. Of course he hadn't; Austin had told him he didn't date. And the little Joe had told him on the topic of his ex had illuminated plenty. Austin knew that kind of pain, knew what it could do to people, in the right circumstances. Or the wrong ones.

That was… interesting.

"Austin?"

Joe was standing in the door to the breezeway; his mother must have gone to hang up her coat.

"You good?" Joe asked. There was a crease in his brow and a splash of something red on his shoulder, likely from dinner. Austin made a note to treat the stain; he was wearing Joe's clothes. He owed him a load of laundry anyway.

He'd let his hair grow out, Austin realized. The sweep of bangs across his forehead almost touched his eyebrows. He must've missed an appointment. Austin thought it suited him, but he also thought—Joe took pride in his appearance. He wore his hair short because it made sense for work, because he didn't have time to spend styling it. If he'd missed an appointment, then what else was he neglecting?

Joe spent so much time taking care of other people. Who was taking care of him?

"I'm good," Austin said, straightening. He slipped Pepa's collar and leash onto the hook next to his coat. "Sorry. I'm good."

"Okay," Joe said. He was still frowning a little, as though he didn't quite believe it, but he didn't challenge Austin on it. "Well, dinner's ready."

He retreated to the kitchen, leaving Austin standing in the breezeway, reevaluating his life.

Days ago he'd told Joe that Paul had to be an idiot. He meant it then, for more than the reasons he'd admitted out loud.

In Austin's entire life, very few people had truly cared for him. His father had loved him, but that love didn't translate to care, not even of himself. Then he died and Austin had gone to live with his aunt. She looked after him, but she was unwell too, and after a while she couldn't do it anymore either. Austin learned independence at a very young age. That was how he survived.

But Joe cared for him. He might not admit it out loud, and he might not care for him the way Austin hoped, but Austin could weather that. And unlike Paul, Austin was not an idiot. If a man like Joe was going to care for him, cook him meals, rescue him from spiders in spite of his own fear, and occasionally take him to bed and make him come so hard his brain leaked out his ears, Austin wasn't going to throw that away.

But after the disaster with Paul, and after Austin's own admission of his nonexistent dating history, he had a feeling it would take a lot of convincing before Joe was ready to commit to something serious.

That was okay, though. Austin was good at being patient.

Chapter Fourteen

JOE LEFT the house early the next morning so he could get a jump on winterizing his clients' gardens and for no other reason. He absolutely was not panicking about Austin meeting his mother or the knowing looks his mother sent his way all night long.

Not that she knew anything. Because there was nothing to know.

Every time Pepa made a move in Joe's direction, Maria had given Joe a look like she knew he lied about her ownership. He hadn't exactly meant to lie about it, but he hadn't told his mother about the dog because she'd never been fond of them, not to mention that owning a dog together spoke of *intentions*. She would read into it and assume Joe was trying to get things that he definitely wasn't. Just because Pepa liked the breezeway didn't mean that Joe was going to keep a whole house for her.

So Joe had pointedly ignored all of his mom's looks and focused on having a nice evening feeding people.

Still, it was weird to see his mom get on so well with Austin. She'd never taken an interest in his friends when he was a child or teen, and she hated Paul. She'd always been better at meeting Joe's material needs than his emotional ones. Watching her make such an effort was weird, but also nice.

But he couldn't avoid Austin forever, because Meg had a swim meet that weekend, and her parents wanted to take everyone out for dinner after—*everyone* including the other party DeeDee had left the house to, who Chris wanted to verbally interrogate.

The restaurant was nice enough to have good food—not so nice that any of the kids would fail the dress code—but from the get-go, Joe could tell things were going to go sideways.

First of all, Meg seated herself between her mother and Will, not leaving an empty space for Alex. Instead, Alex sat across the table from Meg, as if in defiance, and Gavin sat to their left. The only way Joe could sit near Alex was to take the seat between them and Chris, which he couldn't do because Chris was already waving Austin into it and asking questions. So Joe was stuck at the opposing head of the table, one seat away from his tension-filled children.

They made it through the ordering and delivery of their meals with only mild sniping from Meg and Alex, so Joe hoped that whatever was brewing would continue to simmer for one more day.

Joe was distracted by his dinner and watching Will casting longing looks kitty-corner toward Austin, so he didn't hear all of the conversation, but he definitely heard the end of it.

"That guy on Meg's team wasn't bad either—Hammerhead," Gavin said.

"Hammerhead?" Meg asked with a frown.

"Yeah," Gavin explained. "Guy with his eyeballs practically on opposite sides of his head?"

Meg's frown deepened. "That's not a very nice thing to say."

Gavin looked abashed.

"What's it to you?" Alex asked. "Why do you care what anyone says about it? It's not like you like him."

Meg's fork clanked against her plate as a dark flush spread over her face. "Being a decent person isn't dependent on experiencing romantic attraction." She paused for effect. "Obviously."

Joe's breath whooshed out of him. Right for the nuclear option. He met Chris's eyes, then Cheryl's, trying to gauge if either of them had the slightest clue what their kids were fighting about. Looked like a no.

Super.

"Meg," Cheryl said sharply.

Alex's chair scraped against the floor as they stood up quickly. For half a second, Joe expected them to throw their drink in Meg's face, but they just said, "Excuse me, I have to use the bathroom. If I can find one that'll let me in."

Joe watched them go, his mouth half open in shock. Finally he looked at Gavin. "Do you...?"

Gavin's face was pale, his eyes round. He shook his head.

Joe looked at Will. Will was concentrating so hard on his short ribs that Joe thought he might be attempting a molecular breakdown. No help there.

He looked at Meg, who was still furiously red.

She pushed away her plate. "I'm not hungry anymore."

Fantastic.

"Meg, you just had a swim meet. You need to eat—"

"I said I'm not hungry."

Fuck it. Joe turned his gaze to Chris and attempted to communicate telepathically, *I'll handle the other three if you take Meg.* "Should we get the check?" He glanced around at the half-full plates. "And some takeout boxes?"

It was a long, awkward drive home. Will squashed into the middle of the back seat. All three kids stewed in silence. It smelled like leftovers.

Austin drove in silence, tapping his fingers on the wheel, the radio turned low. The speakers crackled so much Joe could barely make out the tune, never mind the lyrics.

Finally Austin let out a breath. "You know, I hate to side with the kids," he said, "but if this is your idea of a date, you really do have no game."

In the back seat, Will made a noise that might've been a laugh or might've been some kind of audible wince. Gavin howled.

Alex continued to stew.

"Don't worry," Joe said. "I'm not in the habit of bringing moody teenage chaperones on my dates."

His voice carried every ounce of his displeasure. Good. Let it. Alex should know he was pissed. They were going to be having a long talk when they got home.

Actually, fuck that. They could have it now. When they got home, Joe wanted a beer, a shower, a cuddle with the critters, and his bed.

"You want to tell me what your problem is, Alex?"

They huffed. "Of course you're siding with *her.*"

Was Joe imagining it, or was there a little extra vitriol on that pronoun? "Uh, yeah," he said, "because from where I'm standing, you're being a real asshole for no reason." He mentally awarded himself two points for not saying *bitch.*

"Fine, whatever. Can we talk about this later? I don't want to get into it with everyone."

"Maybe you should have thought of that before you made a scene in front of 'everyone' at Meg's big night." Jesus, raising teenagers was tough when you didn't have any actual authority.

More silence from the back seat, broken only by the sound of chewing. Gavin had not given up on his french fries, even though they had to be stone-cold by now.

Then a sniffle.

Ah, fuck.

Then an unexpected low murmur from the driver's seat. "Why don't you sit this one out?" Austin suggested. "We'll be home in ten. I'll get it."

Joe cast him a sideways glance as they passed under a streetlight. "What?"

"It's—no offense." The corner of his mouth turned up in a sad parody of a smile. "Just… I think I've got more applicable experience in this case, all right?" He paused. "Plus, you look wiped."

Joe wanted to argue, but he was, in fact, wiped. He sagged into his seat—God, next time they were taking the truck, even if that meant the kids were even more squished; this car was so uncomfortable—and leaned his head against the window. "Thanks."

Austin flicked his blinker to exit the traffic circle. "Hey, what are house husbands for?"

Chapter Fifteen

THEY'D CARPOOLED from the house, so Austin took them all back there. Alex tried to make a run for it, jumping out and stomping to Gavin's car, but Joe moved faster. He grabbed Gavin and hauled him into the house for cookies. Will followed behind without prompting.

Scowling, Alex tried the passenger door and glared harder when it didn't magically unlock. Gavin had the keys. They weren't going to be able to hide in his car.

"Hey, kid," Austin opened with. Maybe he'd luck out and Alex would open up without more prompting.

Alex glared. "Not a kid."

Or not.

"Okay, noted. No calling you a kid." He eyed them up and with a shrug said, "Okay, since you're not a kid, why don't you come in for a beer and talk about it."

Alex narrowed their eyes, clearly trying to figure out the trap.

"No trap. Just beer and an ear."

"Fine."

Alex followed Austin into the house through the back door, and he left them in the breezeway with Pepa and the kittens.

"Take her out for a pee," Austin suggested, then proceeded to find Joe and the boys in the kitchen. Gavin had a glass of milk and was eating a chocolate chip cookie with a dedication that spoke of emotional snacking.

"Gavin, can you take Will home?" he asked.

"What about Alex?" Gavin frowned.

Austin shrugged. "Sticking around for a bit. We'll make sure they get home okay."

Gavin clearly didn't want to leave, but Joe smiled comfortingly and said, "It's okay, Gav."

He managed to get both boys out the door with a bribe of more homemade cookies and promises they could return tomorrow if they wanted.

Once the boys were on the road, Austin pointed Joe toward the shower. Joe shook his head and muttered, "Your funeral," and disappeared into the bathroom with a change of clothes.

Figuring conversation might come more easily if Alex came to him, he poured himself his own glass of milk and sat down to munch on a cookie.

Austin considered what his plans to make this cohabitation permanent and living with Joe's cooking might have on his waistline. Maybe they could put an elliptical machine in the breezeway.

"Where is everyone?" Alex stood in the doorway, Ozzy cradled in their arms like a baby and Pepa, Walker, and Dallas waiting at their heels.

"Joe's in the shower. Gavin's taking Will home."

"Oh."

Austin pushed the cookies in Alex's direction. Alex and Ozzy sat down. Pepa placed her head on Austin's thigh, Dallas asked to be picked up, and Walker wandered off to stalk Joe until he emerged from the bathroom.

And now it was time for Austin to put his money where his mouth was and see if his instincts about Alex's attitude had merit. "So," he said after Alex had nibbled their way through half a cookie, "as one poor kid to another...."

Alex stopped chewing and gave him a look.

"You're looking at a former foster kid."

"Oh."

"Though I never lucked out enough to find a Joe."

Alex resumed chewing. Then, "Didn't you offer beer?"

Austin snorted, grabbed a bottle, and placed it on the table.

Apparently that was all it took to break the seal. "Just—Meg gets *everything*, you know? Like, she's born to parents who have money, and she's got this natural talent for swimming. Gets headhunted for a full ride to amazing schools even though her parents could've paid to send her wherever."

Yeah, Austin had guessed right. He nodded neutrally and debated a second cookie.

Who was he kidding? He picked one up.

"Sucks," he offered. "But, like... you know life's not fair. This isn't news to you. Doesn't make it any easier, but...." *But it doesn't explain your kind of over-the-top reaction.*

"Yeah." Alex crossed their arms and blurted out the next part. "But, like—I don't even know what I want to do with my life, and Meg has this passion and her parents and this promised scholarship, and she's gonna have, like, a career path and sponsorships and just—everything all planned out. I don't even know if I'll go to college or university, and that's—fine. I mean, I think I'm fine with it. I know that's not Meg's fault, but now she's being all *weird*."

And that was where the train of thought screeched to a halt. Austin waited to see if Alex would pick up steam again before prompting, "Weird how?"

"I don't *know*," Alex all but wailed. "And she keeps dragging me to all these feminist events, and it hurts." They sniffled and wiped at their nose. Austin made a note to loan them a clean sweatshirt later. "Like, she brings me to these places filled with women and for women and about women, and I don't know if I fit in there now and I feel weird and dysphoric. And…."

That was already a lot; there was an *and*? "And?"

"Sometimes it feels like she's trying to say something," they admitted.

Ouch. Austin winced. He could guess, but he still cocked his head and asked, "Like what?"

Alex's voice cracked, just a little. "Like she wishes I still thought I was a girl."

These cookies should have more chocolate in them. "That sounds like it would be painful." Austin chewed another bite, thinking things over. He didn't want to dismiss Alex's concerns, even if he thought they were probably projecting, but he didn't want to confirm them either. The best advice he could give was the hardest to follow through with. "So… look. I can't say I've been there, because I haven't. Still, it strikes me that not everyone stays friends forever, but they definitely won't if they don't talk about shit like this."

Alex pulled a face, clearly not enjoying Austin's advice.

He shrugged. "You don't have to listen to me. I'm just some idiot who knows your single dad. But I'm also someone who's never had this many friends because I was too busy hiding. So maybe don't be like me." He paused. "And like… not to take sides, but if Meg doesn't know what's going on in your head right now, how's she supposed to be a good friend to you? It's not like feminist issues only affect women. I'm pretty sure that's, like, a whole thing, right? Intersectional feminism? Like how trans men still need gynecological care or whatever?" He thought that was a vast oversimplification, but getting into details didn't seem necessary and was also outside his comfort zone.

Alex pursed their lips. "I guess." They picked up their beer and took a tiny sip.

"Maybe you could ask Meg if she wants to go to a queer event instead next time." He paused. "After you explain and apologize, I mean. Because...."

"Because I was kind of a raging bitch?" Alex suggested, a little wetly.

"I probably would've phrased it differently."

Alex sighed, sipped their beer again, then said timidly, "Can I have milk instead?"

Austin grinned as he stood up and clapped them on the shoulder. "Of course, kid. Come on, let's find something dumb on TV while we wait for your dad. You want to crash on the couch? I've got some sweats that'll fit you. Well...." He glanced down at the shirt he'd inherited from DeeDee. "Some of them are pre-preowned."

By the time Joe got out of the shower, Austin and Alex had settled on *It's a Wonderful Life*. The lights of the Christmas tree cast the cozy living room in a cheerful glow. Aside from that and the television, the room was dark.

Alex was sprawled across the couch, already cuddled under a blanket, their eyelids drooping. It must've been an emotional day, Austin thought. Austin had chosen the armchair instead. Joe glanced at the couch, then the chair, then shrugged and grabbed a cushion from near Alex's feet and plopped it next to Austin's legs so he could use the front of the chair as a backrest.

"Good?" he murmured.

Austin inhaled. It was a new kind of intimacy, to feel the residual heat of a shower on someone else's body. He could smell Joe's shampoo— something with apples. He wanted to touch his hair. "Good," he agreed. Alex's breathing was deepening. "I'll tell you about it later."

Joe leaned his head back against the chair, tilted his head up. The column of his throat made a long, beautiful line, mottled with red and green and blue and magenta in the lights from the tree. "Thank you," he said.

Austin still hadn't figured out the specifics of making Joe fall in love with him. He didn't have any experience to draw on. But being there for the kids seemed like a good place to start, and it wasn't hard when he had Joe's example to draw from.

Besides, he liked them. Sure, they were unholy terrors and they gave him and Joe an unending amount of shit and most days basic gratitude was beyond their grasp, but they loved each other and Joe. They deserved kindness and good things and adults who cared about them. And maybe one day they might love Austin too.

Austin cleared his throat. "Don't mention it."

THE DAYS leading up to the holiday flew by. Between his shopping and menu planning, Joe was glad the weather had turned cold and snowy, unsuitable for landscape work. It gave him more time to finish all the other things on his to-do list.

Shopping for the kids was easier than usual this year. He found a deal on an older-model die-cutting machine for Gavin so he could make his silly T-shirts himself. For Alex, a pair of Mulan socks and a used smartphone, an upgrade from their current model, which couldn't hold a charge for more than a few hours.

Will was getting used bedroom furniture and a house key.

Joe was still turning over what to get Austin. Everything felt either too impersonal or just the opposite, like if Joe gave him that kind of gift Austin would take one look at him and *see something*.

Which was stupid because there wasn't anything to see. Joe had been careful about that. He and Austin were friends who owned a house they were fixing up together, and in a few months, they'd sell it and go their separate ways.

Not that Joe had figured out yet how they were going to go their separate ways when they had a dog and three kittens to consider.

When Joe got home the evening after another long day, he was surprised to find the house full of delicious scents. Not to disparage Austin's cooking....

Okay, totally to disparage it. It didn't usually smell so herby and garlicky and layered. He still leaned toward eggs, toast, and reheated meals.

Joe followed his nose and found Austin pulling something out of the oven.

"You cooked?" he asked, probably sounding very rude, but it smelled amazing.

"Only in the technical sense," Austin laughed. "I picked up some ready-to-heat stuff at Schinkels—garlic bread, lasagna, and roasted veggies." He motioned to a foil-wrapped packet and a covered foil pan. The delicious smells were all from the lasagna, then. "Just gotta heat the rest while this cools." He opened the oven back up.

"Not that it doesn't look and smell amazing," Joe said, "but buying lasagna for an Italian? Bold move."

Austin froze, hand still on the oven door after having shut it, and shot a startled look at Joe. "Uh."

Joe waved his concern away. "I'm joking. And also starving and grateful. I never turn away dinner cooked by someone else."

"Good," Austin said, though he shot a look at the pasta. "I didn't think—"

"It smells amazing. Stop worrying. Now. I'm going to change while the rest cooks so I don't have to eat in my work clothes."

Joe beat a hasty retreat, feeling like a heel. He'd only been teasing, but now he wondered if he hadn't blundered into another one of those social blind spots of Austin's that he seemed to have thanks to years of foster care and that Joe couldn't seem to stop finding.

Shaking himself, he quickly washed and headed back to the kitchen.

Where he found Austin holding an unopened bottle of wine and staring at it uncertainly with flushed cheeks.

Joe paused and blushed himself. Drinking red wine together seemed ill-advised, and clearly he wasn't the only one who thought so. Maybe they should just have water tonight?

Pepa, noticing his return, hopped in Joe's direction, alerting Austin to his presence. So Joe swallowed his embarrassment and asked, "Trying to decide on drinks?"

Austin took the out and said, if a bit strangled, "I wasn't sure about pairings."

"Right," Joe said with forced cheer. He knelt to pet Pepa, and in a bid to be totally normal while not thinking about Austin's perfect cock, asked, "Er, what did they tell you about the lasagna?"

Austin put down the bottle of wine and lifted a paper from the counter. "Beef with béchamel sauce."

"Ah, well, white wine it is, then."

"White?"

"Yeah." Joe stood and headed for the fridge. Thank God. White wine was good. He could do that. It didn't make him horny. "Red wine for red sauce, white wine for white."

"Oh," Austin said. "That seems kinda... racist."

Joe snorted. "What?"

"Like with like. Kinda exclusionary, is all," Austin pointed out.

Joe rolled his eyes and pulled a white from the fridge. "It's about flavors, not about color matching."

Austin shrugged. "If you say so. I still think it sounds sus."

"Wow." Joe paused, then resumed his search for the corkscrew. "Sus, huh? Maybe you're spending too much time with my kids."

"I don't know," Austin said, faux speculative. "You ever think you might be the problem? Maybe you just attract people who like to give you a hard time."

You gave me a hard time, all right, Joe thought. If he hadn't already uncorked the white, he might've thought twice about it. Maybe he couldn't be trusted with any alcohol right now. Instead he said, "Oh sure, blame the victim."

They plated up and brought their food into the dining room to eat.

"We should get a kitchen table," Austin commented. "It feels weirdly fancy to eat out here."

"Even on this battle-scarred old thing?" Joe's table had been a hand-me-down already when his mother got it.

"Less the furniture, more the surroundings." Austin gestured at the dark hardwood floors, carefully restored wainscoting, original crown molding. God forbid they ever got any water damage in here, because Joe wasn't paying to fix that. It would all have to come down. With the fresh coat of paint they'd put on the top half of the room, it did feel grander than the table warranted. "Besides, now that you can actually *see* the window in the kitchen, it has better light."

Joe looked pointedly toward the exterior door behind Austin, where it was very obviously dark and had been since before five o'clock.

Austin rolled his eyes and nudged him under the table. "It *will* have better light, then," he amended. "Besides, if we're going to host Christmas dinner for… twelve?"

Joe did some quick calculations. "Kids, us, Starling, Linda, and I think Gavin's parents are coming… and Alex's mom might come with their stepdad. And my mom."

"Thirteen," Austin said. "Plus a dog and three cats." He gestured around. "They ain't gonna fit in here."

"I wasn't planning on setting Pepa a place at the table."

Austin quirked a smile, something fond and almost impish. "Liar."

Joe found himself flushing. It must be the wine. Tannins or something. He cleared his throat, took another sip. "I mean, you're not wrong about the table. But…." Austin lived here too; Joe might as well get his opinion. "I was thinking—a big island? I've got a couple nice slabs of black walnut." His grandparents' neighbor had a tree fall a decade ago; Joe and his nonno had helped clear it up. His grandfather had the boards milled and gave Joe half for his help, but he'd never had time to do anything with them. "They'd make a fantastic tabletop."

Austin made a show of checking his watch. "I mean, yeah, but you're gonna want to get on that ASAP if you expect people to eat at it in two weeks."

"It's just sanding and glue," Joe protested. "Well, and figuring out a base, I guess."

Austin tapped his fingers on the table. "Not wood?"

Joe waggled his hand back and forth. "Not fancy turned legs, anyway. That's where the time would come in."

"Metal ones?" he suggested. "Like… this house is kind of a hodgepodge, right? Hundred-year-old house, fifty-year-old addition, thirty-year-old pole barn. There's some unused metal pilings in the garage, probably from when the addition was built. And what might have been a basketball net once. I could weld some."

Joe tried to picture it. It would either be really cool or a complete disaster. "Farmhouse industrial?"

"Sounds like something your mom would hate."

Joe grinned. "What, you think she goes around to her clients' houses suggesting they paint *live, laugh, love* on the bedroom walls?"

Grinning, Austin reached for the wine, lifted the bottle in offering. Joe realized his glass was almost empty and nodded for the refill. "Maybe not *painting*," he said. "Maybe she just, like, drives around with a few extra knickknacks, you know. Throw blankets. Candles. Framed embroidery."

They finished sketching out table/island plans over dinner, but when Joe headed to the kitchen to clean up, Austin stopped him. "Actually, uh, I need your help with something first. Can you grab the dog treats?"

Joe did an about-face and grabbed the bag from the top of the fridge. "She's not still taking any medication, is she?"

"No. She finished those a few days ago, which you know."

Joe turned with treats in hand to see Austin holding a contraption.

Joe raised an eyebrow at the thing in Austin's hands. "You trying to tell me something about your nighttime activities?"

Austin looked down and blushed. Apparently he hadn't considered how the strapping and buckles might appear. "Oh my God, no. It's for Pepa. Obviously."

"Oh, right. Obviously," Joe said and did not make any crass jokes.

He opened the treat bag and Pepa hobbled in, tail wagging and tongue lolling.

Austin greeted her with affectionate coos and knelt next to her. Joe sat down and gave her a treat, as directed, then gripped her collar to help hold her still.

Austin fitted one end of the thing over her amputation stump and—

"You got her a prosthetic?" Emotions warred within Joe. Affection toward Austin for doing such a sweet thing, guilt for not having thought of this himself, worry that it wouldn't work.

Austin didn't answer at first, too busy buckling the straps around her rump and waist. "Made it, actually," he said distractedly.

"You made her a leg," Joe repeated. His heart and stomach did a weird flipping, growing, shrinking thing. How much research had been involved in that? How much trial and error?

Austin grunted and tested the fit of the straps. He tightened them and checked again. Joe kept feeding Pepa treats to keep her occupied, which worked beautifully. Finally satisfied, Austin leaned back and encouraged Joe to do the same.

Joe released her collar. Pepa sniffed the floor and took a step forward in search of more cookies. Since she hadn't yet gotten accustomed to her lack of hind leg, she tended to move it as if it still bore weight, so she moved the prosthetic and accidentally dragged it forward. Pepa froze and turned back to look at her stump. She took a hesitant, limping step forward, testing it out, letting it bear some of her weight. Then she took several exploratory steps. Suddenly she was running about the room, whining at a happy, delighted pitch.

She stopped to press into Austin, crying and licking his face, then tore off to spin around the room.

When she galumphed in the direction of the three curious kittens who had arrived to see what the fuss was about, Walker naturally was happy to join in on the zoomies, and Dallas tried to get a better look at Pepa's new leg. Meanwhile, Ozzy hissed in alarm and jumped up onto the couch so he could watch from safety.

"I think she likes it," Austin said in an impressive understatement, like Pepa wasn't losing her mind with joy.

Joe kind of wanted to kiss the dumbass. And also maybe punch his shoulder for being so ridiculous.

Austin had built Pepa a prosthetic. Joe couldn't even guess how much work had been involved, and he'd done it without help—or at least without Joe's help.

Pepa finally calmed down enough to beg for more cuddles, which she did now, pressing her body so hard into Austin's that she toppled him from his crouch. He went down laughing and rubbed her ears and called her a good girl as her tail whipped everything within range. She settled down with her head in his lap, but the tail kept going.

Austin's cheeks were pink with pleasure, and he kept crooning and petting her, going for her belly when she turned onto her side. "Sweet girl, you deserve it, don't you." When he stroked his fingers through the ruffled fur on her tummy, she kicked the prosthetic out, the way dogs sometimes did by reflex if they had an itchy spot.

It hit Joe then. Austin was a mechanic, but that wasn't just his job. It was who he was, it was what he did. They'd inherited a dilapidated home and Austin wanted to fix it, make it into something homey and functional, something with purpose. He'd fixed up the record player too, sold that off to finance their ongoing renovations once Joe took the two hours to replace the bubbled wood veneer. Now he'd apparently moved on to healing living, breathing things.

Joe's heart was doing something dumb and treacherous in his chest—something it hadn't done in months or maybe years, something he'd thought it might never do again. It felt like it was beating too fast, suddenly, like it had run around the breezeway with Pepa wagging its tail. And now, he realized in horror, it was lying with its head in Austin's lap.

If Joe had realized Austin building Pepa a prosthetic would heal Joe's dumb broken heart too, he could've braced for it. But how could he have anticipated this? Jesus.

He sank to the floor, because a whole half of Pepa's belly was going unrubbed while Joe had a crisis, and that was just not acceptable.

He cleared his throat and kept his eyes on Pepa's fur. "Where'd you learn to…?"

Except then Austin answered, and Joe had to look up, didn't he? His eyes were deep and soft and fond. He shook his head knowingly. "I told you. You can learn anything on YouTube."

Joe swallowed the lump that had risen in his throat. "Think there might be more soul in this than there is in my cooking."

Austin flushed at the compliment. Joe wanted to throw himself off the roof. His heart might have given the green light, God knew his dick had been revving the engine, but his head was still in the driver's seat, screaming and pumping the brakes. But, "I don't know," Austin said. The words came out bolder than Joe expected, though he couldn't have said why he thought Austin would be shy about the compliment. "Pretty sure that celebratory dinner you made was as close as I've come to a religious experience."

Joe did not have the slightest suspicion that Austin was talking about the risotto. His ears burned. "Um." Jesus Christ. He swallowed again. He needed… space. Room to breathe. A pillow to scream into. Starling, maybe, to talk him off the ledge he'd sleepwalked onto. "I actually forgot I need to, um. Call Starling about—the wiring. I better—yep."

Joe didn't run away. That would be undignified and also highly suspicious.

He did lock himself in his bedroom and settle himself as far away from the door as he could, so as to avoid being overheard, and pulled out his phone.

"Hey, Joe," Starling greeted casually.

"I'm going to fall in love with him," Joe blurted out.

"Oh-kay," Starling said slowly.

"Not okay," Joe whisper-shouted, cognisant of Austin still in the house. "Starling, he built Pepa a prosthetic leg." It came out something like a wail.

Starling hummed in acknowledgment, like Joe hadn't provided her with the most damning piece of information that anyone could have uttered. How was Joe supposed to stay strong in the face of that?

"Don't just *hm* at me."

"What would you like me to do?"

"Offer advice."

"For what?"

"My problem."

"Which is?"

Joe let out an agonized groan. "That Austin is incredibly hot and sexy and cute and I'm living with him and will fall in love with him. Starling, I can't fall in love with him. That would be a horrible idea. Absolutely horrible."

"Oh, absolutely," Starling agreed dryly.

Joe groaned and buried his face in his free hand. This was disastrous. He couldn't be in love with Austin. He didn't want to be in love with anyone right now, let alone with the worst possible candidate. Between the living together and working together fixing the house they owned together, he was a bad idea on paper. And that didn't even get into the fact that Austin wasn't interested in dating or relationships.

Falling in love with Austin would lead to heartbreak.

Joe told Starling as much.

Well, he tried to.

But he might not have expressed himself very clearly, since Starling just hummed once more and didn't offer much by way of horror or advice.

Finally he got fed up with her lack of response and huffed indignantly. "Starling."

"Joe," she parroted in the same tone. "Are you done being dramatic?"

Joe gaped. "*Dramatic?*"

Oh, wait. He heard it now.

He huffed again. "Fine. Yes. So done being dramatic, Starling."

"Watch the sarcasm," she shot back, amused and warm. "Joe. Tell me honestly you didn't see this coming."

Joe swallowed. "You already know the answer to that."

"I do," Starling agreed. "We've had this conversation before. Has anything changed since then?"

He let his body sag against the wall, tilted his head back so he was staring up at the ceiling. He was looking forward to having that light fixture work, for sure.

Had anything changed since the day after Joe let the red wine do the talking?

Well, Austin had met Joe's mother, for one. Built the dog a prosthetic. Started looking at Joe with fond, hot eyes. Brought home dinner. Debated over wine pairings with red ears, like he was thinking about what the red wine did to Joe.

"Yeah," Joe admitted, a little hoarse.

"Have you talked to Austin about those changes?"

Joe made an indignant noise.

"Yeah, that's what I thought, dumbass." He could hear her rolling her eyes. "Here's a thought. You don't actually need my advice."

This was not something Joe ever expected to hear from her. "I don't?"

"No. You need to sack up and have an actual adult conversation with the guy you want to bone about how your heart is fragile and he's not allowed to toy with your affections."

For fuck's sake. "Now who's being dramatic?" he grumbled.

"Joe. He calls you his house husband. He made you adopt four animals in two days. It is possible you are not the only U-Haul lesbian in the house. Do you get me? And you deserve to be happy. It has been *so long* since you were happy. I want that for you. If Austin can do that for you, I will help you mail save-the-date cards, okay?"

Joe's stomach tried to exit through his mouth. "What if I'm not ready?"

"Then don't sleep with him. Babe. I love you. But you are so bad at communicating in a relationship, it is, like, pathological. Be honest. If he's coming on too strong, tell him to back off."

"But what if I don't actually want him to back off?"

Oh God, that sounded like a whine. That *was* a whine.

Starling, at least, thought it was funny, if the laugh in her voice was any indication. "José Giuseppe Joseph Romano, are you telling me you want to be *wooed*?"

Oh *God*, was he?

Oh God, he *did*. "Fuck," Joe whispered. He *liked* the way Austin was treating him now—the flirting, the extra consideration. He liked the idea of maybe making him work for it a little. He liked the way it made him feel, like he was worth spending time on, even if they didn't end up in bed together.

Historically, Joe made moves. That was *his thing*. He had game, whatever Gavin thought, even if it was currently a little rusty.

He wasn't used to this end of things. He liked it.

Starling cackled. "The work boot is on the other foot now."

Joe groaned in frustration.

"Look, you have three options—talk to Austin, move out, or do neither and keep your fingers crossed that everything works out."

She was probably right, but Joe didn't have to like it.

Chapter Sixteen

AUSTIN HAD a plan.

It was a good one too. A sneaky one.

Step one was getting Joe to join him on a visit to the local Christmas market.

Austin floated it as a convenience that could be entertaining. Austin definitely wasn't motivated by the romantic nature of the market—he only wanted to visit so he could buy some local honey and pick up gifts for Christmas, that was all. And he needed Joe's input because Joe knew the kids better than Austin did.

So on Saturday Austin launched his campaign and, with little urging, managed to get himself, Joe, and Pepa out of the house.

Pepa was a bit of a cog in the works for Austin's plan, but Joe suggested it and Austin didn't know how to say no when he couldn't give his real reason.

At least the market was perfect for finding gifts for the kids.

First they looked at jewelry, and Austin was instantly drawn to an asymmetrical necklace in the colors of the ace/aro flag, with green at the top, white, gray, and black in the middle, and purple on the bottom.

"Meg will love it," Joe confirmed.

Next, in a stall filled with knitting, Joe cackled when Austin picked up the socks with humping reindeer.

"If you don't buy them, I will."

Austin clutched the socks to his chest and mockingly joked, "Hands off my present. I saw them first."

"I won't take it," Joe laughed, hands up. "Though maybe I should. You'll be Gavin's favorite after you give him those."

"That's the plan," Austin said cheerfully. He waited just a few beats and then added, slyly, "I refuse to be the wicked stepmother."

Color rose into Joe's cheeks. It was so charming Austin wanted to kiss them, but he held back. That wasn't slow, and Austin was committed to slow.

Joe was more skittish than a mouse in a cat café. He turned toward the next stall. He still had to find something for Will and Alex, and maybe Starling.

This one held more knitwear, and Austin picked a matching hat and scarf with colorful stripes. It wasn't exactly rainbow, but it was close enough, and Joe agreed that it shouldn't get Will in trouble with his parents but would be a fun fuck-you to them. Especially since Will was in need of new gear, which apparently his parents hadn't noticed, even if Joe and Austin had.

The reward of finding gifts would have warmed him on its own—never mind the mere fact of having so many people to appreciate at Christmas—but the happiness on Joe's face, the way he smiled softly at the bag dangling from Austin's arm, was a delightful bonus.

Austin was starting to despair that he wouldn't find anything for Alex here. The problem was Austin had an idea but didn't know how to implement it. Over the past couple of visits, Alex had taken an interest in Austin's work on the table legs. They had asked about the welding and even offered to help, to act as an extra set of hands. Austin suspected it might be more than a passing interest for them and wanted to encourage Alex's exploration of different crafts. He suspected they might find a passion in the trades, but it wasn't Austin's place to give unsolicited advice. Still, he could help them by giving more opportunities. He just didn't know how. He couldn't exactly gift Alex a welder.

Then, at one of the final shops, he found it. The artist did metalwork jewelry, repurposing old cutlery into artistic pieces as well as stamping and shaping metal into cuffs and bracelets. But most importantly, they had build-your-own DIY kits. Each one had a strip of leather, a strip of metal, thread, and three stamps to make your own bracelet. Joe and Austin pored over the options for the stamps and eventually settled on bronze and brown for the color and a set of geometric shapes that would give them opportunities to make their own pattern. If they liked it, Austin would happily buy more stamps—maybe a full alphabet.

At that point, Pepa announced it was time for a bathroom break and dragged them outside to find a series of bushes to pee on.

"Wow." Joe looked around the exterior of the community center for the first time, and Austin took a moment to be glad of the brisk wind whipping off the Detroit River, which gave him an excuse for the pinkness in his own cheeks. "I didn't know this was here."

"It's new this year, apparently." Around the building and parking lot, down by the riverfront, the town had built a walking trail. It had booths set up selling hot cider and chocolate, and one that rented skates. Refrigeration coils under the path kept the trail frozen, and dozens of people were skating on it, kids with parents, couples holding hands.

He'd needed to do some shopping, sure, and Joe's input helped, but this was what he really wanted to bring them here for. He'd had a whole plan and everything. Act surprised to see the rink, casually mention he'd never skated before, wait for Joe to suggest they try it—let him think it was his idea—get Joe to hold his hand. Cliché? Yeah, but he was pretty sure it would work. Joe might be skittish, but he let Austin get away with a lot and never called him on any of it. Austin thought he was enjoying himself.

Pepa put a crimp in that plan, though. They couldn't skate with the dog. Austin didn't want to risk any of her remaining paws getting injured by a stray blade.

Too bad. But Pepa needed a walk anyway. They could take her through the park instead, look at the light displays at least, even if it wasn't dark yet.

Just as they were heading that way, Fate intervened with a Linda ex machina.

"Boys! And Pepa," she said brightly, squatting to give her star patient her due attention. "Doing some Christmas shopping?"

"Just finished. Bags are in the car."

She straightened up and offered a smile. "Off to have a skate, then?"

Oh, bless Linda. Austin needed to get her something really good for Christmas. "Well, we can't, with the dog," Joe started, and Austin saw his window and added, "I can't skate, actually."

Joe gaped at him. "What?"

Austin shrugged, feigning nonchalance. He let Joe draw his own conclusions. Skates were expensive; it wasn't like anyone was going to pay for Austin to play travel hockey growing up.

"That's just...." Joe looked at the skating trail. He looked at the skate rental booth. He looked at Pepa.

He looked at Linda.

"Hey," Joe said, "would you mind sticking around for a little while? Maybe taking Miss Pepa for a quick constitutional? They let pets in the building too, so if you haven't gone shopping yet—"

Austin was glad Joe wasn't looking at him, because he definitely would've clocked the smug expression right away. Linda did—she glanced at Austin and then visibly clamped down on a smile. "I'd be happy for the company," she agreed. "What do you think, little lady?"

They handed off the leash, and Pepa trotted gamely after Linda while Austin let Joe steer him toward the skate-rental booth.

"What if I don't want to skate?" Austin asked innocently.

Joe gave him a flat look. "It's new this year, apparently," he echoed, an obvious mimic of Austin's earlier words. "Which means you knew it was here. And then you just casually mention you've never been skating?"

So Joe *did* see through him. Austin smiled, faux innocent. "Does this mean you're paying for the rental?"

Joe elbowed him and told the booth attendant their shoe sizes.

The skating track was decently busy, which meant they didn't have to deal with too many teens and preteens showing off, trying to run each other over. Austin hid his smile in his scarf when Joe insisted on checking his laces before they got on the ice, then let Joe pull him to his feet and lead him onto the path.

He didn't wobble.

He didn't let go of Joe's hand either.

He felt more than saw Joe glance down between them, and kept his eyes straight ahead, even if the smile showed through.

"Never skated before?" Joe said incredulously.

Austin hummed, tugged Joe around a slow-moving group of children. "Yeah, man, I don't know why you bought that. You know I grew up north of Toronto. Even poor kids can buy used skates. Yard sales exist."

Laughing, Joe put on a burst of speed and put them even again. "So, what? This whole thing was a ploy to hold my hand?"

Finally Austin couldn't resist. He looked over to find Joe smiling, blushing. His hair ruffled in the wind; he probably should've put a hat on, but he was too vain. "Maybe," Austin admitted with his own grin. "It worked, didn't it?"

"Kinda convoluted," Joe said. "You could have just asked."

Austin looked at him consideringly. "Could I?" His tone serious now.

Joe licked his lips. "Yeah."

"And you'd be into that?"

Joe snorted. "It's handholding, not handcuffs."

Oh, really? "You could argue it's more intimate, in a way."

"Oh, could you?" Joe asked, a clear parody of Austin's earlier question.

"Joe." Austin shot him a look. Now that they'd started this conversation, he was suddenly desperate to know Joe's answer. So much for sneaky wooing. "Can I date you?"

They were still holding hands, still gliding forward. Joe's cheeks were already pink from exercise in the cold, but Austin thought they were growing darker.

"Yeah. You can do that." He looked bashful. "I think—I mean—the last few days have been good."

"Yeah?" Austin couldn't have stopped the grin if he tried.

"Yeah."

They skated a few loops around the path and then decided to call it for the afternoon. They sat down on a bench to unlace. "So." Austin glanced at Joe. "How'm I doing so far?"

"Top marks for the market and the skating. Deductions for the scheming."

Austin worked his skate off. His toes were freezing and his arches ached. He'd missed this. "Hey, now. You have to admit you're kind of skittish." He paused. "So what is that? An A? A plus?"

Joe waggled his hand, smirking just a little. "A minus."

Austin whistled under his breath. "Wow, tough grader." He tangled his fingers with Joe's again and tugged him toward the parking lot. "Come on. Let's go find our dog."

At home, they set their purchases on the table and got to wrapping. Austin's thighs ached pleasantly from the exercise, and he knew he'd be sore tomorrow, but it was a satisfying feeling. They placed the gifts under the tree, and Joe fed the animals while Austin cleaned the litterboxes. Then they were both exhausted, so they washed up and had tomato soup and grilled cheese for dinner, defending their plates from Pepa and Walker, Austin tucked against the arm of the couch and Joe slotted between his legs, leaning back against his chest while *A Charlie Brown Christmas* played.

They hadn't even kissed since that night with the wine, and Austin was kind of desperate to do it again. But he was also enjoying the slow, easy comfort that was *living* with Joe, touching him with no deeper purpose than because they both liked it. Maybe this was why people had pets.

He had the sudden unbidden mental image of Joe sitting at his feet the way Pepa did, looking up at Austin with big trusting eyes. He immediately pushed the thought aside. They were taking this slow.

Besides, he supposed it was Joe's turn to top next.

Although—

Watch the damn movie, Austin told himself as he plucked Joe's empty soup mug from his hand before he could fall asleep and drop it on the floor. He set it on the table behind him with his own empty dishes, then pulled the blanket from the back of the couch and spread it over— well, over Joe, mostly, and Austin's feet, but Joe was covering the rest of him. The December chill couldn't get him at all.

"'M not gonna fall asleep," Joe protested, voice thick with exhaustion.

"Maybe I am," Austin said. This couch was really too comfortable. No wonder Alex fell asleep so quickly the other night.

"Mm," Joe said, and then for a very long time, he said nothing.

Austin closed his eyes and wondered how he'd lived almost thirty years without him.

Chapter Seventeen

MID-DECEMBER BLEW by in a flurry of snowflakes and last-minute preparations. Austin's skill set—or lack thereof—made him ineligible to help Joe bake, but he had a good eye for creating equal-sized cookie-dough balls for Joe to bake ahead and then freeze so he didn't spend the two days immediately before Christmas exhausting himself.

By mutual agreement, Joe and Austin were taking things slower on the physical side. But just because they weren't fucking didn't mean there was no intimacy. Joe hadn't done so much cuddling and handholding since he was a teenager. He wondered if Austin had ever gotten to enjoy this stage as a kid or if he'd thrown himself right into clubbing and one-night stands. Austin had probably been pretty at eighteen—he would've had plenty of older men lining up with offers to show him the proverbial ropes.

Possibly also the literal ropes, if Joe were being honest.

He should ask Austin which it was, he reflected—about the cuddling versus clubbing, not the bondage. (Okay, maybe also the bondage.) He'd probably get an answer. They'd shared plenty of trauma by now.

All the quiet domesticity was easy to fall into, though. He loved this part of dating—having someone to eat dinner and watch TV with. It was *nice* just spending time together. Joe didn't remember the last time he and Paul had done something like that. He'd forgotten the way it could feel, learning someone, letting them learn you, knowing you were headed somewhere good without being in a hurry to get there. It was a giddy, effervescent thing; it bubbled up inside him like a laugh and wrapped around him like a hug.

Joe felt like a teenager with a crush. When he told Starling—half sheepish, half proud—about their talk while skating, she cooed like a parent whose child took first prize at the science fair.

"Proud of you, babe," she said. And then, because she was Starling and couldn't resist, she added, "Even if it was definitely Austin who did the talking."

Joe didn't bother to defend himself. He didn't have a leg to stand on and Starling never let him get away with shit.

"So does this mean you're finally going to chill out now that you're getting laid again?"

And really, he wished she *would* let him get away with it, just this once, because his silence told her everything.

"Joe... are you *not getting laid*?"

He felt his face burning. "We're taking it slow," he said, mortified.

Starling cackled. "I can always count on you to make me laugh, even on a rough day."

"Glad my pain amuses you."

She snorted. "Waiting to have sex and somehow landing yourself in a decades-in settled married life of bills, children, and no sex is not pain, it's fucking hilarious."

"Ha ha," he said dryly, but he didn't actually mind, not when she spoke with such joy.

"Other people have real pain and troubles." She sounded too earnest for a moment as she said that, like something specific was on her mind.

"Everything okay?"

"Just... I'm not fully sure, to be honest. My sister called and—I don't know yet."

"What's going on?"

"It might be something, it might be nothing, but the waiting sucks."

"Uh...."

"I don't want to talk about it yet. I do, however, want to mock you for embodying two lesbian stereotypes at once—U-Haul and bed death, which you shouldn't be able to do at the *same time*."

"This feels discriminatory," Joe protested. "Are you allowed to say that to me?"

"I sleep with women, so yes. Now tell me more about hosting Christmas. I need to know about this domestic disaster in the making."

"Thanks for the vote of confidence," Joe said, but he told her everything all the same.

AUSTIN DIDN'T open the garage on Mondays unless he had an appointment. Which, thank God for that, because there was no one in the office to have this breakdown to.

He flung himself into the comfiest chair in the animal clinic break room and threw his head back to the ceiling. "Linda, I'm losing my mind."

"Not to be too dramatic or anything," she said dryly. He didn't even have to move his head; just closed his fingers as he felt her press a cup of coffee into his open hand. Linda was a goddess.

He was going to have to move to ingest it, though. He righted himself enough that he wouldn't end up wearing the bean juice and smiled her way. "Thanks." The color of coffee and cream was just how he'd fix it himself. He took a sip for confirmation. "Perfect. And I'm *not* being too dramatic."

"Of course not." She waved for him to continue his story, then retrieved her ballpoint from her ponytail and pulled the day's crossword over.

Austin took another fortifying sip of caffeine and then set the cup aside and got back down on the floor to examine the scale Linda had asked him to take a look at. He pulled the screwdriver he needed from his own ponytail. He had to admit it was a handy place to keep a tool. "I'm not kidding. I don't know if I'm in heaven or hell."

Linda began filling in the first crossword answer. She never looked up when she did this; she was in the zone. "Right. You going to give me real details anytime soon, or are you trying to give me conversational blue balls? Quit teasing."

"Oh, *speaking of blue balls.*"

Something plastic hit him in the back of his head as he unfastened the first screw. For a second he thought she'd thrown her pen, but no, just the cap. Crossword time could not be derailed so easily.

But she didn't ask. She must have reached the limits of her indulgence.

Austin sighed and started on the next screw. He was pretty sure the scale just had a loose wiring connection. All he had to do was take this plate off and find it. "Joe *kissed* me this morning." He paused, because damn it, Linda, sometimes a man has the right to be a little dramatic. "He kissed me like we'd been married seventy years and didn't have our teeth in yet."

He finished with the second screw and popped the plate off. Above him, he swore he heard Linda's pen stop scratching against the newspaper.

Finally she said, "Come again?"

Austin huffed. "I'd *like* to, but we haven't had sex since that first time. The granny kiss is the most action I've seen in weeks. And, like, I was enjoying taking it slow. Am. I *am* enjoying it. But I am also—as previously stated—*losing my god damn mind.*"

The pen noises did not resume. A click as the ballpoint hit the table. Then Linda's head appeared around the side of it. She blinked owlishly at him from behind her reading glasses. "I'm—sorry, are you telling me you and Joe aren't sleeping together?"

Yes. Yes, that was kind of the whole point and problem. "Duh," Austin said.

Linda took her glasses off and squinted at him. "Okay. But you're both—you both enjoy sex. This is not a relationship where you're not having sex on purpose."

"That's correct." Austin didn't know where the disconnect was happening.

"And you've had sex before. Together."

"Yes," Austin said impatiently. "Before we were boyfriends." He immediately wanted to gag. He sounded like a tenth grader.

Linda took a deep breath. "Before you were…. When exactly did you get together?"

"Like, officially?" Austin wrinkled his nose and thought about it. "Um… the Christmas market?"

Linda leaned too far forward and the chair wheels scooted back, almost sending her face-first into the table. She caught herself by slamming her palm down hard. "You morons adopted a tripod dog and three kittens *before you started dating?*"

"Linda! I can't change the things Past Austin has done, but Future Austin would like to not drive into a ditch because he was thinking about how to get Joe to kiss him like that every morning for the rest of his life!" Jesus Christ, that wasn't any better. "And also in the sexy ways. Ways that end in orgasms. Just, I don't know, also the domestic everyday 'okay, I love you, bye' kiss." He closed his eyes and leaned his head against the scale, knocked his forehead against it a few times like he could beat some sense into himself.

"Here's a thought," Linda said dryly. "You could have this conversation with your boyfriend. Or better yet, just kiss him and put both of you out of your misery."

Austin sighed and clicked on his penlight. Sure enough, one of the wires had come loose. Easy fix.

He grabbed the needle-nose from his tool roll and went to work.

He couldn't spend the whole day at the clinic, even if Linda had enough projects to keep him busy in trade for kitten checkups and their first shots. Christmas Eve was the day after tomorrow, and Austin still hadn't finished the legs for the island. Or, he *had* finished them, but then he realized he'd mistakenly assumed the garage floor was level, which it wasn't, so unless he wanted the table to wobble, he needed to even that out.

Alex met him at the house just after lunch, and Austin lent them a pair of the heavy-duty coveralls he wore when welding and a set of heatproof gloves.

"We're only off level by a fraction of an inch," he explained, "so we're just going to compensate with these."

Ordinarily the table would've needed two sets of mounting hardware—one to attach the tabletop to the legs at the head of the table, and one for the foot. But in this case, the foot of the table was getting a double layer to make up for the bow in the garage floor that Austin had forgotten to account for. Rookie mistake.

Alex adjusted their safety goggles. "Cool. So do we weld them both at once, or…?"

Austin glued them first, then flipped down his face shield and welded the sides. Then he handed off the shield and coached Alex through attaching the plates to the leg. They had steady hands and much better patience than Austin had when he learned, and when they stepped back to let Austin inspect, he couldn't even find anything he wanted to touch up.

"Nice job." He paused. "You want to do the other one too?"

Alex grinned brightly and situated themself before pulling the shield back down and lighting the torch.

Before they knew it, the legs were done, and Austin and Alex carried them into the house. The things were as heavy as the tabletop, and assembling it anywhere but on-site would be nonsensical, so they set the enormous hunk of metal in the kitchen to await assembly. But it looked a bit sad without its other half. Not that Austin could fix that, since he didn't know the status of it. So for now, Austin's legs were without their top. Heh.

Alex agreed to stay for dinner—some of Joe's leftovers—and accepted a cup of cocoa while they waited for Joe to get home.

They were sitting together at the dining room table, drinking their cocoa with whipped cream and crushed candy canes. Alex wasn't exactly a talkative kid, but they were quieter than usual as they sipped their drink and fiddled with a spoon. They opened their mouth as if to say something, then sighed and took a sip of cocoa. Austin was starting to wonder if they were building up to something when the front door opened and Pepa and Walker bolted from the kitchen.

"Looks like Joe's home."

Alex nodded. "Can't sneak in, can he?"

"Nope. Walker's a stalker," Austin agreed and stood up to pull the leftover enchiladas out of the fridge.

Alex had to run after dinner—they realized they'd forgotten about an assignment that was due the next day—so it was just Joe and Austin cleaning up the kitchen.

"Good day?" Joe asked. He waggled one of the empty cocoa mugs with the dregs of candy cane.

"Treat after Alex helped me finish the legs for the table. Well deserved. They're a natural with a welder."

"Yeah?" Joe asked, voice full of dad pride.

"Yup. Was able to finish the legs up faster than expected. They're all ready to go. Just need the top."

Joe waggled his eyebrows, and Austin snapped him with a towel.

"Well, lucky for your bottom, the top's ready to go. I polished up the wood last night."

Austin groaned and definitely did not think about Joe getting well oiled wood into his bottom. "So we could assemble it tonight?"

"If you wish," Joe said amiably.

Forty minutes later, they stood admiring their new kitchen island.

Joe gave the surface one last polish, not that it needed it, and stepped back next to Austin. "Not bad."

"If you do say so yourself," Austin teased.

Joe knocked their shoulders together and grinned. "We make a good team."

The table's mix of their skills—of wood and metal, natural and man-made—was impressive. It worked in a sort of seamless way that felt counterintuitive. Looking at the table set Austin's heart thumping with a rush of affection. Without thinking, he turned, wrapped his arms around Joe's neck, and kissed him.

Joe groaned into the kiss and snaked his own arms around Austin's torso to pull him closer.

"Furniture-making get you going?" he gasped.

Austin huffed. "Nah, just your wood."

Joe laughed and pulled him in for another kiss. "Keep making jokes like that and it'll get you laid," he warned.

"Mm," Austin hummed and tilted his head back to give Joe access. "What about heavy petting on the couch?"

"Oh, that I can definitely do," Joe promised between nibbles. They shuffled toward the living room, neither of them wanting to let go. So it was several minutes before Austin found himself stretched out on his back with Joe's solid weight above him, a dirty mirror of their cuddle the other night. He could get used to Joe the personal heater, especially if he kept being so obliging. "You like this," he murmured against the skin of Austin's neck.

Sure, if by *like this* you meant all Austin's blood had rushed to his dick and he'd lost voluntary motor function below the waist. His hips kept hitching up toward Joe without his conscious input. Austin didn't think he could be blamed; Joe had a pretty mouth and obviously knew how to use it, and guys exchanging hand jobs in bar bathrooms didn't tend to go right for Austin's throat like this. It was the novelty factor.

Having Joe's weight pinning him to the couch wasn't terrible either.

"Yeah, baby," Austin managed, much smoother than he expected, "I like it."

Joe scraped his teeth up the side of Austin's neck. "Not baby," he grumbled. The sharp pressure of a bite followed, just enough to hurt in the good way, as Joe shoved his thigh firmly between Austin's legs.

Someone made a desperate sound—they were close enough together for Austin to have plausible deniability—and Austin worked one of his thighs open to better slot Joe between them and hooked his ankle around Joe's back. He couldn't *touch* Joe properly like this, but he could score his nails over Joe's scalp to the back of his neck until he shuddered. "No?" *God*, he felt good. Joe's thick, solid thigh made a perfect surface to rut against, and the pressure against his balls and taint sent something zinging through Austin's body.

"Hnn." Joe had released Austin's neck, but he left his head tucked there, his breath hot and tantalizing in Austin's ear, which somehow felt even better than the pressure on Austin's dick.

"You, uh—" Joe tongued his Adam's apple. Austin forgot how to make words for a handful of seconds. Then, "You want a substitute?"

It wasn't like Austin had forgotten their first trip down this road. Joe wanted Austin to say his name, repeatedly. Austin couldn't blame him; everyone liked a little ego stroking. But Austin had never gotten to *tease* a partner, and he was enjoying it. "One that's just for you?" He curled his fingers in Joe's hair and tugged a little, pulled back until he could see Joe's face. "How about 'sweet thing'?"

It wasn't supposed to be *serious*, but Joe flushed scarlet to the roots of the hair Austin was still holding and thrust down against him a little too uncontrolled to be on purpose, and—okay, right, Joe wanted Austin to call him *sweet thing* while they made out. That got him hot.

What the fuck, why did that make Austin's brain feel like it had boiled over?

Joe kissed him again, and Austin decided he didn't care, even if this meant he couldn't use this new knowledge to his advantage.

But then Joe pulled away, still bright red, and squashed himself sideways on the couch next to Austin instead of on top of him. Not ideal—now Austin was cold, sliding dangerously toward the floor, and sadly dick-frictionless. "What—" he squawked.

Joe wrapped an arm around him before gravity could finish him off and pulled him back onto the couch, on his side this time, so their chests were pressed together. "Sorry, uh."

Austin blinked.

Joe's cheeks were scarlet. "I'm too old to dry-hump to orgasm."

On the one hand, Austin *definitely* wasn't cold anymore. A wave of heat had just washed right over him. He'd been enjoying himself, obviously—he was hard and there was a damp patch in his underwear—but he wasn't in danger of coming in his pants.

Joe was, apparently, which was… surprising. Hot. Interesting.

"What got to you?" Austin asked. It had to be something. Austin's neck was pretty nice, but not have-an-orgasm-about-it nice.

"I'm not answering that," Joe said. "You got enough ammunition tonight."

Fair. Austin would figure it out soon enough. "Okay," he agreed. "Different question—do you think I can get off the couch without falling on my ass?"

Chapter Eighteen

AFTER NEARLY coming in his pants because Austin called him *sweet*, Joe got a reprieve from further potential sexual embarrassment. Not because Austin had failed to accidentally uncover any previously unexplored kinks—Joe wasn't sure yet if it was the word *sweet*, the mild degradation of *thing*, or just the praise that got him going, and frankly he wasn't ready to look into it—but because they hadn't had the time for any more R-rated action.

Between their day jobs and the upcoming holiday, they hardly had enough energy to drag themselves to bed, let alone do anything other than sleep there.

By the morning of Christmas Eve, Joe had readied everything that could be prepared in advance and all that was left was the day-of work. Which was still plenty.

Joe wasn't making the Feast of the Seven Fishes, because he didn't want to bankrupt himself financially and physically, but he had planned a menu of a light charcuterie board, caprese salad, lasagna, and fish as the main course, and a mixed platter of season-appropriate sweets for dessert, which included panettone, cookies, and Nanaimo bars (Gavin's favorite).

Then Austin accidentally rewrote the menu. It wasn't his fault. He'd been eyeing Joe's shopping list and asking questions about various items, when he said, "Well, it's not like I'd know much about traditional. I don't remember ever having a turkey-dinner Christmas."

Exercising an impressive level of restraint, Joe did not pull Austin into a hug or vow to reform the entire foster system or throw out all of his plans for Christmas dinner right then and there. Instead, he hummed softly and said casually, "Oh, that's too bad." And started making plans.

Doing a whole turkey dinner the day of would be impractical, especially since he'd need the oven for the lasagna. But that didn't mean they couldn't *have* turkey.

Joe had been wanting to try spatchcocking a bird anyway.

Austin had decided to close his shop from December 24 to January 1 excepting emergencies. He'd even made a sign for the door that suggested customers call and leave a message if they felt they couldn't wait until the New Year.

"You don't think people will take advantage?" Joe asked skeptically. He himself had closed his own business doors with the promise to only call his employees in the event of storm cleanup.

"Nah, business is usually slow that week. Most people don't want to leave their houses. Might as well just officially take it off this year instead of unofficially."

"Except for being on call," Joe pointed out.

Austin shrugged. "If it's not a real emergency I can book them in for January, but if it is… I wouldn't want to strand a senior citizen or single parent without a car over the holidays." He said it like it was no big deal, like it didn't prove what a massive sweethearted softie he was.

Fortunately, dinner prep went smoothly. It helped that they opened a bottle of wine—white; Joe wasn't stupid—to keep them merry as they worked, Joe micromanaging everything in a way that would've made him hate himself at work but which he couldn't help in the kitchen.

"What's in the Crock-Pot?" Austin asked at around four thirty. Guests would be showing up at any minute.

Oh God, Austin could not find out about the turkey until someone else got here to act as a buffer. If Joe had to look at his big brown eyes filled with some kind of Christmas-adjacent emotion inspired by Joe, Joe would… well, he probably wouldn't be answering the door for any guests. "It's a secret."

By some stroke of luck, Starling arrived a few minutes later, carrying a jug of her homemade Irish cream and a gallon of apple cider. "I brought refreshments." She set them on the dining table and kissed Joe's cheek, then swept Austin into a hug. "Merry Christmas. Eggnog's still in the car."

"I'll get it," Austin volunteered.

"Meow," agreed Walker, and Joe decided it was time for the animals to be sequestered in the breezeway lest they (A) escape or (B) stick their faces in one of the various dishes Joe was setting out. They'd put a tablecloth on top of the piano and were using it to host trays of appetizers;

the sideboard in the dining room was doing double duty as a bar. Soon enough the entire kitchen counter would be covered in food too.

Joe left Starling and Austin in charge of setting up the drink station so he could finish the gravy. He left it on the burner to warm, checked in on the lasagna, taste-tested the dressing, and grabbed the charcuterie from the fridge.

By the time he returned to the dining room, Linda, Gavin, Alex, and Will had arrived. Starling was pouring Linda a glass of her Irish cream, while Gavin and Will poked at the presents under the tree, looking for theirs like they were eight instead of eighteen.

"No presents until after dinner," Joe called.

Alex turned and smiled at him. "Merry Christmas, Joe."

He smacked a kiss on the top of their head as he set down the tray. "Merry Christmas. Your parents still coming?"

"They're just getting the presents."

Rebecca and Trevor came in carrying bags of gifts, clearly having brought enough for not only the kids but also the adults.

Rebecca hadn't made a great first impression on Joe, but in the past three years she'd gotten sober, found a steady job, and met and married Trevor. Joe didn't really know him, but he seemed to genuinely enjoy doting on his wife and stepchild.

"Rebecca, how good to see you."

She smiled at Joe's greeting and pulled him into a hug. "Joe. How have you been?"

"I've been great. Kept busy, but good."

"I'm glad to hear it." Rebecca was one of the first supporters of his landscaping business, sharing his contact details with everyone she knew and providing references.

"Alex tells us this old house is keeping you busy," Trevor said.

Joe laughed. "And Alex too. Come. Get a tour."

They stopped at the tree where Alex, Gavin, and Will were fooling around, taking sneak peeks at presents and trying to guess their contents.

"No touching." Alex smacked Gavin with the back of their hand, and Gavin turned puppy-dog eyes on them. Alex stayed firm. "You agreed to those rules."

"But Alex, ba—"

Alex placed a hand on his face and pushed. "Put that face away, you cheater."

Joe was just finishing up the tour and thinking he should check on Austin in the kitchen when his mom arrived.

"Oh, Joe, it looks wonderful. You've done such great work on the place. And the decorations are lovely."

Joe gave a little smile and admitted, "Most of them came with the house. Also, the kids helped a lot. Gavin and Will were responsible for the mistletoe." He nodded down the hall. Bunches of fake mistletoe hung over every conceivable doorway and a few non-doorways. "It seems DeeDee was a fan."

His mom chuckled. "Somehow, that seems apt for the woman."

Joe bit his tongue on agreeing that mistletoe was the low-key version of leaving a house to two queer single men. Instead, he smiled and said, "Yeah. It fits."

This last was said as they walked into view of the tree, and Gavin, sensing a conversation to snoop on, turned and asked, "What fits?"

"DeeDee's love of mistletoe is in character."

Gavin's eyes lit up. "Isn't it great? Of course, participating in mistletoe kissing is totally voluntary. We don't want anyone feeling uncomfortable."

God, Joe loved his kids.

"I'm sure she's not planning on kissing anyone she doesn't want to, dumbass," Alex said, but couldn't hide the fondness in their voice or gaze.

"Hey, peer pressure is real. Everyone should know that the mistletoe is just for fun and not a requirement."

The next few hours were chaos of the best kind.

Drinks and appetizers were worked through while Joe finished dinner prep, and then they all sat around the brand-new table to plow their way through the various dishes.

When Joe placed the plate of sliced turkey in front of Austin, he gazed up at Joe with hearts in his eyes and eagerly reached for it. Totally worth the effort, Joe thought—even later, when the turkey clearly failed the popularity contest next to the lasagna and Austin admitted that he didn't really like it, even smothered in gravy.

"It's just so dry," he muttered softly to Joe with apologetic eyes.

Joe didn't take offense. "Turkey is the worst bird."

Meg arrived as they were finishing dinner, and everyone gathered in the living room to distribute presents.

Wrapping paper littered the room by the time Alex pulled the final package from under the tree and handed it to Joe. "For you and Austin."

Joe lifted an eyebrow, wondering what on earth the kids thought they should share as a present, but he didn't ask. Asking might get answers too close to the truth or questions he wasn't ready to answer. So he opened the bag and pulled out four hand-painted ornaments. Each live-edge wooden disk had a portrait of one of the animals on one side. On the back, each had a similar inscription—*First Christmas 2025*.

Joe was not going to cry over this. He was not.

"Will found this local artist who does them for pets and babies," Gavin explained, all eager puppy. "So we sent them pictures and they made them up."

Walker's portrait showed him sitting on a flannel-clad shoulder—it must've come from a picture Austin had sent the kids. Pepa's featured her prosthetic. Joe ran his thumb over each picture and then handed them to Austin to admire.

It wasn't a perfect night. Joe's mom committed a party foul by dropping a full glass of generously spiked eggnog on the dining room floor; at least Austin had insisted on plastic cups, for cleanup's sake, so there was no glass to sweep up, just a rag to run over it. The bathroom doorknob had fallen off again, so Austin had stuffed one of Pepa's tug toys into the gap, and if someone wanted privacy they had to hold the rope while they used the toilet. Austin regaled everyone with the months-old story of Joe's heroic bathroom rescue, including the anticlimax where Austin saved himself, and Joe's mom cackled and threatened to tell Joe's uncles, who all worked in construction, that he'd forgotten how doorknobs worked.

"Wait, didn't you actually work for them a couple summers?" Gavin asked. Joe could still take his Christmas present back.

"Oh, shit, you did. I remember that," Meg put in. "You kept showing up to swimming lessons with black thumbs."

Austin's eyes lit up. "Are you telling me that you work with chainsaws every day but you can't swing a hammer?"

"You *literally* watched me frame the floor in the kitchen—"

Will, like a little sleeper agent, piped up from somewhere behind a mountain of wrapping paper. "I showed him how to use a hammer."

"Betrayer," Joe gasped theatrically. "That was supposed to be our secret."

"This is excellent, actually," Joe's mother said under her breath to Starling, who was squashed in at her elbow. "Getting to tell my brothers a ten-year-old taught my adult son something they didn't? Blackmail material for life."

"I think that story deserves dessert." Austin stood and went toward the kitchen. "Nobody get up, it's crazy in there. I'll bring it out."

The wrapping-paper mountain suffered a small avalanche. "I'll help." Will shook his leg to get free of the ribbon wrapped around his ankle.

There was still tension between Meg and Alex. Things had been better since the dinner-out disaster—Joe was sure Alex had apologized—but they weren't totally solved. Alex even helped Meg put on her necklace. Joe held his breath when Meg opened her gift from Alex, which turned out to be tickets to a queer feminist film that was screening at the university, but Meg smiled and thanked them and it all *seemed* genuine.

Cautious optimism, Joe thought as Will and Austin passed out dessert plates and Alex and Gavin started a spirited discussion about whose slice of tiramisu was bigger.

Somehow they dragged Starling and Linda in to adjudicate, while everyone else was busy just *eating* it and making appropriate noises about how good it was, so Joe was the only one paying attention when Will bumped into Austin in the kitchen doorway, one heading in and the other out.

For a second Joe couldn't parse Will's flushed face, but then he followed the line of his eyes up to the mistletoe hanging in the doorway, and—ah.

Austin caught Joe's gaze over Will's shoulder and gave a tiny shrug before pressing a kiss to Will's cheek.

Will went red to the tips of his ears and looked around furtively, as if to check whether anyone saw, but Austin was already back in the kitchen for another set of desserts. Joe took the opportunity to turn to Linda and answer her recipe questions, pretending he hadn't been looking. Will didn't need an audience for this.

The party went strong until nine o'clock or so, when Joe's mom and Alex's parents started looking at their phones to check the time, hiding yawns behind their hands. Joe expected the kids to still be going strong, but Gavin was slouched on the floor with his head against Will's knee, and Meg kept dozing off in the armchair with Starling, doing that thing where her head would dip toward her chest and then she'd jerk it back up again. The final straw was when Alex emerged from the bathroom clutching their stomach and admitted, green-faced, "I think I ate too much chocolate."

The kids and parents headed out after a perfunctory tidy and several rounds of hugs. Starling and Linda stayed behind to help put the kitchen to rights, and by ten the house mostly looked as it had before the whirlwind of revelers descended. Austin took Pepa out for a short walk, and Joe released the kittens on a new pack of catnip mice to try to get some of their crazies out before bedtime.

"I can't believe you have four pets all named Junior," Starling teased as Dallas vaulted over her slippered foot to reach her fuzzy prey. "You fucking sap."

"Wait, four?" Linda asked. "I mean, I know about Pepa—"

Starling pointed at the cats in turn as Joe's ears heated. "Ozzy, as in a nickname for Austin. Dallas, as in another city in Texas that isn't Austin. And Walker, as in *Texas Ranger*."

Linda laughed. "Oh my God. That explains Austin's face when you named them. I thought you were taking it slow."

Joe was saved from needing to defend himself by the sound of the back door opening. He stood up. "Okay, well, it's been fun, but it's time for you to get out of my house."

"Why?" Starling asked, mugging. "I thought you were taking it slow—"

Joe put his hand right over her face and pushed her toward the door. "Oh my God. Begone, wench. Austin! Come say goodbye to the guests who've overstayed their welcome!"

Thankfully, it seemed Starling and Linda didn't need an engraved invitation to the driveway. They waved them off at the door, and then Joe closed it behind them, locked it, and pressed his back against it.

Austin met his eyes and shook his head, exhaustion legible in every line of his body. "People do this every year?"

Joe made a noise of assent. "Next year we're getting takeout."

He would've panicked about the assumption, but Austin snorted around a yawn and corrected, "Next year we're getting a dishwasher."

"Now we're talking." The yawn caught.

Joe had hoped they might have time tonight for another movie, some quality making-out-on-the-couch-like-teenagers, but he didn't think it would be very polite if he suggested it and then yawned into Austin's mouth or fell asleep and drooled on him.

"Bedtime, I think," Austin said before Joe could decide. He stepped forward into Joe's space and kissed him—a soft, gentle promise of a thing that left Joe swaying forward, leaning into his space. It ended almost as soon as it began, but Austin didn't pull away immediately.

Joe pressed a kiss to the curls at his hairline and inhaled. He smelled like turkey dinner. "You going upstairs?"

"Mmm," Austin agreed. "Tonight I am."

Oh. Joe swallowed. That was very specific. "And tomorrow?"

He didn't get an answer, unless you counted a pointed once-over and a spine-melting smile that felt very much like a promise.

Chapter Nineteen

CHRISTMAS DAWNED white and chilly. Austin squinted out his bedroom window at the too-bright world and the large fat flakes falling from the sky. A bit of Christmas magic.

He pulled on layers, dressed Pepa in her prosthetic, and headed out.

His girl ambled through the snow, and Austin meandered after her, phone in hand so he could take pictures. Dog prints in the snow, big fat snowflakes, Pepa with snow on her muzzle, the trees, the house.

Pepa seemed to have had enough of the snow and was leading Austin on a meandering loop back toward the house when a voice behind Austin said, "Can't say I blame her."

Austin looked over his shoulder at Joe and grinned. "She was having fun, but her paws must be getting a bit frozen." He shoved his phone back into his pocket and smiled. "It's probably past time to bring her back in."

Together they followed Pepa around the yard, when Joe suddenly stopped. "Is that Starling's truck in Linda's driveway?"

Austin followed his frozen gaze and, huh, yes, that indeed was Starling's truck parked behind Linda's Subaru. Well. Good for them.

"Did we accidentally set up my bestie with our new neighbour?" Joe sounded confused.

"Looks like it." Austin had to admit that Linda and Starling made sense. They had similar senses of humor—and neither of them had time for Joe's or Austin's shit.

"What the fuck."

He looked over at Joe's gobsmacked face and chuckled. "You can't say you're that surprised. I mean, they did spend most of last night mocking us and getting on like a house on fire."

"But…. Linda… didn't she say something about an ex-husband?"

Austin gave Joe a look. "Seriously?"

"Okay, yes, I know, this is a bad look on me." Joe waved his arms a bit. "I'm just surprised."

"So I see."

"Oh, shut up." Joe shoved his shoulder playfully. "I guess you knew Linda was bi, then, O wise one?"

Austin gave him a flat look. "Her favorite Christmas movie is an episode of *The X-Files*, Joe."

"There's no reason to be mean."

"I don't know why you're having a crisis here. Don't you want to live next door to your bestie?"

Joe spluttered. "Starling's not moving in—is she? They just got together yesterday, right?"

Austin laughed and took Joe's hand, then gently guided him away from their neighbor and back home.

The light mood carried them through the rest of their morning as they got ready to join the Romano family Christmas.

Austin had no idea what to expect from the event. It turned out that the Romano clan was huge. Nonna ("Do not call her Mrs. Romano, Austin, it's Nonna—*always* Nonna") hosted the event in her six-bedroom, four-bath mini mansion. Austin shot Joe a look when they pulled into the long driveway of the Amherstburg property. Austin was pretty sure he could see the golf course from the front yard.

"Joe, does your family have money?"

Joe coughed. "Nonno used to say he was 'not rich, just comfortable.' He died a few years ago, but Nonna hasn't exactly been a worried widow."

"Riiight. I can see that."

"Stop staring at my nonna's driveway and help me carry stuff into the house." The stuff in question was food, food, and more food, and also a beautiful wreath and potted plant for Nonna, who deserved a hostess gift.

Joe's family didn't otherwise do presents at this gathering. Austin was surprised, since he knew how much Joe enjoyed spoiling his own kids, but when he had asked about it a few days prior, Joe admitted that there were too many of them to try.

"How many young cousins do you have?" Austin asked, alarmed.

Joe's answer was wry. "We're Italian Catholics."

Austin digested that information. "Is that your way of saying that you don't actually know?" Joe didn't answer; instead he walked away. "Joe? Joe, how many people are going to be at this event? Joe?"

Christmas with the Romanos was like being in a Christmas movie, Austin decided. The whole event was noise and laughter and food. Austin was barely in the front door before he realised trying to keep track of names was going to be impossible.

The day left Austin buzzing with warmth in a way he hadn't experienced since the death of his great-aunt. Joe's family didn't question Austin's presence, just accepted that he was there and deserved to be treated with the same welcome and affection as anyone else in the house.

Austin found himself happily engaged in conversation with Joe's uncle Luca for nearly an hour once he learned that Luca was the owner of the Ferrari Roma Spider in the driveway—Austin cried inside about him driving it in the snow—and Luca learned that Austin was a mechanic. They even tramped outside so Luca could show her off and Austin could drool over her engine. Austin might not have made his whole personality about cars, but he couldn't resist the power of this engine or the classic lines of a Roma Spider's body.

They probably would have stayed outside even longer if Joe hadn't come out to drag them to the dinner table.

If Austin had thought the spread at their place was incredible, Nonna's offerings overwhelmed him completely. He couldn't identify half the dishes, but he tried every one of them anyway. Joe had obviously gotten his cooking abilities from Nonna, and he also obviously had a way to go to catch up to her, and when Austin voiced that thought out loud, Nonna beamed at him and cupped his cheek like Austin was one of her own grandchildren.

"You're a nice boy," she told him. "Not like that Paul." She tutted and turned her attention to Joe. "Giuseppe, you keep this one around."

Joe went scarlet as Younger Female Cousin Number Seven snickered. Austin got a slightly envious look from what's-his-name's pregnant girlfriend, who was apparently going to be persona non grata until either her particular Romeo Romano put a ring on it or the kid entered the world and became eligible to be showered in Nonna's love. He couldn't blame the girlfriend.

He couldn't blame her baby daddy either. What kind of insanity would a wedding in this family even look like if Christmas was an event of several dozen people? He didn't imagine Nonna would be satisfied with a small affair.

But it was too early to get anxiety about that. That would be putting the cart firmly before the horse. Austin had plenty of time to panic about nuptials later.

But he couldn't help thinking about it as dinner ended and people dispersed to various regions of the house. There was a pool table downstairs, and ping-pong, and the youngest kids—children of Joe's cousins—took over the TV room to play some kind of board game. Austin volunteered for kitchen cleanup with the mom-to-be, thinking maybe they could help each other out, but Uncle Marco—possibly her baby-granddaddy?—shushed her and sent her off to have a nap, saying he'd take her place. She did look exhausted, and she thanked them both profusely as she snuck off, presumably to one of the many guest bedrooms.

Cleanup promised to be a long, terrible job until Austin got a proper look at the kitchen and realized Nonna had *two dishwashers*, which was the most over-the-top rich-person thing he could think of but for which he was immediately grateful. Plates and cutlery went in one, serving dishes in another, which left Austin and Marco just a football field length's worth of pots and pans to hand-wash.

"How'd your man get out of this?" Marco teased as they started rolling up their sleeves.

"I think someone dragged him off to play pool," Austin admitted. "But I don't mind. Uh, I need a minute to decompress, really."

"We are a lot," Marco agreed. "I heard you've been fixing up the house?"

They chatted easily as they blasted through the dishes, first about renovations, then the Romano family construction business. "You let me know if you ever need anything. Tile, fixtures, whatever. Rich people are *always* changing their minds after their shit gets ordered," Marco said.

"Definitely let me know if anybody decides they don't want their dishwasher," Austin answered before he could help himself, and Marco cackled.

They got halfway through the mess before Maria and Uncle Luca came to spell them off, and Austin went downstairs to watch Joe finish wiping the pool table with Older Male Cousin Number Five.

It was *nice*, Austin thought, this kind of wild, affectionate family affair, even if it was boisterous and overwhelming in a hundred different ways. But maybe his favorite thing about it was that dinner had been scheduled for three so everything could wrap up early to get the wee ones and their great-grandmother to bed at a decent hour. Uncle Luca saw everybody off at the door with a bottle of his homemade red wine— Austin caught Joe's eye as he accepted theirs and felt heat lick up his spine—and then they were free, sent off into the night together.

For the first few minutes into the drive, they didn't say anything. Austin used the time to recalibrate; he was half sure he'd been shouting all night to be heard and just hadn't noticed. His ears hurt.

But once the noise in his head quieted, he started thinking instead— about the Ferrari in the driveway… and the Lexus, and the Land Rover, and Uncle Marco's Escalade. Joe's mom had a Cadillac too, but a car, not an SUV, several model years old.

Obviously, none of those uncles were driving their fancy sports cars to their job sites, except maybe Marco if he was picking up a crew, so those weren't their daily drivers. But Joe just had his work truck, steady and reliable, no frills unless you counted the heated steering wheel and seats, which when Joe's work sometimes included removing icy fallen trees, Austin did not.

"Hey, Joe," Austin said without engaging his brain.

"Mm?"

"Are you the family poor kid?"

Joe barked a laugh. "God, probably. Why, you thinking about leaving me for Uncle Luca? The way he looked at you when you were talking about the Ferrari, I thought he might propose."

Speaking of heated seats, Austin flipped his on and snuggled back against the headrest. "How dare you. You've seen the car I drive. My affections cannot be bought with money or automobiles. Only houses and house pets and asshole teenagers."

He felt more than saw Joe's eyes on him as they passed under a rare streetlight on a back country road. "Bullshit," Joe said. "You're also a slut for homemade dinners and red wine."

God, Austin liked him so much it felt like he might burst with it. It was a heady feeling and a terrifying one. Austin had never had a boyfriend before, but he'd never had a family either—never had so much to lose if this went sour.

Please, please don't let it go sour.

"Tell you a secret," he said, a handful of tire rotations before they reached the driveway.

"Mm," Joe said again.

Austin nudged the bottle braced between his thighs. "The wine's not really necessary."

Linda had messaged midafternoon when the Romanos were serving up the Christmas feast, which Austin hadn't seen until his kitchen self-banishment.

I've stolen your dog for the day so you don't have to worry about her. The cats are in the breezeway. Merry Christmas and see you in the morning!

Now Austin thought warmly of her as he considered the empty house that awaited. Nothing and no one stood between him and Joe enjoying each other the moment they walked in. The moment they shed their boots and coats, Austin pounced.

He twined his arms around Joe's shoulders and pulled him into a scorching kiss. After two days of family time and Christmas cheer and tradition, Austin was warmed from toes to head, full of happiness and affection like he couldn't remember. And he had Joe to thank.

He had very specific thoughts about how to thank him.

"Fuck," Joe whispered, sucking bruises into Austin's neck.

Austin moaned and agreed, "Yes, that."

Joe chuckled. "Thinking about fucking me again?"

Austin had definitely thought about that since the first night. But he was also aware of the deal they'd struck. He licked his lips and said, "I think it's your turn."

Joe froze, then pulled back enough to look Austin in the eye. "Are you sure?"

Austin didn't bottom with his random hookups. He didn't trust them enough to be so vulnerable. But Joe wasn't a random hookup.

Instead of answering aloud, he leaned in for another kiss. Hopefully the passionate press of lips and tongue would hide his uncertainty. Besides, it didn't need to be his favorite physical experience if it brought him closer to Joe in this specific intimate way.

Joe gripped his hips and guided him backward, pushing and shoving him with a clear goal in mind, but when Austin pulled back to gasp for air, he found they were farther from the master bedroom, not closer.

"What?"

"I had an idea about you and the table."

Austin swallowed, flushing at the thought. "The table?"

"Well, you did make it hip height for me."

"Oh." He swallowed, flushing with heat. "A happy accident."

"Think our work is strong enough to hold you?"

"Only one way to find out."

"I've got faith in us," Joe said, and then he gripped Austin under the thighs and hoisted him onto the table.

Austin grunted and pushed his tongue into Joe's mouth to muffle it. Manhandling hadn't been a major feature in his sex life before, but it looked like Joe was keen to make it a regular occurrence.

The next few minutes passed in a blur of kisses and touches and hasty clothing removal.

"The problem," Austin gasped as Joe bit his neck.

"Hmm?"

"Wha—? Oh, the problem with the table is the lack of, of lube—oh!"

Joe pulled back and arched an eyebrow. "That's not a problem," he asserted. Then he pulled up a chair as if settling in for a feast and then… got eating.

Austin arched his back, stunned by the touch of Joe's tongue against his hole. He'd never—

Joe didn't seem to have any such inexperience. He pressed in so he could lick, swipe, and stab. With nothing else to grab apart from the smooth surface of the island, Austin tangled his fingers in his own hair and gasped at the ceiling, stunned. His thighs trembled under Joe's hands, Joe's fingers pressing into the muscle as he held Austin open. *There's a tongue— that's Joe's tongue in my ass, oh my God.* The filthy thought made it hotter. So did the dirty, sloppy, wet sounds Joe was making. The longer he ate, the louder he got, and the louder Austin got in turn. He couldn't… he—

Joe pulled back gasping and—Austin peeked down between his legs—looking at Austin's wet hole. Austin slammed his eyes shut and shuddered. A trembling moan escaped him when Joe placed a teasing, closed-mouth kiss to the twitching muscle.

"Good?" Joe breathed, the word a hot whisper on wet, stubble-burned skin.

Austin let out a shaky laugh, incredulous. As if Joe didn't know. Austin would be lucky if Linda hadn't heard him moaning. "Yeah, sweet thing, feels real good, but you're gonna need to work a little harder if you want me to take your cock." If they had to abandon the plan to fuck on the table, well, there was always next time.

"I can work harder," Joe promised the top of Austin's thigh.

Maybe Austin should've phrased that differently. It was the lube situation he was worried about, not Joe's work ethic. But he didn't need to; a second later Joe mouthed sloppily at the base of Austin's cock and a plastic click echoed through the kitchen.

Austin twitched at the sound, felt Joe smile into the crease of his thigh. "Did you… did you have lube in your pocket all day?" *At Christmas with your family?*

The blunt pressure of a fingertip sliding in the wet mess around his hole. Joe sucked gently at his balls. "Wanted to be prepared."

"To fuck me as soon as we got in the door? I'm—" Joe pushed the finger inside. Austin breathed through it, let his thighs fall open farther. It felt—strange, but good. "I'm flattered."

The strangeness evaporated in a spark of pleasure as Joe curled his finger up to press on Austin's prostate. Precome blurted from his cock as his hips tried to thrust upward, but he didn't have any leverage; his heels were hanging off the side of the table.

At least until Joe decided Austin's left thigh was in the way of him getting fingered properly, and propped it up on his own shoulder.

"Okay?" Joe asked, hoarse and breathless, like he was the one with two fingers in his ass and Austin's mouth between his legs, sucking bites onto his thighs.

"Good," Austin told him, shamelessly using Joe's shoulder to lift his hips. Fuck it, he basically asked for this, and Joe's fingers—he was playing Austin a lot better than he played piano, and he was pretty good at the piano. The world started melting around the edges. Austin scrabbled his nails against the tabletop. He felt like he might fly off it. "One more."

Joe obeyed immediately, no second-guessing, which Austin appreciated even if the stretch burned. But he couldn't focus on that when Joe was fucking three fingers into him, not particularly carefully, but controlled enough to hit the right spot every fourth stroke or so, so that Austin's dick was hard and leaking. He could feel the precome dripping down his cock, over his balls, down to where Joe was fucking in and out of him.

Austin couldn't have said what did it, if it was the squelching noise, the breadth of Joe's fingers, or just weeks of anticipation, but *something*—the slack-jawed expression on Joe's face, the way he was looking at Austin like his own personal Christmas miracle—was the last straw. He leveraged his right foot up too, hooked it around the back of Joe's neck, nudged him up. "Joe." He meant to sound demanding; the word emerged plaintive. "Give me your cock."

He didn't know what he would've done if Joe hadn't scrambled to pull himself to his feet, to lube his dick with a hand Austin could see plainly, even in the dark, was shaking. Begged, maybe, but he didn't want to, and Joe didn't seem to need it. He pulled Austin toward the edge of the table with two hands under his ass, and holy fuck that was Joe's cock sliding between his asscheeks, nudging against his open hole—

"*Fuck*," Joe said brokenly as the tip of him pushed inside.

Fuck, Austin agreed as he arched his back on the table. Pleasure rocketed up and down his spine, and he curled his leg to pull Joe forward. His *hearing* went out, his eyes rolled back in his head, his muscles clenched, and—

Joe's hips slapped against his ass and the head of his cock ground into Austin's prostate.

"God," Austin said—thought he said—he didn't hear the word as it escaped him, but he shaped it on his lips as his breath caught in his throat and his dick spasmed between them, shooting up his chest.

Above him, Joe stilled, chest heaving, eyes dark and wanting as he ran them up Austin's body. "Did you just—?"

Austin didn't have the blood to spare for a flush or the brain space for embarrassment. His body still crackled with electricity. He wanted more. "Don't *stop*," he demanded, light-headed.

Joe swallowed audibly but didn't argue. He gently rolled his hips, as if testing Austin's ability to keep going. But Austin hadn't been lying; the body was as willing as the mind.

As Joe slowly pressed back in, his cock slid over Austin's prostate once again, sending shivery sparks to the tips of his toes. Austin arched his back. God, it was—

He was a panting, shivery mess. He couldn't believe…. Austin had known in theory that bottoming felt good for people. But he hadn't anticipated how all-encompassing it would be. The stretch of his hole, the heat, weight, and girth of Joe's cock inside, pressing against him, each bump against his prostate, the wet slick slide of skin, the sight and feeling of Joe between his thighs.

If Austin had known, maybe he'd have done this before today.

"Yeah, darling, that's it," Joe panted. "Fuck, you feel so good."

Austin tried to say, "so do you," but Joe thrust back in at a new angle and pushed a long, high moan out of him instead.

Then again, Austin didn't think it would have been as good with anyone else. Joe hungrily watched him, raking his eyes over Austin and responding to every twitch and sound Austin made, trying to get his thrusts just right to make it good.

"Yeah? Like that?"

"Yes," Austin managed. "There. So, so good." He arched his back again and pressed his hips up into Joe's thrusts. It felt too damned good. He turned his head, pressing his cheek into the table, trying to ground himself, to cool down, but each press of Joe's cock had his head spinning, his cock jerking and drooling.

He pulled his hair and said something. He didn't know what—he couldn't hear himself over the pounding of his own blood.

His second orgasm caught him as off guard as the first.

Neither of them touched his dick, but Joe rolled his hips in several short, hard thrusts that rammed Austin's prostate, and his muscles tightened and clamped tight around Joe's dick. His legs flexed and pulled Joe tight to him. Austin's cock blurted all over his stomach but didn't go soft. It stayed angry red, bumping his belly, as Joe fucked him through his spine-melting orgasm.

"Fuck, darling. Did you come again?"

Austin whimpered. He'd tightened enough that Joe's cock felt bigger, thicker inside him, but no less delicious.

"Do you need me to stop?" Joe held himself still, trembling with the effort.

The thought of Joe thrusting was overwhelming, but the thought of him pulling out was unbearable.

"No." He managed to make his mouth work for words. "I want you to come inside me." He lifted his spaghetti arms to cup Joe's flushed face. "Please, sweet thing?"

Joe's hips were hitching before Austin could brace himself, and soon they were pressed together chest to chest while Joe chased his orgasm.

Austin wrapped his arms around his shoulders and dug his nails into Joe's back and moaned.

Joe lost his steady rhythm, then pushed in hard and froze, and warmth filled Austin. Joe buried his face in Austin's neck and his hips hitched and everything was so much wetter, and—God, Joe hadn't grabbed a condom. His come was in Austin's ass and leaking out of it. That was so hot.

Joe crumpled, panting against him. Austin stroked his hair and ignored his drooling hard cock pressed between their bellies.

Joe eventually pushed himself up so he hovered over Austin and kissed him, sloppy and sweet. Then he locked their gazes. "You're still hard."

"Yeah." Austin's voice cracked. His body had never done this before.

Joe kissed him again, then pulled his dick out in a slow, wet slide.

Austin whined.

Joe sat back between his thighs and moaned at what he saw. "Fuck, darling, you're covered in it." He swiped up some of the come leaking out and pushed it back in with two fingers.

Austin's brain short-circuited. "Who—" He whimpered. "Whose fault is that?"

"*Mine*," Joe growled. Then, before Austin could say anything else, he shoved his fingers against Austin's prostate and swallowed his cock. The warm suction and unerring fingers brought Austin to one more brain-melting climax.

He lost control of his mouth and said… *something* while his hands clenched in Joe's hair and his thighs tried to clamp around his ears.

When he came back to himself, Joe was watching him from his vantage point, his cheek pressed to Austin's thigh and his fingers still in his ass.

Austin flushed red—or would have if he wasn't already sex flushed. "What?"

"So," Joe said, "you forgot to mention that your prostate is magical."

Austin threw one limp arm over his face. "Can you forget to mention something you didn't know?"

Even with his vision blocked, he could feel Joe's eyes on him. A moment later Joe lifted his arm away from his face. His expression was unreadable. "Are you telling me," he said quietly, "that you've never bottomed before and you let me *fuck you on the kitchen table like an animal*?"

"*Let*? I was there for the decision-making process," Austin protested, salty. He had a bit more agency than that, thanks. He definitely remembered giving several key directions, all of which Joe had followed to the letter.

But then Joe's expression went sharp and smug and—"Does that mean no one else ever made you come three times?"

God, he was going to be insufferable, but it was hard to be mad about it. "Nobody else is as good at following instructions as you." Austin definitely deserved some of the credit.

Joe snorted. "I'll take it." He pursed his lips as he considered the tableau of Austin, the table, and three loads of come. "You did make kind of a mess, though."

Now *that* Austin wasn't taking all the credit for. "I had some help."

Joe flushed as he trailed his eyes down Austin's body—his dick wasn't getting hard again without chemical intervention, no matter how that gaze made Austin feel—until it rested between Austin's legs, at which point he seemed to realize he hadn't just fucked Austin on their kitchen table, he'd fucked him *raw*. "Jesus, uh—" He swallowed. "Guess we got a little carried away, but it's—I'm so sorry, I promise I—"

Austin put him out of his misery. "Joe. I'm gonna go out on a limb and guess you were tested when you figured out Paul was cheating on you."

Joe exhaled shakily. "Yeah, obviously. Right after and then again a couple months later."

"And I'm gonna go a little farther out on that limb and say those test results were either negative of anything serious or you got treated for the clap or whatever—"

Joe flushed. "They were negative," he muttered. "Jesus."

"—because otherwise you would've told me about it before we fucked the first time. So we're fine." Because Austin was not going to say *it was hot*. Joe's ego did not need any stroking at this point. "Other than someone's gonna have to disinfect this table, and I think it should be you."

"I think I have to peel you off it first," Joe offered after a moment.

"Maybe get a towel," Austin suggested, "'cause, like, if I stand up—" He was going to leave a trail all the way to the bathroom, was what he was getting at.

"Yeah, uh…." And then Joe bent and pressed his shoulder to Austin's chest, grabbed his arm, and stood again, now with Austin slung over his shoulder. "Maybe I should just…?"

"Jesus," Austin laughed. "You better not drop me."

Joe didn't drop him. He carried him all the way to the bathroom and deposited him in the shower, then retreated to resanctify the kitchen table before their come could become a permanent part of the finish.

Austin was debating whether to get out of the shower or plug the drain and sink into a relaxing bath when the curtain pulled back and Joe climbed in with him, half hard again.

"Keep that thing away from my ass." Austin might've had a good time, but there were *limits*. But Joe just grinned and kissed him and then buried his face and his teeth in Austin's neck, his cock rubbing between their bellies until he spilled between them.

Breathing hard, Austin fumbled one-handed to turn off the water, which was running lukewarm. "All right," he said, "is this a side effect of that whole 'taking it slow' thing, or is this just, like, part of actual dating nobody told me about?"

"Fuck if I know," Joe said without removing his head from Austin's shoulder. "I definitely never made Paul do that three times in a row."

Austin snorted and nudged him aside so he could grab their towels.

They dried off, and Austin stole one of Joe's hoodies and a pair of pajama pants because he didn't trust his legs to take him up the stairs. Then he popped a couple Advil in anticipation of a new and interesting set of aches tomorrow and looked for something good on TV while Joe went to collect Pepa from Linda's. The kittens had been released from their breezeway prison and took their time inspecting the house, as if to make sure Joe and Austin hadn't burned the place down in their exile, then lined up to greet Pepa and Joe at the door.

It was sweet. Domestic. Utterly ruinous too, to know life could be like this—fun and hot and overwhelmingly filthy sex, preceded by a nice family dinner and followed up with a shower and cuddling on the couch watching *The Muppet Christmas Carol*. Austin's life had never been so full.

So naturally the peaceful evening was interrupted by frantic knocking at the front door.

Chapter Twenty

JOE LAY loose-limbed on the couch, playing with Austin's unbound hair while he pretended to rewatch Gonzo narrate a Christmas classic.

He was too pleasure-drunk to focus that intensely on anything. Well, other than the memory of Austin laid out on the table, begging and squirming on Joe's cock. Joe had always considered himself more verse than anything, but after tonight he understood the appeal of exclusive topping. To do otherwise almost felt criminal. A waste of that delicious ass.

Mm, speaking of, maybe Austin would be willing to let Joe kiss it better in the morning? He probably wouldn't want to take Joe's dick again so soon. Joe remembered the days after his first time. Which, he couldn't believe Austin hadn't told him. Well, he could—it was totally in character. Maybe Joe should have guessed, what with the way Austin seemed to blow hot and cold on the idea.

Joe was mid sleepy-morning-rimjob-fantasy when the knock startled Pepa to her feet. She looked toward the front hall, and Joe and Austin shared a look. It was late on Christmas Day. Whoever, whatever, was at the door couldn't be good news.

Dread formed a pit in Joe's stomach. No. Not today.

He pushed those thoughts away, refusing to borrow trouble, and hoisted himself off the couch.

"Should I—"

Joe shook his head. "I'll holler if I need help."

He swallowed and metaphorically crossed all his fingers and toes before he gripped the doorknob and swung the door open.

Will stood on the porch, a backpack slumped at his feet.

It had apparently started to drizzle at some point after Joe got home with Pepa, and Will was wet and bedraggled. His boots were caked in mud, and he shivered as he stared up at Joe. He didn't have to say anything. They both knew what had happened. The thing they'd both been dreading and preparing for. Joe just opened his arms and pulled him in.

Will tucked his face into Joe's neck, and Joe held him close and ignored the slight tremble running through the gangly frame. Will was still shorter, though his last growth spurt had brought him eyes-to-nose with Joe, and Joe was beginning to suspect his most fragile baby might end up the tallest.

"Joe?" Austin stood down the hall, watching them with guarded, unhappy eyes.

Will tensed in his arms, though he kept his face hidden.

"Austin, can you make up some hot cocoa? I've got a craving," Joe said as neutrally as possible. Once Austin had slipped into the kitchen, Joe ushered Will to the bathroom, where he could dry off and change.

"Do you have everything you need?" Joe nodded toward the bag Will had clutched in his hands.

Will nodded. "I kept it packed by the door just in case...." Just in case his parents found out he was gay and threw him out of the house without giving him time to pack.

"Okay. Shout if you need anything."

Joe found Austin in the kitchen, staring blankly at three empty mugs while the kettle steamed next to him.

"Hey."

Austin jumped. He smiled wanly at Joe. "He okay?"

"As he can be. It's not like we didn't know this was coming."

They'd made up three cups by the time Will emerged from the bathroom, and he'd quietly accepted the hot drink. After some whispered debate, they brought Will to the living room and settled him onto the couch.

"So, Will, do you want to talk, or do you want to watch ghostly Muppets harass Michael Caine?"

"Muppets, please," he all but whispered.

By the time the credits rolled, Will was curled up in the corner of the couch looking small and vulnerable. Joe wished he could fix this problem like he had helped fix Will's backstroke.

Austin picked up the dirty dishes and announced he would take Pepa out for one last pee.

"C'mon," Joe said to Will. "Let's get you settled upstairs."

He had already seen the bedroom Joe had outfitted for him, just yesterday in fact, as Joe had presented it as a gift.

But Will hadn't seen the items already in the dresser drawers. Joe tried not to make it a big deal, kept his voice soft when he pulled one open and said, "Just in case you don't have any pajamas."

Will looked at the contents of the drawer. Then with shaking hands he pulled open the rest of them. There were some new pairs of socks and underwear, as well as some hand-me-downs from Joe's wardrobe and a few items unearthed from the house. In the top drawer, next to the new underthings, were a folded rainbow sweatshirt and a T-shirt that read, in bubbly multicolored letters, *My Dad Loves Me*.

Will burst into tears.

Unthinking, Joe lunged in his direction and wrapped Will up in a tight hug.

After several long moments, Will pulled away and angrily wiped at his cheeks. "They didn't even let me grab my keys or phone."

"I'll buy you a new one," Joe promised.

Will snorted. "You shouldn't have to."

"I know. But I will."

"It's not fair."

"I know."

"I hate them!"

"Totally valid," Joe agreed, instead of *me too*. Of all the challenges he'd faced as an ad hoc parent, this one was by far the biggest, most dramatic, and yet probably the one that Joe was best prepared for. From the moment Will had come out to him, Joe had been preparing for this. That included reading parenting guides on how to support grieving teens.

Will slumped, the fight leeching out of him. "I don't hate them," he whispered.

That's okay. I'll do it for you. Joe placed a comforting hand on his shoulder. "Also valid."

Will took a shuddering breath and managed a small smile. "You know you're really good at this dad thing, right?"

"You know you make it easy, right?"

Pain flashed across Will's face, but he didn't argue.

With one last hug and promises to be right downstairs if Will needed him for anything, Joe said good night and went to find Austin.

Because—well.

Austin liked the kids, sure. He was great with them, even. Joe thought hanging out with them might even have some kind of healing built in, since he doubted young Austin had much opportunity to actually *be* a kid. But Joe didn't think suddenly becoming the de facto parents of a teenager was in the same league as adopting a bunch of animals. Austin might be okay with Will living here in theory, and he might tease Joe about being a teen dad, but that didn't mean he wanted to date a dad for real.

You'd think they actually would have talked about this. But they hadn't, so now Joe had to go destroy the dregs of the afterglow with serious relationship talk.

A knot formed in his stomach.

It had to be too much, didn't it? Austin hadn't signed up for this. He'd—

"Hey."

Joe blinked. Somehow he'd made it down the stairs. Austin waited at the bottom, still wearing Joe's sweatshirt and pajama bottoms. They were too long for him, flopping halfway over his feet. "Hey. He's, uh…."

Austin opened his arms.

Joe fell into them, clinging tightly. "Jesus," he whispered, shaking. "I hate them—I hate them *so much*, what the fuck. He's just a kid, he's their *kid*. They're supposed to love him. Why can't they—"

"Hey," Austin said again, a rough whisper in return. "He's got you, right? It's gonna suck, but it'll be okay."

Joe's eyes burned, and he buried his face in Austin's hair. "What the fuck am I doing?"

"What you always do. Taking care of people."

He swallowed against the hope rising in his throat. "It's not—it's not exactly taking things slow, though, is it? If you don't want—"

Austin pulled back, took Joe's face in both hands. "Hey." His eyes were dark and serious. "You think I didn't know this was a possibility? The kids have been invading the house since day one. You think—what, I'm going to be upset you're making sure a kid doesn't go through the hell I went through? You think the way you are with those kids isn't half the reason I even—"

He cut himself off. *Going slow*, Joe reminded himself and forced a breath into his lungs.

"Okay, yeah." He nodded. Austin didn't let go of his face, but he did thumb away a drop of wetness. Fuck, Joe was a mess. "But that's not the same as, you know, 'surprise, honey, we have a teenager now.'"

"Eh," Austin said, deliberately casual. "He's in grade twelve. He's gotta be mostly self-sufficient, right? We'll figure it out."

We.

"Okay," Joe said again. "Okay. Jesus, what a fucking day."

Austin huffed. "You said it." He bent Joe's head toward him and kissed his nose. "Come on. We should get some sleep. I have a feeling it's going to be a busy day tomorrow."

Chapter Twenty-One

IF AUSTIN were being perfectly honest with himself—which he was inclined to avoid this morning—he would admit he was freaking out.

It wasn't just Will moving in. Austin had anticipated that, even if he'd hoped for Will's sake it wouldn't have to happen. It was that, *plus* their Christmas party, *plus* meeting Joe's enormous extended family of uncomfortably wealthy people, *plus* transcendent sex that had his brain leaking out his ears, all coupled with the knowledge that *slow* had well and truly gone right out the fucking window.

Also, they hadn't told the kids they were dating, but given that Austin had slept in Joe's bed last night and not his own, which was in the room next to Will's, it certainly wasn't going to be a secret for long, and he didn't know how that was going to play out considering he was 95 percent sure Will was sweet on him.

Joy.

But he couldn't freak out. It wasn't his place. Will, who'd basically been disowned last night, got to freak out. Joe, who was going to be Will's primary point of support and parent and whatever, got to freak out. Austin, whose participation in this situation was basically "roommate," did not get to freak out. He just needed to be there when Joe and Will did.

It was a lot to suddenly shoulder when he'd spent so much of his life alone, but he wouldn't trade it, so he'd have to figure it out.

He woke up sore, Joe still passed out next to him. The critters weren't stirring yet, so it must still be early. He didn't hear anything from upstairs either.

He hauled his ass out of bed and went to find something to eat so he could grab a couple Advil without upsetting his stomach. Then he took Pepa out for a pee, fed the cats, and put the coffee on. He might not be a morning person, but Joe would need the sleep this morning more than Austin did.

To his surprise, Will stirred before Joe. He crept down the stairs almost silently, then paused at the bottom, like he wasn't sure if anyone else was awake.

"In the kitchen," Austin said softly. "Coffee?"

A moment later Will shuffled in, puffy-faced, hands stuffed in the pocket of his oversize hoodie.

"Hey," Austin offered when Will didn't say anything. "Uh, Joe's not up yet, but there's bread for toast and cereal in the pantry."

Will nodded wordlessly and helped himself to a bowl, a mug, cereal, milk. He was putting them on the table when Austin realized they were going to eat breakfast together at the table Joe fucked him on the night before. "He's not, like, getting sick or anything?"

"No, no, just, uh… long couple days, you know? With all the cooking." And fucking. And emotional upheaval. Austin spotted a splash of white on the table and had a second of pure, hysterical panic before he realized it was milk.

Another nod. Will picked up his spoon. Then, finally, he raised his eyes and looked Austin in the face.

Or, well. Austin *expected* Will to look him in the face, but his eyes sort of stopped when they got most of the way there, on the side of Austin's neck.

The side Joe had fastened his mouth to in the shower last night.

Austin had never checked if there was a mark, but from the expression on Will's face, he didn't need to.

Will's eyes went wide—or as wide as they could given the amount of crying Austin suspected they'd done last night—and his face paled as he put together the pieces. "Oh my God. I didn't—um. I didn't want to like—interrupt—"

Of all the fucking days for Joe to sleep in. "Hey, no," Austin said. "You definitely didn't." Will was several orgasms too late to interrupt, but he didn't need to know that. "And even if you had—it's not like we'd be mad about it."

We, like him and Joe, a unit. Was that the wrong thing to say? Was he, like, rubbing it in?

Was he being pretty ridiculous, because Will obviously had bigger things to be upset about right now than Joe and Austin?

"Right," Will said after a moment, giving Austin absolutely nothing. He pulled his cereal toward himself.

The encounter gave Austin hope. Living with a teenager would be weird, but ultimately everything would work out. They'd have some awkward moments, but they were all adults or mostly adults and they could get through them.

The optimism lasted until Will's sulk wore off, which was about day three.

Austin didn't mean to sound callous. Will was certainly entitled to a whole range of emotions right now, and most of them were negative. Austin had been there himself.

But on day three the grief turned to anger, and with no appropriate targets around, Will snapped at Joe and Austin instead. Of course he did—Austin understood. For the most part, he let the hostility wash over him. Austin had grown up in the system. Will couldn't say anything Austin hadn't heard in a group home. He and Joe and the kitchen could weather a few slammed cupboard doors.

There were other challenges too. More than once, Joe went to the refrigerator to start making dinner only to find the ingredients had been consumed by a hungry teen. They would have adjusted to that with no problem if not for the sudden increase in the grocery bill. Austin had always been frugal, shopping sales and discount grocery stores, but Joe had grown up with money. When he cooked, he liked his creature comforts and fancy ingredients.

Finally, Austin had to wonder what was going to happen when it came time to sell the house. Three guys and four pets—would they find a rental that could fit them all? Or would he and Joe go back to living separately? The ugly apartment over Austin's garage had never held less appeal.

Austin didn't know what would happen. But he did know that something had to change. They couldn't afford to live like this.

A WEEK AFTER Will moved in, Joe curled up with Austin in bed and asked, "Do the fairies ever swap eighteen-year-olds with changelings?"

Austin snorted. "It hasn't been that bad."

Joe pulled back enough to look Austin in the eye. "You can't believe that."

"I think maybe stress is making you exaggerate a bit." Austin carved his fingers through Joe's hair, making him melt under the attention.

"Maybe a little," Joe admitted, because Will wasn't acting like a whole new person, but he was definitely being more teenagery than usual.

Will had always been quiet, but for the past seven days he'd become downright sullen. He joined Joe and Austin for meals when called, but said little. He spent his time holed up in his room unless the kids were over to drag him out. Gavin, Alex, and Meg were a blessing, as they dedicated their holidays to distracting and cheering up Will.

Three days after Christmas, Joe drove Gavin and Will to his parents' house in the hopes of retrieving Will's stuff, but Gavin and Will were blocked from the house while Will's dad screamed that he'd thrown everything out.

Gavin practically had to carry Will back to the car, where Joe had sat waiting in the naïve hope that the kids would have more luck without his presence—Will's parents never cared for Joe—but once home, Will yelled and raged and threw a few rocks at trees in the yard while Gavin stayed by his side and Joe watched helplessly from the house.

The days following that encounter were the worst. Joe was willing to give Will latitude—God only knew how heartbroken and angry Joe would've been in his place—but it wasn't easy when the kid was using his quick wit and sharp tongue to cut. He could draw blood when he wanted, and lately that seemed to be *all* he wanted.

"Maybe things will get easier once they're back at school?" Austin suggested hopefully.

Spoiler alert—they were not.

First of all, Will was an even worse person in the morning than Austin. Second, he took the world's longest showers and somehow managed to use all the hot water. On Will's first Tuesday back in classes, Joe had resigned himself to a lukewarm-at-best shower in the steam-filled bathroom, only to look into the tub and find an inch of water, the drain clogged in a suspiciously familiar way.

"You know what," he said out loud, "I can skip a shower this morning." He poured a cup of bleach into the tub. He could deal with it later. And then, after dropping Will off at school, which he had to do every morning because none of the buses came out this far and there was no one in carpooling range, he went to Shoppers and bought an enormous bottle of lube and a nine-pack of Kleenex, which he set in the middle of Will's bed with a note that just said *The pipes in this house are too old for that.*

What else was he going to do? This situation was challenging enough for everyone without confronting someone for jerking off in the shower.

A week into the new routine, Joe was thinking about the practicalities of buying Will his own car.

"You can't reward his bad company with a car," Austin said dryly over his glass of wine.

Will was at Gavin's, working on a school project, so they had the house to themselves for the first evening in two weeks.

"It's not because of that," Joe protested. Austin arched an eyebrow. "Okay, not just because of that. Being tied to a high-school schedule sucks." It was more than just a little inconvenient. At least Will was old enough to wait around for a ride if Gavin wasn't up for driving him home.

"We could split the driving," Austin suggested, but Joe shook his head.

"I can't ask that of you."

"Who's asking? I'm offering."

"I know. But I'm saying no. The last thing you two need is to be stuck alone in a car together every day."

Their relationship was strained enough as it was. Will didn't seem to know what to do with Austin or how to cope with his feelings. Hell, Joe doubted Will fully understood his own feelings right now, and whether he was jealous of Joe for being with Austin or of Austin for stealing Joe's attention when Will so desperately craved it. Joe suspected that it was more the latter than the former, as he doubted Will had been any more serious about Austin than he would have been about a crush on a teacher. He could remember how early crushes felt more comfortable the less attainable they were. Still, seeing Joe and Austin together was clearly not easy for Will, and as a result, Austin was getting less conversation from Will than Joe was.

"Will and I have history. We'll survive this. I don't want to mess up the chances of the two of you getting along in the future." Joe really hoped there was a future for the three of them, and he didn't want to do anything that put it at risk.

So Austin didn't offer any more carpooling, but he put his foot down on the car.

"We don't need it, and we can't afford the insurance. Not if we want two working baths someday."

"Fine," Joe huffed.

Another downside to having a live-in teenager? It curtailed their sex life to quiet and rushed hand- and blowjobs. But he forgot all about his moody son when Austin smirked and called him a good boy.

Joe flushed but met Austin's gaze. He licked his lips. "Want to take advantage of the empty house to see if three orgasms is standard for you?"

Austin turned scarlet. "Be still my heart." But he put down his wineglass and headed for the bedroom, so Joe figured he was into it.

Turned out Austin was also into having a dick up his ass even without the novelty. He was just as loud and sensitive, and he writhed so beautifully on Joe's cock that Joe nearly threw his back out trying to obey each wordless direction for how to make Austin feel good.

Three orgasms? Not a fluke.

"I wonder if you could do four or five," Joe mused, face smushed into Austin's neck.

Austin grunted.

"Though we can't test that when Will's home. You're also a screamer."

Another grunt, and Austin flailed a limp arm in Joe's direction. Joe caught it and laced their fingers together.

"Asshole."

"You're great too, darling," Joe crooned and kissed his cheek.

In a moment, he would drag himself out of bed so he could start the cleanup. Gavin had texted earlier to say he'd drop Will home around nine, so they only had a couple of hours to get presentable. But for now he was content to enjoy the reprieve from sullen teenager that their bed offered.

At least he was until the phone rang.

"Tell them I'm dead," Austin grumbled, digging his face under a pillow.

Joe fumbled on the nightstand. "It's not for you."

One of his feet nudged Joe's shin. "Tell them you're busy taking care of me because I'm dead."

But it was Starling, and Joe had spent weeks stockpiling ammunition about her supersonic relationship with Linda, and blasting her about it was his preferred expression of joy, after fucking Austin into Jell-O, so he picked up. "Well, if it isn't the pot calling the kettle."

"Hi, Joe," Starling said, all false brightness. "Surprised Austin let you off your leash long enough to get to the phone."

The volume must've been loud enough for Austin to hear, because he raised his hand with one finger pointed.

"He says fuck you," Joe relayed.

"I'd say it back, but I know what your post-sex voice sounds like. Will out today?"

"You and Starling need to set boundaries," Austin grumbled.

Joe soothed him with scalp scritches. "For now," he said. "What's up? Haven't seen your truck at Linda's in *hours*. Trouble in paradise?"

"Not our paradise," Starling said. "My sister called again."

Uh-oh. Joe sat up. Next to him, Austin turned over, eyes suddenly serious. "Bad news?"

"I mean," she waffled. "It's not good news? So, uh, my nephew's going to need surgery, in Toronto, like… soon. Basically as soon as he gains enough weight."

Joe's heart skipped a beat. "Oh my God. What's wrong?"

"I don't know exactly? Something with his heart, I guess. The good news is the doctors are confident they can fix it, it's just… scary, you know? Bad enough for me. I can't imagine how Skyler feels."

"Can we help at all? I could make a casserole or something."

"I'll check their fluids and tires before they drive up," Austin offered, and Joe relayed that too.

"Thank you, guys. I'll let you know, okay?"

The conversation petered out quickly. Joe imagined it wouldn't be long before Starling pulled back into Linda's driveway for a different sort of comfort, and he hoped it helped.

Fortunately, Will came home in something approaching reasonable spirits for once. He and Gavin had been paired together on a project for their marketing class—something about designing a website. He spoke four whole voluntary sentences about it, unprompted even.

Maybe Will just needed a little more normalcy. A school routine, seeing his friends. Obviously he wasn't going to get over his parents' assholery overnight, but progress was progress. An evening where Will didn't cry or act like he wanted to make Joe or Austin cry? Joe would take it.

And the timing was good, because when they were sitting around the table after—Gavin's mother had sent Will home with a tin of cookies to share, and he must really have been in a good mood, because he'd actually done it—Joe's phone chirped again, this time with a weather alert.

It wasn't anything apocalyptic or even unusual. Winter weather advisory. Surprise! It was winter in Canada and weather happened. Locally the forecast called for a few centimeters of snow or potentially freezing rain.

But a hundred kilometers north, they were bracing for a wicked ice storm *bracketed* by snow. The radar looked gnarly. Joe whistled under his breath.

Austin peered over his shoulder. "What's up?"

Joe tilted the screen so he could see. "Think I'm probably going to have to go up London way tomorrow." It wasn't unusual; lots of local crews did that during the winter. London was firmly in the snow belt where Windsor wasn't. Cleaning up after the storm would be an all-hands-on-deck situation.

Austin whistled under his breath. "Nasty."

"Can I see?"

Joe slid the phone across the table to Will. "It's looping, but that's the prediction. If it's accurate, the ice is going to take down a lot of trees. I'll probably bring a crew up for a couple days." He had the number of the cleanup coordinator for London-Middlesex. He made a note to text her if she didn't message him within the next ten minutes.

Will frowned as he pushed the phone back. "Won't it be dangerous to drive up there?"

"I'm not going anywhere until the 401's been plowed and salted," Joe promised. The highway was always cleared first. "But my guess is they'll need help to clear roads and driveways." He paused. "Power might go out tonight, so we should turn the heat up, and I'll lay a fire in just in case. Charge your phone now, okay? Will, if it gets too cold upstairs, the couch is pretty comfortable."

"I'm going to take Pepa out," Austin said. "She's not a fan of getting snowed on. Hey, do you think I could make her a snowshoe for the prosthetic?"

At that, Will almost smiled. "Are you gonna make her matching ones for her other legs? 'Cause otherwise I'm not sure there's a point."

Joe snorted. "Sorry, I just had a mental picture of Pepa buried in the snow except for the prosthetic."

"Oh, she'd be so unhappy." He shook his head. "Maybe I'll just get one of those fake grass pee pads for the front porch. It's not like we use it for anything else."

And then he was up and gone, Pepa trotting at his heels. She always knew when Austin was about to take her for a little walkabout.

That left Joe alone with Will for what might be the last time in a while. Joe opened his mouth to say something—*please try not to bite Austin's head off while I'm gone*, maybe, or *I'm glad you're being less of a dick today*—but Will beat him to it.

"He's just like that, isn't he?" He shook his head as the door closed behind Austin and Pepa. "'Oh, she hates the snow, I'll make her snowshoes and get her a dog potty.' What the fuck. No wonder you're in l—uh, sleeping with him."

Joe carefully decided to focus on the sentence Will had completed, rather than the one he deliberately hadn't. He cleared his throat. Might as well strike while the iron was hot, or whatever. "You know that just because Austin and I are together doesn't mean I love you any less, right?"

Will flinched as though Joe had slapped him, but his posture softened again immediately.

"I know that," Will said. He poked at his empty plate.

Joe waited him out. Giving him silence to fill often worked better for getting Will to open up than asking probing questions.

"I do," he repeated. "It's just...." He wouldn't meet Joe's eyes. "It's hard to see you, knowing my parents wouldn't... couldn't...."

Ah. Joe could see how living with two happy queers after being made homeless for his own sexuality might be painful. "You know that Austin and I don't expect you to feel any particular way or to, like, be happy all the time or for us or anything."

"Yeah, I know," Will said again, but Joe couldn't escape the certainty that he'd eased some tension.

"Just maybe try to take the angst out on inanimate objects and not us?" *Or the shower drain*, he added mentally.

Will gave a wan smile. "I can try."

Chapter Twenty-Two

AS PREDICTED, Joe headed out the morning after, leaving Austin and Will alone together, which meant, despite Joe's good intentions, Austin was now Will's ride to school. For two mornings in a row, they sat in silence, listening to Austin's new favorite podcast. At least they didn't have to rely on his singing voice to fill the silent car.

The first night, Austin suggested they heat up leftovers when they got home, and he barely got an answer before Will stomped upstairs.

"Guess not, then," Austin said to Pepa as he took her outside.

Will eventually crept down for food, but they didn't talk. Or rather Will said nothing and Austin respected the kid's space. Though he noticed that Will wasn't exactly alone. Apparently Ozzy had a new favorite human.

Austin figured Will deserved a little unconditional love, and also cuddles. The poor kid could do with all the physical affection Ozzy could dish out.

Of course, Will was more than happy to join him for dinner the second night after Austin stopped for pizza on the way home.

Joe did his best to keep in touch, but he was busy all day and only managed a few short texts during breaks. Austin and Joe sneaked in a late-night call on the first day, but he was too tired on the second night, so Austin wasn't alarmed at first when he didn't hear much on day three. In fact, he wasn't alarmed at all until just before day five.

When Joe called, Austin cheerfully answered, "On your way home, sweet thing?"

"Well," came an unfamiliar voice, "I will be as soon as I can get my boss home safe and sound."

"Uh," Austin said intelligently as his face flamed.

"Joe's passed out in his passenger seat," the voice continued. "We're parked at his place. Managed to get your name out of him before he dozed off, though."

"What's wrong with him?" Visions of the worst flashed through his mind's eye.

"Other than being a self-sacrificing idiot? Just a cold." He snorted. "Refused to take the morning off. I finally convinced him to take a nap after lunch, but he wouldn't let me take him home early."

Austin groaned. "All right. Thanks for calling. I'll come get him. Hey, you want something from Timmies on my way there as a thank-you?"

"I've eaten nothing but for five straight days, man. If I see another Timbit, I'll hurl. Thanks, though."

Austin snorted. "Fair enough. See you in ten or so." Then he hung up and shouted, "Will!"

He usually made a point of not shouting, so instead of ignoring him, Will scrambled to the top of the stairs to look down. "What? What's going on?"

"You have your driver's license, right?"

"Uh, yeah?"

"Great, put on your coat and shoes. We gotta go pick up Joe."

Ah, there was the surly teenager. "What do you need me for?" Then a pause as pieces started coming together and some of the color drained from his face. "Wait, why does he need a ride?"

"Apparently someone let him work too hard and now he's passed out in his truck because he got sick. I need you to come so we can get him *and* the truck home, 'cause you're probably going to have to use it to drive yourself to school."

"Oh my God. Typical Joe." Will clomped down the stairs. "Leaves us to starve for a week, and when he comes home he's too sick to feed us?"

"Maybe wait until we know he's not actually on death's door to start making jokes," Austin said as he nudged him toward the door. "Come on, his coworker can't leave until we get there."

If he bent the speed limit on the way up Walker Road, Will didn't say anything. Not that that was unusual.

When they were a minute or two out, though, Austin had to prompt a dialogue. "Do you remember seeing any cold medicine in any of the cabinets?"

Miracle of miracles, Will seemed to actually think about it instead of simply sassing him. "Uh, I think maybe some DayQuil and a couple Halls."

No good for nighttime, and they'd definitely need a stockpile from the sound of things. "All right. You want to take Joe home or stop at Shoppers for drugs?"

A streetlight ticked by.

"I've got homework," Will said finally, "so I'll take Joe, I guess."

"You just want to drive the truck."

He couldn't see Will smile, but he thought he heard the trace of one. "Maybe."

In the parking lot at Romano Tree and Landscape Service, Austin shook hands with Greg, Joe's foreman, and let him know he and Will would handle Joe from here. "Uh, I'm assuming everyone's got a few days off coming, after this?" Austin asked.

"Yeah, and I can check messages on the work number. We'll take care of it."

Fantastic, because Austin had no idea how Joe ran his business. "Great. Drive safe, eh?"

Then, because he couldn't send Joe home with Will without checking on him, he opened the truck's passenger-side door.

Joe was dozing, his breath shallow, eyes closed. In the cab light, Austin could make out a faint sheen of sweat on his brow. When Austin brushed his fingers over his forehead, he was burning up. Definitely sick. "Hey, sweet thing."

Joe groaned and cracked open one eye. "'Stin?"

"Yeah, it's me." He pressed a kiss to Joe's forehead, because he couldn't resist. Will, who was climbing into the driver's seat, huffed and rolled his eyes.

"Pretty sure Greg said it was a cold and that Joe wasn't dying," he said with the smug assurance of a teen.

"'Ill?"

At first Austin thought Joe was protesting the fatality of his illness, until he noticed the way Joe was tilting toward the driver's seat. He snorted.

"Yes, Joe, Will is here too. He's the one who's going to take your feverish ass home while I go stockpile drugs."

"Drugs?"

"Not the fun kind," Austin said regretfully. "Go back to sleep, sweet thing. You might as well catch some Zs while your son drives."

Will snorted again and started the truck.

"Drive safe," Austin said with one last stroke of Joe's hair.

"Aw, man, and here I was planning on drag racing down E.C. Row."

Will must have driven exceptionally carefully, or maybe he just hit all the red lights, because he was still attempting to coax Joe out of the truck when Austin pulled up with a bag full of NyQuil, Tylenol, Halls, ginger ale, and juice.

He might have gone a bit overboard, not knowing which comforts or brands Joe would want.

"Oh thank God," Will said when Austin hurried up. "I can't get him on his feet, and he's too big to carry." Will might be almost as tall as Joe, but he was rail-thin with the stretched-out look of a teen who'd been through a recent growth spurt.

Austin nodded at his car. "Why don't you get the stuff into the house while I see if I can talk this lump into moving. Just, uh, maybe don't go back to your homework before confirming I don't need help dragging him in?"

Will huffed and abandoned Austin to his charge.

"Joe," he murmured, and Joe groaned. "There you are. I need you to get up onto your feet and into the house, sweet thing. Once you're up and in, I'll tuck you into bed, but I need you to walk for me."

Joe groaned but managed to help Austin get him upright. Austin slung his arm over his shoulders and pressed another kiss to his burning forehead. "Good boy."

Joe gave a pitiful whimper but did his best to drag his feet up the stairs to the side door.

"He's alive," Will said as he opened the door for them. Despite his sarcastic words, his face was a picture of relief.

"Mostly," Austin joked back. "I'm going to get him straight into bed and dope him up with NyQuil."

Will nodded and locked the door behind them. "I left the stuff in the kitchen." He fidgeted with the hem of his sweater, looking like a too-young stereotype of a handwringing parent.

"Perfect. Thank you. You can go back to your homework. I'll yell if I need anything." He tried to smile reassuringly, though it might have come out strained given that Joe was leaning more and more heavily against him.

"Right. Okay." Will nodded again, then with one last look at Joe, loped up the stairs to his room.

Getting Joe undressed and into bed wasn't nearly as fun as it had been on previous occasions, and not just because his flushed, burning cheeks and fever-glazed eyes weren't sexy. Joe alternated between helpfully unhelpful—trying to take off his own clothes and getting in Austin's way—and directly unhelpful—deciding he needed to go to the bathroom for a pee when Austin had only succeeded in getting one and a half boots off his feet.

But eventually he had Joe drugged up and cocooned in his bed with three kittens around him, purring contentedly as they snuggled up to their own personal space heater. Austin wondered how long the situation would last before Joe kicked off all his blankets in a feverish haze, but he wasn't about to chase the cats away if they were bringing comfort.

He did, however, keep Pepa from the room, as she was too wide-awake and hungry to be a nursemaid.

A few hours later, Austin was cuddled up with Pepa on the couch and reading when Joe shuffled out of his room. His hair was a riot of bedhead and his face was still flushed, but he had left the blankets behind, which boded well for his fever.

"Hey," Austin greeted softly, and Joe wavered on his feet. "What do you need?"

"Bathroom. Drink. Bed?" He looked so befuddled that Austin wanted to cuddle him. Instead he ushered him to the bathroom and asked which drink he preferred.

A few minutes later, Austin was helping Joe back into bed, this time with a can of ginger ale on the nightstand. Joe blinked up at him and asked, "Stay?" So Austin settled next to him over the covers.

Joe groaned about that, but Austin didn't think trying to sleep next to Joe all night would benefit either of them.

"I'll stay until you fall asleep, sweet thing, but I need to rest in my own bed tonight."

Joe just burrowed in as close to Austin as he could get, then fell asleep to Austin finger-combing his hair.

Okay. Now that Joe was out, Austin needed to plan.

Joe was a grown adult. He probably didn't *need* constant supervision just because he was sick. But Austin didn't want to leave him alone either, and Will had to go to school tomorrow. Austin could close the garage for another day. He didn't have anything important on the schedule, just some routine maintenance things with regular clients who'd hopefully forgive him for rescheduling if he said he had a family emergency. He'd just ask his tenant to put the "Please Call for Appointment" sign back up.

Maybe there was a project or two he could tinker on in the garage to pass the time, just because he'd never been good at sitting around.

But he couldn't keep the garage closed indefinitely. Not with Joe off work, Will and the pets to feed, and the heat to keep on in this place. They definitely needed to look into improving the insulation in the spring, because Austin didn't think the air-conditioning bill was going to be any more fun.

Maybe the kids could hang around this weekend while Austin caught up at the shop. With any luck, Joe would be on the mend by then.

But that would only work if Austin didn't get sick too, so he peeled himself out of Joe's sweat-sticky embrace, popped a vitamin C in the bathroom, and trudged up the stairs to bed.

Chapter Twenty-Three

UNFORTUNATELY, JOE'S condition did not improve by morning.

Austin woke a few times in the night to deep, rattling coughs that echoed through the house. Will, at least, didn't look like he'd slept badly, though when Joe coughed like that while they were both seated at the breakfast table, a little of the pre-Christmas Will shone through, timid and anxious. "That doesn't sound good."

"I'll see if there's a clinic open later." Assuming he could get Joe to agree to go… or carry him to the car if he didn't.

"Okay." Will worried his lower lip for a moment. "Text me if he gets worse?"

Ah, Austin thought. Right. This might just be a cold, but Will had just lost his entire family in one fell swoop. "You want me to tell you what color his snot is too?" he asked, hoping to lighten the mood. "I can take pictures."

"Don't be gross." But he looked a little lighter when he grabbed his bag from the hook by the door and left in Joe's truck, so Austin would take it.

Half an hour or so later, he checked on Joe again and found him awake but glassy-eyed. "Hey. Still alive, sweet thing?"

"Unfortunately." He sounded like a frog.

"You want anything?"

Joe took a rattling breath. "Actually…." He pushed back the covers. Underneath, his T-shirt was stained with sweat. Now the whole room smelled vaguely of sickness. "Maybe help me get into the shower?"

"Maybe you can sit on the floor of the tub so you don't die?" Austin offered as a compromise, taking his arm.

He got Joe set up in the bathroom, then stripped the bed, cracked the window, and put on a fresh set of sheets.

He made Joe eat a piece of bread and drink a glass of orange juice, then pumped him full of cold medicine and put him back to bed when he started to shiver. "I'm going to take Pepa for a walk, but I've got my phone, so call if you need me."

"I'm allowed to *voice call you*," Joe said sleepily. "You must really like me."

"I think I probably wouldn't be able to decipher your texts," Austin said honestly.

"Pff." But his eyes were already closed.

The day fell into an odd routine. Austin did a few chores, then checked on Joe, tried to get some liquids into him, made sure he hadn't spiked a worse fever, and let him fall back asleep. He sent Will a message around lunchtime letting him know nothing had changed.

He never did make it out to the garage to fidget with one of his projects. He didn't want to be that far away for that long, get into the kind of mindset where he was focused on his work and wouldn't hear his phone. Instead, he put a nature documentary on Netflix with the volume low and googled recipes for chicken soup.

He was debating if he could get Will to pick up soup noodles on his way home or if they should just make do with rice when someone banged on the door.

Austin had barely made it to his feet before the knock came again.

"Joe? Will said you're home today, so—"

Austin crossed the dining room and pulled open the side door. "Hey, Alex. Shouldn't you be in school?"

They pushed inside, running their hands through their hair. Austin suppressed the urge to ask them where their hat was. They'd *just* gotten out of a vehicle; they hadn't had time to get their ears frostbitten. And Austin wasn't their mother. "Is Joe home? I need to talk to him and he wasn't answering my texts."

"I mean, yeah, he's home," Austin said. "He's in bed, though. Passed out. You could talk to him, but, like, you might as well talk to a wall. He's pretty out of it even when he's conscious."

"Fuck!"

Pepa, who'd wandered in to say hello, nudged Alex's thigh in a quest for affection. Alex ignored her, which made Austin nervous.

"Do you want to come in?" he asked after a moment. Dumb question—they were already inside—but he wasn't sure what else to do to preempt the panic pouring off them.

"No, I—" They ran their hands through their hair again. Their undercut needed a touch-up. "It's fine, you know, uh—I actually don't think I wanted to talk to Joe anyway, right, because, like. How many times in my life am I going to have to disappoint my dad, right? I mean, at some point the bit is going to get old—"

"Come inside," Austin said more firmly, closing the door to the elements. "I'll make tea."

Alex laughed, but the sound was manic, brittle. "I don't, uh. I don't know if—can you drink tea? If you're, like, pregnant?"

Austin's brain screeched to a halt, along with his body, and for several long seconds, he stared, frozen, at Alex as he rapidly assimilated all the thoughts created by that one statement—discovering they were sexually active, hysterically wondering if they knew about condoms or the pill, realizing he suspected he knew who the baby daddy was, and also Joe was too young to be a grandpa but damn he would look good holding a baby.

"I don't know," Austin finally managed to say. "I think caffeine might be bad?"

"Oh, good, so now I can feel guilty about drinking coffee," Alex gasped and stared at Austin, wide-eyed and desperate, and looking so horribly young that it shook Austin out of his stupor.

"Right, come in and sit down."

Once Alex was settled at the table with a glass of water and a mug of peppermint tea—their only caffeine-free option and which the internet said was safe for pregnant people—Austin said, "So, you're pregnant?"

"I don't... maybe."

Austin stared at Alex, trying to figure out what to say next. "Um. Maybe.... Why do you think you're pregnant?"

Alex gave him a look. "I know you're gay, but you must know where babies come from."

Austin gave the look right back. "Yes, Alex, I know where babies come from. But you must have reason to worry more than just having had sex with a penis-having person." He paused, and then, because he was apparently a massive hypocrite and also apparently hated himself, added, "An appendage I hope you've been wrapping up."

Alex glared. "We're not stupid. We use condoms."

"Thank God," Austin muttered.

"But condoms aren't, like, foolproof. And I'm late and I feel nauseous all the time and I don't want a baby!"

Shit, Alex looked like they were going to cry. "Okay," Austin said quickly, as if he could forestall that if he could just get the words out fast enough. "First, you don't have to have any babies you don't want to have. There are options that don't involve teenage parenthood. Second, have you taken a pregnancy test?"

Alex sniffed. "No. I can't…. What if someone I know saw me?"

Austin blew out a breath. "Okay. So, first things first. You need to know for sure, right? I mean, no sense borrowing trouble." Like, okay, buying a pregnancy test… not generally a fun time for a teenager, probably doubly unfun as a trans person. And yet wouldn't it still be better than not knowing?

"But then I'll know."

Apparently not. "Uh, yeah?"

"What if it's positive?" Alex wrung their hands in their lap, avoiding Austin's gaze. "Joe will be so disappointed in us."

Because the curiosity was definitely killing Austin even if the cats didn't give a fuck, he couldn't help but ask, "Us?"

Alex tensed, looked around cagily, and then slumped. "Me and Gavin," they whispered.

Austin did not jump up and shout, *I knew it!* because he was an adult who could restrain himself and also he could read the room. "Ah," he said instead. "Does, uh, Gavin know?"

"No, because if I tell him then he'll react and then *I'll know*!" Alex warbled.

Okay, so, add Gavin and his reaction as components of this Schrödinger's pregnancy stress.

"Right." Figuring it was best to leave that aside for the moment— and seriously, how many issues could he just sidestep?—Austin returned to the other thing Alex had said. "Joe's not going to be disappointed."

"He's going to ask us about condoms." Alex pouted.

"Probably, but only because he'll want to know you're being careful."

"We were. But what if he doesn't believe us?"

If this cycle kept up, Austin was going to down the rest of Joe's NyQuil and crawl into bed with him. He was getting a headache. "Have you given him reason not to trust you?"

Alex wiped their nose on a napkin. "No, but—"

"So he'll believe you," Austin said. "And look, it doesn't matter, okay?"

Alex regarded him through watery eyes.

"If you were careful or if you weren't. It doesn't matter. If you're pregnant or aren't. If you have an abortion or don't. Joe is still going to love you. You think anything could stop him? Will's been an asshole on purpose for the past three weeks and Joe would still walk into traffic for that kid without thinking. So just—you can worry about all the rest of it. Your mom, your stepdad, Gavin, *people*. But you don't have to worry about Joe."

And if, on the odd chance Alex's parents reacted badly, well, it wasn't like Austin planned to use his bedroom much once Joe got healthy again. They'd make it work somehow.

Alex squished their face up like they were in pain, and a few tears squeezed out. They dabbed them away with the napkin and took a deep, loud breath that turned into a single sob.

Then they buried their face in their hands for a second and then raised their head. "Okay," they said, voice surprisingly steady. "Okay, that's—yeah. You're right."

"I know."

That got a wet chuckle. Austin pushed another napkin across the table before Alex could reuse the first one. "You're weirdly good at this, you know."

Austin's cheeks heated. "Nah," he demurred. "It's not *weird*. It's just—I know what I'd want someone to say to me. And it turns out I can say it to you because it's true."

They nodded and balled up the second napkin. "Well, anyway… thanks."

"You're welcome." He paused. "Uh, do you… want me to go buy you a pregnancy test?"

But apparently he hadn't worked an actual miracle, because Alex shook their head. "No, uh, I'm still not ready for… that. But thank you. I should probably get back to school. I asked Will to borrow the truck during my spare period, but I've gotta get back because we're doing exam prep in chem."

Right—the kids had exams next week, on top of everything else going on. "You want to wash your face first? I can find you a cloth."

"Thanks."

JOE HATED being sick. He hated feeling weak, he had never gotten the hang of lazing around in bed, he didn't sleep well when he couldn't breathe, and the feverish flop sweat? Awful.

But Joe had never been *this* sick. He could barely muster the energy to be miserable.

He slept a lot. Every once in a while, Austin coaxed him to eat some bread or Cup-a-Soup or down some orange juice, which burned Joe's throat. Joe didn't like being looked after either, but he had the feeling he wasn't much work at the moment because he couldn't even *do* anything. He spent the days with his eyes closed, more passed out than asleep. He coughed up great, disgusting green globs of phlegm.

Thursday morning—was it Thursday? The days had all run together—when Austin woke him up and pulled the covers back, he hissed.

"Jesus, Joe, what the fuck?"

Joe blinked heavy eyelids and tried to breathe past the elephant sitting on his chest. "Whassamatter?" The word trailed off into a rattling cough. "Can you—help me get up?" He swung his legs over the side of the bed, but then he had to pause, because he was light-headed. "I gotta... pee."

"I'm taking you to the hospital," Austin said. "Your fingernails are blue."

Slowly, Joe held his hand in front of his face. Austin was right. That probably meant something bad.

Joe didn't want to go to the hospital, but he also didn't want his fingertips to fall off. "Okay," he agreed after a moment. "But can I pee first?"

Will was getting ready to head out for the day when Austin dragged Joe to the front door, and the poor kid's eyes just about bugged out when he saw Joe's frail shuffling walk.

"Joe?" he asked in alarm.

"We're going to the hospital." Will nodded frantically, and before he could offer, Austin pointed a stern finger in his face. "You are going to school. We'll be in for a long wait, I'm sure, and there's nothing you can do."

"But—"

"School. I will text as soon as I know anything."

Will reluctantly left, and Joe focused all of his attention on following Austin to his car. The ride to the emergency room passed quickly, which was probably a bad sign, because Joe was pretty sure it was a twenty-minute drive.

It seemed like another bad sign when the nurse at the front desk took one look at Joe and hustled to get him into a bed.

Joe tried to track what was happening, but it was useless. Thank God for Austin.

"Sweet thing." Someone brushed Joe's sweaty hair off his forehead and caressed his face. "Open your eyes for me, sweetheart," a soft voice murmured, and Joe struggled to obey.

He squinted up at Austin, who slowly unblurred and came into view.

"There you are. The doctor has questions, and I don't have answers. Think you can help us out?"

"Try," Joe said, because he would. He brushed at his face with a weak arm only to find his attempts to get rid of the unpleasant tickle hampered by tubes and wires.

"Shh, stop that. No, Joe, stop. You have to leave the oxygen tube where it is. Yes, you have an oxygen canula in your nose because your levels were low—that's why your fingers went blue."

Joe twitched his right arm, his hand heavy and unbalanced.

"You have an IV and oxygen monitor on your hand. Stop tugging."

"Why?" Joe croaked.

"Because," said a new voice, which held warmth despite the clear crispness of the tone, "your lungs are failing to move oxygen through your system. The IV is helping to hydrate you for now, and soon will pump you full of antibiotics."

Antibiotics. For a cold? "'Fection?"

"We've taken blood, and I'll send you down for a chest X-ray, but I'm pretty confident both tests will say the same thing—pneumonia."

The doctor wasn't wrong. Within the hour, she was tutting over his chest X-ray and ordering a course of antibiotics.

"I want him to stay overnight," she said to Austin, apparently having decided to cut Joe out. Not that Joe minded. It was a relief not to be responsible for this. "I'm not happy with his O2 levels, and I want him under supervision."

"But he should be okay to come home in the morning," Austin clarified.

"I'm optimistic, yes. So long as he responds to the antibiotics, the night on oxygen and fluids should be all he needs to kickstart his recovery."

Satisfied that everything was taken care of, Joe drifted off to sleep.

He woke again to the sound of Austin's voice. He cracked an eye open and spied him standing by Joe's bed and gently stroking Joe's unencumbered left hand. "… says he should be fine with antibiotics. Keeping him overnight is just a precaution. They want to make sure…."

Joe blinked, and Austin was kissing his forehead. "Sweet thing, you with me? I hate to wake you, but I don't want to just disappear. I have to go home for the night, check on the kids. Yeah, Will too. Sleep tight and I'll see you in the morning."

Joe groaned, unhappy, and Austin shushed him. "They have my number just in case, but go to sleep and I'll be back before you know it."

He closed his eyes and tried to follow Austin's advice, but the nurses were cruel villains conspiring against them. They woke Joe several times in the night, taking his temperature and fussing with his IV. Each time, Joe grumbled and tried to complain, but sleep took him back under too quickly.

Still, when he woke up the next morning, he felt crusty and unrested, though more clearheaded than he had in days. Not that he felt sharp, but the world didn't have a hazy unrealistic feel.

It took him a moment to figure out why he was awake, and when he finally registered his full bladder, he wondered how he was supposed to fix that. After another few seconds, he remembered the call button beside the bed, and soon an orderly showed up to help with his issue.

As if needing Austin's help hadn't mortified him enough. Now he was relying on strangers.

And yet he barely had the energy to feel frustrated at his own helplessness. He'd been awake for five whole minutes in a row, which was more than he could say for the previous day, but he still felt like garbage. Like he could fall back asleep at any moment. He wanted a shower and real clothes and his own bed, but he was too tired to do anything about any of it, which made him want to cry.

He definitely shouldn't cry, though. He was having enough trouble breathing, even with the antibiotics and the oxygen cannula.

Ugh.

He'd hoped to get sprung early, but no such luck. Fortunately Austin had the foresight to bring Joe's phone and a charger so he could keep him apprised. *Still waiting on doc. They think after lunch.* Considering the state of the provincial health care system, Joe was surprised they weren't shoving him out the door so they could give the bed to someone else, but maybe the doctors were all busy with actual crises and didn't have time to decide if Joe was healthy enough to go home.

Ok, Austin wrote back. *Need anything?*

Aside from a new immune system and a functional set of lungs? *No thx.*

Lunch was a dry turkey sandwich, a banana, and a Jell-O cup, like Joe was in some kind of bad sitcom. He managed the banana and the Jell-O, but the sandwich was too dry on his throat and took too much effort to chew, so he gave up after two bites. He wasn't that hungry anyway.

Finally, around two, the doctor from yesterday popped in. "Ah, Mr. Romano." She pulled the chart from the end of his bed—the one the nurses had been updating all night, waking Joe up every time—and flipped through it, then walked over to the IV pole where his oxygen monitor was and checked that too. "How are you feeling this afternoon?"

"Scale of one to ten? One." He turned his head and coughed a little. "But yesterday was, like, minus three, so."

"Well, the good news is your numbers are looking a lot better. Fever's under control, oxygen levels are improving. I'm going to write you a prescription for some antibiotics and oxygen for home use, but you can go home. If you get worse again, though, you'll have to come back, and if you're not able to get yourself up and around in a week, I want you to see your GP."

Joe would've promised his firstborn child to get out of the hospital. He didn't like Gavin that much anyway. "Whatever you say, Doc. You're the boss."

Somehow he still fell asleep again before Austin arrived to take him home.

Chapter Twenty-Four

AUSTIN SLEPT like shit with Joe out of the house.

It didn't help that the pets didn't understand where he was or why he wasn't home. Pepa jumped to her feet any time a car passed outside, on the off chance it was Joe. Walker followed Austin around forlornly and threw a fit when Austin tried to go upstairs and sleep in his own bed, because Walker didn't want to be alone in Joe's. Finally Austin switched out the sheets and gave in.

Then there was being the contact person for everyone who cared about Joe—his employees, his mom, his dad—who Austin had never met because he lived in Ottawa doing, like, fancy diplomat shit—his kids, Starling, even Linda. Everyone wanted to know what was going on and when he'd be home and what his diagnosis was and the treatment plan and his projected recovery and the last time he'd had a bowel movement.

Okay, Austin was exaggerating, but only a little.

And then there was the part of his brain that couldn't stop thinking about how fragile Joe had been—the insistent, paranoid part of his brain that always had to consider worst-case scenarios, the part that had always insisted Austin keep an emotional distance from people and have a backup supply of SpaghettiOs handy just in case.

Weak enough he'd needed Austin's help getting out of bed. Feverish enough he'd barely been able to string words together. So tired he'd barely been able to finish a glass of juice before he nodded off again.

Fingernails turning blue.

Austin had worried about their relationship moving too fast, about how he would handle it if they broke up. He'd never even considered what it would do to him if he lost Joe to something more permanent until a few days ago, and then he was too busy looking after Joe to think about it.

But then Joe was in the hospital, and suddenly he wasn't too busy anymore. It was like he couldn't *stop*.

So he slept like shit and woke up to Will slamming cupboards in the kitchen—charming—and a strong smell of ammonia, which…. That seemed bad? That seemed, like, go-back-to-sleep levels of bad.

But he didn't want to miss a call or text from Joe saying he was ready to come back home where he belonged, so. Time to face the music.

Austin dragged himself out of bed and found Will in the kitchen glaring at the open fridge.

"You trying to cool down the whole house?" As the words came out of his mouth, Austin realised two things. One: He sounded like someone's parent. Two: Snark was probably not the best way to ingratiate himself to an emotionally fragile grumpy teen.

"It's not like the fridge is doing anything else useful right now." Will glared.

Right. Because Austin forgot to go grocery shopping yesterday. He was pretty sure they didn't have milk, cereal, or bread. "I can get to the store—" Austin started.

Will finally slammed the door shut and huffed. "If I leave now, I can stop at Timmies."

Probably a good idea. "You have cash?"

"Of course." He rolled his eyes.

Austin did not grump back. He hadn't even found the source of the ammonia smell yet, and already he wanted to go back to bed. "Okay, well, that's breakfast solved. I'll get groceries before I go back to the hospital."

Will paused on his way to the door and asked as if he didn't care about the answer, "Is Joe coming home today?"

"Probably," Austin said. "I haven't heard from him yet, but yesterday they were confident that he would."

"Good." Will continued on his way out. Austin supposed he should be grateful that Will actually yelled out a "Bye!" before he slammed the door behind him.

In a state of foolish optimism, Austin checked the fridge and found nothing he wanted to eat for breakfast either.

With a sigh, he shut the fridge and figured he might as well take a page out of the kid's book and leave the house for breakfast. But first he should find the source of the smell.

It was cat pee. It had to be cat pee. But how one of them had managed to pee on the wall, Austin had no idea.

Sighing, he grabbed a garbage bag and a roll of paper towels. Once he'd sopped up the mess and then washed the walls and the floor—all the while carefully not thinking about what he was cleaning—Austin washed his hands ten times and dressed.

He checked his phone before leaving and again once he reached the grocery store, but there were no updates from Joe.

The first text arrived while Austin was in the middle of the bread aisle. Joe was conscious but not yet discharged. Austin heart-reacted the message and then put his head down to get shit done.

Unfortunately, between his lack of sleep and his anxious desire not to miss anything from Joe, concentrating proved difficult, even if all that required his attention were groceries, laundry, and animals.

It was just about lunchtime when his phone rang. Austin lunged for it—it must be Joe.

Starling Bell.

Austin slumped. He didn't want to talk to Joe's best friend right now. He'd been keeping her updated, and he didn't have anything new to say about Joe's condition.

Then again, she'd never called before.

Worry gnawed at his belly. He wasn't sure what emergency would make her call Austin, but something had to be—

"Hello?"

"Austin, hi." Starling's tone sounded heavy.

"Shit—I mean. Uh, what—what's wrong?" Jesus.

Starling barked a laugh. "Yeah, I guess calling you isn't subtle." She sighed. "Look, I hate to do this now. I mean, I would hate to ask anyway, but especially right now when Joe's out of commission—"

"Starling, what's wrong?" Austin's heart couldn't take this beating about the bush.

"I need my money. Or the money you owe me for services rendered." Austin cringed. "Ugh, sorry, that sounded—" Another sigh. "Sorry, sorry, I'm not usually so bad at this, but I'm really—I know I agreed to wait until you guys sold the house, but—"

"Maybe you could tell me about it?" Based on the rambling, Austin figured *something* had happened. He'd wondered what they would do if they changed their mind about selling—something he and Joe should probably talk about soon. Until now he'd figured they could cross that bridge when they came to it. Or didn't come to it. Or didn't sell it.

It seemed like the bridge had come to him, though.

"My sister's kid had to go to Sick Kids and—I mean, they're okay, but the recovery's going to be longer than they thought. Which means two weeks of unpaid leave, and there's housing for them in Toronto, sort of, but there will be expenses and—" She blew out a breath.

"And you need the money we owe you to support your sister." Just because the treatment might be covered by OHIP didn't mean living expenses suddenly disappeared.

"Yeah," Starling agreed, sounding relieved.

"Right, okay." Austin had no idea how they would cover it, but he would find a way. "Can you send me the bill? I'll have to take a look, figure things out." He chewed his lip. "Look, honestly, I'm not sure if we can pay it all right now, but I'll let you know as soon as I can about how much and when we can get you the money."

"Thank you," Starling said sincerely. "Seriously, Austin. The timing sucks, I know—"

"It's not your fault," Austin countered.

"I know, I know. I just hate to add anything to your plate right now."

"Starling, don't—" Austin's phone buzzed, and he pulled it away from his face to check. "Oh thank God."

"Austin?"

"Sorry, text from Joe. He says he's about to be sprung from the hospital. I've got to go."

"Yes, yes, go. Say hi from me. And tell him to get better and to stop getting old-people illnesses!"

"I'll, uh, do that," Austin said, though he didn't think he'd pass along the last part. At least not in so many words. Maybe in a couple months, when he emotionally recovered from his boyfriend almost dying of pneumonia, he could joke about it.

The drive to the hospital was a straight shot down Walker Road, which gave Austin plenty of opportunity to think as he managed to hit all thirty-seven stop lights. He didn't have a ton of money in savings. How much did they owe Starling? He should've asked before. Now he didn't want to look at his phone. Maybe they'd have no choice but to sell the house sooner rather than later and find somewhere to live in the meantime. Or maybe they could get a mortgage. They could swing that, right?

A joint mortgage wasn't exactly taking things slow, of course.

Never mind. Joe first. Financial crisis later.

The inoffensive walls and bland art of hospital hallways all looked the same. Austin got Joe's room number mixed up and did a double take when he poked his head in and found a tiny Asian woman instead of Joe, but then he heard a familiar laugh echoing down the hall and made his apologies.

Austin had a lot on his mind. He couldn't remember the last time he'd put in a full day's work or gotten a full night's sleep. But the stress and exhaustion evaporated, if only for a moment, when he walked into Joe's room to find him sitting up in the bed with color in his cheeks, taking breaths without rattling.

It took Austin a minute to get his own lungs to remember to breathe as the relief washed over him, but then he cleared his throat and knocked on the doorframe. "Hey. I heard you're getting sprung."

"Mr. Taylor!" The doctor turned toward him, smiling. "Good, I need a witness for these care instructions. I've got some printouts for you to take home as well, but I want to go over everything and give you a chance to ask any questions."

Austin *wanted* to finish crossing the room and put his hand on Joe's forehead, feel for himself that the fever had been defeated, listen to his heart and lungs up close, then throw him over his shoulder and get the fuck out of here before he could catch a secondary infection. Barring that, a hug would be nice. It had been too long since Joe touched him.

But he sucked it up and listened to the doctor's instructions, asked his questions, took the printouts and the prescriptions, and finally wheeled Joe down to the elevator, accompanied by a nurse.

"I could walk," Joe muttered, but Austin had seen the way he swayed on his feet in the three steps between the bed and the chair, and decided that was a poor idea.

"Liability issue," said his nurse sweetly. "It's not personal."

Austin was fifty-fifty on whether the guy made that up, but Joe seemed to buy it, which was all that mattered.

The health-care supply store was a few blocks away. Austin ran the prescriptions over to the pharmacy across the street first, then went in to grab an actual oxygen tank—who knew you could get those for home use?—while the pharmacist worked on filling them. Joe stayed in the car. He might have better color, but he still looked like one of the kittens might take him out by accident.

Austin purposely didn't look at the receipt when he handed his credit card over. That was a problem to deal with when the bill came.

Finally he got Joe and his new accessories home and was about to put him to bed when Joe said, "What's that smell?"

Just… fuck. "Fucking cats," Austin groaned. He grabbed a blanket and muscled Joe onto the couch instead. "One of them peed in there last night. I didn't have time to get the smell out yet."

He shot Linda a text before he started, just in case this was less an accident and more a sign of something wrong with one of the cats. God knew how he'd figure out which one. Smart money was Walker, but it could've been any of them. Dallas could be a little terror. He wouldn't put it past her.

Finally either Austin got the smell out or he went noseblind. He set a fan up in the corner to dry the area and went back out to the kitchen to start on dinner.

He was just taking the meat out of the fridge when his phone buzzed with a reply from Linda.

Probably one of the boys marking his territory. Neuter surgery should fix it. You'll want to get that scheduled before marking becomes a habit rather than an instinct.

Austin sank down at the table. Great. One more problem they could solve with money, if they had any.

He needed to go back to work. But even if he did—his business was supposed to support *him* and *itself*, not him and itself, three cats, a three-legged dog, a teenager, and Joe. And sure, Joe would be back to work in a week or two, and that would take some pressure off, but it didn't solve anything *now*.

The garage had been Austin's dream, once upon a time. He'd spent his whole life relying only on himself, and that carried over into his decision to own his own business. Austin had been convinced that making it as a business owner would mean he'd beaten his past, or something stupid like that.

Now it was just one more thing to worry about on top of pets and Will and food and his bank balance—and most importantly, Joe's health.

He couldn't put any of this on Joe until he was on the mend. Joe was worried enough about needing to be taken care of, for once, instead of doing the caregiving. Austin just had to hold it together for a couple weeks. He'd managed it his whole life.

Right now, that meant taking care of dinner.

Austin stood up and turned around. Pasta wasn't that hard. Brown meat in pan, add sauce, boil water, cook noodles. It wouldn't be as good as Joe's, and it definitely wouldn't touch Nonna's, but it would feed them, and maybe Will would stop looking at Austin like he was some poser adult. Austin never thought he'd miss the days Will could barely look at him without flushing.

It took him a minute to register the fluffy orange body on the countertop. "Walker, *no!*"

Walker ignored him and shoved his furry little face deeper into the tray of ground beef. He refused to give up his prize until Austin bodily hauled him away. Even then, Walker stretched out his neck and tried to grab one last mouthful.

His face was smeared with raw beef, and Austin stared at his "bloody" orange mouth and sighed. Awkwardly, he managed to keep hold of Walker with one hand and grab paper towels with the other. Not that Walker really let him clean his face, but at least he managed to get the worst of it. Then, only feeling a little guilty about it, Austin threw the cat onto the front porch.

Walker gave an indignant "Mreow!" but Austin didn't budge.

"You can come back into the house once you've cleaned your face of raw meat, you menace," he declared through the glass.

The cat gave Austin such a scathing look, he was grateful looks couldn't kill, and then settled in to bathe. Or maybe just to get all the delicious flavor from his whiskers.

Back in the kitchen, Austin eyed the mangled beef. Since he hadn't yet cooked it, it was possible it was no more unsafe for human consumption now, but his stomach turned at the thought.

With a sigh, Austin threw the beef into the trash and cleaned up the mess left by his biggest problem child. Or was that second-biggest? Did Will count?

Mess cleared, he eyed the rest of the ingredients. His minimal desire to cook had been squashed.

Fuck it. What would it hurt now if they ordered out? What was another fifty bucks? He fished out his phone and ordered pizza. Hopefully Will would be less likely to grumble about another night without homecooked food if he saw his favorite on the table.

Will still grumbled, but at least he didn't stick around for long. After inhaling two slices and asking after Joe's recovery, he slumped with relief and then took three more slices up to his bedroom.

Austin wasn't thrilled about the idea of food crumbs upstairs—they only just got rid of mice—but he was less thrilled about the idea of picking a fight. Or spending more time with a moody teen who would probably follow up the fight with pointed and aggressive eating of pizza.

So Austin let him go and instead checked on his patient.

It shouldn't have been a surprise that Joe's first day home set the tone for the next few. Austin did his best to balance domestic and business needs while also playing nursemaid to a Joe who vacillated between gratitude and adoration to Austin for taking care of him, and frustration and humiliation at not being able to care for himself. Checking on Joe and fetching him something to drink or eat, or reminding him to take his medication, would either end in Joe asking, "What would I do without you?" or snapping, "I can do it myself!" and then promptly failing to do so.

Austin bit his tongue and reminded himself that Joe was sick and miserable and feeling guilty and horrible on top of that. Snapping back wouldn't help.

The day after Joe got home, Starling emailed Austin the invoice, and the dread hollowed out his stomach. His savings didn't have near enough to cover that amount. Still, in a fit of optimism, or maybe delusion, he signed into his bank account to check the numbers, and discovered they were worse than expected. Shit. Looking at the balance and the recent transactions, he spotted the issue—the e-transfer he'd expected last week with monthly rent from his new tenant hadn't been deposited.

If he didn't move some money around, the next time the mortgage on the garage came out, he'd be in the negatives.

Shit. *Shit.*

Letting out the space was supposed to improve his financial state, but it couldn't if he didn't get the rent on time.

Though a garage that was never open wasn't helping him stay solvent either.

Less than half a year ago, that business was a proud mark of Austin's success and independence. Now it was causing him headaches and had been bumped so far down his list of priorities he wasn't sure when he would get back to it.

Frustrated, Austin slammed his laptop shut and scowled at the kitchen cupboards.

Restless energy suddenly filled him, and he stood up abruptly. Then paused. What to do with all this energy? He could walk Pepa, sure, but that didn't actually appeal. He wanted—he wanted—

He wanted Joe to pin him to the bed—or maybe a wall?—and fuck the restless energy out of him until he was a spent puddle of twitching exhausted muscles.

Fuck.

Well, not fuck. That was another problem too far down the priority list to address or even acknowledge, other than the fact that it was making him a little cranky.

Once Joe was settled back to sleep and Austin was sure he was breathing easy and not about to wake again, he turned his focus on dealing with one of the many tasks that needed doing.

He left a note by Joe's bed saying he was on a grocery and pharmacy run, and then headed out. Maybe he could actually make something edible tonight. If he bought more beef—and guarded it better—he could make pasta.

The drive through Essex did him some good. Feeling indulgent, he sifted through the change in his cupholder and located the three bucks he needed for a ten-pack of Timbits. If nothing else, at least he could count on some simple carbs to cover the hard edges of his feelings. Besides, it was never a good idea to grocery shop on an empty stomach.

But these days nothing he did for himself ever went unpunished. He turned back onto Main Street out of the Tims drive-through and made it a total of two blocks before he had to hit the brakes. In front of him, a minivan had stalled. The driver had put her four-ways on and was standing next to the road, tugging at her hair like she had no idea what to do.

Which, yeah, even if she *did* know what to do, Main Street just before rush hour wasn't a great time to have a breakdown—mental or automotive.

Austin put his own four-ways on and pulled over. "You need some help?"

When she turned, he could see she had her phone to her ear on the other side, but she must not have been getting an answer, because she lowered it when she saw him. "That would be great, actually. I'm not sure what happened, just all of a sudden the wheel went unresponsive and it was like driving a tank."

"Power steering issue, probably," Austin said. "Engine was fine?" The van was still running, now that he was looking.

"Yeah. I just kinda freaked out."

"You have CAA or anything?" If she did, they'd come out and tow her for free, and she wouldn't have to worry about it.

But she shook her head. "Never thought I'd need it."

Austin had her pop the hood so he could do a visual check for any obvious issues, then stuck his head into the car and pulled the cover off the fuse panel so he could check that too. "Power steering still looks the most likely," he said. If he had less on his plate, he'd have offered to take a look himself, but right now he had enough going on. "There's a dealership down the street a couple blocks. If you want, I can drive it there for you. You can follow in my car. They'll probably have a courtesy shuttle, if we hurry." Dealership service departments were usually only open until four thirty or so.

"That would be amazing."

Two minutes later, Austin pulled the van up in front of the service bay at the dealership. The van's owner, whose name was Cheryl, parked his car in the side lot. Austin waved her over as the service manager came out to greet them.

The service manager was a grizzled middle-aged man with a beard and a shirt with *Bobby* embroidered on the pocket. He shook hands with Austin and Cheryl and asked, "What can I do for you?"

Cheryl looked at Austin. "Uh, he thinks my power steering died? So I guess can you fix it and what's it going to cost me?"

Bobby nodded. "Sure, I can get you a quote for that. It won't be done today, though. If you leave your keys, I'll have the courtesy shuttle drop you off somewhere."

After Cheryl followed his directions to the lounge where the shuttle driver waited, Bobby turned his attention to Austin. "Power steering, you said?"

"Like she said, it handles like a tank." Austin shrugged. "I popped the hood and checked the fuses, and there's nothing obvious there. She didn't mention any leakage, so my guess is the belt." He wouldn't have been able to see that just from peeking under the hood.

Bobby tilted his head. "You a mechanic?"

"Most days," Austin said wryly. "Didn't have time to drive her out to my place, though. I gotta get dinner on the table."

"Huh." Bobby nodded and held out his hand to shake again. "Well, you ever decide you're tired of working for yourself, we're hiring."

Austin opened his mouth to turn him down, then changed his mind. "Thanks," he said instead. "I'll keep that in mind."

He needed that, he thought as he got back on the road toward the grocery store. Something that made a difference. A genuine compliment. One little thing to go right.

So of course, as soon as he pushed his cart up to the checkout at the store, he realized he didn't have his wallet.

Fuck. Had he left it in his car? Had Cheryl taken it?

He'd had it at Tim Hortons—or, no, he'd used spare change from the cupholder for that. When had he used his wallet last? When he'd picked up the pizza the other night?

Yeah—and he'd taken Joe's truck, because Will had gotten home after him and parked like a dick. Austin could visualize his wallet now, sitting exactly where he'd left it in the center console of the pickup.

Fuck his life.

Mortified, he pulled his cart out of line and put the perishables back. He left the cart out of the way, in the vain hope that maybe no one would reshelve his groceries in the next hour. It was fine. He'd just go home—Will would be back from school by now—pick up his wallet, go back to the store. Easy. No harm, no foul. Dinner wouldn't even be particularly late.

Sure enough, the truck was there when Austin pulled into the driveway. It locked automatically, so Austin had to go inside to grab the keys.

They weren't on the peg by the door, though. Joe's truck had a push-button start, so Will probably just left the keys in his pocket.

Ugh. He could brave a teenager's lair for the two seconds this would take. It would be fine.

He wasn't taking his boots off, though. Fuck that. The house was a disaster anyway. A little more mud wouldn't make a difference.

He'd almost made it to the bottom of the stairs when his foot slipped out from under him.

"Jesus, what the—" Somehow Austin caught himself on the railing, grateful he and Joe had fastened it extra-securely after last time. His heart was still pounding in his chest when he looked down and saw the pee-stained wall and the little yellow puddle that had almost killed him.

"*Fuck*," he said feelingly. The last thing he wanted was to clean up more cat piss. And now it was on his boots, which meant he was going to track it upstairs when he got the keys.

"Will!" he bellowed instead.

Belatedly, he realized Joe was probably sleeping. Or *had* probably been sleeping, until now.

Thumping came from the second story. A few seconds later, the creaking of an ancient wooden door. "What!"

That was when Austin smelled it. Something other than the cat pee. Something thicker, more cloying.

God, his nose had to be playing tricks on him, right?

Austin chose to believe his nose was playing tricks on him. "Can you bring me the truck keys, please?"

More thumping as Will appeared at the top of the stairs. Austin half expected him to just throw the keys down, and maybe that would've been better for everyone. Because as soon as Will got close enough for Austin to see his face, he made out the red-rimmed eyes, the dilated pupils, and the unmistakeable stench of pot smoke.

"Are you fucking serious right now?"

Will crossed his arms and scowled—whatever the drug's effects, making him less obnoxiously moody wasn't one. "I'm an adult."

Austin barked a humorless laugh. Only an eighteen-year-old would think that Will's current and recent behaviour was a mark of maturity. "Clearly being voting age didn't make you less stupid. What are you thinking, smoking pot in this house right now?"

"The fuck do you care?" Will sneered.

Austin sneered back. "For starters, you have an exam tomorrow, unless you lied about that. Who gets high in the middle of final exams during grade twelve?" Second semester started next week, and Will had a full course load. There would be no do-over for these first-semester classes without summer school.

"Not like I'm smoking at school before taking it." Will rolled his bloodshot eyes.

"No, of course not. You're just smoking a floor away from Joe, who has pneumonia. It's not like he's on a *highly flammable oxygen tank* and can barely breathe as it is!"

Will blanched—clearly not having thought about that—but then firmed his jaw. "Not like I was smoking next to him."

"So you haven't learned about how smoke travels in your science classes?" Guilt flashed over Will's face, but he didn't back down. Austin tried to take a calming breath, but the deep inhale only reminded him of two facts, or rather, two smells—pot and cat urine. "So I guess it never occurred to you to use your pot-smoking time to do anything else. Like clean up cat pee." He gestured to the floor. "Or do the laundry or cook dinner or vacuum."

Will stared back mulishly.

Austin impatiently pushed hair out of his face and rubbed at his temple, trying to ease the building headache. "Fuck this. I'm driving you to and from your exam tomorrow. You're going straight to school and coming straight home afterward, continuing next week. And we'll be laying down more house rules."

Any lingering guilt left Will's face as he scowled deeper in outrage. "You can't ground me!"

"The hell I can't!"

"You're not my real dads!"

"No!" Austin snapped back. "We're just the ones who love you!"

Will paled and swayed, and Austin, standing in cat pee and nauseous from the scent of weed, needed to get out. He spun and stomped out of the house, pausing only to drag his disgusting boot through a pile of cleanish snow, and then flung himself back into his car and took off. He needed space to cool down, to think, to escape from the house and everything in it. To breathe.

He hated yelling. Hated the thought of being like those foster parents who had frightened him as a child. And yet... he hadn't been able to help himself when he saw what Will was up to.

Teenagers got high. Austin had been one. He knew. But the panic and betrayal he felt at the sight of *Will*—smart, capable Will, who was supposed to make better choices than Austin had at that age—high on a school night, burning *anything* in the same house as Joe and his damaged lungs and his *extremely flammable oxygen tank*.... Austin didn't know what scared him more—Will's recklessness with his future or with Joe's health.

It didn't help that Will was doing something so self-indulgent when the floors hadn't been vacuumed in days and the laundry—clean and dirty—was piling up and Austin was standing in cat pee after a failed grocery visit. Austin was drowning in shit to do, none of which he'd asked Will to help out with because Will was supposed to be studying for his exams, and instead Will was getting high before dinner.

Tears blurred his vision, and Austin pulled over to the side of the road. No sense getting into a car accident on top of everything. He felt hurt and stupid and ridiculous sitting here sulking like a kid after a fight, but for several minutes, he couldn't seem to do anything else.

But only for a few minutes. He had responsibilities to attend to. He couldn't afford to break down.

Chapter Twenty-Five

JOE WOKE to the sound of activity beyond his bedroom door and a surprising almost-rested feeling. It had been days since he'd last woken up not feeling miserable and exhausted. He might not feel *good*, but he wasn't on death's door. So that was an improvement.

Since he was feeling slightly less horrible, he should probably find out what the noise was about. Also, he needed to pee. Again.

Joe shuffled out of his bedroom and all but ran into a mop-wielding Gavin, who was wearing headphones and lip-syncing. Judging by his dance moves, Joe suspected the music was Beyoncé.

None of the questions that came to mind were more urgent than his bladder. But when he'd managed to pee without wanting to fall over, he decided he should take advantage of his sudden stamina to have a quick shower.

Five minutes later, he exited the bathroom with a towel around his hips and heard Meg and Alex puttering around in his kitchen.

Nope. Joe still wasn't ready to deal with whatever this was. He went to his bedroom for clean clothes.

When getting dressed still didn't totally wear him out, he figured he was out of excuses. He shuffled back out of his room and asked the now-four teens in his kitchen what the heck they were doing at his house on a Friday at….

"Twelve twenty-three? Shouldn't you all be at school?" Joe glared. Though the effect was probably lessened by his need to lean heavily against the counter.

"Wow. Will wasn't lying, you really were sick," Gavin said around his mouthful of… something he shouldn't be speaking around.

Joe arched an eyebrow, too tired to verbalise his request for more information. Standing was fine, but standing and talking was apparently too much.

"We haven't had classes in a week," Alex explained. "Exams."

It was exam week? Joe needed to sit down. He'd lost time in there somewhere. Vaguely, he reminded himself to call Greg when he could, find out what he needed to do to keep the business running. Probably he needed to do payroll, at the very least.

Joe shuffled along to the table and lowered himself into a chair. Will came along shortly and wiped the table in front of him. A moment later Meg set down a mug of tea. "Are you hungry?"

Actually, for the first time in long enough that he didn't want to think about it, Joe was starving. "Yeah. Do we have anything that's not dry toast?"

"Nonna made manicotti and Italian wedding soup," Meg offered. "Gavin picked it up. Alex and I are making rice and green beans and chicken. The internet says they're good if you have a sensitive stomach."

Manicotti sounded like a bit much, but Joe was sure Austin and Will would appreciate it. The rest of the kids too, if Nonna had packed her usual portions. "Soup first, if that's ready," he decided. "Chicken and rice and beans sound good too. I'll definitely have that for dinner if there's any left. Thank you."

At the stove, Alex preened.

Gavin put the soup in the microwave, the headphones now hanging around his neck.

"So, uh…." Joe didn't want to sound ungrateful, because whatever was happening here, it was awesome. In the time he'd been sick, he'd definitely been mood-swinging all over the place. He had a hard time accepting help, but he'd definitely needed it.

And the person who'd been helping the most was conspicuously absent. Joe barely remembered most of the past week. He hoped he hadn't said anything to run Austin off.

"Where's Austin?"

Gavin, Meg, and Alex exchanged wordless glances. Then Alex looked at Will, who nodded with slumped shoulders, and the other three left the kitchen as he took over watching the stove.

Ominous.

"He went to work," Will said. "I think."

In the dining room, Gavin, Alex, and Meg divided up tasks. Gavin volunteered for litterboxes, Meg for walking Pepa. Alex said they'd check on the laundry and fold it if it was dry.

Joe snapped his attention out of the twilight zone and back to Will. "You think?"

Will poked at the chicken in the pan. "We're not exactly talking."

Oh good. Joe had gotten healthy just in time to mediate a family crisis.

The microwave beeped. Will retrieved the bowl of soup and brought it to the table, along with a spoon, and then returned to the stove to turn the burner off.

Joe picked up the spoon and stirred the soup. The familiar comforting aroma of one of Nonna's best-loved recipes wafted up to his nose. "Why?"

"I think…." Will dropped into a chair across from Joe. "I think I fucked up."

That seemed likely. Joe took a bite of soup. Oh God yes. Real food. He tried to pay attention to Will as well. "Oh?"

Will hunched. He'd gotten tall in the past two years, but now he seemed to be making himself small. "I haven't been very good. Um, to live with. Especially when you were away, and then when you were sick. I just—I didn't help at all. And I got mad when Austin didn't do everything for me. And when he wasn't you. And then I—"

He shut his mouth with a click.

Joe let him hold his silence for a moment while he shoveled in a few more spoonfuls. His stomach did not protest, but he should probably slow down anyway, just in case. He didn't want to see the soup a second time.

"What is it?" he finally prompted.

"Last night Austin caught me smoking weed in the house and flipped his shit."

Will probably should've offered Austin the weed, after the couple weeks he'd had. No doubt he needed to unwind a little.

Then Joe's brain reminded him what today was. "Ah. On the night before an exam when he thought you should be studying?"

"In the house when your lungs were barely working, I think was his main objection." Will rubbed his index finger over an invisible imperfection in the tabletop. "I didn't think about it. I didn't think about *you*. Just like I didn't think about how hard it was for Austin having to do everything for you, and the pets, and me, and try to run a business. I was only thinking about myself, and I could've… whatever. If I fail an exam, that only affects me. But everything else…."

Joe's stomach prompted him for more soup. He obliged. Then he had to ask. "When you say flipped his shit…?"

"He yelled. Loudly." Will hunched over a little more. "I'm surprised it didn't wake you up. He said he was driving me to school and back for the next week like—like he was grounding me. I told him you weren't my real dads."

Joe winced. "Not your finest moment, bud."

"In my defense," Will said miserably, "I was high."

He didn't sound like he thought it was a particularly good defense, so Joe left it alone. "What did Austin say?"

Will buried his face in his hands. His shoulders shook.

Alarmed, Joe let his spoon clatter to the table. He couldn't move very quickly, but he got up anyway and scuttled around the table so he could put his hand on Will's shoulder.

Wordlessly, Will turned and buried his face in Joe's midsection, wrapping his arms around his waist.

Joe's eyes stung too.

"He said—" Another full-body shudder. "He said you were just the ones who *loved* me, and I couldn't—I've been such an *asshole*, I don't deserve—"

God damn it. Joe was too dehydrated to want to cry like this. "Hey. *Hey*." He pulled Will closer. "Will. Yes, you do, okay? God knows what you're going through isn't easy. We get it. You think either of us is perfect? I've seen Austin eat SpaghettiOs out of the can Will."

Will snorted a snotty laugh into Joe's hoodie. Oh well. Alex could bring up a clean one from the basement. "But I was—I was so mean to him. I thought, if everyone's going to leave me one day anyway, it'd be easier if—if he already—but he said *we*, Joe, he said *we love you*, and I—"

Joe looked up at the ceiling. It didn't help. Will sobbed against his belly. "Sorry, kid. You're stuck with us, so let's try to make the best of it, okay?"

"Okay," Will gasped, nodding.

Joe ruffled his hair. "Good," he said. "Now, uh, I'm glad we had this talk, but I really have to sit down. Pneumonia is no fucking joke."

He resettled into his chair and found Will, red-eyed and blotchy, watching him with concern.

"I'm going to be okay. The meds are working." Will nodded to show he understood, but he didn't look convinced. Figuring distraction was the best course of action, Joe took a conversational left turn. "So, I don't think you ever explained what's going on with all this." He twirled a finger around to indicate everything.

Will shrugged and broke Joe's gaze. "I asked everyone to come over and help so we could get it all done today. I'm not gonna ask them to every time. I know I need to, like, be better and help out more. I just couldn't do it all myself this time."

After taking a moment to chew on that, Joe said, "Look, your home here isn't contingent on you being good or pleasant or helpful. We won't throw you out if you don't help us vacuum. But we definitely appreciate the help, and it's probably not a bad idea to figure out a system for chores so everything's clear and feels fair."

"Okay." Will nodded seriously and then gave a shadow of his trademark sassy smile. "And I know you won't throw me out for being a bad house guest. If you were going to, you'd have done it already."

Joe snorted. "Yeah, probably."

By the time Austin got home an hour later, Joe had shuffled his way to the living room couch, and the kids were halfway through their plates of manicotti and an episode of *Stranger Things*.

"Uh, hey," Austin said slowly as he eyed the scene. Joe tried to see it from his perspective. If he'd walked in to find Austin ensconced on the couch in a cozy blanket cocoon with warm tea, drowning in teens who had sprawled over the remaining couch cushions and the floor at his feet, with the smell of chicken and Nonna's manicotti on the air, he wasn't sure he would know what to focus on first.

"Hey," Joe croaked. "The kids took care of dinner."

"I can smell that." Austin sounded dazed as he took another look around. "Why is everything clean? And why are you out of bed?"

"I'm out of bed because I woke up and didn't feel like hot garbage, so I celebrated with some food and a walk to the couch."

"The house is clean because we cleaned it," Gavin added helpfully. "I mopped."

"You mopped." Austin looked like he might faint.

"Yes, he mopped, and we vacuumed and cleaned the kitchen, did the laundry, cleaned the litter boxes, made and/or brought dinner, and walked the dog," Meg added.

"Oh. Why…?"

She rolled her eyes. "Because Will called and said you were both being big dummies. Will promises not to pretend housework isn't a thing from now on, and you should promise to ask for help in the future."

Joe bit back the smile that wanted to burst out at the look on Austin's face. There was nothing like being scolded by a teenager for a failure to successfully adult. He wondered if his own expression was so poleaxed when they served him the same judgement.

Figuring he should rescue his boyfriend from the trials of teen parenting—he'd missed out on several opportunities to do anything boyfriendly over the past two weeks—Joe patted the couch next to him and said, "Why don't you grab some food from the kitchen and join us in some mindless TV, babe? I'll even share my blanket."

Austin did just that, and thankfully missed the shocked looks sent his way by Gavin, Meg, and Alex.

"Did you just—"

"You did."

"Does that mean—"

Huh, apparently Will hadn't spilled those beans. Impressive.

"Yes. It does. You were right, he's too cute not to date."

"I knew it!"

"Yes!"

"So, like, the wedding is next week?"

"Wait—Will. You knew?"

"Well…."

"Oh my God! Betrayer!"

"Wait, does that mean he's kicked out of the betting pool?"

"Betting?" Austin stood in the doorway with a plateful of pasta. "Who's betting?"

"The children, and probably others, presumably about our romantic prospects."

Austin froze with his fork halfway to his mouth. "Uh… what?"

"Apparently we won someone money by getting together."

"Oh." Austin cocked his head. "Should we, like, do something about that? I feel like you should scold children for betting on something personal and tell them it's very bad and wrong, but honestly, I don't care."

Joe laughed. "Me either. If they'd run away to Vegas, maybe I'd have something to say about it." He winked at the kids as Austin settled next to Joe on the couch, their thighs and shoulders pressed together.

Alex flushed and looked down at their lap, and then up again too quickly for Joe to figure out who or what they were looking at. No one else seemed to notice, and the atmosphere was too nice to disrupt by poking anything with a stick. Especially after the past couple weeks.

Austin's thigh was warm and solid against his own, and Joe let whatever was happening go. Right now he had his crazy family around him and he could breathe all right for the first time in weeks. That was enough.

"So hey," Meg said slyly, as they paused between episodes for a bathroom break, "if you and Austin are together, that means there's a bed going totally unused upstairs, right?"

Alex was in the kitchen making popcorn, as per tradition, but Will and Gavin whipped their heads around to look at Joe.

"Yeah…?"

"So we can totally have a sleepover, right?"

Joe opened his mouth to object—surely they were too old for sleepovers, especially now they could drive themselves around; surely their parents would want them home; this was very last-minute and they hadn't brought toothbrushes—but his eyes caught on Will's, open and pleading and bright for the first time in weeks. God damn it.

He sighed. "It's Austin's bed," he said pointedly. "So you'll have to ask him if it's okay if two of you sleep in it." He paused. "And no horny shit."

Meg wrinkled her nose. "Gross."

When Austin emerged from the bathroom, Gavin and Meg set upon him. Will hung back, obviously still feeling some guilt. Joe figured the two of them needed space to talk it out, but it didn't look like that was going to happen tonight.

"*Please*," Gavin said, all puppy-dog eyes.

"Yeah, please?" Meg echoed. "I've been training so much I barely get to see anyone."

Alex entered with the popcorn. "What's going on?"

"Sleepover," Meg said. "Austin's totally going to let us share his bed 'cause he's sleeping with Joe anyway. Right, Austin? Alex and I need to catch up."

"How come I get stuck with Will?" Gavin grumbled. "He kicks in his sleep."

Will shoved him with a shoulder. "Sleep on the couch, then, dick."

Austin sighed and looked at Joe. "I'm going to say yes to this, aren't I?"

Joe shrugged. "Probably."

Austin returned his attention to Meg. "You're changing the sheets yourselves. And Ozzy's probably going to want to stay with you, so leave the door open, okay?" She had claimed Austin's bed as her property just days after her adoption.

"Of course."

"And you have to shut up if we tell you to. Joe still needs his sleep."

Joe could probably sleep through the five of them singing karaoke to "Bohemian Rhapsody" in his living room, the way he'd been going lately, but let Austin pretend he was exerting some control.

"And, uh, no drugs or alcohol."

"Whatever," Meg said, taking one of the popcorn bowls from Alex. "You only have gross beer anyway. Are we good? Can we start the next episode now?"

Chapter Twenty-Six

Austin shepherded Joe to bed shortly after the girl with the superpowers got her eighties makeover. His eyelids were drooping, and Austin wasn't carrying him in front of the peanut gallery. He didn't trust Gavin not to wolf-whistle, and that would set Pepa off.

While Joe brushed his teeth and climbed into bed, Austin checked all the water dishes and took Pepa on her nightly yard inspection. He was looking forward to spring, when he wouldn't have to freeze his ass off for ten minutes while she decided where to pee. Maybe after the thaw they could fence part of the yard so she could do this unsupervised. Now that Austin had fixed his cash flow problem….

Finally Pepa had watered the bushes to her satisfaction, so Austin let them back inside. The kids had turned the TV off—apparently *Stranger Things* was a whole-family ordeal and they were only allowed to watch it as a group—and he could hear murmured voices and giggles from the second floor.

The kids should have this. Especially Alex. A night of being a regular teenager would do them some good.

He unbuckled Pepa's prosthetic and stroked her ears as she got cozy in her basket by the fireplace. Then he brushed his teeth and slid into bed next to Joe, who flopped around with his hand until he found Austin's shoulder and then leaned over to kiss him, close-mouthed.

Probably for the best. He was still kind of mucusy.

"Mm," Joe mumbled. "Night."

Austin closed his eyes.

It had been a busy day. He still couldn't quite believe he'd done something so impulsive, and done it so quickly at that. But he didn't have any regrets.

That morning, he'd thought about Bobby's offer at the dealership. He'd thought about Joe's mom's interest in Austin's garage, how she'd mentioned property in that area was desirable and that she'd always be able to find a buyer if Austin ever wanted to sell. Months ago, Austin had pushed it out of his mind. Back then he had no intention of selling.

But now? Austin's priorities had changed. He already owned a home. That home and the family inside it kept him plenty busy. He had enough responsibilities. He wanted a job he could get paid for and then go home to what really mattered.

So he called Maria, and she called her buyer, and then Austin called Bobby, and at the end of the day, Austin didn't own a business anymore.

He thought he might feel sad about it, but he didn't.

He hadn't had much time to process it all. He'd gone out and done what he needed to do, and he was still working through how he felt about it when he came home to find the house clean and Joe on the couch, looking better than he had in weeks. Will had stuttered out a sincere apology when Austin picked him up from his exam, but they hadn't had time to really talk before Austin needed to head out again.

They probably still needed to talk.

And he needed to talk to Joe too, but that was going to be a different conversation, harder to navigate. Joe felt bad enough for the help he'd needed in the past few weeks. Austin didn't need to add anything else for him to feel guilty over, especially considering that this particular issue meant an overlap of business-and-home decisions that might lead him into a Paul spiral.

It could wait until Joe was well enough to go back to work.

Austin closed his eyes and let sleep take him.

THE NEXT morning, Austin stirred awake and wondered why he wasn't still dreaming.

Their bedroom door creaked open, and he realised he'd heard a soft knock. "Austin?"

He lifted his head and squinted. Alex stood in the doorway, looking—Austin didn't know how to describe the look. Tentative but stubborn, apologetic and happy.

They stepped into the room and continued the confusing body language by pulling their sleeves over their hands and then smiling. "Uh. I got my period."

It took a second for the importance of that comment to land. "Wait." Austin jerked up, pushing his head and shoulders off the bed. Behind him, Joe grunted. "Really?"

"Yes."

"Awesome," he breathed. "Uh, not that I'm not thrilled, but this couldn't wait until... not 6:02 a.m.?"

"I don't have any supplies." They grimaced, embarrassed. "Don't suppose you have some extra?"

"Uh." Austin did not. But... well, Joe had hair ties in his car. "Did you check the bathroom cupboards?"

Alex nodded.

Austin was loathe to do it, but he couldn't leave Alex waiting.

"Joe," he said softly, and stroked his hair. Joe grunted. "Joe, wake up for me."

"Ungh. Wha—?"

"Pads or tampons. Do you have any?"

"You bleeding?"

Alex snorted, and Austin smiled. Clearly Joe wasn't awake yet. "No, but Alex is."

Joe's eyes fluttered open and he looked at Austin, then Alex. "What?"

"I got my period. Like, off schedule. So...."

"Oh." Joe flailed with the duvet and tried to sit up.

Austin put a hand on his chest. It was laughably easy to keep him lying down. "Just tell us where to find them."

"Right." He rubbed his eyes and stretched as though that might help him remember. "Uh... bathroom, basket on the shelf over the toilet. And I think the rest of the boxes are in the linen closet."

"'Kay, thanks. I'll go look." Alex slipped away.

Joe turned his increasingly wakeful gaze on Austin. "Why is Alex so happy about getting their period off-schedule after six and a half years?"

"Uh, well." Shit. Alex had flown the coop, and now Austin had to explain. That didn't seem fair. "There was some... concern... that they might not get it for a few months."

"For a few...." Joe inhaled sharply and swung his legs out of bed. "That little—"

Austin scrambled and got an arm around his waist. "Give your brain a minute to catch up before you go wringing Gavin's neck, okay?"

"*Gavin?*" Joe whisper-screeched. His sickly pale skin had gone blotchy red. "I was going after Alex for not telling me. Are you saying *Gavin*—" He took a handful of loud breaths. Austin didn't think it was the remnants of pneumonia. "I've told them about condoms *so many times.*"

"Yes, and they used them, but condoms are not infallible." Austin brightened. "Although hey, in this case, they were not defeated, so. Congratulations on your successful sex ed lectures."

"I'm too young to be a grandfather," Joe said unhappily, finally relaxing back into his pillow.

Austin patted his shoulder. "Fortunately you're not going to be one, so you can relax."

But while the stress and adrenaline might've leeched out of him, the unhappiness persisted. "Why didn't they come to me?"

Austin curled his body toward Joe's and tugged him closer. "While you were out of town or while you were dying of plague?"

"Yes," Joe said mulishly.

Austin snorted a small laugh and kissed his forehead. "Your kids love you. They trust you. And they don't want to disappoint you. But they're still kids. They're not ready to be parents. And sometimes that means they're not ready to talk about the possibility with *their* parents."

Joe reached for Austin's hand, still wrapped around his waist, and brought it to his lips instead. "Neither were you, but you seem to be doing okay."

Something warm and soft curled in Austin's chest. "I'm flattered, but I don't think that's exactly the same thing. I definitely would've run the other way if you were expecting quadruplets."

Joe scrunched his face. "I'm trying to be upset about that, but *I* would've run if I were expecting quadruplets. I'm pretty sure I'm eligible for Mexican citizenship."

Austin wasn't clear on how that would've helped. "Which means you can't blame Alex for not wanting to talk about it, especially before they had the guts to take a test. They didn't even tell Gavin."

Joe's eyes went soft. "But they told you."

"Yeah, well." Warmth spread across Austin's cheeks. "Apparently none of them are afraid of me despite my tough-guy exterior."

Joe cackled. "Oh no, Will definitely is, but in the 'scared and horny' way."

Awful. Austin was trying to forget about that.

"Anyway." Joe shook his head. "Did I miss anything else important while I was on my deathbed?"

Austin should tell him, but he didn't know how. It would change things if Joe knew how Austin had paid Starling's bill. Austin didn't want Joe's apology or his pity. He didn't even want his money. He just wanted to keep living this small, quiet life in their quilting project of a house, with their pets and their horde of children and the love Austin never dared to even hope for.

"No," he said. The lie slipped out easily, uncomplicated. "I mean, unless you missed my dick."

"Of course I missed your dick," Joe said instantly. Then after a beat, "Well, I did when I was away. I wasn't really conscious enough to miss your dick while sick."

The creak of stairs told Austin that Alex was headed back to bed.

"Well... since you missed my dick and we're both awake at this ungodly hour...."

Joe barked a laugh. "I think I'm well enough to lie back and think of England."

AUSTIN WOKE up again before eight to the feel of being watched. Pepa wagged her tail once their gazes locked, and he gave in to the inevitable and rolled out of bed with a grunt. Joe slept on, thank goodness.

He'd passed out almost immediately after coming and barely stirred when Austin cleaned him up. Clearly, he still needed extra sleep.

It was almost ten by the time he surfaced, first to use the bathroom, and then to join everyone in the kitchen. By that time, the kids had decimated Austin's pancakes—the only dish he'd acquired any skill at in months—except those he'd stashed away for Joe, and were giggling over the remains.

Naturally, once Joe was conscious, the marathon continued.

Starling found them on the couch mid-episode, the TV paused so they could argue over which character was the most annoying.

"I'd say this wasn't how I expected to find you, but... let's be real." Starling stood at the end of the couch, having divested herself of boots and coat without anyone noticing her arrival.

"Starling!" Joe said with delight and no move to stand up. Apparently even he knew better than to play good host right now. "You're just in time for our debate."

"Sounds like it. What are we arguing about?"

"Maybe," Austin broke in before the debate could resume, "before we continue to badger Starling for her opinions, we should ask her if she'd like to have a seat?"

"As if you need to ask," Starling said with a wave of her hand. "Though I should probably get to the point since I was actually on my way home." She shrugged and lifted up the reusable bag hung at her side. "I bring gifts from Linda—homemade muffins from her now more reliable oven." She winked at Austin.

Naturally, the kids stopped listening after *muffins*, and Gavin tore into the Tupperware inside the bag and exclaimed, "Chocolate! Ooh, blueberries! Sweet!"

"Stop." They all looked at Joe. "At least pretend to have manners. It's almost lunchtime. Can we serve them up properly?"

Gavin pouted, but he replaced the lid and carried his prize into the kitchen, trailing after Meg and Alex, who were already musing over menu options, and denying Will a view into the tin, despite his best efforts.

"You didn't just stop by to feed my children," Joe prompted.

"Well, not *only*. Though Linda really did want to send those over. She also sent a message," she added with a look in Austin's direction. He girded himself. "Next time, ask for help, you hapless sad sack."

"You'll be surprised to hear that you're not the first one to tell me that," Austin said dryly.

Starling snorted and looked at her nails, faux casual. "What about pig-headed martyr? Anyone call you that yet?"

"Starling," Joe cut in, but Austin waved him off.

"Not in those words exactly, no."

"Well, they should have."

"Yes, thank you." Austin wasn't unaware of his need to do some self reflecting as to why he didn't reach out for help or why all his new friends and family thought that was stupid of him.

Starling eyed him and then relaxed, dropping the act. "Good. Because I'm too grateful to actually lecture you." She sat on the couch next to him and hugged him. "Since you're also my new favorite person."

"I am?"

"Of course you are," she said, jostling his shoulder. "Skye and Brady are safe and sound in Toronto."

"Wait." Joe shifted to look around Austin. "What happened while I was down for the count?"

"Your boo, despite his stupid overworked martyr complex, found the time to listen to my woes and pay me for the work on the house."

"What?" Joe shot Austin a look, but before he could ask how, Starling kept talking.

"Which I needed for Skye and Brady."

That caught Joe's attention. "Wait, what's the update on that? You said your nephew—"

"He's getting treatment at Sick Kids." Joe paled. "He's fine. Well, not fine, but the prognosis is good. The doctors are happy with his initial response and hopeful he'll be back home in a couple weeks good as new, sort of."

"But the money?"

"I wanted to help—my sister is living in Toronto for two weeks."

Joe cringed, obviously having caught on to the issue and Starling's views on the matter. He asked more questions about Brady's health, which Starling answered in detail. Clearly the issue had been weighing on her. By the time the kids started bringing food into the living room, Starling was shaking her head at their invitation to join and saying she should get back on the road.

"Thanks again, Austin." She kissed his cheek and then the top of Joe's head. "Have fun being cozy sloths on a Saturday, I guess."

"Thanks for looking after her when I couldn't," Joe said quietly during the brief moment when the kids were out of the room, fetching more provisions.

"What are boyfriends for? Besides, it's not like it wasn't also my wiring." He waved a hand about the room.

"I'm not sure the old stuff would've been able to handle the load of this many teenagers charging their devices," Joe said wryly. "Although the real issue would've been they each would've had to charge them in a separate room."

"We'd have tripped and died over the extension cord situation, probably," Austin agreed, relaxing somewhat. It didn't seem like Joe was going to pry further—to ask where Austin got the money, or offer to pay him back, or anything else that would leave Austin choosing between lying, deflecting, and the awkward truth. "Hey, while the kids are distracted—think there's enough manicotti left for a grown-up's lunch?"

Chapter Twenty-Seven

BOUNCING BACK from pneumonia didn't happen as seamlessly as Joe hoped. He might finally be ready to shower, put on clothes instead of pajamas, and leave the house, but prolonged physical activity still exhausted him. When he went out with his seasonal work crew to clear snow, he had to use the self-propelled blower and leave the shovel cleanup to someone else. The cold air made him cough, and he had to use an inhaler. And when he got home, he usually ended up falling asleep on the couch for an hour or so before he had the energy to think about dinner.

Walker, at least, loved this development, as it meant he got his favorite cushion in his favorite room of the house for long enough to have a very satisfying nap. And landscaping work for Marco and Luca's buyers was mostly design at this stage, which Joe could do at home on his laptop.

True to his word, Will had stepped up around the house. He totally took over litterbox and pet-feeding duties. He and Austin traded off dinner dishes, and the three of them rotated laundry, with Joe getting off easy once he was back to doing most of the cooking, and he usually fell asleep before ten.

All in all, Joe didn't have anything to complain about aside from the condition of his own body, so he felt extra petulant about being so grumpy he couldn't fuck Austin the way they both liked. Austin never gave the slightest indication of dissatisfaction, and Joe couldn't exactly complain at being ridden so enthusiastically his headboard left a dent in the plaster. But his own inability to pick Austin up and rail him six ways from Sunday on their kitchen table, fuck him into multiple orgasms, and then pour him into bed did kind of grate on him. He felt like he'd set an expectation and now he couldn't meet it.

Considering that he'd left Austin in charge of the house, a financial disaster, a teenager he didn't sign up for, four pets, and his own sickly ass for a couple weeks, he owed Austin better than what he was currently capable of providing. But he'd get there.

In the meantime, he needed to figure out his own financial disaster.

The landscaping crew didn't have much to do during the winter, except in the case of a snow or ice storm, so the business didn't have a lot of expenses in terms of salary. Joe had secured a few contracts to clear snow at local businesses—salt sidewalks, that kind of thing—but it was really only enough to keep him and one other employee busy, without much left to pad the business account. Since Joe hadn't worked, he'd had to pay two people and hadn't been able to put anything away.

Which meant paying Austin back his half of the bill for Starling's work would require time. But Joe didn't want to leave it unpaid. He hated owing money. He could take some out of savings—the kids didn't know he had a little put aside for them for next year, and he could replenish it when they sold the house....

Or they could sell the house now and he could pay Austin back. But then what? If they didn't live together anymore, the life they'd built in this house would die too. And it was one thing to end up living together by accident and quite another to intentionally go out and buy somewhere else to live.

They could rent someplace, maybe. If they could find someplace that didn't mind that they had four pets between the two of them.

In any case, selling the house seemed like Joe's only financial option, even if he didn't want to do it, and it was what they'd agreed upon, so he sucked it up and asked his mom for that book she had on staging and her list of things to do before selling a house.

He was flipping through it at the kitchen table while he waited for the sheet-pan fajitas to finish—not exactly like Abuela would've made but easy to clean up and Joe was tired, God dammit—when Austin's car pulled in.

Ever since Joe got sick, Austin had been coming home from work earlier. He used to come home between six thirty and seven, but now he often pulled into the driveway around five. Joe didn't know how he was managing that, considering the amount of money he'd just splashed out, and he didn't know how to ask.

By the time Austin came into the house, he'd ditched the coveralls, which usually meant a messy day at work. Maybe someone's oil pan exploded on him or something. "Hey." He stopped in the kitchen and leaned over for a kiss. "Smells good in here."

"It's nothing fancy," Joe warned. Even Austin couldn't fuck up this recipe. Well—okay, he probably could. He definitely didn't know how much seasoning to use on chicken.

Austin detoured to the cupboard to start setting the table. "You forget I'm measuring by the SpaghettiO standard. What else do I need to get?"

"Shredded cheese, sour cream, and the tortillas."

He was well-trained enough by now that Joe didn't have to remind him to bring the panini press to the table so they could warm the tortillas.

"Call Will down for dinner?" Joe asked.

"Mm-hmm." Austin took two steps out of the kitchen and shouted up the stairs. "Will! Food!"

Joe sighed. "I meant go *get him* like a civilized person. I could've done that," he complained.

Austin snorted. "Been doing your lung exercises? 'Cause last I checked you couldn't out-shout a mouse, sweet thing."

Unfortunately, this assessment proved to be all too true the next day when he failed to answer his mother's cheery greeting as she let herself in the front door, because he was in the bathroom.

At least Pepa kept her entertained while he flushed and washed up. Also they'd fixed the door handle properly this time, so he didn't have to worry about accidental walk-ins.

"Mom, I wasn't expecting you this morning," Joe said when he found her in the living room sweet-talking Pepa. She'd never been a dog person, and certainly never one who cooed at them.

"I know, but I was gathering some information about house listings, and I thought, why email all of it when I could just pop by and tell you in person?"

Joe narrowed his eyes at her. His mother loved him, but she didn't have a history of being casually affectionate or thoughtful. Her love usually came in the form of money or material possessions rather than time. She'd been trying to do better these past few years, but she still wasn't a "just popping by" sort.

"Oh?"

"Yes, so why don't you come sit with me and talk staging."

Joe wrinkled his nose but followed directions. "Coffee first. You want a cup?"

"No." The answer came so quick and firm that Joe sent her an alarmed look. "Already had a cup this morning," she said brightly.

Joe shook his head and got his own cup of morning stimulants, then rejoined her and Pepa.

"So, what did you want to talk about?"

"Well, as you know, staging is an important part of selling. And you'll want to think about how to go about these things. There are a few companies that I can recommend that take care of everything, or if you want, there are places that rent furniture so you can do it yourself."

"Hm." Joe hummed into his coffee. "Well, I'll have to talk to Austin about it, since we'd be splitting the fees, but send it all my way so we can look over stuff." The thought of more bills terrified him, but at least they could likely put these off until it was time to sell the house—which would solve those cash-flow issues.

She made a note in her book and then asked something else. Joe kept answering her questions, mostly with the same answer as the first—for her to email him the details.

"Mom, not that I'm not happy to see you, but most of this stuff can wait," he pointed out twenty minutes later. "I mean, we're not planning to list for a few more months, and you know we want you to be the listing agent. You have time to share all this."

"Right, yes." She smiled. "Never hurts to get a jump on things."

"True. But all of this could have been done over email." Most of it was contact details.

His mother shifted in her seat and then shrugged. "I guess I was just in the mood to see you."

"Right." It wasn't that he didn't believe her, but he wasn't sure what to make of it. "Well, whatever the reason, I'm happy to see you. Nothing like an overnight stay at the hospital and an oxygen-tank prescription to make you appreciate seizing the day," he said jovially.

His mother's face twisted unhappily. "Your father had to talk me out of storming the hospital," she admitted.

Joe started. His *father*? "You talked to Dad?" As far as Joe knew, his parents had hardly spoken for the past two decades. Theirs had been a love match to start, he thought, but they'd also been young and unready for the realities of a marriage, two busy careers, and a child. Their divorce was the first in either family, and despite their amicable split, the disappointment of the in-laws meant they didn't spend time together. At least, Joe didn't think so.

"Your young man called to tell me your fingers had turned blue and you were in the hospital. Of course I called your father."

Put like that, it made sense. Still.

"You talk often, do you?"

His mother shrugged and busied herself tidying up her work things, tucking her pen and notebook into her portfolio. "Now and again. It's hard to cut ties completely with the father of your child."

"Right," Joe said. It wasn't like he thought they *never* talked.

Her phone pinged then, and she checked it. A smile tugged at the corner of her mouth as she read and typed back.

"All good?"

"Hm? Oh, yes. But I should probably be going. As much as I'd love to stay here all day, I've got places to be." She stood, and Joe followed her to the door and watched her don her boots and coat. "Besides, if I leave now, I'll have time to get a cappuccino on the way to my appointment." She kissed his cheeks and, with a gloved finger wave, headed for her car, giving Joe no time to process what she'd said, let alone to question her very un-Italian choice of a lunchtime cappuccino. Only children drank that after breakfast.

And she'd refused a coffee just minutes before.

Well, if she'd decided to talk to his dad again and try to be a more active parent, maybe she'd also decided the rules about drinking only espresso after nine in the morning didn't apply. Who knew? It wasn't like Joe was going to tattle to Nonna.

He puttered around a bit for the afternoon—bought groceries, vacuumed the never-ending furballs from under the couch—until it was time to pick up Will from school and deliver him to his new part-time job at Tim Hortons.

"You're not paying rent," Joe warned when Will sprung this on him.

"Duh," Will said, "I'm saving for college," and Joe didn't have an argument for that, so the discussion ended.

By three thirty he had dinner in the Instant Pot and Pepa hankering for a walk, and for the first time in weeks, Joe felt up to the job and the weather was warm enough that it didn't make him cough. He buckled on her leg, clipped the leash to her collar, and off they went.

They were on the return trip when Joe heard the familiar cranky rumble of Austin's piece-of-shit car, but it was coming from the wrong direction. He stepped farther into the ditch, thankful that enough snow had melted he could see where his feet were going and not risk tumbling in headfirst, and cocked his head as Austin pulled over to the side and rolled down the window.

"Hey, stranger," Joe said, leaning down. "Going my way?" At his feet, Pepa whined and jumped, obviously having smelled her favorite human. She didn't have to make it so obvious that Joe was the spare.

Austin held up a Tims cup. "Had to swing by and see if Will's barista skills were up to snuff." That explained why he hadn't hit up one of the two Tim Hortons on the way from the garage to the house. "You want a ride?"

Joe looked down the road. He was maybe a hundred feet from their driveway. "I think I'll chance walking it." He was enjoying the exercise. Then he looked back at Austin. "New coveralls?" He usually preferred black or gray; these were ultramarine.

"Ah, yeah." He gave a half shrug as he glanced at them. "Boxing Day special."

"It's a good color on you." It really wasn't—honestly it kind of made him look like he was turning blue—but Joe had never claimed to be an impartial observer.

"Yeah?" Austin flicked his gaze up and down Joe's body like he was checking him out, which was a bit ridiculous since Joe was wearing a puffer jacket and a hat, but maybe Austin couldn't be impartial either. "You sure I can't offer you a ride?"

Well. Joe smirked. "Race you home?"

JANUARY BLED into February, with the end of March and the optimal window to list the house creeping closer. Joe's mom started stopping by more frequently, and items Austin could only categorize as staging props appeared. Scented candles in every room. Fluffy white towels that stayed in the linen closet with the tags still on, a note that read DO NOT USE pinned to the top. A burlap table runner in the kitchen, a bowl of fake fruit (why couldn't they just use real fruit? It wasn't like they wouldn't eat it), fancy wrapped bars of soap.

Austin was of two minds about the whole thing. On the one hand, the bathroom and Will's bedroom particularly were improved with the application of scented candles. The table runner dressed up Joe's beautiful walnut showpiece and made the kitchen feel *homey*. The soap wrappers had a whimsical farm animal print that DeeDee would've appreciated, and Austin smiled whenever he saw them, even though they took up valuable counter space in the tiny bathroom they all shared.

On the other hand, it was hard not to resent all the little items that kept reminding him that eventually this wouldn't be his home anymore, and he didn't have anywhere to go.

He did try, one evening when Will was at work and he and Joe were lying in bed, and Joe was making eyes like he wanted to fingerbang him to another orgasm, as if to make up for the time they lost when Joe was sick, as if Austin were in any way unsatisfied after riding Joe very thoroughly. "Hey, uh…." He caught Joe's hand before it could start to wander. "Have you thought about what you're going to do? With Will, I mean."

Joe shrugged and turned his body closer to Austin's. "There's room for him at my place. Once we get a closing date, I can give my tenants notice."

Right, sure. Because Joe had always made sure he had a place where Will could crash if he needed to. The barndominium would probably be great for Pepa too—not that Austin had ever been inside, but the open-concept main floor would be nice, and the yard was already fenced, so she could go outside unsupervised.

"Right," Austin said after an awkward moment. Did it sound like he was fishing for an invitation to come along? *Was* he? "Makes sense."

"But," Joe allowed, "I don't want him to, like… panic about anything. There's no reason he needs to think about us selling until we have a firm plan of what's happening next."

Austin would like to make that plan now, but he couldn't explain why without telling Joe he'd sold the garage, and he still didn't quite know how to do that. "That's fair but, like… maybe stop leaving your staging crap and selling checklists all over the house, then."

Joe grunted. "Good point." He loomed over Austin. "But definitely a tomorrow problem."

The following morning, Austin's day off, he stood in the kitchen and locked eyes with Pepa. He was alone in the house, if you only counted humans, so he gave in to temptation.

"This is the kind of shit that doesn't have a manual. How am I supposed to know what to do?"

Pepa wagged her tail.

"Right, experience." Austin sighed, rubbed his face, and then consulted a doctor.

Linda arched her eyebrows when Austin showed up on her doorstep, but she let him and Pepa into the house and offered them coffee.

"Let me get this straight." She rolled her eyes when Austin snorted. "You and Joe are living together, own pets together, are dating and sleeping together, and you want to know when you're allowed to tell him you love him?"

"When you say it like that, it sounds stupid," Austin complained.

"Right, the way I was saying it is the problem."

"The problem," Austin said, talking over Linda's snort of amusement, "is, like—Joe's last relationship was a train wreck, so we're trying to take things slow, but my last relationship was *never*, so I don't know what that means. At the start, we said we'd sell the house in the spring, and he's doing stuff to prepare for that, but telling him 'I sold the garage so we can live here forever' is, like, going to give him an aneurysm."

"Honey," Linda said slowly, "I hate to break it to you, but there really is only one solution here."

"What?" Austin didn't like her tone.

"Talk. To. Him."

He thunked his head onto the kitchen table and groaned. "I was afraid you'd say that."

"You don't have to open with 'I want to have your babies,'" Linda snarked. "Just say you want to talk about things because that's what adults do in adult relationships. They talk about expectations and boundaries."

"I was afraid you'd say that too," Austin grouched. "Why is adulting so hard?"

"Don't look at me. If I understood people, I'd have become a human doctor."

Maybe that was why they got along so well. Austin had just picked machines instead of something living. Neither of their patients could talk—not unless Linda had patched up any parrots—and somehow that made fixing them easier instead of more difficult.

Linda clearly had the patience of a saint, because when Austin continued silently lamenting all the choices that had led to this moment, she offered, "I don't know why you're having such a hard time with the idea of telling him what you want." He wasn't looking at her, but he could hear the smile in her voice anyway. "I'm sure he responds well to that kind of direction."

Austin had a mental flash of telling Joe he wanted to make the en suite bath usable and Joe's dick getting hard in response. God. The behavioral conditioning would turn them both into monsters. Austin would get spoiled in every way and Joe would be so come-dumb they'd all die of starvation.

"Maybe too well?" Linda prompted when Austin didn't reply.

He groaned and buried his head in his arms.

"Just start slow. Like… 'Hey, Joe, is it cool if we go get screened for STDs and promise not to sleep with other people so we can stop wasting money on condoms?'"

Austin slithered off the chair and rolled under the table.

"The consequences of your own actions can still find you under there." As if to prove her point, she pushed back from the table and crawled under with him. Her knees popped alarmingly. "Austin. If you haven't even talked about that, you're not moving slowly. You're standing still."

Ouch. He let that land and sink in, because if he didn't he was afraid he'd find out in a few weeks or months that she was right. And the danger there was that the world would move on without him.

Then he took a deep breath. "The thing is," he said finally, "I can't pretend anymore. That this isn't serious for me. I'm not standing still, it's just… there isn't any farther to go."

Linda squeezed his hand. "It's a reasonable boundary, you know. Not pretending he means less to you than he does. If you don't think you can talk about it, you could just stop pretending and see what happens."

Blinking, Austin considered that. What if he stopped holding back in front of people? What if he kissed Joe whenever the urge struck instead of only when he was trying to start something in bed? What if, when Joe was making dinner to the standards he'd returned to, postpneumonia, Austin stopped biting back things like *I love how intense you get about Parmigiano Reggiano versus Romano cheese* just because they had the L-word in them?

Joe didn't have to reciprocate now. Austin could wait—as long as he knew Joe wanted to one day. That they wouldn't remain stuck in this weird limbo place forever. That meant more to him than the house. And if Austin practiced that, he could ease into the words thing. Maybe he could even casually drop into conversation that he'd sold the garage. He couldn't go backward.

He could only move toward a future and hope it had room in it for him and Joe together.

JOE SAT in the Timmies parking lot with his engine off and the cabin slowly cooling. Hopefully Will would be let off shift soon, because Joe was all for not idling to save the planet, but he didn't want to freeze his balls off to do it.

Maybe he should have gone inside, but he was trying to give the kid some space. He'd shown up once to do the teasing proud dad thing, making a big deal out of Will taking his order—just enough to be embarrassing but not enough to make Will quit and refuse to speak to him again.

But as much as Joe didn't want to embarrass Will further, it was fucking cold and the kid's shift ended five minutes ago, according to his dashboard clock.

Joe sipped his drive-through coffee to warm up and pondered the best way to entertain himself. He could text Austin, but the guy was still at work for at least another thirty minutes, and given that he'd apparently permanently cut back on his hours—a fact Joe felt guilty about and that Austin wouldn't talk about, thus ramping up his guilt—Joe didn't want to distract him and take away any *more* working minutes.

Maybe he could call Starling?

"Ugh, it's almost as cold in here as it is outside," Will griped before he was all the way in the cab.

Joe rolled his eyes and said cheerfully, "Well, if you didn't leave me waiting out here for ten minutes, it wouldn't be an issue."

Will glared as he buckled his seat belt. "It's not my fault that I have to change and shit after my shift is done."

Joe turned on the engine. "Note to self: Show up fifteen minutes late from now on unless the weather is nice."

"You're such a dad," Will groaned. Then, before Joe could say anything to prove or disprove that statement, he asked, "What's for dinner?"

Teenagers. "Too tired for fancy. Austin's picking up a roast chicken and fresh bread, and we're making a salad."

"I can't believe I ever thought Austin was cool," Will said. "You two are the most boring married couple I know and it's barely been six months since you met."

Hands tightening on the steering wheel, Joe flushed. His mouth went dry. He and Austin were not "married." "We're not—" he started.

Will flapped a hand. "Whatever. Legal paperwork. You're good as. Though Gavin's gonna be super pissed if you don't have a summer wedding. He wants to throw wildflowers when he's flower girl."

"Wildflowers—girl—what?" Thank God Joe was stopped at a red light and could check his ersatz child for signs of insanity.

Will looked like his usual sassy self. He rolled his eyes. "He called dibs. The rest of us are holding out for groomspeople, but you know Gav. I think he just wants to throw shit."

"Will—" A horn honked behind them. Joe jumped, checked the light, and hit the gas. "Austin and I are not getting married. We haven't even—we're taking things slow."

A long, echoing pause filled the truck. Joe didn't take his eyes off the road, but he could feel Will's gaze.

"I'm sorry, what?"

"We're taking—"

"I heard you," Will sassed, "I just can't believe you."

Joe didn't want to know. He didn't want the answer. He should run away from this conversation right now.

Instead he asked, "Why not?"

"Joe. You live together with five dependents, four of which are ten-to-fifteen-year commitments. Austin is the emergency contact in your phone, which everyone knows now because that's who Greg called when you had pneumonia." Will kind of sounded like he was trying not to laugh. Joe steadfastly kept his eyes on the road and tried to breathe. "He has your mom's phone number. *You took him to meet Nonna.*" Will was *definitely* trying not to laugh.

"That was…. He didn't have anywhere else to go at Christmas. I'd do that for anyone."

"Right, sure," Will said distractedly.

Another red light. Joe blinked and risked a look over. "Who are you texting?"

"Like I'm going to keep this to myself."

In the cupholder, Joe's phone lit up, and lit up, and lit up.

And lit up.

Oh Jesus. They had another five minutes of drive to go. Five minutes during which Joe couldn't defend himself and the kids could roast him unchecked until he was nothing more than charcoal smoldering in the grate.

It wasn't that Joe was unaware of the fact that he and Austin had skipped past a few relationship milestones on the cohabitation and joint-property-ownership fronts. But he hadn't thought about what that meant for their relationship and its level of seriousness.

No, scratch that—he hadn't *let* himself think about it. Because after Paul, Joe was gun-shy. No one would have accused Joe of having had good luck in relationships. In fact, Starling would tell anyone, Joe included, that his taste in people sucked. Mostly because Joe had a tendency to read people wrong—crush on the lesbian, be serious with those who wanted one-night stands, fail to see the interest of those who were genuine. But Paul had been a truly spectacularly bad choice. Looking back, Joe could see he'd invested too much, held on too long.

Will kept his peace for the rest of the drive home, and Joe was almost grateful for that until he parked and realised Will's nose had been buried in his phone the past five minutes. He left the truck without saying anything, and that fact had Joe reaching immediately for his own phone.

The chat was still firing—the kids typing so fast he could hardly catch up.

Gang, folks, siblings. Joe says he and Austin are taking things slow
What?
Huh?
More info, doesn't compute
That is what he told me! No summer wedding because they're quote taking things slow

....

What?
You told him that makes no sense right?
Joe, you know you shouldn't smoke while at work right? Or before driving?
Or after having pneumonia?
He's not high, just dumb
You own pets together!
More importantly
They own a house!
They adopted Will!
Austin came to my swim meet.

It's like not wanting to get married 6 months after meeting a guy isn't a valid life choice, Joe wrote back. Seriously, he'd think the kids would be happy he wasn't rushing into anything.

He headed into the house and found Will in the kitchen, typing on his phone, a carrot stick poking out of his mouth like a parody of a cigar. Joe probably should have been more afraid to look at the chat.

He's talking to your uncle Marco about redoing the en suite in your bedroom, you absolute buffoon

Home reno and collaboration with extended family
Your boring homelife is nauseating

What was nauseating was this conversation. The evidence was damning, and Joe couldn't ignore what it all added up to. Not that it kept him from trying.

He just doesn't like sharing a bathroom with a teenager.

Will tore his eyes away from his phone to give Joe a Look. Then he typed out, *Every time you talk about home staging, he looks like you kicked Pepa in front of him.*

More laughter and mocking followed in the chat.

Joe slumped into a kitchen chair and rested his head against the table.

"I'm in love," he whispered to himself. His phone stopped vibrating. "I'm in love with Austin."

"Uh, yeah?" Will said, taking the seat opposite him. "Did you seriously not know this?"

Joe groaned. His phone had gone suspiciously quiet. Desperate for the distraction, he asked about it.

"I told them you were having a breakdown because apparently this was somehow news to you, so they should cut out the teasing in the group chat until I could figure out what level of breakdown we were talking about."

Jesus Christ. At least he'd done *something* right.

"Should I get you a drink? What's the protocol?" He paused. "Or, like, I could call Starling?"

"Jesus Christ," Joe said out loud this time. "Don't put me on the news. You guys already sunk my battleship, okay?" Nobody else needed to use him for target practice today.

Will frowned. "Sure, whatever. But… I don't get it. Like… 'Oh no, I'm in love with my husband who wants to build me an expensive luxury bathroom.' Boo hoo."

Husband. That word again. Joe was going to start tearing his hair out.

"Uh," Will went on before Joe could get further into his breakdown, "that came out meaner than I meant it to. But, like… love is good, right? Like, the dream? Please don't make me talk to you about how hot Austin is. That would be so awkward."

"Oh God."

"Right?" Will said. "So like… beer? Is that the move? Or is that the first step on the path to alcoholism?"

"No beer," Joe decided. Nothing foamy should touch his stomach right now. His digestive system was already throwing a rager. He needed to take a minute.

When the moment had passed, Will got up anyway and went to the fridge. He returned a moment later with a glass of water, which he put in front of Joe, and then he started taking vegetables out of the fridge. "I still don't get what's so bad about this."

"I'm not *good at it*," Joe blurted.

There was a loud clatter. Joe looked up to see Will had dropped the knife he'd been using to chop up a cucumber. "*What*?"

Fuck, he should've kept his mouth shut. Now he had to explain, or—or he'd end up with Will trying to make him feel better. Will was his *kid*. Will had just gotten disowned. Joe couldn't put his own bullshit trauma on his kid.

"Joe." Will looked like he'd been gutted. "You are really, horrifyingly good at love, okay? You're the reason we know what that is."

"I'm good at loving people," Joe corrected. "I'm not good at keeping someone in love with me."

He didn't look up from the table.

Will picked up the knife and put it in the sink before sitting down across from him again. "This is about *Paul*?"

He said it so incredulously Joe had to look at him. Will was looking at him like he'd grown a second head and then punched it in the face. "People who don't learn from their mistakes repeat them."

And Joe had tried so hard not to repeat the mistakes he'd made with Paul. He'd tried to keep his hands and his heart to himself. With Paul everything had moved so fast. He'd gotten swept up in it. And at the end of it all he'd lost Paul, had to leave his job, walked away from the house where he was already envisioning their future.

"Austin and Paul aren't even the same *species*."

"Maybe not now," Joe allowed. "But their closets look kind of the same."

Will frowned again. "Is that, like, a—what are they called? Euphemism? What does that mean?"

"No, it's not gay code, it's—I mean they both liked to go to the clubs a lot. So they had lots of clubbing clothes."

Now Will was just flat-out staring. "I have literally never seen Austin wear anything other than coveralls and flannel unless it was something he obviously stole out of *your* closet. Or DeeDee's." He paused. "Do you think he'd let me borrow some shirts?"

"I think I'll definitely need that beer if he does." God, soon Will wouldn't even need a fake ID to get into clubs. Joe might as well have become a grandfather after all. He could feel arthritis settling in. He had the sudden urge to check the backs of his hands for liver spots.

Will rolled his eyes. "Okay, but the point is, obviously Austin's not going out clubbing at the moment. He's picking up dinner. Just like he picked up dinner when you were sick. Like he washed your sheets every day and missed work and shit taking care of you. Because he loves you. And he's *not* like Paul."

Once when Joe got strep throat, Paul moved back in with his parents for a week.

Joe took a deep breath and forced the residual panic from his brain just as Pepa perked up in the dining room and started barking.

Austin was home.

Will stood up and went back to the counter to finish with the vegetables. "This conversation isn't over," he warned.

"It definitely is."

Before Will could protest, the door opened, admitting a gust of cold wind, the scent of roasted chicken, and Austin, dressed in ancient jeans and one of Joe's sweatshirts. He set the grocery bags on the table and then bent to give Pepa her due attention. "Hey, pretty girl. Did you miss me?"

Pepa wagged her tail so hard it made a repeated thunking noise against the leg of the dining table, echoing the thud of Joe's heart.

God, he was dumb.

Apparently having guessed that Joe had not recovered from his trauma, Will piped up, "Hey, Austin."

"Hey, Will." There was a double thwack of boots hitting the mat, and then Austin entered the kitchen. He ruffled Will's hair, set the chicken down on the counter, and made a beeline for Joe. "Hey, sweet thing."

Joe tilted his face up automatically for the soft kiss Austin planted at the corner of his eye. "Hi."

"Brought you some dessert."

The plain white box Austin slid onto the table smelled like butter and chocolate and pastry. Joe eased open the flap with his thumb and tried to devour the contents with his eyes. "Are these from—"

"That place you like on Erie Street, yeah." So Austin had driven forty minutes out of his way to get Joe's favorite cannoli. No—longer than that, if he left from the garage to pick them up; that drive would take at least a half an hour at this time of day. "I still think Nutella is disgusting, but it's cool, I can eat the ricotta or lemon one."

Joe felt Will's eyes on the side of his face like a laser, practically etching *I told you so* into Joe's skin.

"Thank you," Joe said, a credible imitation of a normal person despite the emotions crowding his chest.

"You're welcome. So—are we spoiling our dinner, or are we going to pretend we're adults?"

Chapter Twenty-Eight

NOW THAT Will had pried Joe's eyes open, he was seeing all kinds of things he hadn't noticed. When Austin folded his own laundry, he often left his clothes inside-out, but he knew it drove Joe crazy, so he turned Joe's right-side out. He never complained about buying Joe's fancy coffee creamer (which Joe denied using to the rest of the Romanos because he didn't want to be mocked forever). He called every day on his way home from work to find out if Joe needed him to pick up groceries or Timmies or a stray child.

Every time Will caught Austin doing one of these things now, he met Joe's eyes and mouthed *He loooooooves you* or, for variety, made exaggerated kissy faces.

Even the horribly awkward conversation Joe had to initiate about paying Austin back for the electrical work went well.

"I just have to move some stuff around," Joe said. He didn't want to touch the money he'd put aside for the kids, but considering he was on a limited income until spring came around and landscaping picked up, he didn't have much choice. "I'm sorry it's taken this long, I—"

Austin caught his hands before he could gesture any further. "Hey. Take a breath."

How could he? How could Joe take a breath when Austin was right in front of him looking at him like that, with those big soft dark eyes so full of—

He took a breath.

Austin squeezed his fingers. "It's okay. Really. I know you're good for it. It can wait."

But *something* wasn't right.

Like—Austin always called when he was leaving work, but he kept getting home too soon. The drive should've lasted ten more minutes. And when he got home, he always went right into the garage and changed, even though it was absolutely fucking frigid in there. If he was only worried about tracking in dirt or oil, he could've changed in the breezeway, which was at least a seminormal temperature, even if they didn't burn wood in the stove as much now that the pets were all recovered and housebroken.

And there were other weird things. Austin used to drive Joe nuts with the Facebook message tone on his phone, always people wanting to know garage hours or make appointments or whatever. Now Austin was getting phone calls instead. Who got phone calls anymore?

No one their age liked talking on the phone unless they had to. Or were hiding something.

Paul's phone habits had changed in the months leading up to their breakup. Only afterward did Joe realise he was trying to avoid the paper trail of text messages. Though if Joe were the type to snoop, the call log would have been just as incriminating.

Joe's brain screeched to a halt as he considered the implications of what he'd just thought, but then he shook it off. There was no way Austin would do that to him. Not Austin, who was gentle with the kids and the animals and smiled at Joe like he hung the moon.

Right?

NOW THAT the thought had occurred to Joe, he couldn't seem to shake it. So much about Austin's routine had changed. When it was just the earlier return home or traveling from a different direction, Joe could wave it off as Austin changing things up to adapt to their new circumstance and Joe's illness, but it wasn't just that. Austin was hiding something. Changing before he came inside, secret phone calls, and now he was being… weird.

Like bringing Joe the cannoli or offering to drive Will to school, or taking care of the massive bathroom spider without fussing or asking Joe to do it. Like he needed to make up for something.

Joe thought about bringing it up, but what was he going to say? "Hey, why are you being so nice to me?" That was an objectively insane thing to say to your boyfriend.

So Joe kept his mouth shut.

As February wound into March, the weather warmed and Joe started booking summer work. New money, more money, coming in was essential for the health of Joe's bank account. Not to mention that more consistent work outside the house and property would be good for Joe's mental health. He'd never been very good with idle hands, and while normally the fixer-upper would be a great way of keeping busy, it wasn't exactly distracting Joe from his troubles. Not when each decision was tinged with repeated reminders of his future. He could make everything to his taste as much as he wanted—he wouldn't be the one living here.

Of course, the dwindling days of winter also meant something else—early acceptance to higher education.

Joe still didn't know what Alex was planning, but he suspected there might some trade-school forms hidden away. Gavin was also a mystery, to himself as much as anyone else. Fortunately he was totally sanguine about having no idea what he wanted to do with the rest of his life and happily talked about taking time off and getting a job. Or "the real-life experience of capitalism," as he called it.

"I'll come work for you," he'd started telling Joe the year before, with an easy grin and promises to behave. Of course, recently he'd started to talk about working for Austin instead, especially whenever Austin was more lenient than Joe in enforcing boundaries. Austin hadn't agreed to anything, but always encouraged Gavin to explore his options and not feel the need to just go work for his dad.

But Will and Meg had sent out applications, and while finances were likely to curb Will's options, the sky was the limit for Meg. The kid was Olympic-hopeful level of talent, which meant she'd have her pick of Canadian and American schools. Not that Joe was willing to risk jinxing things, but he was pretty sure she'd get a full ride. She was smart enough for it too.

So it was hardly a surprise when Meg texted the group chat one afternoon with a shot of an early acceptance from the University of Michigan.

And naturally, since Joe was a spiralling stressed-out emotional mess who loved feeding all of his adopted children, he texted back the date and time for a celebratory dinner.

AUSTIN KNEW how Joe got about dinners. He suspected part of it was hereditary—he'd experienced a Romano family dinner, after all, and Nonna made Joe look like an absolute beginner. So in the days leading up to the event, he made it a point to get home on time, pick up a few extra chores, run the vacuum a little more frequently. He had more energy now than he'd had in years anyway, probably from a combination of working fewer hours and eating better food, though the quality of sleep he got passed out next to Joe factored in too. After work one day, he even went by the hardware store and bought a plastic bin to go in the fridge, which he labeled in Sharpie: FAMILY DINNER SUPPLIES. DO NOT EAT.

Will got a look at it when he was getting out the condiments for dinner one night and gave him bombastic side-eye, but Austin just said, "Your father is under a lot of stress," and went on with his sudoku puzzle.

Will closed the fridge and the side-eye became a staredown Austin could feel right through the feeble protection of the newspaper. "You could fix that."

He set his pen down. "I'm trying," he pointed out, gesturing to the fridge. He hadn't reorganized the thing and made himself promise implicitly to lay off the three pounds of cheese because he was worried about his cholesterol.

The stare did not abate.

"What?" Austin asked when Will didn't offer anything further.

He shook his head. "Nothing." But Austin thought he heard him muttering under his breath as he returned upstairs. "Un-be-fuckin'-lievable."

Austin had to work the day of the dinner, but the kids were all coming over right after school, so he cleaned up and changed at work and sent Joe a text—*call if you need anything on my way home*—and then got in his car.

The phone remained silent, so it was only a short time before Austin pulled into the driveway. He parked in front of the pole barn, next to Meg's little Chevy, and did his best to skirt the half-frozen puddles and slush piles on his way to the door. Not that the kids had bothered, judging by the melting goo pooling on the boot mat.

Austin added his own to the pile and poked his head into the kitchen, which already smelled like Joe's enchilada casserole. "Hey."

Four heads looked up from the table, two from the floor—the kids, Pepa, and Ozzy, but no Joe. Meg and Gavin waved; Alex nodded. Will huffed.

Tough crowd. "Where's Joe?"

"Went to change his shirt," Will said shortly.

God, did Will have something up his ass again? Austin hoped not. This was supposed to be a night for celebrating. He glanced at the stove timer. "Cool. Hey, help me set the table?"

It was another three minutes before Joe came in, face pink like he'd just scrubbed it with cold water. Austin hooked an arm around his waist before he could get to the kitchen and pulled him in for a kiss. "Hey. Enchilada sauce accident?"

Joe blinked at him as though he didn't know what Austin was talking about. Then he looked down at his shirt. "Oh. Uh… yeah."

Austin frowned. "Are you feeling okay? You're not getting a fever again, are you?"

Joe batted his hand away from his forehead. "I'm fine," he promised. "Can we eat?"

That wasn't like him, to be so short, but maybe he was stressed. Maybe he'd gotten enchilada sauce on one of Gavin's hilarious tree pun shirts. "Guess we better before the kids decide Pepa looks edible."

Joe snorted. "I think they'd eat Will first."

"Harsh."

Dinner was—well, the food was good. Austin had questioned the wisdom of inviting Alex to a dinner to celebrate Meg when the two of them still had bouts of sniping, but Joe pointed out he couldn't very well invite Gavin and not Alex without Alex feeling left out, or Gavin deciding not to come, and they figured they had to risk it.

And honestly Austin thought it was going okay until Meg asked Alex if they ever finished that rainbow sweater they were knitting.

It seemed like an innocuous question to Austin. Certainly no one else at the table seemed to think it landed like a grenade. Even Alex barely reacted, only shrugged disinterestedly. "I'm not really into knitting anymore."

Maybe Meg's question flew under the radar, but Alex's answering tone did not. Gavin and Joe both raised their heads. Austin caught himself ping-ponging between expressions, trying to gauge what was about to go down. Should he clear the table of projectiles?

"Oh." Meg deflated a little. She'd eaten a little over half her plate, which Austin knew by now was not enough to sustain an athlete of her caliber. The girl's appetite was impressive. "You never said anything. I thought maybe we could do, like, our knitting thing next year. Like we used to, but on Skype or Facetime or whatever."

That was a fucking friendship overture. Austin might not have a lot of friends, but even he could see that. And Alex was stabbing their plate like it had personally insulted them.

Still, Meg went on bravely. Austin felt like he was watching a car wreck in slow motion. "We could do something else instead," she offered. "Like, remember when we all had to quarantine and we went online and binge-watched *iCarly*—"

Alex's palm landed flat on the table. Will jumped. "That show's for little girls."

Meg's slam echoed theirs like she'd just been waiting for those words. "Yeah," she said coolly. "Except for how anybody can like anything, because gender's a social construct."

Alex's mouth dropped open and they flushed deep enough to highlight the trio of freckles by their nose.

"Like, whatever," Meg went on before Alex could defend themself. "I get why you didn't want to tell me you thought you might be pregnant, because that shit's scary even without the gender dysphoria. So whatever. It hurt, 'cause I thought we were friends, I've been *trying* to be friends, I've been trying to understand what you're going through. But it's like you realized you weren't a girl and somehow that meant you couldn't do anything girly. Like have *girl friends* or talk about boys or fucking *knit*. Which is so stupid! Will talks about boys! Lots of people knit! But you ditched all the hobbies you thought were too *femme* and you ditched *me*, and I dare you to tell me it's made you any fucking happier."

"People change," Alex snapped back. "I'm allowed to not like stuff anymore."

"That's not what I said!"

"You don't get to decide for me!"

"Exactly! Neither should anyone else! So why are you letting *society* have a say?"

Alex opened their mouth, shut it, opened it, then shut it again. A tense silence bubbled around them, and Austin wondered if now was the time to cut in. Or maybe he and Joe should make a run for it. This felt like not the kind of conversation to be hashed out around parents.

"You thought you might be pregnant?" Everyone turned to Gavin, who was pale and staring wide-eyed at Alex, all wounded puppy. "Why didn't you tell me?"

The table swiveled back to Alex. At least Austin wasn't the only one watching this play out like he'd scored front-row seats to the taping of a soap opera. Will looked like he wanted popcorn.

"I—I—because Schrödinger's pregnancy! Not knowing was less terrifying and I was already stressed, which is why I skipped my period in the first place." Alex hugged themselves, but now that the dam was broken, they couldn't seem to stop. "I was stressed about school and exams and what'll happen next year and fighting with Meg and whether or not you liking me means you think I'm a girl and—"

"Wait, I've been banging you for months and you still think I'm *straight*?"

"Banging," Will whispered, almost gleeful. Joe groaned softly and glanced longingly at his glass like he wanted something harder to drink than fizzy water.

"What?" Alex looked poleaxed.

Gavin shrugged. "I don't have, like, a label or anything. Maybe I'm just Alex-sexual."

"Alex-sexual," Alex said. "That sounds dumb."

"What? I've been in love with you since I was eight, so the question's kind of, like, mote, or whatever."

"Moot," Joe said quietly.

"Yeah, that." Gavin snapped his fingers and pointed at Joe.

Silence reigned as everyone took all that in. Austin spent several agonizing heartbeats achingly, furiously jealous that Gavin could say that so easily. Like it was so obvious that he wasn't telling anyone anything they didn't already know. Unconcerned with whether it was too soon (how could it be?), sure Alex would want to hear it.

Then Joe picked up his glass and eyed his water and Austin reminded himself this was not about him. "I understand why people exploit their families for money on YouTube now."

Will snorted, still looking gleeful, probably because today he was in no way part of the drama.

Giving up, apparently, Joe reached back for a bottle of wine on the sideboard. "Christ, does anyone else want a drink?"

"Not the red," Austin said, because that was the last thing they needed.

Joe grunted and stood, heading for the white in the fridge, Austin assumed.

Meanwhile, Gavin and Alex were sort of just making eyes at each other. Alex hadn't acknowledged Gavin's confession, but Austin suspected that had more to do with the audience than a lack of reciprocation.

Joe returned with a bottle of white, as predicted, and two glasses.

"So, now that Gavin's acknowledged that liking you doesn't make you a girl," Meg said—Austin winced, but Alex just rolled their eyes, so maybe that wasn't too harsh—"can we talk about how you're totally still allowed to like what you want and shit?"

Joe handed Austin a healthy glass, and he drank deeply and braced himself for what came next.

Alex frowned. "You might have a point about the knitting. And still being able to like it. Just. You get why it's hard going to feminist stuff that's all about *women*, right?"

Meg frowned back. "I mean, I know some of it is women-based, but. like, men and enbies can be feminists too. And," she said, picking up steam, "you thought you were pregnant—which is why intersectional feminist issues like abortion rights should still matter to you."

Alex frowned deeper and pushed their food around their plate. Everyone else at the table held their breath. "Okay, so maybe I was having a bit of a dysphoric freak-out," they admitted. "I'm allowed to say no to stuff and it not be, like, a total rejection of you. But also, I could try to be better about, you know, talking to you about my feelings and not saying no to everything."

Meg burst into tears. Alex stumbled over themself getting out of the chair and getting to Meg, and then the kids were hugging and crying together. It hit Austin suddenly that *this* was who Meg and Alex were as friends, and that he'd never actually seen them being their true selves, at least with regards to their friendship.

He glanced at Joe and caught him trying to covertly wipe tears from his eyes. How much stress had Joe been carrying around, worrying about two of his children not getting on?

"Time for dessert?" Austin asked in an undertone. Joe nodded and stood, but as he walked to the kitchen, tension crept back into his shoulders. Austin had no idea what could possibly be bothering him now, but maybe he could lighten the mood and bring a bit of humor back. "Teenagers. All that drama. Glad we're too old for that shit." He chuckled and bumped their hips together.

Next to him, Joe went rigid.

Did he hit a sore spot? Austin didn't remember him having any bruises. "Hey. You okay?"

The dessert plates clanked onto the counter. "Why wouldn't I be?"

"Because you just totally froze? And because those are your favorite plates and you're always really careful with them?" Too late, Austin realized that was probably a rhetorical question.

"I'm fine," Joe snapped.

This was such an obvious lie it left Austin grasping for a rebuttal. He was blaming his total shock for the fact that the next words out of his mouth were, "Okay, maybe I was wrong about being too old for drama."

One of the kids dropped a utensil. Otherwise the house went silent.

Then Will said, "Actually I think we're gonna wait on dessert— take Pepa for a walk before it gets too dark, you know?"

The other three fell over themselves to agree and scampered out of the house. Austin didn't think they'd ever moved so fast, not that he was watching them. He couldn't tear his eyes away from Joe.

But Joe wasn't having the same problem. As the kids left, he turned his back to Austin. The wine bottle went back in the fridge. The magnet holding Will's work schedule fell off with the force of Joe closing the door.

What the fuck.

Austin could no longer keep the question in. "Are you going to tell me what's going on?"

Joe whirled around. "Shouldn't I be asking you that?"

Apparently hanging out with the kids and three cats and a dog had taught Austin a lot about patience. "Joe. I don't know what you're talking about. Can you please tell me why you're upset?"

For a second Joe only gaped at him. Then he said, "Because you're hiding something!"

Oh fuck.

"Did you think I wouldn't notice when you started changing in the garage when you got home?" Joe's face contorted. "Or that you changed your work hours? No way you're working as much as you used to. And the number of times I see your car coming home from the wrong direction—"

So he knew. He knew Austin had sold the garage and he was pissed because Austin hadn't told him. But why hadn't he said anything before now?

Finally Joe stopped pacing and faced him head on. "Just give it to me straight. Are you cheating on me?"

Wait, what the fuck? "*Why would I do that?*" Austin said. "I *love you!*"

Oh Jesus. He probably shouldn't have shouted that.

Joe gaped at him, red-faced. "Um," he said.

What the fuck? Austin repeated in his head.

"But the—the work hours? And the clothes changing? And the phone calls. And you didn't want red wine—"

"We have a houseful of kids," Austin pointed out, because that seemed the most pressing issue. "Sorry for wanting a *little* privacy in our sex life, which I absolutely will not get if you drink red wine, sweet thing."

The endearment slipped out. It felt awkward at a moment like this, when Joe was being, frankly, kind of insane. But Austin couldn't help it. Obviously Joe had worked himself into a frenzy. Now Austin had to talk him out of it.

Joe blinked and licked his lips. "But—okay, and last weekend you didn't want me to, uh...."

"Fuck me into a coma at ten o'clock on Saturday morning?" Austin filled in. Because yeah, he'd stopped Joe from trying to make him come more than once. "And... what, you thought I was *saving it for someone else?*"

Joe averted his eyes.

For fuck's sake. "Babe. I love how well you know my body and how good you can make me feel, but if you want to fuck me like that, you need to tell me in advance so I can clear my schedule for the rest of the day, because I'm too stupid afterward to *watch TV*. Take some pity and wait until the afternoon at least."

Joe made an embarrassed noise that he muffled in his sleeve, half turned away. His ears were bright red too. After a moment he turned back and met Austin's gaze. "And, uh, and the changing, and the... coming home from the wrong way...?"

Austin had to tell him now. He would've done it weeks ago if he'd known Joe would jump to this kind of conclusion. "Sweet thing." He held out his hands. Joe took them. "I sold the garage."

Joe's mouth dropped open. "What?" And then: "Why?"

He shook his head, pulling Joe closer. He wasn't allowed to try to get away. He wasn't allowed to feel guilty about this. "You were sick. Starling needed the money we owed her. I was trying to figure out what to do, if I could borrow against the house, but I think I'd need your sign-off on that 'cause we're co-owners, and then I remembered your mom mentioned she had a client who was looking for commercial property on that section of Malden, so...."

"My *mom* was in on this?" His voice cracked, and shame crept into his expression, and he tried to take a step back. Austin kept gentle hold of his elbows. "If you—where have you been going?"

"*Work*," Austin said. "Uh, the dealership in town happened to be hiring. It was fate, I guess."

Joe took a deep breath. He was taller than Austin, and broader, but right now he seemed tiny in Austin's arms. He was better at hiding his neuroses than Austin had given him credit for too. Austin wouldn't make that mistake again. "Why didn't you tell me?"

Austin cupped his cheek. "I knew you'd feel like it was your fault, and I didn't want that. And you were so determined we had to take things slowly. If you thought I sold the garage for our relationship…."

Groaning, Joe closed his eyes and leaned his head into Austin's touch. Something inside Austin started to unwind. Joe was getting closer, not farther away. "I've been so stupid."

"Hey." He bent forward until their foreheads touched.

"No, Austin. Fuck, I'm so—if I'd just *asked*—"

"I could've told you about the garage at any time," Austin said gently.

Joe opened his eyes only to narrow them. "Don't let me off the hook. I've been such a *baby*."

"You maybe should get some therapy," Austin said lightly. "I think my fancy new insurance might cover that, actually."

JOE LAUGHED wetly, wondering how in the world this conversation had ended up here. Austin wasn't wrong. He probably *should* invest in therapy if a few presents had him freaking out this badly.

He was still processing the conversation from most to least recent, because his brain could only handle so many surprises at once, so he started with a weak attempt at a joke to divert attention from his sniffling. "Putting me on your insurance isn't exactly going slow, since I don't really qualify as a dependent." He couldn't bring himself to let go of Austin's hands to wipe his eyes.

Austin shrugged. "No. Putting you down as my domestic partner on official paperwork is definitely not slow, but I'm tired of slow. I'd rather be honest about what I want."

Honesty.

Joe didn't want to go slow anymore either. Had they ever even really done that, or had they only lied to themselves about it? From day one Joe had known he could have feelings for Austin. He'd told himself he'd keep on his guard, but he hadn't. He didn't want to.

He wanted to be here, in this house, with Austin, being honest about what he wanted.

Joe's brain processed a little farther back. What Austin wanted was Joe. Because Austin loved him. And Joe had kind of left him hanging.

"I, ah." Austin squeezed his fingers. "I love you too."

A smile took over Austin's face. "Yeah?"

Joe nodded, feeling the pressure in his chest ease at the admission. "I think I have for a while, but I didn't let myself think about it."

"Flattering," Austin said dryly, but he didn't look angry. The smile didn't even leave his lips.

"I'm sorry I've been kind of, uh… irrational." He swallowed. "I know you're not Paul. I think I just… I got in my head and assumed the worst and—"

"Sweet thing"—Joe's breath hitched to hear that name said so tenderly—"your behavior is totally understandable."

"Still dumb, though."

Austin cupped his face and brushed his thumbs along Joe's cheeks. "I'm not saying I wanna do this again, but I won't hold one moment of temporary paranoia against you."

"Ha, thanks."

There was no choice but to kiss Austin then. Austin moaned into his mouth and twined his arms around Joe, who was suddenly keenly aware of how long it had been since the last time Joe hadn't been an anxious mess while they made love. Suddenly he desperately wanted to go to bed and make Austin feel good in all the ways they'd talked about. After all, it was after dinner—Austin couldn't complain about being too useless until bed at this time of day.

Then the sound of the front door opening interrupted those thoughts.

Joe groaned and buried his face in Austin's hair. "Why did we have kids, darling?"

Austin chuckled. "Your idea," he reminded Joe, scritching his nails pleasantly through Joe's hair. "I'm attached now, though, so why don't you plate that dessert, and then later tonight, after they've gone home, you can fuck me through as many orgasms as you'd like." He paused and then added, "Sweet thing," whispered right in his ear, which sent delicious shivers through him.

"Right. Dessert. Then orgasms."

AUSTIN FOLLOWED through on his promise to let Joe have his way, so Joe felt no shame about sleeping in the next morning. In fact, he felt no small amount of pride at waking to Austin's slack face and leaving him snuggled under the covers to go make breakfast.

Thank God Will had opted to spend last night at Meg's place. He'd originally said he was leaving to stay with Gavin, but one incredulous unhappy look from Alex put an end to that.

Since the house was gloriously free of teenagers, Joe decided to go wild and crazy and make a french toast and bacon breakfast that wouldn't be hogged. He and Austin ate in the kitchen in their boxers, standing up, trading syrup-sticky kisses that eventually needed to be showered off.

They took a lazy walk with Pepa and played with the kittens, Joe sitting on the couch and Austin on the floor, leaning on his legs; they passed the laser pointer back and forth. Finally even Ozzy tired of the game and climbed into Austin's lap instead.

Joe wanted to pet something too, but Walker and Dallas had abandoned them to investigate criminal insect activity in the basement. He contented himself with running his fingers through Austin's hair.

"You're gonna ruin my curls," Austin complained halfheartedly, pushing his head deeper into Joe's touch.

"I'll wash it for you again later."

"That's not good for curly hair," Austin grumbled, but he didn't move, so Joe didn't stop. He half felt like he could hear Austin purring.

Some combination of the sex and the breakfast and the release of tension from last night, or maybe the soft, damp warmth of Austin's hair sliding between his fingers, made him brave. Or maybe it wasn't bravery. Maybe it was hope. He swallowed. "Austin."

"Mm-hmm."

He took a fortifying breath. "I love you."

Now Austin tilted his head back, smiling. He couldn't reach Joe's mouth from that angle, so he caught his wrist and pressed his lips to that. "Yeah, sweet thing. I love you too."

Okay, Joe. Now the rest of it. "I don't want to sell the house."

For a second Austin froze. Then he carefully removed Ozzy from his lap and turned around, taking Joe's hand in both of his. "Okay," he said softly. His eyes were warm. "We won't sell the house." Like it was that easy.

Joe wished it were. He swallowed. "But I, uh, I can't pay you back yet, if we don't. Landscaping work will pick up soon, but—"

Austin rose and pressed a finger to his lips.

Joe swallowed again.

"I don't need it," Austin said. "I told you. It can wait." He pursed his lips. "When you were a kid, did you ever imagine where you'd live when you grew up? What you wanted your house to look like?"

"Sure. Doesn't everyone?"

Austin shrugged. "Maybe not the way you think. See, because I had dreams, sure, but I'd been poor my whole life. I wanted a dream I could make come true. Big houses cost money. So I thought, you know, I'd probably live in an apartment. If I was lucky maybe I could buy one instead of renting. And then I thought, well, what if I have a business? Maybe I could live there. And that's what I did. But all those dreams? They were black and white, sweet thing. Just me alone in a place to call my own. Four walls and a roof and hot running water."

Joe swallowed. Austin had sold that dream for him. "Baby—"

"Not done," Austin said gently. "I'm trying to tell you I never even let myself dream of this—not just a place to live but a home and a partner and a family that loves each other. Not until a little old lady grandparent-trapped me into it. I have never been so rich. So all that worrying you're doing? I get it. I did it already. I made my choice, and I have no regrets."

Joe blinked away the sting in his eyes. "Okay," he rasped. "I get it. I just… I hate owing you. It's, like, probably pathological."

"Probably a little toxic masculinity at work too," Austin suggested. Which…. Joe's family was loving but pretty traditional. It was a fair cop.

Joe sighed. "Yeah."

Austin turned his hand over and kissed his palm. "Thank you."

"For what?"

He shook his head. Joe really had made a mess of his hair. "I never wanted to sell the house."

"Oh." He'd played that close to the chest. Well, Joe was the one who wanted to go slow. Talk about working against your own interests. He smiled. "I should probably talk to my mom."

He rang her up and arranged for an after-lunch coffee. A few hours later, he sat at her kitchen table and broke the news.

To her credit, his mom didn't even twitch or try to talk him out of it, just raised an eyebrow and nodded. "So are you hoping to keep both properties long term?" Ever the real estate agent.

Joe rubbed his face and sighed. "Selling the barndominium and setting up shop in the barn on our property would make the most sense. But I've owned it less than two years, so listing it...."

"Might not be the right move," she finished for him. Commission would eat up too much of what Joe could get out of it. His mom could give him a break, but that would make the property less attractive to agents representing buyers, since their cut would be smaller too. "Well," she said slowly, "if you can get the business set up at the farmhouse, then you could always lease the barndominium to another business until selling makes sense."

Joe nodded. "Yeah, I figure that's the best short-term plan, but I'm not sure our pole barn is suitable for running a business. Might take more than a couple of months to make the move. During which time I'll have to pay the mortgage and spend money and time fixing up the new place, when it's just gearing up to busy season."

"Joe," his mother *tsk*ed.

"I'm well aware that I don't have to go to banks for a loan and family will help me out." He blew out a breath. "I just... goddammit, I managed to get here on my own."

She let the silence hang between them for a moment, as if gathering her thoughts. Then she said, "Not that I want to deny you all of your lovely achievements, but you do realize you've had help. Your friends and family and inheritance from your grandfather were the reason you never had to take out loans in the first place."

Joe opened his mouth, then shut it. Well, shit. What was with his loved ones calling out his bullshit these past twenty-four hours? Clearly Austin had a point about that need for therapy.

He dropped his head to the table and blew out a breath.

"Yes, fine. Point taken. I will make sure to call someone if I need the help and will consider the benefits of an uncle loan over that of a bank."

She patted his head. "Good boy."

Before either of them could say anything else—probably for the best; he was having a moment of uncomfortable dissonance—her front door opened and a familiar voice called out, "Good news—I caught an earlier flight and got you those weird pickles it apparently can't live without."

Joe lifted his head and stared, bewildered, in the direction of the front door, waiting for the appearance of the man who owned that voice.

A beat later, cheeks pink and hair windswept from the late winter weather, Joe's father stepped into the kitchen, carrying a jar of pickles and smiling. But he jerked to a stop when he caught sight of his son sitting at the kitchen table. Which was beyond weird, since Joe would have sworn that the only reason his dad would have had to return to his previous marital home was to see his son, not his ex-wife. But clearly he hadn't known Joe was there.

"José!" A smile overtook his face, and he swept forward. Despite his confusion, Joe rose quickly, happy to see his father no matter the circumstance, and let himself be pulled into his father's embrace.

Julio Gonzales Vasquez was a large man. He'd been slim in his youth, so said the old photographs, but had thickened out in his thirties. Joe had only ever known the six-foot-plus linebacker of a figure that stood before him now. Despite his own height, Joe took after his mother's side, and his stomach and jaw showed no signs of broadening like his father's. All of which meant that, despite his age, his father's hugs were just as warm and comforting and protective as they had always been.

"Dad, what are you doing here?" Joe moved to fill a mug with coffee.

"Oh, well," his dad hedged, like he wasn't sure how to answer. That made no sense. His father had spent his entire career working in the diplomatic service. He always knew what to say.

Joe turned to see the most incongruous sight he'd ever seen. His parents were sitting together at the kitchen table like they hadn't done in almost twenty years, looking like something out of Joe's childhood memories—except for the gray around his father's temples and the fact that his mother was apparently so hungry that she couldn't even wait to get a fork and was using her fingers to eat warm pickles straight from the jar.

Joe handed his father the cup and then sat down. Maybe he was still dreaming? He cast baffled looks from one parent to the other, trying to figure out what was going on. Not that his parents noticed—they were too busy having some sort of silent communication.

They must have come to an agreement, because his mother turned her gaze from his dad to her jar of pickles and dipped her French-manicured fingertips into the brine to grab another. "Your father came to visit me. We've decided to give things another go."

Twelve-year-old Joe would have been ecstatic at the news. Sixteen-year-old Joe would have scoffed and asked them if they were deranged.

Adult Joe was just confused. "What?"

"We've been seeing each other for a few months," his dad explained. "A lot of what went wrong for us the first time had to do with our youth. Neither of us really knew ourselves or what we wanted or needed."

"But you do now?" Joe said slowly.

"Yes," his mother said simply.

"And what you want is to date each other." The words felt weird in his mouth.

"Well," his dad said, "we were thinking about getting married again. I've put in for retirement from the service so I can move back here to be with your mom."

Was it April Fool's? No. It was still March. Joe stared at his dad, then his mom. Despite their smiles, neither of them looked like they were joking. No, they had silly love-struck expressions as they stared at each other, besotted. Joe loved his parents—he wanted them to be happy—but he couldn't help but worry that this would end in heartbreak for everyone. "Marriage? Isn't that... rushing things?"

"Maybe a little," his mother conceded, "but with your father's citizenship and upcoming retirement, it makes sense to move up the timeline so it's all sorted before the baby arrives." She took another bite of pickle.

Joe stared. "*Baby?*"

"BABY?"

A bubble of hysterical laughter floated up through Joe's chest, and he giggled. Austin watched him with confusion and alarm. "Baby!" Joe confirmed with a gasp, and then laughed some more.

"Your mother is pregnant." Austin seemed to be struggling to grasp the concept as much as Joe. "And your dad is the father."

"Yes," Joe gasped.

"What the fuck."

"That's what I said."

"Sorry, but like, isn't your mom too old?" He winced then, maybe worried he'd been offensive.

Joe snickered. "I asked that too. Apparently forty-eight isn't, as evidenced by baby." He sobered. "Doctors are keeping a close eye, though. Did you know anyone over the age of, like, thirty-five is considered geriatric when it comes to growing babies?"

"I did not know that."

"Dad says they're going to have lots of visits to make sure all is good, but she seems fine so far."

They sat in silence for a long moment as they both considered that news.

"Whoa."

"What?"

"You're going to be a big brother. Like, biologically this time." Austin grinned. "How does it feel?"

"Fucking surreal," Joe said, then had another round of hysterical laughter. "Jesus Christ, I've gotta tell the kids they're getting a new aunt or uncle and they might have to babysit." Gavin would be so mad if Joe got a sister and Gavin didn't get to be flower girl at the wedding.

Okay, probably he and Austin should talk about getting married before he booted Gavin out of the flower-girl job. Just because they already had four kids, three cats, a dog, and a house didn't mean they should jump right to marriage.

Besides, it might be polite to let his parents get remarried first.

Joe's life was ridiculous.

Chapter Twenty-Nine

CLEARING THE air with Joe didn't immediately solve all the problems at the Taylor-Romano household. Will still had the occasional mood swing, the timing of which Austin couldn't predict, though Joe sometimes could. "It's his sister's birthday tomorrow," he said once, and then, one Saturday in early April, "His brother's getting married today."

But Austin wasn't hiding his phone therapy appointments, or the fact that he was driving ten minutes into Essex instead of twenty in the other direction, and when he came home, he didn't have to hide his branded work shirts.

Joe's work picked up too, as his uncles were putting the final touches on a few houses in an upscale residential development. They offered a package that involved a credit to have Joe do a custom landscaping design or put toward a service, and with the spring rains, it was the perfect time to lay sod and plant boxwoods.

On the whole, things were going well. They had the fruits over for dinner twice a month, and Starling and Linda invited them over once a week to play cards and shoot the shit. The Austin of a year ago wouldn't recognize this weirdly domestic parody of himself. The Austin of today only wished he'd let DeeDee Mitchell set him up on a date a little sooner.

He was thinking about his life in vague, satisfied terms as he brought Pepa into the breezeway from a damp Sunday morning walk. She was probably due for a proper bath, given the amount of mud she'd managed to fling all over herself. He was wondering if he could coax her into the tub or if he should risk the moldering upholstery of his car and take her to the self-serve dog wash in town when Will came cursing down the stairs.

"Austin?"

"Breezeway," Austin answered. "Bring me a towel from the linen closet?"

Will appeared a moment later. "Hey." He handed over one of the rags they used for Pepa.

"Thanks." He was kneeling to run the towel over Pepa's legs and belly when he registered the state of Will's clothes. His T-shirt clung to his scrawny chest and shoulders with damp. "What happened to you?"

Will winced. "I woke up like this," he said. "I think the roof is leaking."

Some part of Austin was vaguely impressed he'd slept through getting that wet. Teenagers really would sleep through anything.

Then the implications sank in, and he sighed. "Ah." He finished drying Pepa and unclipped her lead. "Why don't you put on something dry and I'll make coffee and we can figure out how to handle Joe."

WHEN JOE arrived home from a long day gardening, he found Will moping at the kitchen table with his textbooks splayed out in front of him, and Austin tossing a salad at the counter.

"Honey, I'm home," Joe teased, and was rewarded with an eye roll from Will and a wink and a kiss from Austin.

Figuring he might as well eke out the one true joy of living with a moody teen, Joe jumped Will, wrapping his arms around his shoulders, kissing his head and ruffling his hair.

"Joe! Get—off! Joe!"

Cackling, Joe stepped away, and Will's pouting rearrangement of his hair did nothing to dampen his grin.

"God, you're so embarrassing."

"I try," Joe said amiably. "So what's with the homework in the kitchen? Keeping Austin company?"

"Uh." Will shot a look at Austin, who snorted.

"Subtle, kid. Will's been temporarily evicted from his bedroom."

Joe paused, his hand frozen mid-reach to steal a piece of pepper from the cutting board. "What?"

"The roof pissed on my bed."

"*What*?" That statement was more nonsensical than Austin's.

"Will kindly discovered a leak in the roof this morning," Austin finally translated.

"It woke me up," Will added.

"The roof leaked?" Dread curdled Joe's stomach. Any roof leak powerful enough to wake someone up wouldn't be a cheap fix.

"Yeah," Austin cut in. "It's not as bad as you're probably imagining, but it's not great. Before you start panicking, you're going to sit down to eat dinner and I'm going to tell you what I learned today."

"What you learned." Joe had been one step behind on this conversation ever since the roof was mentioned.

"Go grab us drinks while Will cleans up his homework and I fill up plates."

Figuring he might as well do as ordered, Joe saluted Austin and joked, "Sir, yes, sir!"

Five minutes later, they sat round the table and Joe picked up his fork and hesitated to tuck in. Austin rolled his eyes and motioned for him to eat.

"I already called Marco," Austin began. "He swung by to take a look on his lunch break. He insisted. He stuck his head in the attic but couldn't be sure about the full extent of the damage. He's sending someone tomorrow morning to cover it with a tarp and take a closer look."

Joe blinked, surprised. His uncle had already been by?

"He says we'll probably have to decide between a patch job and a new roof, but if we go the patch job route, we're probably just delaying the inevitable."

"Makes sense." Joe rubbed at his forehead. New roofs were expensive, but depending on the size of the patch, it probably made more financial sense to chuck the whole thing and pay now rather than later. "I don't suppose the roof happened to leak gold or diamonds into Will's bed as well."

Austin snorted. "Nah. So we're going to have to make an adult decision."

"Sounds scary," Will put in.

Austin reached over and flicked his forehead. "I called the bank and asked what our options were. The advisor said we probably wouldn't have any trouble getting a mortgage or a line of credit, since we own the house outright."

Joe stared at Austin. A joint line of credit was a big step for a relationship, but it was a heck of a lot better than many of the alternatives.

"There's one other thing to know before we make any decisions."

"Oh God, what else?"

"Marco offered to let us pay in installments. I told him we'd talk about it."

Damn right they would talk about it. Joe's knee-jerk reaction was to say no, but he swallowed the urge and tried to think it through. Did he want to reject the offer because of an illogical need to prove himself or because there was a flaw in the plan?

"Since you're apparently going to keep talking mortgages *and* I have math homework, I'm going to go do that in my—in the guestroom. At least I get credit for thinking about those numbers."

Will loaded his dishes in the washer and skedaddled.

"Did Marco mention how much the new roof might cost?"

"Depends on whether we go asphalt shingles or metal, but anywhere from about fifteen to forty, he guesstimated."

"I don't want to owe him forty grand," Joe said. "It's not about ego. What if something happens and we can't pay him back? I don't want to owe family that much."

"Yeah, I think the metal roof's off the table, so to speak. Even if it does sound cool as shit."

Joe remembered the cheerful patter of rain on the top of Austin's dilapidated trailer and wondered if he meant that literally. It did sound nice. It would probably also keep Joe up at night until he got used to it. "So, conventional asphalt shingles. Maybe they'll have a sale on last season's colors."

Austin nudged him under the table. "That's the spirit."

"You're being remarkably chill about this."

"One of us has to," Austin pointed out. He was gentle about it, but Joe still felt it, and it sent his thoughts whirling.

Joe had been chill once, back when they first got the house and Austin convinced him to fix it up. They'd had some setbacks, like the kitchen floor and the septic system, but he'd rolled with those punches.

He didn't know when he lost that ability, if it happened when he and Austin started sleeping together or if it was later, when Joe got sick and had to rely on Austin for everything, but at some point he'd become so paralyzed that he was no help at all. He'd only had a handful of sessions with the therapist, but she'd already pinpointed the way he stuck his head in the sand when things went wrong, and while they were just starting to work out *why*—God knew that tendency hadn't served him well—that didn't mean he didn't need to work on being more present. He knew if it had been Austin who got sick instead of him, he'd have done the same things Austin did. He'd have handled it. He leaned on Austin too much now because he could.

But that wasn't fair; this wasn't Austin's burden to shoulder alone. They were partners. It was time for Joe to pull his weight.

He managed to press his foot back into Austin's. "It shouldn't always have to be you. Let me talk to Marco too, okay? He's my uncle, after all."

AUSTIN PLACED another tray on the picnic table already laden with food. Joe might have gone overboard, not that Austin would say as much out loud. Austin got to reap the benefits, after all.

Yesterday, they had all headed down to Essex District High School to watch the four kids cross the stage and claim their diplomas. Joe cheered louder than almost anyone else in the audience, much to the kids' chagrin, but none of them turned away when Joe tackled them later with hugs and congratulations. Joe would never say it to the kids, but Austin knew the day was all the sweeter for him since there had been times in the past when he had worried some of them wouldn't graduate on time.

Joe had an excess of joy and energy to share, and with their financial situation more or less handled, Austin had no objections to Joe declaring they would host a late June party. Instead, he smiled and nodded and offered to do last-minute grocery runs and set up the table and chairs in the yard and even borrowed extra lawn furniture from Linda.

"This looks delicious," Maria said, rubbing her swollen stomach. She was almost seven months along. Austin thought she looked like she'd shoved a basketball up her shirt.

"Doesn't it?" Austin shifted a plate, then tucked his hands into his pockets to keep them from fidgeting.

"Think we'll be able to eat it all?" She shot him a cheeky smile, and Austin grinned back.

"Well, thankfully we have separate fridge and freezer. Lots of room for leftovers." Austin figured they'd be eating this feast for days, but at least that meant Joe would have a break from the kitchen after his days-long cooking binge.

"Good point," she laughed. "Though if there are any leftover arancini, don't be surprised if they don't make it to your fridge. The baby is fond of them."

"Speaking of—all going well?"

"Yes." She smiled that glowy smile of the happily pregnant. "Honestly, it's been easier this go-around than my first, which is not something I anticipated. Joe gave me the worst morning sickness."

Austin snorted. "Well, he is something of a morning person."

"Who's a morning person?"

Austin caught Joe around the waist and pulled him in. "Just this terrible guy I know. Always making me coffee in the morning and reminding Will not to forget his homework."

"Hmm." Joe smacked a kiss on his cheek. "Sounds like a catch."

"Actually, he prefers to—"

"Oookay, who let you into the Jell-O shots?" Joe interrupted.

Maria cackled.

"Please. As if I need alcohol to embarrass you in front of your mom." Making Joe blush was its own reward, always. "Speaking of embarrassing—are you gonna give a speech for the fruits? Tell them all you're so proud as they go off to their new grown-up lives?"

Joe wrinkled his nose. "Not really my style. I'll save it for their weddings. Or in Meg's case, her first Olympic gold medal ceremony."

"What are they up to next?" Maria asked.

"Meg's off to U of M, full ride, obviously. Alex got into trade school, so they're going to learn welding and, I don't know, make the big bucks in a factory or create enormous obscene metal sculptures. Could go either way."

"Both," Austin said confidently.

"Definitely both," Maria agreed.

"Will's starting nursing school at the college to get the first two years of credits out of the way before transferring to the university. And Gavin...."

Austin snorted. "Gavin is about to learn the extent of Joe's morning-person perversion doing physical labor five days a week."

"He just wants Alex to see him with a tan and, like, muscle definition."

"I think he wants to be able to take them on an actual date that's not to Tim Hortons." Though Austin would admit some of it might be ogling-related payback. Austin was the one who'd somehow ended up at Bikini Village with Meg and Alex as they shopped for their graduation do—the pool party Meg's parents had thrown. Which unfortunately meant he'd been in earshot when Meg asked, *So what are we going for here? You want to be comfortable and not get a sunburn, or do you want Gavin to have to ice his crotch in public?* Even more unfortunately, he had also heard Alex answer, without hesitation, *Crotch icing for sure.*

He'd seen the swimsuit. He had not, thankfully, been present for the party. However, every so often one of the kids would now say something like, *You know, eggplant is a fruit,* and Gavin would blush and grin sheepishly and Alex would look very smug.

Apparently Joe was having similar thoughts, because he said, "I think I might have preferred it when they were desperately and successfully hiding their relationship from us."

Austin snorted. "Right, babe. Successfully."

"You're mocking my pain." Joe pouted, and Austin patted his hair.

Maria continued to laugh at them. "Payback for all your youthful indiscretions, dear. Karma," she said gleefully.

Joe's pout intensified. "I didn't have any youthful indiscretions."

"That's not what I remember." Joe's dad stepped up to their group and unknowingly mimicked Austin by slipping an arm around his wife and kissing her cheek.

They'd eloped at the courthouse a month prior with Joe and Austin as the only witnesses. Austin was uncomfortable at first, until Maria pointed out that Joe was the only guest the bride and groom wanted and Joe would want Austin with him for support.

Joe stiffened, his posture screaming guilt. "I don't know what you're talking about."

Julio snorted. "No? Am I getting senile in my old age? Because I remember the summer you lived with me in Ottawa before you went to grade eleven—"

Austin was never going to pass up an opportunity to learn about Joe's past shenanigans. "I think I need to hear more about these youthful indiscretions."

"I think you should come help me play host elsewhere, not near my loose-lipped parents." Joe pushed Austin away from the food, and Austin laughingly went along with it.

They bumped into Marco almost immediately, but luckily for Joe and the secrecy of his youthful indiscretions, Marco was eager to talk about houses.

"The roof's looking good."

Austin didn't have to know anything about houses to recognize a man admiring something he felt ownership over. He reminded Austin of some of his middle-aged customers admiring their dream cars.

Swallowing a smile, Austin watched as Joe joined him in conversation, unconsciously crossing his arms, a mirror image of his uncle. They leaned back to eye the house as Marco asked about the roof and then their future plans. If not for the imminent arrival of the fruits, Joe probably would have been persuaded to walk the property and show his uncle all the next-ups on the to-do list. Not that it would stop them from doing the tour later. Knowing Marco, he'd want to take another look at the en suite and admire the successful transformation. It did look even better after Joe let his mom help decorate.

Austin was eternally grateful for the extra bathroom, since Will's morning and evening routines seemed to be getting longer the more comfortable he got living in the house. Not that he would be living there much longer.

A week ago, when gathered around the table for dinner, a knock had come on the door, startling Pepa and surprising the humans. Joe answered and almost slammed the door shut again, but he very manfully refrained, he told Austin later, and asked their visitor, "What the fuck are you doing here?"

"I was hoping to see my baby brother," an unfamiliar voice responded, and all the color drained from Will's face.

"Why?" Joe snapped.

"Because I want to make sure he's okay and to tell him I love him."

Sitting across from Austin, Will bit his lip and his eyes watered.

Austin had only gotten as far as standing when Joe, followed by an unfamiliar young man, returned to the kitchen.

"Henry?"

"Will," presumably Henry sighed with relief and strode across the room to pull Will into his arms.

The story came out in broken pieces—how Henry had been forced to wait until after the wedding and he and Tilly were moved into their own place, independent from his parents. With his new wife's encouragement, Henry had left the church, and now he was reaching out to Will.

The result was that, at some point during the summer, Will would be moving out to live with Henry and Tilly. No date had yet been set for the move. Austin wasn't sure who was most nervous and worried about the upcoming separation, but neither Joe nor Will would commit to a timeline.

Austin was jolted out of his musings by the arrival of a car bearing Meg, Gavin, and Alex, Meg honking lightly as she pulled into the last available patch of gravel in front of the pole barn. "Sorry we're late," she half shouted across the yard, closing the car door behind her. "These two wouldn't stop sucking face long enough to get in."

But she was grinning when she said it, any trace of resentment from the past long gone.

"I've got the hose ready," Joe said wryly, "just in case."

They'd talked about offering Gavin one of the bedrooms upstairs for the summer, given how early Joe's crews started work, but the potential of having to deal with teenagers' sex noises kiboshed that immediately.

Alex sniffed. "Please. We're just as likely to need it for you two."

"Nah," Joe said cheerfully. "We've got a room."

Meg and Gavin made dramatic retching sounds.

"Now that you're here," Austin interrupted, "I think we can officially start the party." He caught eyes with Joe. "Right?"

"Oh, aren't we fancy," Maria teased as she eased herself down into one of the patio chairs. Julio put a hand on her shoulder. "I didn't realize this was such a formal affair, with a start time and everything."

Joe's cheeks went ever so slightly pink. Someone who didn't know him might've thought it was just the summer heat. "It's not *formal*," he protested.

"Your shirt has a collar," Meg said judgily. "It's eighty-five degrees out here. In the shade."

"Austin made me give Pepa a bath this morning," Will put in. "And then he blow-dried his hair after his shower."

Gavin looked around the yard at the assembled group. Linda and Starling were in the shade under the oak tree, with Pepa between them, gazing up adoringly at Nonna, who had Davide's plump little girl on her lap. Half a dozen other Romano cousins whose names Austin mostly remembered were milling around too, with their own families, poking around the partly renovated pole barn, stuffing themselves with Joe's homemade biscotti, and chasing their kids around the yard.

"Holy shit," Gavin said, almost bouncing in excitement. "They're finally going to do it."

Alex looked at him, then at Joe, then Austin. They nudged their shoulder into Gavin's. "Maybe we should let them tell us."

"Yeah, Gavin," Will agreed. "Don't be such a know-it-all. Let them tell us."

Joe caught Austin's eye again, and they both smiled. Austin took Joe's hand. "Guess we better tell them before Gavin does it for us," Joe said.

Austin took in the sight of it—their kids, their house, their pets, their extended family, everything he'd been too afraid to admit to wanting, never mind try to build—and found himself suddenly, overwhelmingly grateful to DeeDee Mitchell and her batshit matchmaking plans. "Let him," he said, tugging Joe close enough to kiss. "I have better things to do."

Keep Reading for an Excerpt from
Sheep Calm and Merry On
By Ashlyn Kane!

IT WASN'T unusual to have a white Christmas in Vanderbilt, Michigan.

But it was a little unusual to have a blizzard-like white-out December 23.

Fortunately Devon's trusty farm truck had four-wheel drive and a good set of chains or he would've been stuck in the grocery-store parking lot until the plows came through, and who knew how long that would take. He might have had to spend the night at his sister's place.

Either way, he was sticking to the bigger roads as much as possible and taking it slow. No point tempting fate, especially since cell reception up here was spotty enough when the weather was good.

And the weather was decidedly not good. Devon kept the truck in low gear and his eyes on the road, the windshield defroster cranked. He should've had the heated steering fixed. He updated his mental priority list to include "fix the heated steering." Check the shelters, break the ice on the unheated water troughs, feed the critters, call the mechanic.

Then he could build a nice fire in the farmhouse woodstove and spend the rest of the night drinking cocoa and wrapping presents.

If his teenage self could see him now, he'd probably think he'd overdosed.

Snow battered the windshield and wind rocked the truck as he crawled along toward his exit. The snow was thick enough that he could only see a narrow sliver of road through the tracks left by other vehicles. The sides of the road were already more than a foot deep. Nasty stuff, and it was only getting worse as the temperature dropped.

Not a good day to be out for a drive, for sure. Anyone who got in an accident out here was in for a nasty night.

Devon had to keep a close eye on the side of the road in order to keep track of it under all the snow, or he never would've seen it—a tiny green sedan that had slid off the road and ended up half in a snow drift. A good two inches covered the roof, so it must have been there for a while.

Cursing, Devon eased on the brakes as he passed and dared a glance over. He couldn't see anyone in the car.

He did see a track in the snow, though, heading north along the roadside. Devon thought whoever'd been driving the car had to be insane, until he spotted the mile marker just sticking up above the snow.

There was a rest area with bathrooms and telephones a quarter mile up the road. Maybe the driver didn't have a death wish after all.

Even with four-wheel drive and chains on his tires, Devon didn't make the turn into the rest area. The lot hadn't seen a plow in hours; if he went up that road, he'd never get out again. So, cursing himself and whatever moron thought it was a good idea to drive a subcompact in northern Michigan in the middle of a blizzard, he stopped the truck, grabbed a set of flashers from the emergency kit and set them on the tailgate, and hoofed it through the snow.

The wind bit his cheeks and eyebrows, and he was quickly in snow up to his knees. *A fire and hot cocoa*, he reminded himself. And a good night's sleep for his Good Samaritan act.

The sun was going down and the temperature was plummeting with it. Devon wrapped his scarf tighter around his face, hunched his shoulders, and pushed into the wind. The sooner he got to the rest stop, the sooner he could go back to his truck and get warm.

Finally he pushed open the doors and stepped inside.

The power was out—no surprise—so it was emergency lighting only, and no heat, though it was still warmer than outside, and at least the wind and snow couldn't get in. Devon squinted into the dim light. "Hello? Anybody here?"

No answer.

"Anybody else here crazy enough to get out of their car in this shit, or is it just me?"

But the snow tracks definitely led here, and now that his eyes had adjusted, he could make out a watery trail in the direction of the bathrooms. Well, that made sense, right? Might as well find a smaller area, try to keep that warm.

He followed the puddles to the men's room, but found it empty. Then he spotted one more puddle in front of the women's bathroom.

Now what? He didn't want to be a creep, but also, leaving without checking on whoever was here was not an option.

He knocked. "Hello?" he called. "Ma'am?"

No answer.

Well, if whoever was in here was dead, they weren't going to yell at him for coming in. He pushed the door open.

At first he thought this room was empty too. Maybe he'd actually driven the truck straight into a hydro pole and hit his head and this whole thing was just him hallucinating during his last moments.

But then he heard a rustle that sounded almost like those stupid helium balloons, the ones people filled up for Valentine's and birthdays and wedding photoshoots, and he tried again. "Is anyone—"

"Jesus!"

Devon's mouth dropped open in surprise, and he fumbled in his pocket for his phone, because duh, it had a flashlight on it. "Uh. Jesus who?"

He swept the beam around the bathroom. When the light hit a spot under the sink, the whole place spun like a disco ball.

"F-f-fuck!"

"Jesus Fuck," Devon repeated. Sure. Why not? "Kind of a lame knock-knock joke." He directed the light at the floor in an effort not to blind whatever tin-foil-covered delusion was lurking in this bathroom. "What are you doing in here?"

"F-freezing to d-d-death."

Devon snorted. Apparently two could play the smartass game. "You want me to leave you to it? Or, like, I can give you a lift back to my place and we can come back for your car when the weather clears."

Pause. Then the funny metallic rustle again, and suddenly Devon's damsel in distress was standing in front of him, a reflective blanket wrapped around his hips like a skirt.

"Uh," said Devon. "Where are your pants?"

Wordlessly, the guy pointed to a stall door. A pair of jeans hung from the top, visibly damp from the knee down, reminding Devon of what he had to look forward to once the snow he'd waded through melted. At least the guy had the presence of mind to bring the emergency blanket from his car.

"Right," Devon said, shaking his head. "What do you say, man? I want to get back in my truck before the snow covers it. I promise I'm not an ax murderer."

He got the impression of dark eyes blinking at him. "That leaves a lot of other kinds of murderer."

Definitely a smartass. "If I wanted you dead, I could've left you here…?" he pointed out, leaving the end of the sentence hanging so the guy would introduce himself. Devon couldn't actually go around calling him Jesus Fuck.

"Noah," he said finally as he took the hand Devon offered. His hands were dry and chapped, but at least they weren't cold.

"Noah," Devon repeated. "I'm Devon. You try the phones in the lobby area? Let your people know you're not dead?"

Noah shivered and pulled his coat around him a little tighter. "Phone's out with the power."

Right, obviously. "All right, well, you wanna leave a lipstick note on the mirror letting everyone know who to blame if you turn up dead?"

Noah snorted. "No, man, I'll take my chances. Even if that does mean putting my pants back on."

Devon left his phone faceup on the counter and turned around to give him privacy. "What the hell were you thinking driving in this anyway, in a tiny little car like that?"

"Mostly I was thinking 'holy shit, I hope I don't die.'"

Fair enough. He didn't owe Devon his life story. "Well, there's a generator at my place. You can call your people from there."

"God, this is disgusting." The slap of wet denim. Then, "You're assuming I have people."

"If you don't have people here and you're driving up I-75 in this weather, I'm the one who should be worried about ax murderers."

Noah snorted. "My parents are in Indian River. Brother moved when he got married. I think he's in Vanderbilt now."

"You think?"

"Never been to his place. I've been in Colorado the past three years."

Was Noah allergic to speaking more than two sentences at a time? Devon gazed up at the ceiling. There was a water spot over by the window. "I'm in Vanderbilt too. Sort of. My place isn't really *in* anything except the middle of nowhere."

"Wow. You're really not good at this whole 'reassure me you're not a serial killer' thing." He paused. "You can turn around now, your virgin eyes are in no further danger."

Devon ignored the quip about his virgin eyes out of deference to Noah's sense of safety. If he replied with a chirp about Noah's virgin ass he'd probably change his mind and freeze to death in this place. "Great. Let's get to my truck before the engine seizes up."

NOAH HAD pretty much resigned himself to a long, cold, uncomfortable night followed by a day that would likely be more of the same, until the power came back on and he could call someone to come get him and tow his car out. He'd had the presence of mind to bring a handful of stuff from the car's emergency kit, but if he were really been smart, he'd have grabbed a change of clothes along with the bottles of water and granola bars.

For the first hour he figured he'd be okay. Then the temperature dropped and the snow came down heavier. The little mylar blanket was not cutting it anymore.

He'd been panicking for a good forty minutes before Devon showed up, to the point where at first he'd thought he was hallucinating.

But nope. He was being rescued or possibly murdered. As long as he had the opportunity to get warm first, he wasn't sure he cared.

Back outside, the sun had set and the wind was still blowing furiously. Noah pulled his blanket as tight over his coat as he could, but he couldn't do anything about his jeans, which froze stiff after a handful of steps. He could feel them chapping against his skin.

But the red glow of emergency lights flashed up ahead, promising the eventuality of warmth and safety and maybe even food. Noah gritted his jaw against his chattering teeth and followed Devon's footsteps.

He expected a beat-up farm vehicle, from what he'd seen of Devon in the dim light of the rest stop—plaid trapper hat, Carhartt jacket, work boots. No-nonsense stuff. Instead Devon waved Noah toward a black Sierra Denali, a couple model years old but still top of the line. Maybe serial killing paid better than he thought.

"Get in and get warm," Devon shouted over the roaring wind. "I have to get the flashers and clear the snow."

Noah didn't have to be told twice. He scrambled into the cab, thanking God or Satan or whoever for remote start and heated seats. Would Devon be offended if Noah took his pants off again? Because he would love to toast his glutes.

He didn't have time to decide before Devon joined him in the truck, snow dusting his hat and shoulders. "Well! That's the last time I leave any Christmas shopping for the last minute," he said bracingly. "You good?"

Noah was not what he'd call good—he was cold and wet and uncomfortable. But he was on his way to fixing most of that, so he just nodded and shoved his hands in front of the vents. "Yeah, man. Let's just get going before it gets any worse out here."

"Can't argue with that."

Even in the well-equipped truck, they made slow, careful progress, occasionally hitting patches of ice or snow that sent the truck skidding. Noah felt stupid for thinking he could make it through this mess in his car, but he'd been so focused on getting home for Christmas for the first time in years—on the idea of starting over.

Because Colorado had never really been home.

And now he was so close he could taste it, and he'd almost killed himself getting there. Stupid.

"Jesus, it's a mess," Devon muttered, squinting at the road. "You see any mile markers?"

"I think they're all covered." God, were they going to get lost now too? What a fucking day.

Luckily they spotted a sign for a turnoff, only half covered, and Devon whistled under his breath. "My lucky day I guess."

"Mine too, for sure."

Whatever country road Devon had turned down, it didn't have any street lights. But from the twin black maws on either side of it, it had plenty deep ditches. Devon steered the truck straight down the middle, seemingly oblivious but maybe just concentrating.

"So," he said after a moment. "Colorado?"

The least Noah could do was fill the silence with small talk. Apparently even fancy trucks didn't get radio reception in weather like this.

But he didn't want to get into the whole drama of it. People always thought they understood, or they felt bad for him, or they asked a bunch of questions Noah didn't want to answer. That part of his life was over. He liked where he was now.

Career-wise, that was. He wasn't too keen on the treacherous back country road through the part of Hell that had frozen over.

So he skipped the part people found interesting and said, "I went to school out there," which was also true. Coincidentally, that was after he washed out of the NHL. "Then I just kind of stayed."

"But you still can't drive in the snow?"

Okay, Noah probably deserved that. "I lived on campus," he protested. "And then when I graduated, I got a job at a boarding school, so I lived in the residence there too."

And then he moved in with Tommy, but the less said about that, the better.

"Huh." Devon flipped his turn signal. God knew who for. No one else was nuts enough to be out in this shit. "What were you doing?"

Damn it. That one wasn't so easy to sidestep. "Athletics stuff mostly. Glorified gym teacher." No big deal.

"Yeah? Nice. You moving back to the area, then?"

He must've seen all the shit in Noah's car.

Noah sighed. It was a small area. Devon would find out soon enough anyway. "Yeah. Shitty breakup, great job opportunity. Couldn't pass it up. The job's actually in Traverse City, though."

"Hmm. Teaching?"

God, please don't let Noah's random savior happen to know anyone who worked in education in Traverse City. "Yeah."

Mercifully, the line of inquiry ended as they turned into the driveway of a two-story farmhouse with a patchwork of outbuildings—a barn, a detached garage, a shed…. Noah didn't know what to call the other one. A second barn?

Either way, Devon pulled up to the garage and pressed a button, presumably to open the door. When nothing happened, he sighed. "Power's out. Be right back." And went to open it by hand.

The interior of the garage didn't reveal much. There was a block heater for the truck, the typical pieces of scrap wood you found on any working farm. Nothing that said *human entrails! Turn your insides to your outsides!*

It was possible Noah was cold enough to have gotten delirious, because the idea made him giggle. Maybe Devon would roast him alive. That would be nice.

"One more question," Devon said when he was unlocking the side door to the house. "How do you feel about dogs?"

"Uh," said Noah, but he didn't have time to say anything else before a black-and-white blur bounded outside.

For the time being, it was ignoring Noah, concentrating instead on Devon. Its tail wagged furiously as Devon petted at it. Noah thought he'd try to shoo it back inside. Instead, the dog accepted exactly four seconds of pets and then booked it toward the field, ignoring Noah entirely.

"Uh," Noah said again. "Do you need to go get it?"

"Nah, he'll be back in a few minutes. He's gotta see a man about a couple dozen sheep." He gestured for Noah to enter first. "C'mon, we're letting the heat out. Get inside. I'm going to go start the jenny."

With basically no other option, save running into the field after the dog, Noah obeyed.

He couldn't see much. Nothing new there; the most he'd seen in the past couple hours had been the inside of Devon's garage when the truck headlights illuminated it. But there was a rechargeable flashlight plugged in and glowing faintly nearby, so he grabbed that and flicked it on.

He was standing in a small mudroom off the farmhouse kitchen. The floors looked original—worn but clean. The room contained a chest freezer, a washer and dryer, and at least four different coat racks affixed to various walls, some hung with dog leashes and others with winter clothes, rain gear, and extra sets of keys. Noah wrangled himself out of his coat and hung it up, then set his boots on one of those fancy electric boot-drying racks. Talk about creature comforts.

Noah looked at the dryer, then down at his wet jeans. He thought about walking around a stranger's farmhouse in his underpants.

And decided to risk it. He wasn't going to freeze to death in Devon's house in the next half hour. It was, like, a balmy sixty-two degrees in here. Devon probably had a blanket somewhere, or a spare pair of pants. He shoved his jeans into the dryer and walked farther into the house.

It was a nice place, but lived-in. Sections of the kitchen cupboards had worn paint. The floor in front of the sink and the fridge dipped a little, as though too many people had stood there washing dishes or deciding on a midnight snack. Beyond the kitchen, a little dining room held a bay window with a view of what Noah assumed, but couldn't tell in the current weather conditions, was a field.

Off the dining room was a living area that looked over the front porch, and to the right, a hallway. That seemed like the likeliest place to find a blanket or pants, so Noah pushed open the first door, expecting to find a linen closet, and found a small office instead.

The lights came on.

It took Noah a moment to adjust to the sudden brightness, though the room itself was done in subdued dark-green paint and walnut wainscoting. Floor-to-ceiling shelves held seemingly everything *except* books—kids' trophies, larger ones, medals, framed photographs.

The ones closest to Noah were of sheep.

Not cute little lambs. Not the sweet, docile-looking puffballs of cartoons and cozy documentaries about Norway. Massive, fat, curly-haired cowlike beings, with wrinkles on wrinkles and fuck-off horns and teeny tiny faces poking out from their wool hoods. Terrifying demon sheep.

Judging from the ribbons on display next to and in some of the photographs, *prize-winning* terrifying demon sheep.

Noah guessed Devon hadn't been making a euphemism when he said the dog was going to see a man about several dozen sheep.

The next shelf seemed to be dedicated to the dog, a black-and-white border collie with one ear that went straight up and one that flopped over halfway. Every picture spoke of the genuine affability only certain dogs could pull off—eyes bright, mouth open in a humanlike smile, tongue lolling.

But it was the third shelf that brought Noah up short. The shit in this shelf, he actually recognized.

Scan the QR Code Below to Order!

ASHLYN KANE always wanted to be the class clown but never had the guts to come out of that teacher's-pet shell. Now she channels her need to make people laugh into contemporary and paranormal m/m romance. Her 2019 release *Fake Dating the Prince* received a coveted starred review from *Publishers Weekly*, which called it "as sparkling as a diamond engagement ring."

An editor by day, Ashlyn enjoys DIY home decor, music, container gardening, and long walks with Indy, her 90-poundchocolate lapdog. She became an avid hockey fan at the age of 28, to the surprise and delight of her father and grandfather, who thought maybe it skipped a generation. Neither of them can explain why she hates their team.

Sign up for her newsletter atwww.ashlynkane.ca/newsletter/

Website: www.ashlynkane.ca

Follow me on BookBub

MORGAN JAMES is a clueless (older) millennial who's still trying to figure out what they'll be when they grow up and enjoying the journey to get there. James started writing fiction before they could spell and wrote their first (unpublished) novel in middle school. They haven't stopped writing since. Geek, artist, archer, and fanatic, Morgan tends to pass free hours with imaginary worlds and people on pages and screens—it's an addiction. They live in Canada, where they're Alfred to their cat's Batman.

Follow me on BookBub

HOMECOMING
for BEGINNERS

*It's just a house
until you fill it.*

ASHLYN KANE

When Ollie Kent arrives on the front steps of the Morris mansion, he's six months out of the military and the brand-new single parent of an eight-year-old cancer survivor. Now they're starting over back in Ollie's hometown, where he's lined up a job as a live-in caregiver for old man Morris.

So it's kind of a downer when a very hungover, mostly naked man about Ollie's age answers the door and tells him old man Morris kicked the bucket.

Tyler Morris left town at sixteen as a pariah. Since then, he's built a good life for himself as an EMT. But even in death, his father has to get in one final screw-you: Ty can either return to his hometown and act as executor of the family fortune, or let it all go to a hate group.

Between an unexpected job offer and unexpected roommates, coming home doesn't go the way Ty expects. But Ollie and Theo bring the cold, lonely mansion to life, and golden-boy Ollie provides good cover for the town's scorn. The only problem is, Ty's falling head over heels for the world's sweetest and most stubbornly independent single dad, and if he wants to keep Ollie around, he'll have to convince him to let Ty help.

SCAN THE QR CODE
BELOW TO ORDER!

HOCKEY EVER AFTER · BOOK ONE

WINGING IT

Falling for his
teammate wasn't in
the game plan....

ASHLYN KANE
MORGAN JAMES

Hockey is Gabe Martin's life. Dante Baltierra just wants to have some fun on his way to the Hockey Hall of Fame. Falling for a teammate isn't in either game plan.

But plans change.

When Gabe gets outed, it turns his careful life upside-down. The chaos messes with his game and sends his team headlong into a losing streak. The last person he expects to pull him through it is Dante.

This season isn't going the way Dante thought it would. Gabe's sexuality doesn't faze him, but his own does. Dante's always been a "what you see is what you get" kind of guy, and having to hide his attraction to Gabe sucks. But so does losing, and his teammate needs him, so he puts in the effort to snap Gabe out of his funk.

He doesn't mean to fall in love with the guy.

Getting involved with a teammate is a bad idea, but Dante is shameless, funny, and brilliant at hockey. Gabe can't resist. Unfortunately, he struggles to share part of himself that he's hidden for years, and Dante chafes at hiding their relationship. Can they find their feet before the ice slips out from under them?

Winging It is the first book in the hot, hilarious, heartfelt Hockey Ever After series. If you like witty banter, friends to lovers, and sports romance, you'll love *Winging It*.

SCAN THE QR CODE
BELOW TO ORDER!

"There's plenty of charm to this second chance romance."
—*Publishers Weekly*

THE ROCK STAR'S GUIDE TO GETTING YOUR MAN

ASHLYN KANE

When Jeff Pine rents a cabin in the hometown he's been avoiding for fifteen years, he just wants some time away from his rock 'n roll world to figure out his life. Instead he runs into his former BFF—and the inspiration for dozens of love songs—on the first day.

Facepalm.

Park naturalist Carter Rhodes is a cinnamon roll dressed like a lumberjack. Fame and fortune don't turn his head, but the snarky little nerd who followed him around as a kid? The guy who makes him laugh when he's grieving and relax when he overextends himself? Not the rock star, but *Jeff*? That guy has a chance.

Jeff has always known Carter is it for him, but he's facing a tour with increasingly hostile bandmates, a looming album deadline, and the suspicion that their label is up to no good. Can he find the courage—and the time—to write a true love song with Carter?

Scan the QR Code
Below to Order!

String Theory

Ashlyn Kane & Morgan James

For Jax Hall, all-but-dissertation in mathematics, slinging drinks and serenading patrons at a piano bar is the perfect remedy for months of pandemic anxiety. He doesn't expect to end up improvising on stage with pop violinist Aria Darvish, but the attraction that sparks between them? That's a mathematical certainty. If he can get Ari to act on it, even better.

Ari hasn't written a note, and his album deadline is looming. Then he meets Jax, and suddenly he can't stop the music. But Ari doesn't know how to interpret Jax's flirting—is making him a drink called Sex with the Bartender a serious overture?

Jax jumps in with both feet, the only way he knows how. Ari is wonderful, and Jax loves having a partner who's on the same page. But Ari's struggles with his parents' expectations, and Jax's with the wounds of his past, threaten to unbalance an otherwise perfect equation. Can they prove their double act has merit, or does it only work in theory?

SCAN THE QR CODE BELOW TO ORDER!

THE INSIDE EDGE

ASHLYN KANE

What does a work-life balance look like to recently retired professional athletes?

Ex-hockey player Nate Overton is trying to find out, but dipping his toes in the gay dating scene post-divorce is a daunting prospect even without the news that his show is on thin ice. Before he can tackle either issue, he skates headfirst into another problem—his new cohost. Former figure skater Aubrey Chase is the embodiment of a spoiled rich playboy. He's also flamboyant, sharp, and hot as sin.

Aubrey knows how important it is to get off on the right foot. He's just not very good at it outside the rink. Having spent his life desperate for attention, he'll do anything to get it—even the wrong kind.

For Nate and Aubrey, opposites don't so much attract as collide at center ice. But while Nate's everything Aubrey has scrupulously avoided—until now—Aubrey falls suddenly head over heels, and Nate's only looking for a rebound fling. Can Aubrey convince Nate to risk his heart again, or will their unexpected connection be checked at the first sign of trouble?

SCAN THE QR CODE
BELOW TO ORDER!

www.ingramcontent.com/pod-product-compliance
Lightning Source LLC
Chambersburg PA
CBHW061921130726
47908CB00016B/531